THE

WOLF'S

DEN

Connie Senior

Published by Bitingduck Press
ISBN 978-1-938463-83-9
eISBN 978-1-938463-86-0
For information contact
Bitingduck Press, LLC
Altadena, CA
notifications@bitingduckpress.com
http://www.bitingduckpress.com

"Sometimes things fall apart so that better things can fall together."
~ Marilyn Monroe

Chapter 1: A Werewolf Comes Home

August 1992

WARM AUGUST DAYS ON the Maine coast had pushed the weeds in the vegetable garden to riot stage. Caleb jabbed ferociously at the deep root of a weed that had fountained up amidst the flowering pumpkin vines, pitiless, although his own uprooting had taken place only the previous day.

As he knelt, working his hands into the soil to fight the numbness of jet lag, the pungent aroma of moist, dark loam sent him back to the greenhouse in Castle Arghezi, the remote Romanian castle destroyed the previous year by a vengeful vampire who had taken the lives of those Caleb loved—and who now might be menacing his old hometown.

The fall of the castle had set him on the path that led back here to Bar Harbor, where he'd spent much of his childhood. The town hadn't changed much in his six-year absence: tourists thronged the ice cream parlors and t-shirt shops and clogged the streets with rented bicycles, which wasn't much different than when he was growing up. But against the bland backdrop of summer visitors, lives had been lost, and now a rogue werewolf pack hunted a shadowy group of vampires. Barely a day back in Maine, Caleb wasn't yet sure how he was going to prevent more deaths.

He tossed the weed onto the growing pile, recalling the greenhouse as he'd last seen it: twisted metal window frames, shattered glass, desiccated, leafless trunks poking up from pots, dust and leaves covering the slate floor. He had protested when his adopted Romanian family had accused him of running away from Maine, but wasn't there some truth in that? Now he had fled Romania after making a disaster of that, too, only to find that Sophia, his one surviving childhood friend, hadn't forgiven his absence. She'd given him a little more than twenty-four hours to find a hotel room and get out of her house. Could he blame her?

From behind him, the wooden gate to the back yard creaked open.

"Caleb?"

Standing, he rubbed his hands together to dislodge the clinging dirt before slowly turning. At first, he didn't recognize the woman framed by the tall white picket fence, squinting at him in the bright sunlight, one hand shading her eyes.

"It *is* you," she said, dropping her hand and giving him a tentative smile.

Toby's mother. He recognized her now, although she had lines at the corners of her eyes and had put on weight. Years ago, she had accepted the shy, socially awkward boy Caleb had been and had treated him like another son. How jealous he'd been of Toby, his friend who could do no wrong and who had a kind, pretty mother.

"It's been a long time," Trudy marveled, stepping forward and letting the gate bang shut behind her. "Sophia says you've been abroad."

Caleb, aware that he'd been staring at her, looked down at his hands, palms dark with soil and dirt packed under his fingernails, and futilely wiped them on his jeans.

"Yes, I was in Romania—in the mountains, a remote place. It's a long story about how I got there," he said uncertainly. When they were kids, Toby had never told his mother that his best friend was a werewolf. But she wouldn't have believed that werewolves existed, and Caleb didn't think she'd believe him now if he told her that he'd spent the last six years leading a pack in the Transylvanian Alps and becoming proficient at hunting and killing vampires.

"Fintonclyde asked me to come back, because there was—Because he wanted my help to—" He broke off as he stepped through the fence surrounding the garden and fumbled for a few long moments with the wire loop that served to latch the gate. He couldn't think of a way to complete the sentence that wouldn't sound absurd or just plain crazy, so he said simply, "Anyway, here I am."

"You look, well, different somehow," she said hesitantly, advancing across the grass toward him. "Grown up."

At that moment, Caleb didn't feel grown up, but like the motherless boy Trudy had taken under her wing. He stepped toward her, extending one hand tentatively and then pulling it back, pretending that his hand was too dirty.

"I'm older," he said with a weak chuckle, trying but failing to sound nonchalant.

"Aren't we all, dear," she answered gently.

"Are you still teaching?" he asked, feeling the need to fill the silence with uncomplicated pleasantries.

"No, I had to give that up after losing Toby. I had some…problems," she said, looking away for a moment. "I mostly help my husband Tom run his business these days."

"Oh, right. And he's here to look at the, uhm, plumbing or something."

"This is such a lovely place," Trudy observed with a vague wave of her hand toward the hulking Victorian house, "and I'm sure it'll do well as a B&B. Sophia's wanted to fix it up ever since she inherited it from her aunt, hasn't she? I know things were a little rough for her for a few years after what happened, but…" She pursed her lips, but continued with a bright smile, "Tom will figure out what she needs. Will you be staying on to help her?"

"She doesn't seem to want my help," Caleb murmured, then quickly said, "I mean, I'll help if I can, but I don't know how long I'll be here. Things are…up in the air."

They stood two arm-lengths apart, but the gulf between them felt like miles. He wanted to keep talking about anything that would stop him from thinking about Trudy's son, but trivial conversation abandoned him as he saw Toby's deep-set dark eyes and fine, straight nose mirrored in her anxious face, as if his best friend's ghost had materialized before him.

The silence between them lurched into awkward embarrassment as Caleb realized he'd been gaping at an unseen presence.

"Well, I'd better see how Tom's getting along. He's so forgetful these days that I have to check the math on his estimates," she chirped in a brittle voice, and then turned away from him.

"I'm sorry," Caleb called hoarsely. "Sorry I ran away."

She froze, one arm on the gate latch, while his heart hammered.

"I couldn't face it, losing him," he said, taking large, ragged breaths that didn't fill his lungs. "But that wasn't— That's not right. I should have been here with you, but instead I ran as far as I could go. I'm sorry."

As she turned slowly to face him, Caleb saw her eyes glistening with tears. "I miss him every day," she said in a cracked voice.

"I do, too," he whispered, putting his arms around her. "It wasn't fair. It wasn't right. It wasn't…"

Trudy would never know what had really happened to her son six years ago. She thought Toby had died in the conflagration that had claimed their other friend, René, a tragic, freak accident caused by two boys being reckless with fire. Caleb wanted desperately to shield her from the grotesque and horrible truth.

He held her until she stopped shaking, her tears seeping into his shirt. She drew back, took a deep breath, and swiped a hand across her wet cheeks.

"I don't blame you for leaving," she sniffled in reassurance. "I went through a rough patch, after… what happened, but I'm fine, fine now." She laughed self-consciously as she pulled a tissue from her pocket and blew her nose. "Tom was my rock. Without him I'm not sure where I'd be. I had what you'd politely call a drinking problem, which cost me… let's just say almost everything. Tom pulled me through. He's always been so strong, which is why—"

Trudy hesitated, fished another tissue from a pocket, and dabbed it under her eyes. She smiled brightly, grief still lurking at the corners of her mouth.

"About that. Your Mr. Fintonclyde used to dabble in alternative medicine or whatever they call it these days."

"I suppose you might say that," Caleb replied cautiously, amused by her implication that the old man who had raised him was somehow "his" and that the gray-bearded old codger was some sort of New Age guru. "Why? Is something wrong with you?"

"No, not me, dear," she said with a final sniffle, "although I haven't cried this much in a blue moon. It's Tom I'm worried about. For the last month, he's been—I don't know how to describe it—different: tired, forgetful, not thinking clearly. I made him go to the doctor, but they didn't find anything to account for the way he's been acting."

"Isn't there a new disease out there?" Caleb recalled the awkward interview at the US Embassy in Bucharest the previous month. "A blood disease. Romanian orphans are getting it."

"You mean AIDS?" Trudy shook her head. "We thought of that, because when it first started, he was so anemic that he was receiving regular blood transfusions. But they have a test now, and he's negative. So, then I thought, the blood—losing so much blood…?"

"You're thinking of vampires." It sounded silly to say it here in this technological land where no one believed that sort of thing any more. Caleb could scarcely believe his Romanian vampire-hunting castle could ever have existed, even though it was no more than twenty-four hours and two plane rides away.

She shook her head as if she thought that was crazy—which of course she did. "I just thought maybe Mr. Fintonclyde might have some ideas. Could you ask him for me?"

"I'll ask him," he said, although Trudy had vastly overestimated the old man's medical abilities. "Have you been sick?"

"Me? No, I haven't had any of those symptoms."

"What about Tom's friends?"

She pursed her lips thoughtfully before continuing. "Dave has been acting peculiar, too. They go out drinking together, and sometimes they come back a bit, well, not exactly hung over, but… Of course, I don't go to bars with him anymore, not after AA," she said dismissively. "I try to get Tom to stop. He tells me he will, but then… it's odd, now that I think about it."

"Any particular bar where they drink?"

"Oh, that old dive on Main Street, the Lobster Pot. Do you remember it?"

"You know, you're the second person to mention that place today," Caleb said as a slippery, silver-bright thought leapt up before vanishing into the dark waters of his jet-lagged brain. He shook his head, as if that could dredge up the thought.

"Let's go inside," he said finally. "I'd like to meet Tom, and I'll introduce you to Bela, my adopted son."

Chapter 2: Reunion

(Twenty-four hours earlier)

"RUDY, WHERE ARE YOU?"

Sophia stood, sweat trickling down her face and stinging her eyes as she squinted into the late afternoon sun. She took off her straw hat, swinging it to her side with one hand while she wiped her forehead with the back of the other. A small breeze tickled the back of her bare neck, making her glad that she'd sheared off her long, thick hair in time for summer.

"Rudy?"

The boy kept disappearing, hiding from her and from the demons that plagued him. She tried to take care of him—she genuinely tried—but why did he keep making himself scarce? She fanned her face with her hat and listened, but all she heard were lazy clucks from the chickens in their enclosure and the slobbering of the dog, sprawled on the lawn and gnawing on a thick, knotted length of rope.

She blew out a breath, squashed the hat on her head, and exited the vegetable garden, carefully latching the gate so that Fintonclyde's dog didn't nose her way in and rip through the plants again. On cue, the yellow Lab trotted up and nudged her with a wet nose. Sophia distractedly scratched the dog's head, while wondering where Rudy was hiding this time.

The events of the last two months would have traumatized most adults, and Rudy was only an eight-year-old who'd endured the agony of a were-wolf bite and its aftermath, which had effectively made him an orphan. His parents, German mother and Chinese father, had been scientists working at the Jackson Laboratory in Bar Harbor. The father had left the country a few years ago, and Rudy had lived alone with his mother, who hadn't survived the attack by a pack of werewolves at the full moon. His father hadn't been located, so last month Rudy's maternal grandfather had come to Maine to make funeral arrangements and to take the boy back to Germany. Fintonclyde had shown Opa the special condition of his grandson under the full moon. Sophia had not been there, but the day after, Rudy's grandfather had been thoughtful.

"I had a friend who was a—who had that condition," Sophia had explained, as they sat in the back yard on a warm summer evening, watching Rudy throw a dirty, disintegrating tennis ball for Fintonclyde's dog. "It's not so bad."

Opa looked the part of a Teutonic grandfather: a thin, ruddy face topped with white hair and bushy white eyebrows that shadowed cornflower-blue eyes. Curiosity twinkled in the old man's eyes, tinged with concern, when he had asked, "You speak about the boy that Fintonclyde raised, yes? Did he ever have a normal life?"

"He went to college, got a degree, and then…" she had replied uneasily, not sure what to say about Caleb's six-year absence. "You might meet him. Fintonclyde says he'll be here soon." At the time, she'd openly scoffed at Fintonclyde's belief that his expedition to Romania would bear fruit.

"I must return home." Opa had smiled and patted her hand. "Rudy will stay here for now. I have agreed this with Fintonclyde. He will attend school and you will care for him."

"Of course," she had answered automatically, although this was the first she'd heard of the plan. She had bristled slightly at the thought of Fintonclyde making deals behind her back and at his assumption that she'd know how to take care of an eight-year-old boy.

As the youngest of nine children, Sophia hadn't spent a lot of time around young kids. There had been hordes of nieces and nephews when she'd been growing up, but serving as an unpaid nanny to older siblings hadn't been appealing. What she'd wanted was to get out from under the lash of her violent father and away from the inbred claustrophobia of the tiny, isolated village of Tribulation, Maine. Coming to live with her aunt in Bar Harbor had been her road to freedom, or so she'd believed when she was fifteen.

Now she found herself taking care of this little werewolf, while Finton-clyde made the drive down to Boston to collect an adult werewolf: one of her oldest friends, but one she wasn't sure she wanted to see again. Apparently, Caleb was bringing his adopted teenaged son, which her mind refused to reconcile with the image of the Caleb of her childhood memories, who could scarcely take care of himself in many ways.

She slowly surveyed the back yard for obvious signs of Rudy. One of his hiding places was the narrow space between the chicken coop and the fence, but all she could see behind the coop were stacked boards and a partial roll of chicken wire. No boy.

She stepped into the shade of the large, turn-of-the-century Victorian she'd inherited from her aunt, fanning herself with her hat. She wanted to fix the unreliable plumbing, peeling wallpaper, and dusty, neglected rooms to turn the place into a bed and breakfast, but something always seemed to come up. This summer, her plans had been derailed by the unexpected arrival of this orphaned werewolf and her promise to take care of him.

At her feet, the dog whined and picked up one end of the thick rope, knotted in several places and crusted with mud.

"Not now, girl," she murmured, looking into the dog's hopeful brown eyes. "Maybe Rudy will play with you, if we can find him."

Next, she tried the toolshed between the back of the garage and the chicken coop, another place Rudy sometimes hid when she forgot to lock the door. Inside the humid darkness of the shed, she inhaled the smells of decaying grass and moist earth, squinting until her eyes adjusted to the dim interior.

"Rudy?" she called as she edged around the lawnmower. Shovels and rakes clanked softly as she shifted them, but the boy wasn't hiding behind them.

She emerged from the toolshed, remembering to snap the padlock closed, and wondered where else to look. She eyed the crawlspace under the house.

A few decades ago, the original kitchen and old servants' wing had been enlarged. Although the ground floor had grown, the basement hadn't, which meant that at the back of the house there was a crawlspace underneath that extended in about six feet before ending at the foundation. It was damp, full of spiders, and uncomfortably tight for an adult, but could be a good hiding place for a small boy.

Sophia knelt next to the house and peered through the lathwork that sep-arated the crawlspace from the yard. In a few places, the thin boards of the flimsy barrier could be pushed aside. A determined little boy could wriggle his way under the back of the house. She gnawed her lip, trying to decide if it was worth getting a light and probing the darkness.

The boy had good reasons to hide, given all he'd been through. Sophia had tried for years to imagine what it would be like for a werewolf to change during that one night under the full moon. What little she knew came from hints Caleb had dropped when they were younger.

Like an ocean wave that you feel coming, he'd said once. *You sense the change around you, and then when the wave breaks, it pulls you under and you feel like you're drowning, but you come up again, sometimes a long way away, not sure how you got there.*

The memory of Caleb's words made her shiver, in spite of the summer heat. How had that first transformation been for Rudy? The day before the last full moon, Fintonclyde had taken Rudy and his grandfather to the small island he called home, an isolated spot in the Atlantic where a werewolf could run freely as Caleb had done as a child. Rudy had returned the next day even more silent and withdrawn. In the weeks since then, the little boy had not opened up to her. She couldn't get him to sit down for meals; he preferred stealing food from the kitchen late at night. He read the library books she brought him or spent hours glued to a hand-held video game. Fintonclyde's Labrador Retriever was his only friend in the world.

The dog barked excitedly and loped over to the rhubarb patch, where the large, leafy plants lined up next to the house like a long, dark green sea monster.

"You know where Rudy is? Show me, girl," Sophia said, brushing grass from her knees after standing. She swiveled her neck from side to side to peer between the giant leaves until she spied a swath of clothing.

"Rudy!" she called. "What are you doing in there? Come out now."

A head emerged cautiously from the leaves, thick black hair falling over dark eyes, and then the boy stood. After he pushed through the curtain of rhubarb, the dog trotted over and licked his face.

"Hungry," Rudy whined, one arm hooked around the dog's neck.

"We'll have supper soon," she said. "When they get here."

Rudy gave her a frightened look.

"Remember?" she said, irritated, because she'd told him several times already. "Caleb and another boy are coming. Fintonclyde went to the airport pick them up."

"Who?" Rudy asked, hugging the dog tighter.

"They're like you," she answered carefully; she'd told him this several times, too. "When it's the full moon, they…change, they—" She stopped, not knowing how to explain the transformation.

Werewolves didn't remember what happened under the full moon, Caleb had said. Maybe they didn't know they became wolves, not until someone told them. She knew: she had seen the Wolf, had been paralyzed by its piercing howl, had watched the powerful jaws snap tree branches like twigs. How could she explain this to Rudy, who would never know what he became, except through the eyes of others?

From the driveway beyond the fence, car doors slammed. The dog shot across the grass. Rudy took timid steps in the direction of the gate that separated yard from driveway, where the dog had stationed herself, yipping in anticipation and wiggling in a happy dance. The little boy halted about twenty feet from the gate, arms held rigidly at his sides. Sophia's leaden feet refused to move.

* * * *

The old Land Rover hit a bump and bounced, creaking rhythmically as the motion died away. Caleb squinted as sunlight flooded his eyes and painted the right side of his face, making him hot, sticky, and uncomfortable. They weren't on the interstate, but driving on a two-lane road, late afternoon sunlight strobing through pine trees as they headed south.

"Good. You're awake at last," Fintonclyde said, smiling as he peered down at him. At six-foot-three, he'd towered over Caleb during his childhood and now, at twenty-five, Caleb was still several inches shorter than Fintonclyde. Even folded into the driver's seat, the old man loomed.

How old was he now? Caleb wondered. Fintonclyde had always been cagy about his age and his history, but Caleb figured he had to be at least seventy. The old man's shaggy gray hair and bristling beard, which had been neatly trimmed when Caleb had met him a month ago in Romania, were approaching the wild shagginess that usually characterized him.

"I've been asleep the whole time? I barely remember leaving the airport." Caleb massaged the nape of his neck with both hands and heard his vertebrae crack from the effort of moving. Almost twenty-fours of sitting in airport lounges and being crammed into airplane seats had not been kind to his neck or his back.

For the preceding weeks, Caleb hadn't let himself sleep, not deeply, while he'd wrestled with the bureaucracy—Romanian and American—to get the paperwork necessary to take Bela out of the country, worried about the myriad details of the journey from the remote mountain village to Boston's airport, and tried to manage Bela's mood swings. He was as weary as if he'd been walking through the mountains for days, maybe as exhausted as the night he'd arrived at Castle Arghezi six years ago.

"Hmm, yes. I had hoped to have more time for telling you about my plan," Fintonclyde said, giving Caleb a sidelong look of mild rebuke.

"Your… plan?" Caleb asked muzzily, still trying to push away the thick fog that shrouded his mind. When Fintonclyde had showed up in the village last month, he hadn't shared any plan, but had told an incredible tale about disaster in Bar Harbor and hints of an old, powerful vampire recently arrived in town. What had the old man said? *Hundreds of vacationers had to be evacuated and several were bitten.* Caleb wasn't sure what to believe, but he didn't have enough to go on yet to come up with a plan.

"Yes, my plan. Starting tonight, we'll divide into groups and search the town one area at a time."

"Huh?" Caleb was at first puzzled, then incredulous. "So, you're admitting that you have absolutely no idea where the vampires are or how to find them."

Fintonclyde snorted and waved a hand dismissively. "Werewolves should have the natural ability to—"

Caleb cut him off with a laugh. "To what? Sniff out vampires? Sure, there's a grain of truth in that. I can smell a vampire at close range, and the smell lingers for quite a while. I also have years of experience. What about this werewolf pack you've hired? Sure, they chased vampires under the full moon once, but how good are they for the rest of the month?"

"Well, the natural ability should be there," Fintonclyde said smugly.

"They don't have any experience, do they? Look, it's not as easy as you seem to think. Vampires are good at hiding, including hiding their scents or mingling with crowds of humans."

"But vampires only come out at night," Fintonclyde persisted, "so logically we should hunt them at night when there aren't other people around."

Caleb was growing irritated at the old man's arrogance coupled with his lack of basic knowledge. "There are a couple of problems with that. While it's true that some vampires don't show themselves during the day, the old, powerful ones can stand daylight in varying degrees. And where do you expect to find the vampires? Walking around the streets in the dead of night like—I don't know—zombies in a B-movie?"

Fintonclyde scowled at him, then stared through the windshield as if the familiar route needed all his attention. After another left turn, the twists of the road fell into a pattern that tickled Caleb's memory. Signs for Acadia National Park appeared along the road, and then houses, a few at first, then more. They rounded a curve and Caleb saw the sign for the town high school, where he and his friends would sneak in during Christmas break and build snow castles on the athletic field, using magic to sculpt towers and turrets, then gleefully destroying each other's fortresses. All that was from a different time: scenes from the life of a boy who had known so little about the world.

Bela groaned from the back seat, mumbling a question in Romanian.

"Almost there," Caleb answered in English, turning around to see the boy sit up and run a hand through his messy black hair.

"Ugh. This blanket smells like dragon," Bela grumbled. "If we're almost there, can I get something to eat soon? I'm starving."

Caleb knew he should feel hungry, too, but he had a roiling pit of anxiety where his stomach should be. As they drove on, the houses became older and grander, evolving from bland vinyl-sided boxes to shingled Victorians. Neon-lit motel signs popped up, generally proclaiming *No Vacancy*. On the right, Caleb saw the stone church with its square tower that marked the intersection of Roberts Avenue and Mt. Desert Street. Fintonclyde turned left onto Roberts, where the old houses and huge trees crowded the narrow street. Suddenly, a large, two-story house with salmon-pink siding and white trim emerged from behind an oak tree. So much had changed in Caleb's life in the last six years, but the house on Roberts Avenue had been frozen in time.

The Land Rover bounced as it turned into the driveway. Gravel crunched on tires and, in the back yard, a dog barked frantically.

"Here we are," Fintonclyde said with a satisfied smile as he turned off the engine and set the handbrake. "Once you've rested for a bit, we can get the Hellhounds—those werewolves I've told you about—and start the search."

"What?" Caleb asked, still incredulous that the old man believed himself to be a seasoned vampire hunter.

"My plan. The plan I've been trying to explain to you," Fintonclyde said as he pushed open the driver's door, which creaked ferociously. He hopped down, wrestled the door closed, and walked down the driveway with a surprisingly spry gait.

"Your plan?" Caleb called at the old man's retreating back. He pushed open his door and rolled out of the Land Rover, feeling the hours of driving in his aching back and legs.

Fintonclyde turned, one hand on the gate latch, and glowered at Caleb with a look that said, *Foolish boy, you don't know what's good for you.* That look sent Caleb straight back to being twelve. Fintonclyde turned away and pushed the gate open. Inside the yard, a dog barked out greetings and questions about the strange new scents.

"Haven't you heard anything I said?" Caleb shouted. He stumbled in an attempt to catch up to the old man, because his stiff legs couldn't keep up with his growing anger.

A yellow Lab, nearly identical to the one Caleb had grown up with, curiously sniffed at Fintonclyde and the new smells he had brought with him, before trotting into the yard to stand next to a small, thin boy with straight dark hair falling over his eyes who stood with his mouth slightly agape.

Caleb leaned on the open gate for support, while his muscles stopped protesting. Behind him, he heard a door open, followed by a groan and a thud as Bela descended to the driveway.

"Ah, Rudy," Fintonclyde said, as if he hadn't heard Caleb, "I have some people for you to meet."

"Hold on a minute," Caleb said. "You can't just pretend that I'll go along with whatever ridiculous thing you call a plan. You don't know the first thing about vampires or werewolves!"

"Oh, come now, Caleb." Fintonclyde pivoted and gave him that *look* again. "I do have a certain amount of experience—"

"You mean your little experiment raising a werewolf cub, a lone werewolf who never met any of his kind? That's not much to brag about."

Caleb stepped through the gate and quickly scanned the large back yard. Fifteen feet from him, the little boy Rudy watched him silently; the dog appeared to be magnetically attached to his side. Fintonclyde stood between him and the boy like a gatekeeper. Off to Caleb's right, a woman with short dark hair, wearing khaki shorts and a pale blue cotton shirt with the sleeves rolled up to the elbows, observed him warily. This was not the reunion that he'd wanted with Sophia. The desire to run away hit him in the gut and made his legs turn rubbery again. He sucked in a lungful of air and thought, *Haven't I done enough running away?*

"I suppose you have a better plan," Fintonclyde growled angrily.

Caleb's attention snapped back to the old man's glowering face. "I will," he said. "I will once I've had a chance to look around town and talk to that pack, the Hound Dogs?"

"Hellhounds," Fintonclyde said with a derisive snort.

"Right. Hellhounds." Caleb ran a hand through his unfamiliarly short hair and tried out a conciliatory smile. "Give me a couple of days to get my bearings."

Fintonclyde crossed his arms and blew out a harumph. "Don't take too long. The full moon is in three days."

"Thanks for reminding me," Caleb answered sourly, his attempt to placate the old man evaporating.

"Don't think you're going to stay in town for the full moon," Fintonclyde said sharply.

"As jet-lagged as I am, that had not crossed my mind," Caleb shot back.

"Yes, of course, you will need to come out to the island for the full moon. And then we must talk about the plan—"

"Yes, the plan. We'll discuss that after the full moon, but you might as well go back home now, because there's nothing for you to do here before then." Caleb set his jaw and crossed his arms, mirroring Fintonclyde's stiff posture.

"You are making a mistake, Caleb."

"For the last six years I've been responsible for my own mistakes," Caleb answered haughtily, though it sounded hollow once he'd said it, because he knew how much his mistakes had cost him and the people around him.

Fintonclyde narrowed his eyes in a flinty stare, which Caleb returned. After nearly a minute, the old man turned away with a wordless cry of disgust. He slapped a hand on his leg to call the dog, who whined, not wanting to be parted from Rudy, but reluctantly followed Fintonclyde as he brushed past Caleb. Dog and old man collided with Bela in the open gate.

Caleb put his hands on Bela's shoulders, drawing him out of the way to allow passage of the irate old man and the very unhappy dog. The gate swung shut, thumping against the fence.

Sophia slowly crossed the yard toward him. Her thick dark hair, which had hung down her back in a fat braid when they were kids, floated above her shoulders and curled around her neck. She swung a straw hat in one hand and her knees were bright green with grass stains.

"Oh," Caleb said. He let go of Bela's shoulders, then didn't know what to do with his hands, which flopped uselessly at his sides. "You've, uhm, cut your hair."

"A while ago." A frown twitched across her forehead, and she absently tugged at a curl with one hand. "You look changed… different, but good. I mean, you look healthy, so wherever you were must have done you some good."

Caleb struggled to answer, knowing that the longer he stared at her, the more likely it was that she'd think the mountain air had messed with his mind. He couldn't fit his six years in Romania into a tidy narrative involving fresh air and exercise when the reality had been a jumble of friendship and fighting, of learning and loss.

He took a deep breath and began again. "Sorry. It's been a long day, a long few days actually. I may not be at my best."

Sophia bit her lower lip and glanced away from him toward Rudy, rooted in place like a garden statue. She sighed and her familiar green eyes flicked back to Caleb's face.

"But here you are," she said and gnawed her lip again.

"And this is Bela, my son, adopted son." Caleb waved a hand in Bela's direction, then fixed his eyes on the smaller boy. "You must be Rudy. We've come a long way to meet you."

Rudy nodded solemnly, his large, dark eyes fixed on them, but fidgeting with his hands as if he wanted to run away.

Bela took a sudden big step toward Rudy, calling cheerfully, "Hey, was that your dog?"

"Get away from me!" Rudy shrieked, his high-pitched voice cracking as he stumbled backward.

Sophia glared angrily at Caleb, and then took a step toward Rudy, who had tumbled onto the grass and quickly drawn his knees into his chest, arms wrapped tightly around his legs.

"Wait," Caleb said quietly.

Sophia halted but stood tensely as if ready to swoop down and carry Rudy away at any moment.

Bela closed on the little boy until he stood a couple of feet away. He lifted up his chin and tugged the neck of his t-shirt down, and asked, "Got one of these?"

Rudy froze, mouth hanging open and wide eyes drawn to the scar that decorated Bela's neck from one side to the other.

"Let's see yours," Bela prompted.

Rudy's expression shifted from rigid terror to puzzlement to realization. He unclasped his arms, and then slowly lifted his shirt to expose the livid purple-red line slashed across his pale white chest.

"Yeah," Bela said casually, snapping his t-shirt back in place. "That's a good one. It won't always look like that, though. It'll fade like mine."

Rudy let his shirt fall back down. He didn't take his eyes off Bela's face as he nodded, while obsessively running his hands down his chest to smooth the shirt back into place.

"Are you hungry?" Bela asked, grinning down at Rudy. "Because I'm starving."

"Cookies," Rudy whispered, a ghost of a smile softening his face. "There's cookies in the kitchen."

"That sounds great," Bela said. He thrust an arm down, clasped a hand around Rudy's wrist, and pulled the little boy to his feet.

Caleb let out the breath he'd been holding in. A glance in Sophia's direction told him that she'd been holding her breath, too.

"Yes," she said, suddenly businesslike. "I suppose you'll want something to eat."

Rudy led Bela through the gate, Sophia trotting briskly after them. Caleb followed more slowly. A headache rumbled behind his eyes like a storm cloud about to explode with thunder. His jet-lagged body told him it was the middle of the night, which made the late afternoon sunshine filtering through the trees alien and wrong.

Or maybe I'm the alien, he thought. *What if I don't belong here anymore?*

Chapter 3: Artifacts

Sophia stood at the island in the middle of the kitchen, leaning over a lumpy mound of bread dough. The high ceiling and white-painted cupboards around her gave the room a light, airy feeling, countered only by the hulking, stainless-steel gas range and refrigerator, her concessions to modernity in a kitchen that could have existed in an earlier century. She pounded the dough, curling and releasing her fingers, shoving it hard against the counter with the heels of her hands, turning it to start the cycle again. *Slap-Shove-Turn.*

"An elephant's foot," Caleb said, his voice floating in from the hall. "No, from Africa," he replied to a question from one of the two boys who formed his audience.

From her vantage, Sophia could see into the front room of the house and hear Caleb's running commentary from the adjoining hall as he explained the origin and probable history of the eclectic collection of artifacts she'd inherited from her aunt. She should have sent them all outside. She wanted her house back, free from Caleb's presence, which hung around the rooms like a heavy fog. The moon would be full in two days, and they'd all be going out to Dragonshead Island, Fintonclyde's isolated home off the coast. Then she'd have the house to herself. *Slap-Shove-Turn.*

Caleb wasn't a bad houseguest and had been painstakingly polite since his arrival yesterday. He'd said little so far about his time in Romania, although Bela had exuberantly told wild tales that had captivated Rudy.

Sophia didn't know Bela well enough to tell if the boy was exaggerating, and Caleb hadn't volunteered much. The stories, if true, painted a far different picture of her old friend than she remembered.

Her childhood memories were of a clever, painfully shy boy who had been her friend in a distant era of summer freedom and adventure, but she didn't know what to make of this man, his face tanned and weather-beaten, his brown hair streaked with blond. She could no longer see in him the Invisible Boy who had tried to hide from the world when they were kids.

"—Japanese sword," Caleb was saying, and then he called out sharply, "Rudy, put that back! No swords in the house, but maybe later, if you're good, we can take it into the back yard. Now, this is a rain stick from South America."

Caleb had a knack for getting Rudy to obey him that had eluded Sophia. She wondered if it was because he was male or because he was a werewolf. In any case, Rudy would listen to Caleb where he blithely ignored her. *Slap-Shove-Turn.*

"Toby and I tried to work out where all this stuff came from, because Sophia's aunt wouldn't always tell us." Caleb's voice grew louder as he moved into the front room. Through the connecting door, Sophia saw him squat near the glass-fronted shelves that held smaller and more delicate items kept out of reach of Sophia and her cousins long ago. The two boys crowded Caleb on either side, jostling for a look at the curios.

"Shark teeth." Caleb pointed to one of the shelves. "And this fang comes from some large beast. Fintonclyde says it's not a dragon."

"Definitely not a dragon," Bela piped up, jabbing a finger excitedly toward the cabinet. "Back home, I climbed up to the top of a cliff where a dragon had been nesting and found an old skull. The teeth were nothing like that."

"Wow," Rudy breathed, then hesitantly whispered, "Can I see it?"

"Nah, I had to leave it at home." Bela shot an irritated glance at Caleb.

"As I said, this fang probably isn't from a dragon," Caleb said neutrally. "Toby always thought it was from a manticore. Let's see, somewhere in here there's a... Hmm, I don't see it."

Sophia fixed her gaze on the bread dough, as if it might make a break for it. She looked up to see Caleb standing in the doorway, flanked by the two boys.

"Do you still have that... that thing that used to be in the cabinet?"

Caleb hesitated and then plunged on. "The thing with the long black hair and the—the shrunken head?"

"A shrunken head?" Bela echoed eagerly.

"Oh, that," she scoffed. "I haven't seen it for a while. When I went to Boston, I rented out the house, packed up all of my aunt's things, and put them in storage. I haven't unpacked everything yet. Besides, I was never sure that it *was* a shrunken head."

Caleb chuckled. "Toby and I used to argue about it whenever I came to the house, remember?"

"That was a long time ago," she observed, trying to keep her tone flat and wishing that Caleb would stop bringing up the past. What good would that do anyone?

"Maybe not the first time I was here," Caleb mused. "That was—"

"New Year's Eve," she finished stiffly as she balled up the dough and threw it into a bowl, which wobbled from the impact.

"That's right, New Year's Eve." Caleb smiled at the memory. "Toby talked his mother into letting him bring a bottle of champagne that night, even though we were both underage. I remember that was the first time I ever had a drink. But mostly I remember meeting your aunt and the stories she told us about all the places she'd been. She even told us about going to Romania and looking for werewolves in the mountains, which is an odd coincidence, I've always thought."

Sophia patted the dough to level its surface. She cast her eyes about, looking for the kitchen towel that should have been on the counter. She couldn't find it, which drove her to rattle drawers as she jerked them open.

"That's why you left, was it?" She scowled at him, clutching the towel she'd tugged out of a drawer, and then stared down at the dough, while she obsessively smoothed the towel over the top of the bowl. Caleb didn't speak for a few long moments.

"That wasn't why I left," he said carefully. "For what it's worth, I didn't mean to be away for so long."

"Forget it. The past is past. And you can't bring it back," she snapped.

Caleb took a step toward her, then stopped, looking puzzled or maybe hurt. Sophia gripped the bowl tightly and turned away from him. She set it on a sunny windowsill with a sharp *thunk*.

"Hey," Bela called out to Rudy, lightly shoving the younger boy in the shoulder, "what do you have to eat around here?"

Silently, Rudy pointed to the ceramic cookie jar sitting on the island. He and Bela sidled to the refrigerator, where they opened the door, jostling and rattling the contents.

"If you want milk, get it out and close the door," she called to the boys, then pivoted to face Caleb.

"I can't bring Toby back," Caleb insisted gently, hands outstretched with palms up. "But I'm not going to let him be forgotten. He was a good person. He was my friend and your friend, too."

"How dare you," she said slowly, her face flushing as she gripped the edge of the counter. "How dare you lecture me about Toby. You didn't even stay for the end of his trial. And you don't know what it was like sitting with Toby's mother, repeating that absurd lie that a freak accident killed Toby and René and that it was partly her son's fault for playing with fire. You come back and think you can fix things, but you can't. Some things can't be—" She closed her eyes, biting her lower lip. She wasn't going to cry in front of Caleb.

"Some things can't be fixed," Caleb agreed quietly, his words radiating out into the silent corners of the kitchen like ripples from a stone tossed into still water. "I came back because… well, partly because what happened to Toby and René isn't over yet. Maybe Fintonclyde and the rest of them thought that pinning René's death on Toby would tie everything up neatly, but I've never believed that. We can find out what really happened and—"

"There you go again, lecturing me!" Sophia opened her eyes, glaring at him. "I don't have time for this. The house needs a lot of work. I've got to paint and fix the plumbing and add at least one bathroom upstairs before I can turn this place into a B&B. In fact, I've got a contractor coming by this afternoon to give me an estimate. I'd appreciate it if you stayed out of the way. Really, it'd be better if you found someplace else to stay, with Fintonclyde or… I don't know where."

"Going back there is the last thing that I—" Caleb winced. He looked away for a moment, drawing a deep breath, and said in a forced, neutral tone, "I can help you with the house, with whatever needs doing, and I have to be in Bar Harbor to prevent more of the trouble that happened… you know, already."

She knew Caleb was trying to be careful with Rudy in the room. The little boy didn't need to be reminded about the werewolf pack that had upended his life during their full-moon rampage. But Caleb should have some respect for her feelings as well.

"Get a motel room, then," she conceded, avoiding Caleb's eyes as she mounded the leftover flour, scooping it up in one hand, and then letting it fall back to the counter.

"It's tourist season, in case you haven't noticed," Caleb said.

"Well… go stay with that gang that Fintonclyde brought to town," she shot back, running her hands down her apron to wipe away the flour.

"Look, I don't know even where to find them."

"Get Fintonclyde to draw you a map or something." She blew out a long breath, puffing her cheeks with the effort, then softened. "Okay, stay until the full moon, but after that…"

A sudden stillness settled in the kitchen, a dead calm like the eye of a hurricane that foretold stormy weather ahead. Sophia methodically untied the strings of her apron, pulled it over her head, and laid it carefully across the back of one of the chairs at the kitchen table. Rudy looked up at Bela quizzically, long hair falling across his eyes, silently asking, *did we do something wrong?* The little boy tugged at Bela's sleeve and they both scuttled behind Caleb, heading for the safety of the living room.

"Rudy, over here," she ordered, pulling a chair away from the table. "You need a haircut. I've been saying this for days, and now it's time."

"Noooo!" the boy protested. He'd gone from silent to truculent since Caleb had arrived. "I wanna find the shrunken head!"

Caleb crossed the kitchen and put a hand on Rudy's shoulder. With a tight smile, he said, "You listen to Sophia. If she says you need a haircut, then you need a haircut." Caleb locked his eyes with hers and, in a more serious tone, continued, "In the past, I've only got into trouble crossing her."

"Now," she commanded, gripping the back of the chair with both hands.

Rudy shuffled across the kitchen, dragging his feet and rolling his eyes as if being called into the principal's office. He sat on the chair heavily, looking up at Caleb with one final mute plea.

"I need to go to the bank and see if they still remember my account," Caleb said in a light tone. "Come on, Bela."

"Aw, no," the older boy protested. "I'll stay here and…watch Rudy get his hair cut."

Sophia wrapped a towel around Rudy's neck and retrieved comb and scissors from a drawer. She stood next to the chair, tapping a foot on the floor.

Caleb gripped one of Bela's shoulders. "We could both use some fresh air, and, after the bank, we can walk up to Oceanside for a burger and a frappe."

"A what?" Bela asked.

"Oceanside is what they call a drive-in here. People drive their cars up and order food, American food like hamburgers, hotdogs, and frappes, which are like milkshakes."

"Frappes have ice cream in them and milkshakes don't. I guess you've been away for too long to remember that," Sophia snapped, her irritation with Caleb extending to his vocabulary.

"Of course, I know that," Caleb grumbled, as he pulled Bela toward the mudroom, which led outside. "Let's go."

"I wanna go, too!" Rudy wriggled in an attempt to get free.

"No," she countered. "Haircut."

"Another time," Caleb promised as he and Bela disappeared through the door. "And listen to Sophia!"

Predictably, Rudy stopped squirming once the door had firmly shut and Caleb's voice faded. Sophia stood behind the boy, combing his hair while deciding how short to cut it. She blew out a long breath and snipped half an inch, then another half inch. Better to make it shorter, since she didn't know when she'd get him to sit still again. Once she made the first cut, all she had to do was make the rest the same length without thinking too much. She was tired of thinking.

"Can Toby come over?" Rudy asked, twisting in the chair to look up at her. "'Cause I want to ask him about those dragon teeth or man-mant—"

"Manticore," she corrected. "Turn around and sit still."

As she circled Rudy, making small snips to even the length, she thought about that New Year's Eve ten years ago, and her mind's eye saw Toby and Caleb standing on the front porch, bulky shapes dressed for the Maine winter, wrapped in wool with eyes the only thing visible between scarves and hats. She shook her head, trying to clear away the memories that pushed up like rising bread dough, wild and unrestrained.

"Toby's gone away," she said at last, realizing that she'd been staring up at the ceiling, holding back tears instead of cutting hair. She faced the boy, inspecting the hair that now fell above his eyes instead of into them.

"All done," she said, blinking and running the back of her hand under her nose to stop sniffling. She untied the towel around his neck, carefully folding it to keep hair from spilling onto the floor.

"I want to go with them!" Rudy declared, sliding off the chair and sending wisps of black hair floating gently in the air.

"That'll have to wait for another time," she said sharply. "Why don't you go see if the chickens have any eggs for us?"

The boy glared at her, and then turned toward the door before she could give him a basket or a bag. He'd figure something out, or he'd lose interest in the chickens and find something else to occupy himself in the yard. She thought she knew all his hiding places now.

Sophia stared down at the discarded clumps of straight black hair scattered at her feet, thinking about the few times that Toby had let her cut his curly black hair, which he preferred wearing in a long ponytail like those grizzled old bikers he hung around with. She saw him now, standing with his thumbs hooked in the front pockets of his jeans and rocking on the balls of his feet. *Did you have to cut it so short, Daigle? You're messing with my image.*

Tears leaked from her eyes, ran down her cheeks, and plopped into the mess of hair on the floor. She ground her teeth before stomping across the kitchen to snatch the broom and dustpan. She had stopped crying by the time the floor had been swept clean.

Chapter 4: Oceanside

ALEB'S FEET THUDDED ON the three short steps from the mud-room door to the driveway; familiar steps that he and Toby and René had trod many times, sometimes with soft footfalls when sneaking in to visit Sophia late at night, sometimes with staccato pounding as they ran from the house on some errand or adventure, sometimes bypassing the steps altogether to leap onto the gravel below. Two months ago, he'd have been sure that he'd never walk these steps again, never see Sophia again.

Now he was here, and somehow things had gone wrong. He'd been trying to keep the two boys out of her hair, while coaxing Rudy out of his anxious silence. He had made progress with the little boy and felt sure he would make more when the moon was full in two days. Werewolves, though they didn't remember many details of their Night, forged strong bonds after running together under the full moon. How could he explain that to Sophia?

"Rudy's hair isn't that long," groused Bela from behind him, as his feet hit the driveway, gravel crunching under his boots.

Caleb turned, distracted from thoughts of how to mend things with Sophia. Bela's tangled mop of black hair was getting long, too, or maybe his inherent wildness would always make him look like he needed a haircut. And he'd been growing, Caleb realized. Bela seemed an inch taller than when they'd left the village; something about the shape of his face looked different, too. Bela had turned fourteen while they were in transit, and he hadn't even acknowledged the boy's birthday; he'd been too preoccupied with visas and travel and the hundreds of details he'd juggled to get them here.

The rage that he'd felt at the thought of an old, powerful vampire from Romania invading his hometown had been replaced by anger and frustration at the mess in which he found himself. Barely twenty-four hours back in the US, he had a traumatized little boy on his hands and somewhere out there lurked the gang of werewolves that Fintonclyde had hired to hunt vampires. If that wasn't enough, his one remaining friend in the world was going to kick him out of her house for reasons he didn't entirely understand.

"It's going to rain," Bela complained, head down as he limped down the driveway.

"Maybe, maybe not." Caleb scowled at the dark gray clouds massed overhead. They looked like half-congealed pudding: not ready to rain until fully set. "We need to get out of Sophia's hair for a while."

"You know, those stories you told me about your friends—Toby, Sophia, and René—were all about adventures and stuff, but you never said that Sophia was Toby's girlfriend."

Caleb frowned, stopping in the middle of the driveway. "We were all a little in love with Sophia when we were kids. For a while René had a huge crush on her, which Toby thought was kind of funny. Anyway, Toby and Sophia... well, they started dating, or whatever you call it, when I was away at school, and I didn't think it was, you know, relevant. Did she say something to you?"

"No, but it's so obvious," Bela said, turning to face Caleb by walking slowly backward. "I mean the way she snaps at you whenever you mention him and cries when she thinks we can't hear."

"I miss him, too," Caleb murmured. As he resumed walking, he churned through his conversations with Sophia over the last day. "I should have been there with her... After what happened to René and then that joke of a trial where the so-called elders of Tribulation passed judgment on Toby, I couldn't—I had to get away for a while, and then I sort of found myself going to Romania."

"Yeah, that's another thing," Bela said, digging his hands into the pockets of his jeans. "You always made it seem like you left America for humanitarian reasons, to civilize werewolves and teach kids, but that's not right, is it? You were running away."

"That's not fair," Caleb protested. "I guess you could say I was running from something here, but I stayed in Romania to help our kind. Before I joined Pack Six, people hunted us, because the packs terrorized and murdered humans. I had to do something. I did make life better for our pack, for all the packs in the mountains."

"Hey! Watch it! I bite!" Bela yelped as a tourist, wobbling on a rented bicycle, nearly collided with him at the end of the driveway.

As Bela cursed in Romanian, Caleb pulled the boy close to him. Tourist-clogged streets weren't the best places for werewolves with fraying nerves two days before the full moon.

"The walk will do us good," Caleb said grimly, dragging the reluctant boy as they turned onto Mt. Desert Street, where the parked cars protected them from stray bicyclists, but the sidewalk bustled with people wandering in and out of cafés and t-shirt shops.

"And we, that is I, need to go to the bank to get some money," Caleb said defensively, then tried to lighten his tone. "We can't stay at Sophia's much longer. She made that clear."

"Nice of her not to turn us out until after our Night." Bela laughed nervously, then he asked, "A bank is sort of a place where they store money, right? A big cave or what do you call a room that's like a big cave?"

"A vault?" Caleb smiled. Bela spoke English fluently, but his vocabulary was spotty. He'd grown up in the Romanian mountains where the closest village had less than a hundred inhabitants and existed on a barter economy.

"Yeah, vault. You walk in and they give you money?"

"I have—or had—an account that Fintonclyde set up for me." Caleb slowed at the puzzled expression on the boy's face. He stopped in front of a bike rental shop, letting the shambling flow of people pass them by, and tried to explain. "When I came to live with Fintonclyde, my father gave him money for me."

"He paid to get rid of you?"

"No, he couldn't take care of me after my mother died, but he had insurance money from…" Calen knew the concept of life insurance wasn't going to make sense to a boy who had never even seen money until a few weeks ago. "Anyway, at the bank they'll know how much of the money is mine, and I can ask them to give me some of it."

"Uhm, they have big chests of money in the…vault?" Bela asked, confusion evident in his tone.

"They don't keep all the money in the bank. It's stored, sort of, somewhere else. Anyway, they write it all down in big books," Caleb said. Today wasn't the day to explain computers or more advanced concepts like compound interest. He put an arm around Bela's shoulders and they plunged back into the crowd. "The bank's not far, around the corner. You'll see."

The smooth, gray granite blocks on the face of the Banking and Trust building on Main Street rose before them like an American castle. The high windows and wide front door seemed less imposing than when he'd been a child tagging along behind Fintonclyde or when, as a teenager, he'd come to withdraw money to pay for college.

Inside, the thick carpet, leather chairs, and dark wood paneling were as he remembered. On one side of the lobby, a balding, middle-aged man sat behind a large heavy desk, "Manager" engraved on a gleaming brass plaque, and reverently calculated something using a large adding machine. His shiny head bent down as he wrote the result with precision and an air of satisfaction. On the other side of the lobby, the teller's slots punctuated a long counter, like the crenellations on the top of a castle, in case bowmen needed to fire their arrows.

"How can I help you?" beamed a teller with a flash of white teeth. The young woman's curly brown hair floated over her shoulders and rose above her head like some small mammal about to attack from behind. The badge on her chest proclaimed, "I'm Debbie! Ask me about free checking!"

"I have an account," Caleb began, somewhat overwhelmed by the reception, while Bela stood beside him, mouth hanging open. "I've been out of the country for a few years. I don't remember the number."

"Not a problem, sir," Debbie replied with a pert shake of her curls and a toothy, incandescent smile. "Let's just see some identification, and I'll look it up."

Caleb extracted a battered driver's license and a cleaner passport from his pocket and slid them across the counter.

Debbie squinted at the license that had been gnawed by rodents, buried under a layer of ash from the fire at Castle Arghezi, and only recently unearthed. She pushed the license away with a fingertip before she picked up the passport, which had been better protected. She typed on a keyboard, frowned, and wrote a few numbers on a slip of paper. She excused herself to confer with a stern older woman, whose reading glasses were slung around her neck on a beaded chain and whose coif was a stiff confection of hairspray and respectability. The older woman pursed her lips, regarding Caleb critically. After a moment, she nodded, wrote something else on the slip of paper, and sent the young teller off into the shadowy bowels of the bank.

"Where do they keep all the money? Is that where she's going?" Bela piped up, oblivious to Caleb's gestures aimed at keeping the boy's voice low. "How long will this take? I'm hungry, and you said we were going to get some food."

Caleb glared at the boy, exasperated that he'd have to explain how banks worked again, and was about to launch into a lecture on the etiquette of bank lobbies, when his eye caught a tall, dark-haired man striding into the bank from the street. The way the man carried himself was familiar. The newcomer wore dark sunglasses and an expensive, tailored suit with a casually open shirt collar that seemed anything but casual.

The manager sprang up from his adding machine, crossed the lobby to greet the newcomer, and guided him back to the desk. The stranger took off his sunglasses and coolly regarded the manager, who bobbed as he pumped the visitor's hand in an effusive handshake.

Caleb turned his back on the pair, suddenly intensely interested in a sign on the counter about FDIC regulations. The tiny print blurred and dissolved into a thick white fog. He heard flames crackling and smelled the smoke from Castle Arghezi on that terrible day when much that he loved had been destroyed. Before his eyes, a black-clad figure materialized from the billowing smoke and leered at him with a cruel smile and empty eyes that devoured light like twin black holes.

Bela broke the spell. "Caleb—"

"Not so loud. Don't turn around," he whispered, becoming aware that his white-knuckled fingers gripped the edge of the counter and that his jaw ached from clenching. The teller's return was a welcome distraction from the turmoil in his head.

"Everything seems to be in order, Mr. O'Connor." She smiled reassuringly and slid a new account passbook across the counter.

Caleb fought to keep his hand from shaking as he picked up the book and made his eyes focus on the balance in the savings account. He looked up at the teller without speaking, because the numbers danced and wiggled on the paper as if not entirely real. Although, he told himself, he'd seen things that most people wouldn't think were real at all. Why should he be amazed by mere money?

Misunderstanding his concern, Debbie quickly reassured him, "Interest rates have been falling lately, but your savings account has still done pretty well in the last six years."

"I guess so," he croaked, while she beamed at him, pegging him as a man of substance. "Could I withdraw two hundred dollars?"

"You bet! Are twenties okay?"

The teller counted out "Twenty, forty, sixty, eighty…" and laid ten crisp bills in front of him. He didn't pick them up immediately, because he had been straining to catch any conversation from behind him between the bank manager and the tall stranger.

"I'm sure now that you've returned, you'll want to have easier access to your funds. Have you considered opening a checking account?" Debbie launched into well-practiced patter. "We have several options for checking accounts. With your balance, I would recommend the Platinum Account, which comes with free checking and, this month only, a set of steak knives or a toaster oven."

Caleb took the bills, his identification, and the new passbook from the counter and stuffed them into a pocket, his wallet having long ago been eaten by rats.

"…or perhaps the Gold Account, which does have a minimum balance," Debbie continued, oblivious to Caleb's disinterest. "There's a monthly fee, but it's waived if—"

"Who is that man talking to the manager?" Caleb interrupted, leaning across the counter and keeping his voice low. "I think I've seen him some-where before."

"That's Peter Brody," Debbie replied with syrupy admiration. "He's buy-ing the Haddock Building after the former owner died"—she lowered her voice, clearly enjoying the chance to gossip— "from that flu that's been go-ing around. Most people just get sick, but poor Mr. Haddock was positively ancient and not healthy to begin with. Anyway, Mr. Brody's probably come in to sign the papers." Mistaking his look of consternation for a question, she added, "The building's just down the street, you know, where the kite store is and, of course, the Lobster Pot."

"The Lobster Pot?"

"That bar down in the basement." Her smile slipped slightly as she confided quietly, "Very popular with locals, but maybe a bit too much local color for tourists, if you know what I mean."

"This Peter Brody, has he been in town long? Where's he from?" Caleb asked through clenched teeth.

"He's from Hungary, I think, or someplace around there. He's been here since last year sometime, in the fall maybe, after summer for sure. He must have come into some money to buy that building," she said, cooing like a teenager over her first crush.

Caleb had heard enough. He mumbled something to the teller and grabbed Bela's arm. Then he dragged the boy across the lobby, risking a glance over his shoulder before exiting to the street.

"What was that all about?" Bela asked, twisting out of his grip. "Does this mean we're not going to get anything to eat?"

"Keep walking," he ordered, marching grimly down Main Street. After they turned a corner and were no longer in sight of the bank, he slumped against the side of a building.

"That was Cuza in the bank." Caleb shivered with rage at the thought of a steady stream of tourists passing through the vampire's greedy fingers. "He's no Hungarian refugee, although I'm certain he can convince people of that. He can be extremely persuasive."

"That was him? I never saw him that day when you fought him," Bela mused.

Caleb winced. In his mind, he saw the Great Hall of the castle, its walls obscured by fire, smoke, and the aura of magic. He heard the thunderous crash when the roof beam fell, crushing Alexandru Arghezi, his mentor and friend, and ending his life. The tall, thin figure of the vampire Cuza materialized out of the choking clouds of dust. The high, angular cheekbones, the leering smile, and the empty eyes had been burned into Caleb's memory.

"It's him, all right," Caleb said grimly. "Alexandru and I hunted him for years, but I only saw him one time, on that day. And I drove the stake through him myself."

Bela paced unevenly the sidewalk, not bothering to suppress his limp in the excitement of seeing Caleb's old foe, while Caleb had fallen into a heavy lethargy, his back pressed against bricks and prickling uncomfortably.

"Yeah, and one of our pack was supposed to burn the body. You never saw it, did you? How could you trust that—" Bela switched to Romanian, spewing out epithets, because he didn't have the words in English.

"Scumbag? Son of a rabid bitch? Sheep-screwing coward?" Caleb translated, momentarily distracted by the boy's colorful language.

"Whatever. You get my meaning," Bela grumbled.

"Let's not bring that up again." Caleb flinched at the memory of the familiar argument. "I didn't want to believe that Cuza was really here when Fintonclyde said that a powerful vampire had popped up only a few months after…that day. It was too weird a coincidence. Now it seems that I wasn't being sufficiently paranoid."

"What are we waiting for?" Bela called out, launching himself toward Main Street. "Let's go back to the bank and rip his throat out."

"Killing vampires isn't that simple, and Cuza is an old and powerful one." He grabbed Bela's arm. "No, we're still going to Oceanside. I need to think, and a drive-in burger shack is the last place on earth I'd expect to find a vampire in an expensive suit."

They skirted Main Street as Caleb called up an old mental map of the town, distracting himself with memories of cutting through yards and huddling in alleys with Toby and René years before, often after they'd had pulled a prank on someone and had to make themselves scarce. Now it was Caleb who needed a quick escape, because he wasn't ready to meet his old nemesis.

Why had the old revenant come to Bar Harbor? Not in search of him, since Cuza had been on the Maine seacoast for at least eight or nine months. Caleb hadn't even thought about coming back until last month, when Fintonclyde had traced him to the ruins of Castle Arghezi, spinning that half-baked tale of Bar Harbor monsters. Fintonclyde's story now seemed understated.

Caleb wondered if he'd been recognized at the bank, in which case time might not be on his side, particularly since Cuza had established himself in town and had probably attracted others of his kind.

Where would they hide in Bar Harbor? Hunting vampires in the Transylvanian Alps had been tedious and messy. Caleb and Alexandru had slogged through bat-infested caves or crawled the rafters of barns and attics, but they had known where and when to look. He'd have to investigate the Lobster Pot as a start, and he'd make sure that Fintonclyde wasn't keeping any information from him, as the arrogant old man sometimes did.

After winding through back alleys and private yards, he caught the long-forgotten smell of charring meat and frying grease, which meant summer, which meant they were close. He'd been fourteen when Fintonclyde had let him spend time with Toby in Bar Harbor at summer's end. Some days they'd pick up work at the harbor, scrubbing down the decks of fishing boats or balancing crates of freshly caught fish on the handlebars of their bikes as they made deliveries to local restaurants. They spent any money they earned, often at Oceanside.

As Caleb and Bela emerged back onto Main Street, a low white building came into view. On one side of the building, picnic tables were scattered under shady maple trees.

"This is it?" Bela asked, unimpressed. "Where's the food?"

"Careful crossing the street," was Caleb's only reply as they dodged the slow-moving cars that clogged the entrance to the parking lot, which held about thirty cars plus about a half-dozen motorcycles.

He saw the large wooden sign that he remembered: white with blue letters spelling out "Oceanside Drive-In Restaurant." An American flag hung limply on a flagpole atop the sign and "Bikers Welcome" was written in smaller letters at the bottom. People queued up to place orders at the windows that faced the parking lot, milled nearby waiting for their food, or gravitated toward the picnic tables shaded by large, old trees. The menu, hand-painted on a wooden sign on the side of the building, hadn't changed: hamburgers, hot dogs, lobster rolls, French fries, frappes, sodas, and softserve ice cream.

Bela smacked his lips and drooled as they got close to the wooden counter where orders were taken. "They serve ham and dog?" Bela puzzled as he scanned the menu.

"Hamburgers are sandwiches with beef, not ham, and hot dogs are like sausages. And French fries are—Oh, never mind." Caleb didn't think explanations would do any good. He ordered cheeseburgers (one for him, two for Bela), fries, and blueberry frappes.

As they leaned against the counter, a giant, bear-like man broke through the lines of people waiting to order. He towered over most of the crowd by several inches; the tattoos on his beefy forearms, the bandana wrapped around his head, and the black leather vest shouted out "biker." After the man swaggered past them, Caleb saw the word "Hellhounds" written on the back of his vest in flaming orange and red letters, along with a picture of a snarling dog with long, pointy canines and bloodshot eyes. His gaze followed the biker as he continued to the grassy area under the trees and joined a group of people at a picnic table, all wearing similar black leather vests.

When the food came, Bela tore into the French fries, marveling at how the greasy strings of starch could have come from potatoes. Caleb ate mechanically, hunger replaced by a churn of anxiety as he surreptitiously observed the pack of bikers like a dog stalking dangerous and unpredictable prey.

The giant man appeared to be in his twenties, with a ruddy face that suggested time spent in wind and sun. He stood, legs apart and thick arms crossed, talking to a boy of sixteen or seventeen who gestured with his hands aggressively to make some point. The boy, several inches shorter than the older man, had copper-colored hair escaping from under a backward baseball cap. A second boy of similar age sat on top of the picnic table, boots resting on the bench, reading a book and paying little attention to the others' conversation. Something in the faces of the two boys suggested they were brothers, although the second boy had curly ginger hair and a thinner build than the first.

On the other side of the picnic table, an older man paced while talking to a short woman with sharp, black eyes and long, dark hair in a braid that fell down to her waist. The man was wiry, with thin but ropy muscled arms, a crewcut, and a red, curly beard streaked with white. Years spent outdoors had left his skin tan and leathery, wrinkles fanning out from his eyes. He could have been anywhere from late thirties to early fifties. Something about the way this man carried himself made Caleb think of him as the werewolf pack's Alpha. The woman waved her hands gracefully while speaking rapidly to the man. Caleb wondered if she was also the Alpha.

"This is great," Bela mumbled around a mouth full of cheeseburger, a thin stream of mingled meat juice and ketchup dripping down one wrist. The boy stopped, sensing Caleb's unease, and wiped the back of his hand across his mouth. "What's wrong?"

"Finish your food. I have to take care of something." Caleb nodded toward the group of bikers as he crushed the remains of his cheeseburger in the greasy wrapper and tossed it into a trash can. *Can this day get any worse?* he thought, clutching his paper cup like the butt of a spear. *I have to meet these werewolves sometime. It might as well be now.*

Caleb crossed the grass to the Hellhounds' table, forcing himself to stroll instead of stomp. He smacked his cup on the picnic table and asked, "Mind if I join you?"

Wariness rippled through the group as conversations stopped, and the bikers turned to face him. The boy who'd been reading put the book down carefully beside him. All five focused on him for a moment, and then four of them shifted their gazes to the older redheaded man, whom he'd picked out as the Alpha.

"Been wondering when you'd turn up," the Alpha said with a lazy southern drawl, regarding him with pale blue eyes that glinted like chips of ice in his leathery face. His right arm bore a tattoo of two wolves chasing one another, teeth bared and jaws ready to snap, which Caleb didn't regard as a friendly sign.

The Alpha advanced toward him, closing the distance between them to a few feet, and then walked around him slowly and deliberately. Caleb shifted in response, a complicated dance in which he maintained his eyes on the man circling him without turning his back on the rest of the pack. After the Alpha completed his silent circuit, he planted himself in front of Caleb, hands tightly folded across his chest.

"I'm—" Caleb took a step forward.

"I know who you are, Fido," the man jeered. "You're Fintonclyde's pet dog."

Caleb was stunned, remembering how he'd initially been greeted by Pack Six in Romania. Some insults spanned oceans.

"I've been called that before." Caleb chuckled, keeping his tone light even as the hairs rose on the back of his neck. "But I prefer being called by my name, Caleb O'Connor."

Silence had fallen on the group at the picnic table, while around them the sounds of summer bubbled: the banter between adults and the giggles of children chasing each other around the grass. A barely audible growl rippled through the Hellhounds, but the leader raised a fist to quiet the others.

"Damien Fang," the man grunted, then more forcefully said, "People call me Fang."

Caleb nodded in acknowledgement, biting back another laugh. Was that his true name or an affectation? No matter, he didn't want risk the situation blowing up by asking or, worse, by laughing out loud. "I arrived yesterday and… I've heard about you. I was hoping we could talk."

"What's to talk about? The old man's paying us to do a job and we're doing it."

"I have some experience in…" Caleb hesitated, considering they were already attracting attention from the people around them. "…in what you're hunting. Maybe we could join forces."

"For a cut, right?" Fang barked a laugh, which was echoed by chortles, jeers, and guffaws from the other Hellhounds. "Is that your game, you dog? Ride into town and try to rob me and mine? No deal."

Caleb stepped even closer, nose-to-nose with the Alpha, and quietly seethed, "You haven't been successful so far, because you don't know what you're dealing with." Thinking about the astonishing sum in the new savings account passbook in his pocket, he pivoted. "How much does Finton-clyde owe you? I can match that, if it's money you want."

Fang snarled in response. Caleb saw something big coming at him from his right as the giant lunged, howling obscenities and possibly a name that devolved into an incoherent moan. Both boys tried to restrain the huge biker, one pulling on each arm, while yelling at him to stop.

"Buck! No!" Fang commanded, turning and pushing his open palm flat against the bigger man's chest.

Buck, the angry giant, stopped struggling, but glowered at him. The rest of the Hellhounds were breathing hard as the sound of voices ebbed like the tide rolling out. The surrounding crowd had hushed as well, eyes fastened on them. Caleb forced himself to calm, grinding his teeth, as he watched Fang for a sign of his next move. But before the pack leader could speak, the dark-haired woman stepped in. She glared up at Caleb, hands on her hips.

"You insult us if you think we are going to take money and leave," she said slowly in a low, gravelly voice with a thick, Latin accent. "We lost one of our own fighting *los cadáveres*. No money can bring her back. Vengeance is what we want, not money."

Caleb stood his ground, raising his hands, palms out, in a placating gesture. He stared into the woman's flinty eyes. "I am sorry, sorry for your loss," he said quietly. "Vengeance is what I want, too. One of the…ones you're hunting destroyed my home and killed a friend. If we work together—"

"We got one of those stinking corpses in June," the boy with the baseball cap snarled. "And we're going to finish them off, so why don't you go back to wherever you came from."

From the corner of his eye, Caleb saw a fast-moving streak of curly black hair as Bela appeared at his side, cursing in Romanian.

"Where we came from was full of vampires," Bela exclaimed, switching to English. "Caleb hunted them and killed lots of them. You're going to need his help."

All eyes were on Bela now, who clenched and unclenched his fists, trembling with rage as Caleb flung an arm across the boy's chest to hold him back.

"Well, Fido brought his puppy," Fang drawled. The pack leader folded his arms and inspected the boy. The two younger Hellhounds chortled, the tall biker grunted dismissively, and the steely-eyed woman appraised Bela critically.

"He led the toughest pack in the mountains and took down meaner dogs than you!" Bela yelled.

Caleb was surprised and touched by Bela's defense. However, his fighting skills weren't going to be useful on a pack of extremely irritated werewolves in such a public place.

"I get that you're tough, because you made a kill in June," Caleb conceded, dividing his attention between Fang and the female Alpha. "You want vengeance. I get that, too. But you probably also want to be paid and get out of town before the cold weather comes. I can help you. I spent six years hunting and destroying the Undead in— It doesn't matter where exactly. I know how they think, their habits, the places they like to hide. Look, I don't want to fight you; I want the same things you want."

The sharp-eyed woman murmured something to the pack leader that Caleb couldn't hear. Fang shook his head dismissively, keeping his eyes locked on Caleb's for a long moment in which Caleb forgot to breathe.

"Let's roll," Fang barked to his pack. The Alpha pushed past, shoving Caleb hard enough that he fought to keep his balance. The rest of the Hellhounds stomped after their leader, glaring at Caleb, who stood motionless, one hand clenched around Bela's upper arm, until the gang had mounted their motorcycles, gunned their engines, and wheeled out of the parking lot.

Caleb emptied his lungs in a long, explosive sigh, as he loosened his grip on Bela's arm. "I suppose that could have gone worse."

"What a bunch of jerks," Bela complained, massaging the arm with his other hand. "Hey, can we get something else to eat?"

Chapter 5: The Lobster Pot

OTHING SADDER THAN AN empty bar, dontcha think?"
Mickey looked out across the scattering of tables with upside-down chairs stacked on top, their legs reaching up like bare trees in
winter. On one side of the room, thick curtains, once black but now faded
with age and streaked with dust, hid the window slits that looked out onto
the alley outside. A bar, like a casino, is a place where the patrons prefer not
to know whether it's night or day, which suited some other folks as well.
"Where's the Big Cheese? I thought he was supposed to be back before
opening time."

"He's going to be back soon. Are you ready?"

"Hold your horses, Frenchie," Mickey answered from his vantage behind the bar. "You don't want me to pour the champagne too early, do you?
It'll go flat."

"Will you stop calling me that? It's not my name."

Frenchie thrust his pudgy, annoyed face far enough across the bar top
that Mickey involuntarily pulled back. The Big Sleep made some people
better looking than they had been in life. Frenchie's round, pasty face—a
lumpy moon, the surface marred with craters and mountain ranges—had
not been improved by crossing over.

"Yeah, I know, but it always gets a rise out of you." The slim, dark-haired,
eternally young man chuckled, ignoring Frenchie's scowl as he lined up
eight champagne flutes in front of him on the marble bar top.

"Well, it's mean, and I don't like it," an irritated Frenchie whined, flicking a glance back to the bar as he scuttled from table to table, picking up chairs and noisily setting them on the scarred wood floor.

Mickey took a bottle of champagne from the cooler under the bar and set it next to the glasses with a thud, not caring that it would probably explode when opened. Frenchie was his biggest mistake. When Mickey had encountered the little sap, he had forgotten to count the number of bites, but it wasn't exactly his fault. He'd been desperate back then. Frenchie had been annoying before the change and he was, if anything, more annoying now, especially since he'd been hanging around the Big Cheese like a pilot fish around a shark.

"Where is everyone?" Frenchie moaned, throwing himself onto a bar stool and gesturing to the empty room. "He's going to be back soon, and everyone's supposed to be here. Oh, he's going to be so mad."

The door next to the end of the bar swung open, momentarily letting in clanking sounds from the kitchen, as a tall woman glided into the room. Even wearing jeans, running shoes, and a t-shirt, she carried herself like fashion model on a runway. Her black hair was pulled tightly away from her thin face, and her dark skin almost hid her bloodless nature. Dr. Nina Patel's looks had been improved by crossing over, Mickey thought, though her personality sure hadn't.

"Hiya, Doc." Mickey smirked.

"Dr. Patel to you," she said haughtily, cocking her head toward the kitchen. "I'll be amazed if those two oafs manage to hook it up correctly."

"We got a whole kitchen back there, Doc. Why do you need a special icebox?"

Dismissing him with a shake of her head, she threaded her way through the tables to a booth against the far wall. After sitting daintily, she reached for the notebook resting on the papers scattered about the table and began to make notes.

"Temperature regulation," she said, drawing out the syllables as if speaking to a small child. "I am tired of hauling dry ice from my lab."

Mickey didn't understand what the scientist from the Jackson Laboratory was going on about, and, to be honest, he didn't care. He held his tongue and rearranged the flutes to give himself something to do.

He missed the old days when the basement room had been a speakeasy called the Tin Palace, a high-class joint where a guy could always find pliable mortals, insensible after one too many gin cocktails. The ground floor above had provided cover as a supper club, and in the basement, the jazz band played all night and the alcohol never stopped. An underground tunnel concealed in the kitchen allowed Prohibition-era patrons an escape route if the place was raided and led all the way to the waterfront where "lobstermen" would retrieve lobster traps full of Canadian booze.

The public entrance to the Lobster Pot, as it was called now, was a door from the alley on one side of the building, which led down into a narrow hall so dim, that patrons often emerged through the floor-to-ceiling curtains squinting. The atmosphere and clientele had seriously degenerated over the years, in Mickey's opinion. The current patrons consisted mostly of stingy locals capable of nursing a single beer all night as well as the frequent ghost tours, in which guides brought in gaggles of tourists, telling them tales of the spirits that haunted the bar. Tourists had been known to faint from fright, especially after Mickey had volunteered to show them the "haunted" back room, a dark, spooky place where he could often grab a quick bite.

Frenchie, seated at the bar with head in hands, looked up expectantly at the sound of the exterior door opening. From the hall between the stairs and the main room, they heard the clicking of high heels and the trilling laughter of Lady Agatha Pilkington. Frenchie collapsed again, but Mickey pasted a bright smile on his face.

Mickey had worked for Lady Agatha back in the 1930s as a chauffeur and general fixer at Lilac House, her mansion by the sea. Then she had disappeared for a long time and had yet to repay him for rescuing her from her entombment. In the six years since the rescue, he'd fallen into the old routine of running her errands and killing time while she patronized expensive shops, had her nails done, and flirted with rich tourists.

She emerged through the dusty, maroon curtains at the end of the hall, followed by her companion, Guy de Mornay. Lady Agatha's blonde curls, heart-shaped face, and porcelain skin might have misled mortals to guess that she was in her twenties, although her aura of world-weariness would suggest well-preserved forties. Guy, trailing behind her as usual, wore a tweed jacket and ascot that were ridiculously out-of-place for summer in Bar Harbor. His thinning brown hair was combed over a large, pale forehead, and he had the protruding, oversized nose that the English aristocracy considered distinguished. Lady Agatha carried only an expensive leather purse, while Guy struggled with bags bearing the names of the priciest shops in town.

"Are we late?" she called, removing a pair of large, dark sunglasses as she peered around the room. "There was a delightful sale on Louis Vuitton that I could not pass up and, of course, I had to scour this dreary little town for fabric samples. This establishment is badly in need of redecorating. Isn't that right, Guy?"

"Quite so, quite so," he murmured as he set the bags down, then pulled out a bar stool for Lady Agatha, fussing over seating her.

"How delightful!" Lady Agatha cooed, settling on the stool and nodding toward the line of empty champagne glasses on the bar. "We are all here to celebrate. Even the mysterious scientist."

Nina Patel continued to scribble in her notebook and did not look up or acknowledge the new arrivals.

"Science comes and goes," Lady Agatha began airily. "Time passes, but that doesn't mean much changes."

"Your Ladyship," Mickey interjected quickly, trying to head off another argument between the two women. "Looks like he's not back from the bank yet. Can I make you a gin and tonic in the meantime?"

"Alchemists like that dotty Isaac Newton believed they had the secret of life, and look where it got them, but we know that the secret of life is in defeating death as we have done." Lady Agatha waved a dismissive hand. "Words! Science is just words. Something that we all can agree on is the need for a quiet place where our kind can mingle with mortals. We ought to be discussing redecorating this establishment, as we shall soon own it. The décor has degraded considerably since the thirties."

Mickey silently agreed with her as he sliced a lime and added it to the gin and tonic he'd hastily assembled. A fishing net, frayed and battered by decades in the ocean, hung from the ceiling above the bar, festooned with plastic lobsters and, oddly, shoes. The Lobster Pot had a tradition among the regulars of throwing shoes up into the net after a sufficient number of beers had been consumed. The large mirror behind the marble-topped bar had been obscured by a big wooden ship's wheel flanked with paintings of winking, scantily clad women in sailor's hats. The patterned tin ceiling, hidden by decades of grime and the rough rope nets, spoke of the classier past that Lady Agatha wanted to bring back.

"We need the locals," Nina Patel said, jerking her head up from her notebook to glare at Lady Agatha. "The ones who come back week after week because of the cheap beer, free pool, and, yes, the execrable décor.

Without them I can't complete my statistically designed test matrix."

"Oh, speak English, dear," Lady Agatha said, her voice dripping with honeyed venom.

"Trying things out on our 'herd'," the scientist shot back with a disdainful toss of her head. "Did I use small enough words for you?"

Lady Agatha pointed a long, crimson fingernail at the scientist like a fencing foil and snapped back, "I had a deal in which this little science experiment would be finished by Labor Day and you'd move on—to Boston or New York, I don't really care—where there are ever so many cattle for you to 'herd.' Ugh! Such a vulgar term."

"I'm very close," Nina Patel said. "Just another couple of generations and I'll have it figured out."

"Generations? By the Darkness!" Lady Agatha retorted. "We do live forever, but I don't want to be trapped in this science experiment for decades."

"Not decades." The scientist curled her lip into a sneer. "Months. A mouse generation is only three months."

"So," Mickey said slowly, counting on his fingers. "Six months?"

"At maximum. I want to be gone from this miserable little town as much as you want to be rid of the science experiment, as you call it. I'm short-listed for a position at the Rockefeller Institute, after all." Nina Patel paused expectantly, waiting for some form of awe or approbation. "The Rockefeller Institute? In New York? Surely, you've heard of it. It's the most—"

The outside door banged open, freezing her in mid-sentence. Cuza emerged from the short hall, face twisted in rage as he strode to the bar. He threw his sunglasses on the floor, shouting, *"Fiul unui măgar!"*

"Whoa, hombre," Mickey said placatingly as the others in the room looked mystified. "Not everyone here understands the old mother tongue."

"I do not have words in English for that…that…" Cuza spluttered.

Mickey wondered what had caused Cuza to lose his temper as well as his vocabulary. He spoke heavily-accented English passably well, but this was the first time Mickey could recall him becoming angry enough to be at a loss for words.

"Your glasses, sir," Frenchie stammered, holding out the sunglasses he'd hurriedly retrieved from the floor.

"Was there a problem at the bank?" Lady Agatha put in sharply.

"No, the building is mine," Cuza said airily, pushing away the obsequious

Frenchie and leaning against the bar, struggling to control himself. "But that is not—"

"Ours, you mean to say," Lady Agatha said with a puckered smile. "I gave you the money needed to buy this place. Perhaps that has slipped your mind?"

"Yes, yes," Cuza replied not bothering to cover his underlying rage. "But you gave me power-of-attorney. And I run this bar, if that is acceptable to you, *partner*." The last word was coated in unctuousness with a core of sarcasm, like a chocolate-covered grenade. "That is not important at this—"

"I have no interest in meeting the public," Lady Agatha interrupted tartly, pronouncing the final word as if it had lice.

"You have no trouble meeting with our chosen few, I assume. My brilliant plan means that our kind will never have to hunt for what we need," he said with a self-congratulatory smirk. "But there is something more important that—"

Nina Patel cleared her throat, eyes boring into Cuza.

"Without the efforts of our talented Dr. Patel, this would not be possible," he conceded. "But we must not talk about such trivial things. At the bank, I saw that... *câine turbat.*"

"Oh, do they let dogs into the bank, Boss?" Mickey asked innocently as he ripped the foil from the neck of the champagne bottle.

"Not dog!" Cuza raged. "How do you say in English? *Vârcolac!*"

"Oh, werewolf," Mickey said brightly, amused that the usually hyper-controlled Cuza was losing his marbles. "This town's crawling with those mangy dogs, Boss, you know that, like those biker hooligans. You telling me they let bikers into the bank?"

"Not one of those whatever-you-call-them," Cuza said with irritation. "I do not believe my eyes when I see that disgusting piece of— He calls himself Lupeni last year, but I ask the bank teller for his name and she tells me—how is this possible? —that he is from this town and his name is Caleb O'Connor."

Frenchie squeaked and fell backward, landing with a thump. "Caleb... Caleb O'Connor?" he stuttered, looking up from the floor.

"Ah! You know him!" Cuza shouted, towering over the cringing Frenchie, who had pulled his arms over his head like a shield.

"Maybe," Frenchie muttered, not meeting Cuza's angry stare. "Yeah, sorta. I mean, it was a long time ago. He left town, that's what I heard."

"Why did you not know he returned?"

"I've only been like this... you know, for a few years, and I can't exactly go out in the day yet. Anyway, someone might recognize me in town."

"Ridiculous!" Cuza thundered. "Lurking in the shadows is what we do! And if you are good enough, you take care of anyone who recognizes you."

While Frenchie sniveled on the floor, Cuza, his face twisted in fury, turned on Mickey. "And you! You know this town, yet you did not detect this Lupeni or O'Connor, whatever he calls himself. He worked for your nasty brother. Together those two eliminated at least a dozen of our kind in Romania, including"—Cuza threw a smoldering glance at Mickey—"your sister-in-law Ana Maria!"

Without noticing, Mickey had been twisting and re-twisting the metal harness from the top of the champagne bottle, but now he held himself rigid, as only an immortal could.

"I never seen the guy before, so don't pin this on me," Mickey said, compressing the mangled wire into a rough ball and flinging it to the floor.

"I am sure dear Mickey will help if he can," Lady Agatha said soothingly. "But aren't you overreacting a bit? After that dreadful debacle two months ago..."

"First," Cuza shot back angrily, "that was not our fault. We were surprised by that gang of motorcycle-riding dogs and could not defend ourselves. Second, this Caleb O'Connor has hunted our kind before. That is why he is here. And if he finds one of us, he will not rest until he gets all."

Mickey glared at Cuza and with more vigor said, "Why didn't you get rid of this werewolf back in Romania? Why'd you run away?"

"I did not run away," Cuza replied coldly. "After I had my revenge on your brother, there was nothing left there."

He's evading, Mickey thought. Cuza hadn't provided many details of the fight with Alexandru and the destruction of the castle last year. Given that he liked to brag whenever possible, Mickey suspected that Cuza had been less than victorious and that the new werewolf in town had something to do with it.

"I needed a fresh start, fresh blood. My new ally," Cuza continued, nodding toward Nina Patel, "made a discovery, a very important discovery, that means the mortals give us what we need in a more... modern way."

"Modern!" Lady Agatha sniffed. "You're barely a hundred years on this side of the veil. When you've been around as long as I have—"

"Now that everything's hunky-dory, let's celebrate," Mickey interrupted. He'd heard this argument before, and it always ended badly. He grasped the neck of the bottle and pulled the cork out quickly enough that champagne exploded, fountaining up and splattering droplets on the bar top.

"Oh! Do be careful!" Lady Agatha cried and backed away, stumbling off the stool. Guy plucked a handkerchief from his pocket and scurried over to mop up the spray from her dress with one hand as he steadied her with the other.

Mickey mumbled an apology and filled the glasses, trying to keep his hand from shaking. Hearing about the deaths of the brother and sister-in-law he hadn't seen in decades was unsettling enough; the arrival of this werewolf whom Cuza feared created another dimension of anxiety. As he topped off the flutes, the door from the kitchen flew open, slamming into the wall. A tall, wide figure strode through the doorway.

"What's going on, Boss?" asked Vito, a tough guy from New York City who had come to Bar Harbor for the disastrous party two months ago and stayed. His partner Donnie trailed behind him, silent as usual. Mickey thought the pair looked like a comic-book version of goons: beefy shoulders, thick brows, and perennially vacant expressions. How they had become immortals was a puzzling tale that Mickey did not want to know. But Cuza wanted minions and Frenchie was clearly sub-par in that department.

Mickey pointedly gave the first glass to Lady Agatha as Cuza glared at him. The scientist reluctantly left her notebook and strode to the bar to claim a flute. Frenchie picked himself off the floor and scuttled toward the bar, waiting until Cuza had a glass in hand before taking one for himself. Vito and Donnie tipped back their glasses and started to drink, until Frenchie pestered them to stop.

Cuza, glass in hand, waited impatiently for adulation, but no one was willing to give him what he wanted—which wasn't surprising as he had managed to insult almost everyone in the room since he'd arrived. With a slight shake of his head, Mickey realized he was going to have to be the one to break the awkward silence.

"To the Lobster Pot," Mickey toasted with a weak smile.

Frenchie echoed his words in a squeaky voice, then tipped the glass to his mouth, but spilled most of it down the front of his dirty gray hoodie.

"*To me!*" Cuza called and then drained the glass. He carelessly tossed the empty flute on the bar, sending it spinning. Mickey grabbed it before it crashed to the floor.

"On to business!" Cuza said.

"Redecora—" Lady Agatha began, but Nina Patel talked over her.

"I'm going to be busy for the next few days with deadlines: three grant proposals and a manuscript to finish," the scientist declared, gathering up papers from the table, while Lady Agatha fumed. "Now that the freezer's installed, I can concentrate on more important things and won't have time to run back and forth from my lab all the time." She tucked papers into the book and snapped it shut, then marched across the room. The velvet hangings that led to the entry hall swished and swallowed her as she exited. "Send someone to do a pick up," she called from the hall.

"The rudeness of that...that..." Lady Agatha spluttered, at a loss for words that might be considered ladylike.

"We have a bigger problem," Cuza said, crashing a fist on top of the bar like a judge banging a gavel. "Caleb O'Connor must be eliminated."

Vito grunted and shrugged his mountainous shoulders. "Me and Donnie can take this guy out."

"No, we need to rid ourselves of all the disgusting dogs at once," Cuza said. "The moon is full in two days. That will be the time for hunting."

"I would have thought that the terrible night when those savage beasts attacked us would have made you less eager, not more, to fight werewolves at the full moon," Lady Agatha said.

"We were taken by surprise," Cuza said, "and we had no weapons. This time will be different."

"You want me to bring out the stuff, Boss?" Vito smirked.

"Yes," Cuza answered with a thin smile, waving his hand to dismiss the two goons, who obediently lumbered out of the room. He strolled to the pool table and pushed a ball hard enough to ricochet several times before sinking into a corner pocket. Looking pleased with himself, he turned back to face the others still clustered near the bar.

"Ah, those nights under the full moon, when I stood on the wall of the castle, listening to the wolves howl, picking them off like—how do you say? —ducks in a pond," he proclaimed theatrically. "Do you not remember, Mircea?"

Mickey bristled at the old name he'd left behind in Romania. Persistent memories of the time before the change clamored for his attention, but he swatted them away like gnats. "No, I don't. I left before you kicked out the rest of my family and took over the castle, don't you remember?"

"No? I thought you were there." Cuza shrugged away Mickey's question. "The castle had weapons from many centuries. My favorite was the crossbow. Oh! The wolves shrieked when I shot them with silver arrows."

Distracted, Cuza stared up at the ceiling. The oppressive weight of time could overwhelm immortals, could sweep them away and drown them in an unstoppable tsunami of memories. The silence dragged on, punctuated only by a ping when Frenchie dropped his flute on the floor.

Mickey didn't like to think about the time before the change, fearing the wave that appeared to be drowning Cuza. If he wanted, he could remember the castle where he'd grown up, as well as the tall, smiling stranger who had arrived one day with a vague story of having known his late father. To Mickey, a lonely and impressionable sixteen-year-old, Cuza had become a surrogate big brother, teaching him to hunt when the weather allowed and tutoring him in French and History during the long, cold winter months. Ana Maria, his brother's beautiful, lonely bride, had quickly fallen under Cuza's spell. Perhaps she had been his first victim. She had stopped coming to meals, spending most days in her room, except when Cuza made one of his increasingly frequent visits. Mickey hadn't noticed how much Ana Maria had changed, until late one night when she'd appeared in his bedroom to make his adolescent dreams come true before giving him the bite that changed him forever. After that, his memories were hazy until the night of the third bite, when he'd come awake to the aching thirst for fresh human blood. Terrified about what he might do to his own mother, he'd confessed to his brother Alexandru before running away. Shortly after, Cuza had taken the castle from the family and filled it with his cronies. But Mickey didn't see the point in remembering all that.

"Hey!" Mickey shouted as much to push away his own memories as to get Cuza's attention. "Stick with us here: the castle, the moonlight, the werewolf-hunting."

Cuza smiled at the little group who stared at him with either puzzlement or disgust. He continued smoothly, as if there had been no interruption, "So long ago. Many things were lost when Ana Maria and the others left me. I did not need them! I will build again here, but we must be rid of Caleb O'Connor!"

The kitchen door swung open with a bang as Donnie appeared, carrying several rifles. Behind him, Vito's meaty arms were wrapped around a large, black leather case. The guns rattled as Donnie deposited them atop the marble surface of the bar. Vito set the leather case more carefully near Cuza, who stroked it lovingly before snapping open the brass locks.

The sight of the arsenal roused Lady Agatha, who had been silently looking daggers at Cuza during his rambling speech.

"I fail to see how these brutish tactics will succeed," she said tartly. "In fact, you may draw altogether too much attention toward us. It was you, dear Cuza, who said that lurking in the shadows is what we do best."

"We cannot allow him to live!" Cuza retorted as he opened the black case, reverently pulling aside a cloth to reveal a shimmer of metal. "And if he unites with the other werewolves, then what will we do? No, he must be stopped now. Here is how we start. It is modern, but we must move with the times."

Cuza lifted out a black and silver contraption that, to Mickey's eye, looked more like a harp than a weapon, until he spied the pistol grip and the telescopic sight. A crossbow, then. Cuza gently laid the bow back in the case and picked up a black leather cylinder with a strap along one side. Black feathers on dozens of arrows jutted out, glinting in the light. He removed an arrow, caressing the shaft slowly and sensually.

"The shaft is ash, the straightest possible and," Cuza chuckled as he pointed to the metal tip of the arrow, "silver, you see?"

"Evil Atropos!" Lady Agatha cried, aghast. "I cannot support this horrible plan, which will not end well, mark my words. Come, Guy, we are leaving!"

Guy did not answer, because he'd drifted away from her, carefully examining each gun in the collection.

"Ah!" Guy exclaimed, reverently picking up a rifle, feeling the weight of it in his hands. "We always had a grand time, hunting mortals in the woods. Remember those hunts at Lord Moreton's estate? We'd let 'em loose and then hunt them on horseback. Wound them a bit and move in for a ripping good feed."

"I was never party to such uncivilized behavior," she protested. "Seduction is always a better way."

"Decent," Guy murmured, ignoring her as he raised the rifle to his shoulder and sighted along the barrel. "Well balanced. Yes, this will do."

"Then I count you in," Cuza said as he put the arrow back into the cylinder.

"Sounds absolutely smashing!" Guy replied enthusiastically.

"And you, too," Cuza addressed Mickey. It was not a question.

"Yeah, yeah, sure, Boss. I bumped off a couple guys for her Ladyship back in the day. I can use a piece," Mickey mumbled without enthusiasm, because he had similar reservations as Lady Agatha. To Vito, he asked, "You got a pistol or a revolver? That's more my speed."

"Yeah, got a revolver, you want that," Vito said.

"And ammunition?" Cuza asked.

"I got a guy making those silver bullets like you wanted," Vito answered as he closed and locked the crossbow case.

Cuza pivoted to glare down at Frenchie. "You must find Caleb O'Connor, and you must tell me where he will be at the full moon."

"I guess," Frenchie mumbled unhappily, pulling himself up, rung by rung, on a stool. "He might be staying at Sophia's, if he's in town…"

"Another werewolf?" Cuza demanded. "Do not tell me there are more hiding in this town!"

"N-n-n-no," Frenchie stammered as he gripped the side of the bar like a life preserver in choppy seas. "Just this girl that I—that we knew when we were kids. I could check at her house."

"Not 'could'!" Cuza thundered. "You will find Caleb O'Connor and you will find out if he works with that disgusting pack of motorcycle—"

"Bikers, Boss," Vito tossed over his shoulder as he carried the weapons out of the room.

"Bikers," Cuza said with disdain. "You will find out where those dogs will be when the moon is full. Otherwise, do not bother to come back, for I will cut off your worthless head if you do not bring me what I need."

Frenchie, eyes wide, nodded his head vigorously, but had lost the power of speech. He tugged on the hood of his jacket, shadowing his face, and slunk out of the room.

"Ah, almost opening time," Cuza crowed as he clapped his hands. "Let us make ready to feast."

Chapter 6: The Bagman's Lament

THE VAN BUCKED AS it stalled on the two-lane road. Mickey had thought that he could drive anything on wheels, but he wasn't sure about the stolen delivery van, which had a touchy transmission and a large steering wheel tilted at an odd angle that made turning awkward. A car honked as it swerved around him. Mickey pulled down the bill of his cap jammed his sunglasses into his cheeks, and restarted the engine.

"Undignified is what this is," he grumbled to himself as he wrestled with the awkward steering wheel. Running errands for that crazy scientist was almost as bad as working for Cuza. Lady Agatha had volunteered him, uncharacteristically eager to help the scientist complete her "test matrix"—whatever that was—in the hope that would hasten Cuza's departure from Bar Harbor.

The nightmare had started last spring, when Mickey had emerged from his winter hibernation and found Cuza comfortably ensconced in the town, waiting for him. As Mircea Arghezi, he hadn't worried so much about leaving a trail when he'd fled 1930s Romania, but the world was different now. His old mentor had looked him up.

Winters along the Maine coast didn't present many opportunities for prey, and Mickey slept away the long, dark season. But Cuza didn't know the local habits, and last winter, instead of sleeping, he'd preyed on the few year-round inhabitants of Bar Harbor. The Jackson Lab was busy all winter, and the science crowd were naturally disposed to look pale and keep weird hours. Cuza had finished off a couple of students and turned Nina Patel. Now the pair of them had some sort of "grand plan" promising a steady supply of fresh blood.

Mickey didn't know much about the plan and didn't care, because signing up with Team Cuza would mean working for the person who had destroyed his family. He was willing to tend bar at the Lobster Pot, because it reminded him of bygone days, but he liked working for Lady Agatha—not for a salary but for room and board, which meant a stone coffin in her hidden, underground crypt and a share in the victims of her seductions. He hoped that Her Ladyship was right in thinking she could make Cuza go away—the sooner the better.

Gingerly putting the van in gear, Mickey resumed driving down the tree-lined road, looking for the entrance to the Jackson Laboratory. Low hills covered with solid swathes of green trees rose up around him as he drove out of downtown Bar Harbor. He'd have preferred actual mountains, like the ones he'd grown up around, but hills were better than the long, open vistas along the coast where the ocean and the sky went on to infinity.

About a mile south of town, he saw buildings through the trees to his left. Turning into what looked like an entrance, he hit the brakes, unsure of where to go. He hadn't realized that the Jackson Laboratory wasn't one building, but a collection of two- and three-story buildings; some were red brick like on a college campus, and others bland and modern like at a factory. The Doc had neglected to provide instructions on how to find her lab among this hive of scientists. Maybe she'd thought it should be obvious. Mickey nosed the van toward a red brick building surrounded by a carefully manicured lawn. It was as good a place as any other.

"Aren't you a little young to be driving?" asked the security guard who approached the idling van.

"What can I say? I'm cursed with a baby face. You look young forever, and then one day you don't. It's something I gotta live with." He furrowed his brows, attempting to appear both sheepish and serious at the same time. Looking eternally sixteen had advantages for seduction, but it had drawbacks when trying to impersonate some run-of-the-mill working Joe.

The security guard, a middle-aged woman with a round, doughy face, appraised him critically, then shook her head, as if not believing him was too much effort.

"Well, you can't park your van here, no matter how old you are," she said. "Deliveries have to go to the main loading dock."

"But I'm not delivering anything. I'm picking up a package from ..." He grabbed the clipboard on the seat next to him and flipped through papers, pretending to read. "Yeah, here it is, Dr. Nina Patel. My boss pulled me off my regular route to do this pick-up. This Dr. Patel must've really given him an earful. If you can just tell me where to find the Doc, I'll be out of your hair."

"Oh, *that* one. She's a real pain in the butt." The guard laughed. "But you still can't park here. Do you know where the loading dock is?"

"Not really my regular route, you know?" Mickey attempted to look helpless, giving the guard a smile that generally worked on motherly types.

"Okay, you can pull in over there for ten minutes, fifteen max," she said, gesturing to a parking space with a "Visitors" sign. "But make it quick."

He parked the van and grabbed the clipboard for additional authenticity before hopping out onto the asphalt, shaking his head theatrically to play the part of an irritated errand boy. He shed his sunglasses as he approached the guard who eyed him suspiciously, arms crossed.

"You are going to take me to Dr. Patel's lab," he intoned, locking eyes with the guard. She gasped once, then her body relaxed and her pupils dilated. "Nod your head for yes. All right, let's go."

The guard plodded past the red-brick building toward a three-story, white building, its stark face covered with a grid of blank windows like a hospital or an asylum. Inside the lobby Mickey saw people in white or blue lab coats, a few scurrying like scared rabbits spooked at being out in the open, others strolling more slowly, particularly those in groups of two or three locked in animated conversations. Instead of crossing the lobby, the guard took an immediate right turn toward a doorway and then into a concrete stairwell that led below ground.

Mickey licked his lips approvingly. He always felt better underground. The stairs ended in another door that opened on a long corridor lit from above with the same unnatural, jittery light as in the kitchen of the Lobster Pot.

Large glass windows along the corridor provided views into laboratories where more people in lab coats carried out mysterious tasks in the name of science. To his eyes, some of these rooms looked like a cross between a kitchen and an alchemist's lair with rows of bottles on shelves and black-topped tables cluttered with glassware and strange machines that he couldn't identify. Other labs contained numerous metal cages with mice—dozens or hundreds of them in total—peering out through the shiny steel bars, twitching tiny whiskered noses, which he found as unsettling as the unnatural pulsing light overhead.

The guard, shuffling ahead of him, grew restive as Mickey slowed to stare into the windows. He sensed her breathing coming in explosive little puffs. If he didn't find Dr. Patel's lab soon, he'd have to mesmerize the guard again, which he didn't fancy doing in view of the scientists. But before he needed to figure out how to keep the guard under his control, she turned left and stopped at a solid metal door.

He chuckled to himself, shouldering his way around the guard and opening the door. "Hiya, Doc!" he called cheerfully.

Dr. Nina Patel perched on a stool in front of a black countertop that held a scattering of papers, her ever-present notebook, and a large, luminous screen. And she didn't look pleased to see him.

"Finally! What took you so long?" She scowled at him as if she were doing him a favor by merely being present. "Make it quick, because there's a seminar in ten minutes."

"Sure, Doc, whatever," he replied, stepping into the lab. The overpowering animal smell conjured up a desire to sink fangs into flesh that was both alluring and sickening. How did the scientist stand it? Or maybe she snacked on the occasional mouse.

Behind him, the guard stood timidly in the doorway.

"What are you doing here?" Dr. Patel demanded.

"I should escort him back out," the guard mumbled, frowning in confusion, probably unsure how she'd ended up in this basement laboratory.

Mickey prepared to give her another dose of his special stare, but the Doc beat him to it.

"You're dismissed and close the door!" she ordered, and the guard couldn't seem to scuttle out of the lab fast enough.

"So, where's all the mice?" he asked, tossing the clipboard on the countertop before strolling casually around the room, pretending to inspect the mysterious machines on the counters. Rows and rows of yellow-green numbers jittered on the dark background of the computer screen. He'd never seen the sense of those computer things. Even television confused him, with its ability to mesmerize mortals almost as well as he could.

"Why do you care?" she snapped brusquely, hopping off the stool. "If you must know, they're kept in special rooms, maintained by technicians."

She sneered at the last word, waving a hand dismissively.

Then she turned her back to him, picking up a large, white cube from the floor and slapping it on the counter in front of her. The Styrofoam squeaked as she pried off the top of the cube.

"You're really gonna be done with all this in a few months?" He waved a hand vaguely at the mysterious contents of the lab. "Because, you know, people in town are getting suspicious. Whatever you're doing to them is making them sick, and they're gonna figure out it isn't the flu."

She gave him an irritated look before crossing to a freezer larger than the one she'd installed in the Lobster Pot's kitchen. Glass tinkled inside as she yanked open the door, returning with a rack of vials, each the size of a pinky finger and capped with an orange stopper.

"I told you, I want to get out of this town as badly as Her Ladyship wants me gone," she said as she lifted vials from the rack and set them in little wells in the Styrofoam container. "In fact, some of my colleagues here are getting suspicious. I've had to use it on them, just to keep them docile."

"Chomp, chomp," he quipped.

"Well, that, too." She tossed her head back haughtily. "I'll be out of here as soon as I can engineer a mouse strain that expresses the right factor."

"I have no idea what you just said, Doc, but I like the idea of you leaving town," Mickey said cheerfully. "You and Cuza."

"New York will be far more suitable," she commented as she pulled on a pair of insulated gloves. "More people to prey on and better society."

"Hey, thanks for that," he said.

She walked away from him to a corner of the lab. Foggy tendrils slithered out and flowed along the floor when she pulled open an ice chest. She extracted a piece of dry ice and carried it to the Styrofoam container, wisps of white flowing behind and then vanishing. She slid the dry ice from a gloved palm into the container and swiftly brought the lid down on the steaming interior.

"There," she said, shoving the white cube across the counter toward him. "That should last for a few days. You can come back for more after that."

He scowled at the thought of this becoming a regular job. Then, because he knew it would irritate her, he said, "We're going to need more syringes, too. Maybe a couple dozen."

"Is that so?" she snapped, pulling off the gloves. "Cuza is playing havoc with my lab budget."

He thought at first that she wasn't going to go along with this. In truth, they had plenty of syringes, but he enjoyed seeing the scientist put out. He smiled blandly as she rattled a drawer open, pulled out a white plastic-wrapped package, and slammed it on top of the box.

"Catch you later, Doc," he called on his way out the door.

Chapter 7: Répondez, S'il Vous Plaît

SPIDERS. RATS. PIGEONS. RUSTLING in the rafters.

Bela looked around at the musty-smelling, junk-filled corner of hell to which he'd been exiled. Dusty cobwebs hung everywhere in the garage. He hadn't seen rats yet, but plenty of evidence: gnawed corners of old magazines, nests made of twigs and bits of old furniture stuffing, and the smell. He'd never forget having to eat rats and mice when food was scarce, and that nasty, rodenty stench. *Americans eat much better food*, he thought, *like the hamburgers at that place yesterday*. His stomach rumbled at the memory.

Since they'd returned from the drive-in with those hamburgers, French fries, and delicious ice cream drinks, Caleb had been agitated. He'd told Sophia about the Hellhounds, but had left out the part about seeing a vampire at the bank. Today Caleb had thrown himself into setting wards on Sophia's house, magically blocking the doors and windows. He had told her that it was because he didn't trust the Hellhounds, but he'd sent Bela to the grocery store to buy several pounds of garlic bulbs, which he'd discretely tucked around the house while Sophia wasn't watching.

Bela wanted to help Caleb make the wards around the house. He'd been able to break through most of the magical protections that Caleb had created around the castle back home, hadn't he? He couldn't understand why Caleb didn't want his help now. Instead, he had sent Bela to this cobweb-filled garage, suggesting that he clean out the junk. But how was he supposed to know the difference between junk and valuable stuff?

The garage was detached from the house and wide enough for two cars, although currently it held only Fintonclyde's battered old Land Rover, which he stored at Sophia's when he wasn't on the mainland. The junk (or possibly valuable stuff) took up the rest of the interior. The outside of the garage had been painted at some time in the distant past, judging from the peeling white flakes on the siding. Inside, the unpainted walls were hung with tools, rope, bicycles, tires of different sizes, and objects wholly foreign to Bela. Around him crowded a jumble of boxes, old appliances, and broken furniture. A couple of naked light bulbs dangled from the rafters, not giving much light. In the deep shadows overhead, animals squeaked and flapped and scampered. Late afternoon sunlight filtered in through the open doors, providing more illumination than the bare bulbs.

Bela didn't think the broom and leather gloves that Caleb had given him were going to help much. He'd cleared a patch of the packed dirt floor near the open doors, shoving aside rags, paper, and tiny crunchy skeletons. A fit of sneezing halted the sweeping, but he had laid bare an area in front of a long table that seemed to have been used for doing something mechanical. On the table, he uncovered rusting metal tools, greasy rags, and magazines about motorcycles, possibly related to the tools. Underneath it all, well-hidden and well-chewed by rodents, was a pile of magazines featuring pictures of smiling women wearing little or no clothing, which were more interesting than motorcycles. He made a half-hearted attempt to pile the tools on one end of the table. Maybe if he looked harder, he'd find a box for them. When nothing suitable appeared, he returned to leafing through the magazines.

A dull roaring sound, out of sight but getting louder, made Bela turn toward the open door. He thought of the bass rumbling of a huge lion; maybe those manticores that Caleb had described made such a sound. The appearance of a tire, then the gleam of chrome cut short his more fanciful speculations. He stiffened as a motorcycle nosed up the gravel driveway toward the garage. The rider wore a bandana across his head, ginger curls sticking out from the cloth, and looked familiar from the encounter at the drive-in. Without taking his eyes from the motorcycle, Bela stuck an arm behind him, closing his hand around a satisfyingly heavy metal bar. They hadn't received a warm welcome from the Hellhounds. What if this was the vanguard and the whole pack was coming to take revenge?

The rider, sixteen or seventeen years old, was dressed as he had been the previous day at Oceanside: black leather boots, blue jeans, and black leather vest over a short-sleeved t-shirt. He swung a long leg over the bike and peered into the garage.

"Hey," he called tentatively, squinting into the gloom.

"Hey," Bela responded tersely. That was enough encouragement for the older boy to slouch into the garage, hands shoved in the pockets of his jeans.

"Saw you at the drive-in," the stranger drawled in an American accent different from that of the Maine locals, softer and less nasal. "It got kind of weird, huh?"

Bela hastily put the tool he'd been gripping back on the table, feeling better about his chances since the rest of the biker gang didn't seem to be tagging along. He crossed his arms and nodded, pretending he hadn't been about to run screaming at his visitor, brandishing a makeshift weapon.

"Some of us can be, you know, touchy. But after what happened in June… Yeah, it's been hard." The older boy gave Bela a pained smile. "That your father with you yesterday?"

"I guess you can call him that. I mean, he kind of adopted me when I was little," he replied cautiously. "My name's Bela. What's yours?"

"Oh, yeah, sorry. Damien Fang, same as my father. Some folks call me Junior, though," the boy said uncomfortably, as if the nickname didn't please him.

Bela clearly remembered how Damien hadn't yelled at them or taken a run at Caleb at the drive-in. Instead, he'd tried to restrain the huge guy who could have flattened them without trying too hard. He uncrossed his arms and took a few steps toward the other boy, who responded by stepping sideways.

"Was that your brother with the baseball cap?" Bela thought about the other boy who had snarled at Caleb.

"Yeah. Darius, my older brother. By five minutes, and he never lets me forget it." Damien grinned at an old joke. "We're twins, not identical, though. We're, uh, actually not very much alike."

"I could tell." Bela chuckled, and Damien joined him, though the Hellhound's laughter contained more pain than amusement.

The older boy looked down at his feet, drawing patterns with the toe of one boot in the dusty detritus that Bela had recently swept into a heap. "Did Caleb really hunt vampires like he said? He wasn't just saying that to impress my father, was he?"

"Up in the mountains, where I grew up? There were so many of those stinking corpses," Bela said enthusiastically, waving an arm at unseen mountains. "Caleb knows how to find them and kill them. Well, maybe kill isn't the right word, because they're already dead. You can put a wooden stake through their hearts and that's mostly good enough, but for an old, powerful one, you have to cut off its head and burn the body. Caleb did that lots of times."

Bela wasn't sure if Damien's wide-eyed stare and open mouth indicated astonishment or disbelief, but he kept talking, louder and faster, before the other boy could get in a word.

"And then there was the night that vampires attacked this castle where Caleb lived. We tried to protect the castle—our pack, I mean—and Caleb and my mom had a huge fight with them. Lots of the castle was destroyed and most of the roof collapsed. I didn't see it happen, because I got hurt before the fight." He winced, his foot twinging at the memory, as it always did. "This time, though, I'm going to help Caleb fight. That's why I came. He didn't want me to come, but I made him take me."

"A castle, huh?" Damien said, trying not to sound too impressed, but curiosity got the better of him. "Did they get all the vampires?"

"We thought so. Until yesterday," Bela answered darkly.

"Huh?"

"Caleb went to a bank to get money, right before we met you, and the worst vampire of all from back home walked in. Caleb was shocked, but I wasn't, because one of our pack was supposed to burn the body and he—Well, never mind about that. Anyway, I always thought he got away, and when we found out that there was vampire trouble over here, it seemed to fit. But Caleb didn't buy it, until the bank."

Damien, who had absentmindedly been sorting tools and lining them up on the table by size, narrowed his eyes, saying, "There's more than one of those stinking corpses in this town. We've been trying to find them since…" He pulled the bandana from his head and ran a hand through his hair.

We lost one of our own, one of the Hellhounds had said. Bela knew what that was like. How many leaders had they gone through before Caleb came along? How many pack members had they lost? He could scarcely even remember.

After a silence that had grown from uncomfortable to agonizing, Bela said, "Hey, I'm really sorry about—"

"So, what's all this junk?" Damien asked abruptly, shifting away from Bela's gaze to gesture toward the depths of the garage.

"Not really sure," he answered quickly, grateful for the distraction. "I'm supposed to be cleaning, but it's one giant mess, and I don't know what most of it is or what to do with it. And there's these huge spiders and probably rats, though I haven't seen one yet. I guess somebody knew something about motorcycles once. There's a lot of tools and stuff."

"And what's that under there?" Damien pointed to a tarp at the back of the garage, dusty and streaked with pigeon droppings.

Bela scowled. "Don't ask me. I'm new around here."

He followed Damien, threading a path past a rocking chair with no seat bottom and an ancient washing machine. He sneezed when the older boy yanked on the tarp, sending a plume of dust into the air like a volcanic eruption. The motorcycle underneath had mud-crusted wheels and a black body with a dull silver tank embedded in its center; the black wires and silver pipes snaking toward it made Bela think of a heart with protruding veins and arteries. The motorcycle had two seats, one behind the other, and leather saddlebags next to the rear wheel. A dusty helmet and a pair of goggles hung forlornly from the handlebars.

"German," Damien murmured, squatting down and using his bandana to gently wipe dust from silver lettering on the side. "It says… Zündapp. Never seen anything like this, but my father'll probably know what it is. Who does it belong to?"

"Caleb used to have this friend Toby, who liked motorcycles. Maybe it was his."

"Was?" Damien turned to face him, enthusiasm for the mysterious motorcycle lighting up his face.

"He's not around anymore. He died a long time ago."

"Oh, sorry," Damien faltered, then unable to resist the lure of the bike, he returned to inspecting the motorcycle, rubbing away more dust. "Two opposed cylinders, probably a decent-sized engine… Might be okay or it could have a case of garage rot."

"Huh?" Bela took a step back. "Is that some kind of disease?"

Damien chuckled while staring down at the motorcycle. "Nah. When a bike sits around for too long, bad stuff can happen: the brake fluid goes bad, the brake pistons stick, or maybe the gas tank rusts out. But, hey, if we could get this running, it would be really cool. And restored, it might be worth some money."

"Really?" Only yesterday Bela had learned that there was a lot of money in the world and that having some of it was useful. "I guess I could ask Caleb or Sophia, but maybe not today." Seeing the puzzled expression on Damien's face, he finished quickly, "Caleb is upset about seeing that vampire, and meeting up with your pack didn't make him any happier. I mean, when that huge guy came at him—"

"I don't know what it's like wherever you come from." Damien turned his head, glaring at Bela over his shoulder. "When someone in your pack gets killed, you think offering money's gonna help? It's an insult, dog, a big-time insult."

"He didn't know!" Bela said hotly. "You can't blame him if he didn't know."

"Well, it hurts all the same."

After stuffing the now-dusty bandana in a back pocket, Damien busied himself with the tarp, tugging at corners and snapping away wrinkles, until the motorcycle had been hidden once more. Without making eye contact, Damien strode away from Bela toward the open door of the garage, noisily kicking the chair out of his way.

Bela slowed his breathing, thinking about pack members he cared about. What if Caleb or Mom had been killed fighting vampires? The thought opened a cavernous, aching hole inside him.

"So, my father wanted me to pass on a message," Damien spat, still irritated. The older boy stood framed in the wide door, where the late afternoon light gave his curly red hair the look of a halo, like those saints Bela had seen on the stained-glass windows of the village church.

"What, an invitation to a duel?" Bela snorted, winding his way carefully through the maze of discarded objects. "He didn't look too happy with Caleb yesterday."

"Doña Flóres got him to calm down," Damien said with the divided loyalty that Bela found all too familiar. "I mean, my father runs things, but she, you know, advises him."

"Is she your mother?" Bela asked, remembering the small, dark woman with the fiery temper who had lashed out at Caleb yesterday.

"No. My mother died when we were young and Doña Flóres sort of raised us. She's from Cuba, and they are really harsh to us dogs down there. Anyway, she tells my father when he's being an asshole," Damien concluded sheepishly.

Bela nodded in agreement. "Back home, Mom's the Alpha of our pack. She's not my real mother, but she and Caleb raised me. Anyway, Caleb does what she says, well, mostly."

"Alpha?" Damien asked, looking puzzled.

"I think that's the word in English. You know, the Alpha runs the pack. The Betas take orders. That's just how it goes."

"Yeah, I guess that is how it works, but we don't have a name for it. So, my father is, like, mostly the Alpha, except when Doña Flóres tells him he's being an asshole. And that's what she told him. So, anyway, tomorrow it's the Howling—"

"The what?" Bela asked, confused at first. "Yeah, it's our Night. So?"

"Right, so my father wanted me to ask if you and Caleb would, you know, meet up with us."

Bela ran a hand through his hair. "I don't know. He's hard to figure out sometimes. I can ask him, but I don't know if he'll go for it. He was mad at your father, and there's this little kid we have to take care of. You know, the one that got bitten by your pack?"

"That old man told us about him and about the ones who didn't…survive. But I don't remember, none of us do." Damien frowned. "Is he okay, this kid?"

"Seems to be. He's as annoying as any eight-year-old, but I was probably that way when I was little." Bela laughed, trying to lighten the pained expression on the other boy's face. He remembered the agony of recovering from his own bite and his parents' rejection. They had dropped him off in the forest for the wolves just before the full moon, and even though he'd been picked up and greeted almost immediately, it had still been mighty weird to wake up the next morning amidst a bunch of hairy, naked, rat-eating strangers.

Damien fidgeted, one foot scuffing the gravel of the driveway, and glanced over his shoulder at his motorcycle. "It hurts, doesn't it?" he asked softly. "The bite, I mean."

Bela gaped, speechless for a moment at what seemed like an impropriety, then said, "At first, yeah. I don't remember very much. Caleb showed up and put this really smelly stuff on it and then it got better. Why? Don't you remember? How old were you when you were bitten?"

Damien, in turn, stared at him for a moment, before saying, "Oh, I never… I mean, I was born this way. My mother was, you know, not one of us."

"Whoa," Bela said under his breath. His adoptive mother had told him that werewolves could father children by human mothers, but no one in the pack back home had ever met someone like Damien. He wondered what it would be like to have a mother who wanted you and loved you. He had cried for his parents so much at first, but then strangely seemed to completely forget them. He wondered now if Caleb's story about their being killed on the road after they left the village were true or just a way to get him out of Romania, and decided he didn't much care. For the first time ever, he wondered if the bite had changed him…or if it was the way Mom and Caleb had welcomed their pack newest member. Within just a couple of months Bela had felt so lucky to be a werewolf that his old life had disappeared from his mind, even when his new life had been hard.

"Look," Damien said, sounding embarrassed by Bela's awed reaction. "I gotta get going. Ask Caleb, will you?"

"Where's this going to take place, in case Caleb decides to come? I'm not saying that he will, you know."

"Oh, right." Damien laughed, shedding some of the tension between them. "There's this old farmhouse where we've been camping, kind of out in the boonies. Do you have something I can draw on? I'll make you a map."

Bela turned to the table, poking through the various piles until he found a sheet of paper, the back of a receipt for motorcycle parts, and the stub of a pencil. Damien bent over the paper, explaining as he drew how to find the old farm road and patiently identifying landmarks along the way. Dust fell on the map, accompanied by the sound of rustling and scurrying from the rafters above.

"What's up there?" Damien asked as he brushed off the map. He pointed his nose up at the ceiling and took a sniff, but didn't look any further enlightened.

"Pigeons, probably," Bela commented with a shrug. "Some kind of bird, anyway."

"There," the other boy concluded, satisfied with his work. "We get the grill going around five."

"Grilling? What are you…?" Bela conjured up scenes of torture in his mind and wondered if the depiction of the Hellhound on the back of the bikers' vests was in some way accurate.

Damien didn't seem to notice the horrified look on his face. "You know, hot dogs or burgers, steaks if we can afford them. It's kind of a tradition. You could bring something."

Bela laughed, embarrassed that he had jumped to such a dark conclusion. Back home they'd have rabbit or mutton stew sometimes, depending on what they could get. He remembered times when there was nothing to eat before moonrise. They could have used some hot dogs. A whirring sound cut through Bela's thoughts, as wings fluttered in the rafters above Damien's head.

"What's that?" Damien asked, running a hand through his hair.

"Birds?" Bela said uncertainly, peering up into the shadowy beams.

"That's kinda gross," Damien said, then he shrugged. "I guess I should go, but maybe I could come back sometime and take another look at that bike? I could try to get it running. I bet you have all the tools here. If it'll run, I could show you how to ride it."

"Sure," Bela said, trying to keep the enthusiasm out of his voice. Riding that motorcycle, it wouldn't matter that he couldn't walk without out a limp.

Damien took the bandana from his pocket, shaking it out and then pulling it on his head. His feet crunched the gravel driveway, and then he swung a leg across his motorcycle, gripping the handlebars and firing up the engine with a roar.

Bela stood in the driveway until the rumble had faded, his mind full of hot dogs and fast motorcycles. With a sigh, he finally limped into the house to tell Caleb about the Hellhounds' invitation.

Chapter 8: When Worlds Collide

SLOW DOWN!" BELA YELLED as he squinted at the piece of paper, rotating it left and right as if it would make more sense from a different angle.

"Admit it," Caleb said. "We're lost."

"Slow down!" Bela repeated. "If this stupid truck would stop bouncing, I'd be able to read the map."

"We still have time to get to the harbor and take a boat out to the island," Caleb said as he pulled the Land Rover off the narrow, country road and switched off the engine.

Shaking his head to indicate that he wasn't giving up yet, Bela spread the map across his knees and traced a finger along the hand-drawn lines.

"Maybe we should go back?" Rudy asked timidly from the back seat, cradling a still-warm pan of brownies in his lap as if it were a puppy.

Rudy had balked at going to meet the Hellhounds, even though he'd started to come out of his shell. He answered questions when asked and spoke up on his own occasionally. As a sugary incentive, Caleb had suggested that Rudy help make brownies to take with them. Earlier in the day, the boy had scooped flour and stirred batter under Sophia's watchful eye, then had licked the bowl with an enthusiasm he rarely showed for anything. Now, though, Rudy had relapsed into his former state of wide-eyed fear.

Caleb looked over his shoulder, smiling at Rudy, while asking himself if this had been a good idea. He could have sent both boys to Fintonclyde's island for the night and done this werewolf meet-and-greet on his own. This would only be Rudy's second full moon. Fintonclyde had been there for the boy's first transformation last month and had assured him that the werewolf cub had handled the process well—but the old man was only human, after all.

"Hang on there, buddy," Caleb called. "We'll get this figured out, and then we can eat the brownies."

"Oooookay," Bela said from the front seat. "I know where we went wrong. We shouldn't have taken that last turn. We need to go back."

"You said to take a left," Caleb said with exasperation, turning to face Bela.

"No, I said we're looking for a dead tree shaped like a fork on the left. That's where we were supposed to turn."

"All I heard was 'fork left'," Caleb said.

"You were going too fast, and I was yelling, but you weren't listening," Bela shot back.

Caleb studied the boy's face, brows furrowed in frustration and framed by curls of sweaty black hair. Bela had been enthusiastic for this expedition, despite the open hostility shown by the Hellhounds at their first meeting. This was a bit puzzling, because in the past Caleb had played the peacemaker, while Bela's first instinct had always been to fight. With a grunt, he turned on the engine, put the Land Rover in gear, and pulled back onto the road. As he retraced the last half-mile of the route, Bela hung out the open window, hair flattening against his head.

"There it is!" Bela crowed triumphantly, as he ducked inside to consult the map. "See, there's the dead tree that looks like a fork. Turn right here. I'm sure."

"If we don't find it soon…" Caleb warned, slowing down to make the turn onto a dirt road, which looked like any one of a dozen that they'd already passed, rutted and overgrown with a riot of bushes and late summer flowers.

"We're really close," Bela insisted. "There'll be a gate soon… There it is!"

Caleb pulled the Land Rover to a stop in front of a wooden gate bearing a torn, faded sign that read "No Trespassi". The gate creaked and buckled as Bela swung it open, but didn't fall apart as Caleb feared it might. After Caleb pulled the truck forward, Bela swung the gate closed.

"Only a mile and a half down the road!" Bela proclaimed, pulling himself into the passenger seat and waving the map.

Caleb doubted that the term "road" applied to the narrow, dirt track, which had not been maintained for decades judging by the depth of some of the ruts. Nevertheless, he noted fresh motorcycle tracks ahead and conceded that they did seem to be going the right way. He put the truck in gear. The Land Rover jiggled along the road, generating a wall of dust behind them. The rattling shook Caleb's bones, but Bela bounced happily with every big bump. *At least someone is enjoying this ride*, Caleb thought.

Poplar saplings crowded the dirt track on either side, red rose hips bobbed in the bushes, and blooms of goldenrod, Queen Anne's Lace, aster, Black-eyed Susan, and yarrow waved in the Land Rover's dusty wake. Caleb's mind wandered to the poultices and potions he could make from them, accustomed as he'd been to treating the ails and injuries of his werewolf pack in Romania. Tonight would be the first time in seventy-three months that he hadn't run with his pack in the mountains.

The track turned sharply, and they entered a cleared space ringed with trees. An old house sat to their right, the peaked roof and clapboard siding slumping like an ancient grandma asleep in a chair. A stone chimney poked up, garlanded with a brilliant green vine that had colonized a section of roof. The doors were long gone, the windows dark with a few lonely shards of glass glinting in the late afternoon sun.

The Hellhounds' motorcycles were lined up next to the front porch, where the roof had slid almost to the ground on one side. A battered pickup truck was parked near the bikes and, behind that, a couple of khaki-colored canvas tents had been erected. On the other side of the clearing, opposite the house, sat a small pond, about a hundred feet at its widest, vibrant with green islands of algae catching the sun. At the pond's margins, reeds, cattails, and wildflowers mingled; beyond them, tall pines and oaks mixed with willows and poplars.

Caleb brought the Land Rover to a stop behind the row of motorcycles. The smell of cooking meat wafted toward them from a grill made out of an old 55-gallon drum turned on its side and raised on metal legs. Bela smacked his lips appreciatively and reached for the door handle. Caleb told the boys to stay in the car, resulting in disappointed groans from Bela, though not a peep from Rudy.

The Hellhounds, clustered around the smoking grill, turned to stare at them. One of the younger pack members began to walk toward them, but the small sharp-eyed woman held him back as the pack leader crossed the clearing and planted himself twenty feet from the Land Rover, arms crossed and feet set in a wide stance. Instead of leather, today Fang wore a t-shirt and, over it, an apron with "World's Best Cook" visible beneath the stains of past cookouts. He didn't look welcoming.

"You're here," Fang said after Caleb had jumped out and drawn a few feet closer.

"You invited us," Caleb said warily. Then, trying to sound more placating, "Nice spot. Have you been camping here all summer?"

"It suits us," Fang said. "We don't like being around people, especially not for the Howling."

"No worries about that around here." Caleb thought about the Night in June, when the Hellhounds had not been in an isolated patch of woods, but right in Bar Harbor. Probably it wouldn't be wise to bring that up or to ask how it had happened.

Fang uncrossed his arms, signaling a grudging acceptance. Caleb turned his head to nod at Bela, who eagerly tumbled out of the back seat.

"I didn't have the chance to introduce my son Bela, when we met before," Caleb said, putting a hand on Bela's shoulder as the boy joined him. He wondered again whether this meeting was a good idea. But the Howling, as Fang had called it, was almost upon them. After the pack leader gave a noncommittal grunt, Caleb sent Bela back to the Land Rover to fetch the potato salad and marinated chicken.

"You brought the kid, huh?" Fang asked. "He gonna sit in that car all night?"

Caleb looked over his shoulder. Rudy sat frozen in the back seat, clutching the foil-wrapped pan of brownies like a shield.

"They're not going to hurt us. It's going to be okay," Caleb said softly as he approached the open back door, the words meant to reassure himself as much as the little boy. "I'll bet you're hungry after the car ride."

Rudy's wide-eyed stare fixed on Caleb for several moments, then the frozen mask slowly melted as he looked down at the brownies in his lap.

"Hungry," Rudy whispered, darting a nervous glance up at Caleb. The boy scooted to the end of the back seat, then eyed the ground warily, uncertain how to get out without losing the pan of brownies.

Caleb resolved the dilemma by picking up the little boy, who held tightly to the pan, and setting him on the ground. He closed the truck's door and turned to face the pack leader as Rudy scuttled behind his legs.

"This is Rudy," Caleb said simply.

Fang squatted next to the little boy who stood immobile, the foil-covered pan in front of him for protection.

"What've you got there, kiddo?" Fang asked in a kinder tone than Caleb had heard from him.

"Brownies," Rudy stammered, his arms shaking slightly as he held up the foil-covered pan.

"Made them yourself?"

Rudy nodded slowly, his eyes wide.

The pack leader frowned, scrutinizing the little boy for a long moment. Caleb held his breath, suddenly afraid for the boy, until Fang ruffled Rudy's hair. "I like brownies," he said, standing up. "Let's see if the others like them, too."

Fang took the pan and held out a hand to the little boy. Rudy refused it, clutching Caleb's leg like a squirrel frozen on a tree trunk. Fang shrugged and sauntered away. Caleb and Bela trailed in his wake with Rudy as the scared caboose to their little train. Fang introduced them to the rest of the pack grouped around the grill: his sons Darius and Damien, the female Alpha Doña Flóres, and the bearlike giant Buck.

Rudy peered up at the Hellhounds clustered around him and shrank into himself. Doña Flóres knelt in front of Rudy, taking his hand and whispering solemnly, although Caleb couldn't hear the words. The little boy relaxed and smiled shyly at her, which brought out a broad grin from the dark-eyed woman. She stood, still smiling. Rudy allowed himself to be led as far as a table fashioned from an old door and two sawhorses. She poured lemonade into a plastic tumbler, which Rudy clutched with both hands as he took a tentative sip while his eyes flitted fretfully from one Hellhound to another.

Damien, the ginger-haired boy, took the bag of food from Bela and tossed it on the table. Then he led Bela to one of the parked motorcycles, pointing to something on the engine and talking animatedly. Caleb was surprised to see Bela respond with interest, because he didn't think the boy knew or cared about machines. Darius, Fang's other son, stood with Buck and silently appraised the visitors.

Caleb allowed himself to relax slightly as he joined the Hellhounds' Alpha next to the grill.

"Just don't seem like a cookout without beer," Fang said, handing Caleb a plastic cup of lemonade, "but what are you gonna do, right?"

Caleb nodded. He wasn't sure what alcohol did to the transformation, but the taboo seemed to span continents. As Fang poked hot dogs and flipped burgers, Caleb found the chicken pieces he'd brought.

"Back in the mountains," he commented as he tossed chicken onto the grill, "our pack was happy if we got anything to eat before the, uhm, Howling."

"You're kidding." Fang turned, scanning his face skeptically.

Caleb shrugged. "It got better after the first year. I mean, it was the middle of nowhere: no grocery stores, certainly no hot dogs."

"You really take out all those reeking relics?"

"The what? Oh, the vampires. Well, when I got there, they were all over, but…"

Caleb felt more at ease as he spun tales of vampire hunting in the Transylvanian Alps. The aroma of sizzling meat and the background buzz of conversation soothed his nerves, which had been frazzled by the frantic ride and by fears of another hostile confrontation with the American werewolves.

Maybe this will turn out all right, he thought.

* * *

GUY DE MORNAY, THIRD son of an earl, English gentleman and gigolo, Titanic survivor, and reluctant immigrant to the New World, was in his element. At last. In the old days, his life had revolved around balls, hunting, and drinking blood. Lately he'd barely been getting one out of three.

The promise of hunting excited him as little had in the past eighty years. His companions for this hunt, noisily tramping through the trees alongside him, left much to be desired, but in this land of savages one had to take what one could get.

Cuza, the megalomaniacal Romanian, was bonkers, but at least he had style. Cuza's associates—Vinny and Dante or Vito and Donnie, Guy didn't bother to keep the names straight—knew how to fire a gun, but were not well endowed with brains and had no idea how to move silently through the woods. Mickey, in contrast, could be quiet and clever if he cared to exert himself. It was fortunate indeed that the one called Frenchie hadn't come along. That clumsy coward would certainly have cocked things up.

"Do keep the noise down, chaps," Guy reminded them again. "Werewolves' hearing is frightfully keen."

The little hunting party had driven to within a half-mile of the werewolves' meeting place and parked the stolen Cadillac in the bushes. Mickey had always been handy with cars; stealing them was another of his useful skills. After unloading guns, boxes of ammunition, and Cuza's crossbow, they'd fought their way on foot through the overgrown forest.

Guy missed the well-groomed parks of the English country estates where he'd hunted in the past. Deer and foxes were the usual prey, but those times when he and his vampire chums hunted mortals in the forest had been the best of all. All his friends were gone now. He'd lost one fifty years ago in the attack on Lilac House and another this summer, ripped apart by savage werewolves. Tonight, after the moon rose, he was going to have his revenge on those vicious curs.

Their hearing, nearly as good as that of werewolves, detected the sound of voices before they saw the camp. Guy motioned for the others to halt while he crept close enough to see into the clearing where the motorcycle gang stood around a smoking fire.

"Ah, he is here," Cuza said smugly, coming up behind Guy. "We can begin now."

Annoyed, Guy scowled at the Romanian. "*Now* we get into position and wait until after the moon rises," he muttered angrily. Hadn't they been over this before? Didn't anyone remember the plan? "They will be better able to defend themselves as humans. Everyone knows that once transformed, they are dumb animals. Thus, we do not attack until after moonrise."

Guy turned to the others, whispering, "Spread out. Find a tree for cover that gives you a good line of sight and make yourselves ready. And keep the noise down!"

He pulled on a pair of leather gloves and loaded silver-tipped bullets into his rifle. He wasn't particularly fond of silver himself. After he'd checked the rifle, assuring himself that all was ready, he consulted his pocket watch. Soon he would settle scores.

* * *

WEREWOLVES ALWAYS KNEW WHERE the moon was, even before she rose or when she hid behind thick clouds. That sense grew stronger in the weeks that the moon waxed from new to full. As sunset neared, no one in that isolated clearing needed to say anything. The Hellhounds packed away left-over food, locked up utensils, and bagged trash, while they laughed and joked with one another, Bela joining in. Caleb hung back, watching how the American werewolves did things and thinking about the pack back home. This would be his (and Bela's) first Night away from the Romanian pack. How would the Wolf react?

Every pack had their own rituals before moonrise. The Hellhounds fist-bumped and high-fived each other before scattering for privacy behind vehicles or into the ruined farmhouse. Caleb took the boys with him to the side of the Land Rover hidden from the clearing.

Bela opened the back door, sat on the seat with legs extended, and pulled off his boots. "It'll be fun! You'll see," he said as he tugged his t-shirt over his head.

Rudy stood against the side of the Land Rover like he was facing a firing squad.

Caleb sat cross-legged on the ground, which made Rudy giggle nervously.

"What's funny?" Caleb asked.

"Grownups don't sit like that," Rudy replied, shaking his head.

"I'm different from most grownups." After a silence, in which Rudy screwed up his face in puzzlement, Caleb continued, "You know about the full moon, don't you?"

Rudy tensed warily.

"I think you're smart enough to know that the moon changes as it goes around the earth. Some nights we don't see her at all or we only see part of her. Once a month, the sun lights up the whole moon and she shines all night."

"I know all that," Rudy answered petulantly.

"The night when the moon is full—just one night every month—something magical happens, and I get to be something different."

"Me, too!" Bela put in as he wriggled out of his jeans, then tossed them behind him on the seat.

Rudy's eyes widened and he shivered, putting some effort into hiding his quaking.

"Does that seem scary?" Caleb asked gently.

Rudy jerked his head in a tense nod.

"It can be scary for other people," Caleb said patiently, "because when the moon is full, and I get to be something different, it's so much fun for me that I'm not always polite. That's why I stay far, far away from people. Doesn't that seem like a good idea?"

"I guess," Rudy whispered.

"Another good reason to stay far away from people is that I don't remember what happens. I know I have fun when the moon is full, but, after the sun comes up the next day, I don't remember what I did. Pretty weird, huh?"

Rudy gave a hint of a shrug, appearing to relax slightly.

"I'll bet you don't remember what you did last month when the moon was full."

"When?" Rudy answered quickly, the note of panic in his voice indicating that he knew what Caleb was asking.

"When you and your grandfather went to Fintonclyde's island. The moon was full that night."

After a minute of silence, Rudy said in a tremulous voice, "There were trees, lots of trees. I didn't like them. Bad things come out of the trees when it gets dark."

"But nothing like that happened, right? You didn't see anything in the trees," Caleb said, keeping his voice low and soothing.

"I don't think so," Rudy said softly. "Opa and Mr. Fintonclyde were watching me. They said I'd be safe, but they said I had to sit on a rock and then they went a little ways away. And then—" Rudy shivered, wrapping his arms around his chest, although the air around them was warm.

After a minute or two, the shaking subsided, but the boy's next words came out in fits and starts: "It hurt so much. I thought I was going to—I thought it would be like before."

Caleb sighed. He had only fragmentary memories of his earliest transformations in which his parents would lock him in a small, dark closet. Later memories, when full moons meant roaming the island freely, had washed away the terror he must have felt back then.

"Can I tell you a trick about that? The change—that's what I call it—hurts more if you fight it, if you're afraid of it. It's like jumping into a swimming pool or a pond. Have you ever done that?"

"Yes," Rudy said cautiously, his eyes fixed on Caleb's.

"Right, so if you're afraid when you jump in, you might hit the water really hard or you might forget to close your mouth and swallow a lot of water and then feel like you can't breathe. The harder you struggle, the worse it feels. Well, the change that happens to us is like that. If we're afraid, it hurts a lot, but if we just let it happen, it's easy like diving, not hard like smacking into the water."

"And it won't hurt?" Rudy asked hesitantly.

"It will feel weird, but only for a little bit. After that, we won't remember, and we can do whatever we want."

"Like what?"

Bela, naked and smiling, hopped out of the car and said cheerfully, "Oh, run around, chase rabbits, howl at the moon."

"We're going to have an adventure," Caleb said as he reached out to unlace Rudy's sneakers, "but our clothes will get in the way."

Rudy smiled apprehensively, kicked off his shoes, and slowly peeled away his clothing. After undressing himself, Caleb put everything away in the Land Rover. Anything left on the ground would be fair game for the wolves, who would likely rip it all to shreds.

"Now close your eyes," Caleb whispered.

Frogs croaked in the pond. Crickets sang in the tall grass. The werewolves, still in human form, were silent, although on the inside, they all felt the moon singing in muscles and sinews as she rose, beckoning the Wolf to come out and play.

Caleb Wolf shook himself all over, throwing off the effects of the transformation and the last shreds of humanity like drops of water from wet fur. *Something was wrong.* He had a pack and a place, but around him the smells, the dusky light, and the heaviness of the air were all wrong. Bela hobbled toward him, pressing his nose against his shoulder, and growled softly about the wrongness. Where was the rest of their pack? A cub with outsized paws and floppy ears tumbled in front of his feet and whined uncertainly. Caleb knew somehow that he had to take care of this little one and nuzzled him, learning the smells of the new wolf.

A single howl shattered the silence, then others chorused in response, all unfamiliar. They were in another pack's territory. Cautiously, Caleb edged around the truck to get a peek at where the strange howls had come from. He saw and smelled the other wolves, beginning to form a picture of them in his mind. He tipped up his nose and howled to announce himself, then nudged Bela and Rudy forward toward the other wolves.

The moon slipped through the branches of the pine trees on the far side of the pond, not yet high enough to fully light the clearing. The wolves didn't need much light; their eyes took in blues and yellows, and their keen noses created landscape paintings in a palette of smells instead of colors.

Caleb trotted over to the Alpha, a yellow-gray wolf with a torn ear and scarred flanks. The Alpha, Fang, growled softly and bared his teeth. Caleb stretched out his front legs, dipping his head to acknowledge that he was in the other's territory. Fang touched noses with him, accepting the submission. Fang's two sons were easy to pick out by smell and by their yellow-gray coats, which were not as grizzled and scarred as their father's. The two younger wolves circled Bela warily at first, then all three playfully chased each other in the open clearing. The sleek, black-haired She-Wolf of the pack, Doña Flóres, sniffed Caleb approvingly and then playfully nipped Rudy, rolling him onto his back as the cub squealed with delight. Even Buck, a large, muscular gray wolf, rubbed noses with Caleb, not as angry and standoffish as when human.

Introductions – nipping, sniffing, chasing – were still going on when something seemed to erupt from the ground near Caleb's feet. His hackles up, he sniffed at a stick, quivering in the dirt. *Silver!* He could sense the lunar metal, and he remembered his old pack being attacked with silver. He barked a warning to the others as Fang rose up on his hind legs and yelped in pain. One of the flying silver sticks pierced his shoulder.

Caleb fastened his teeth into Fang's scruff and dragged the pack leader away from the deadly sticks that sang through the air before burying themselves in the ground. Fang snarled and twisted wildly, trying to sink his teeth into Caleb's front legs, while the other members of the pack surrounded them, barking in frenzied confusion. After pulling the pack leader behind the pickup truck, Caleb released him. Fang lay on his side, unable to get up, whining and snapping as Caleb danced around trying to pull at the stick protruding from his bleeding shoulder. Caleb clamped his jaws on the wooden, silver-tipped stick and tugged it free as the other wolf howled. The bloody end glowed faintly with the aura of silver.

A sharp cracking noise momentarily drowned Fang's anguish. Caleb recognized that sound. Humans with metal sticks and silver bullets had hunted his old pack. The Wolf, while not as good a tactician as Caleb's human self, knew that men with metal sticks were dangerous but could be defeated.

He nudged Bela and Rudy toward the house. Bela whined, eager to join the fight, but Caleb growled softly: *protect the cub*. Reluctantly, Bela shepherded the littlest wolf inside the shelter of the crumbling building.

Behind the cover of the truck, the rest of the wolves gathered around Fang, growling with fear and anxiety. Bullets pinged into metal or buried themselves in the ground, sending up puffs of dirt. All the shots came from one side of the clearing, proving that their attackers were not yet surrounding them.

Caleb didn't want to stay trapped or risk that some of the attackers would move around and flank them. He needed to find out more about these mysterious shooters with silver in their arsenal. Behind the truck were two tents, and beyond them, he smelled the pond on the other side of the clearing. The tents wouldn't provide protection from bullets, but they would provide cover.

He had the beginnings of a plan and barked at the other wolves to follow him, but some were too confused or unwilling to leave their wounded leader. One of the yellow-gray wolves who had a gleam of intelligence in his eyes, barked in assent. Caleb touched noses with him to acknowledge, then slunk behind the tents, followed by both of the young brothers.

*　*　*

GUY LOOKED AT HIS watch again, impatient for the hunt to bring him the trophy he desired. He hoped you could stuff a werewolf after killing it or maybe make a rug.

They had spread out in the cover of trees with a good view of the wide clearing, but so far, they'd been unsuccessful. Cuza took the first shot they'd all promised him, but missed. The second arrow was only slightly more successful, taking down one of the smaller wolves, but not killing it. Before Guy could get a shot at the downed body, another wolf dragged it out of sight behind the pickup truck. How quaint: the savage beasts were cooperating. He'd expected them to try to kill one another, although that would deprive him of sport.

All the vampires were firing now: Cuza and the other two to his left, Mickey to his right using a revolver, which was simply ridiculous in Guy's opinion. In between the crack of gunshots, he heard the whining and yowling of the injured wolf. He detected movement, but couldn't get a clear shot because the cowardly dogs were hiding. Bullets zinged as they hit metal instead of flesh. The others kept firing, but Guy waited patiently. The wolves would break from cover, and he'd get them.

Two or three wolves darted from the cover of the truck, but vanished into the darkness beyond before he could line up a shot. They were fast, faster than the hunting dogs he'd once owned. He lost track of those wolves. Perhaps they'd run away into the woods, the craven curs. No matter, he would hunt them down before the night was over.

Guy had been focused on the prey in the clearing, so it took him several moments to notice the snarling to his left, accompanied by shouting from

Cuza's two thugs. They had wanted to take positions close to one another, which Guy had said was a mistake, but those two clods hadn't listened to him. Wolves had ambushed them. Preposterous! How could such beasts, no better than dogs, do such a thing? He raised his rifle and sighted, ready to fire. There were sounds of scrambling through the bushes, then the baying of wolves grew fainter. Had those dimwitted thugs run away? They'd drawn off some of the wolves, at any rate.

"Keep firing," Cuza shouted from his left. "Do not worry about those two. They will take care of themselves."

As Guy shouldered his rifle, two wolves burst from behind the motorcycles, heading for the vampires. The enormous gray wolf charged straight at him, while a smaller black wolf danced and weaved across the space, adroitly dodging Cuza's arrows. Guy's shot caught the gray beast right in the chest, and it seemed to dance for an instant, coming up on its hind legs with the impact. The wolf howled and fell on its side, motionless. Guy scanned the clearing for the other wolf. Perhaps he could bag two in one night!

Guy didn't look at what was close by, until growling drew his attention to the black wolf crouched at his feet, eyes gleaming yellow in the dark. Guy de Mornay never found out if it was possible to stuff a dead werewolf. The leaping, snarling animal with yellow eyes was the last thing he ever saw.

* * *

As CALEB WOLF RUSHED toward a pinpoint of silver light, the vampire holding it smelled familiar. The Wolf had met him before! It was Cuza, the one who had tied Caleb with a silver chain that bit into his flesh, had thrown him into a pit with his old werewolf nemesis, and had hurled fire at him.

Caleb leapt. Cuza ducked out of the way, causing him to hit the ground. He shook his head to clear it, then looked up to see the vampire aiming a bright point of silver at him. He sensed more silver in a tube on the ground at the vampire's feet. He snatched at it, grabbing a strap in his teeth. He ran toward the smell of water, splashing into the pond and shoving reeds aside with his nose. A silver-tipped stick sliced through the water close by. He let go of the strap in his teeth. The tube floated briefly on the water, then sank, leaving only bubbles on the surface to mark its disappearance.

When Caleb emerged from the pond, Cuza was striding toward him, a vague shape outlined in the faint glowing aura that long practice had taught him signified the Undead. Balls of fire flew through the air, conjured by the vampire. One struck his fur, making him yelp. He dove back into the water.

Head held above the water's surface, Caleb saw the gleam of two pairs of wolfish eyes behind the approaching vampire. He couldn't identify the wolves by smell with the sulfurous odor of the pond in his nose. As the wolves leapt, the vampire disappeared. A flutter of black wings retreated upward: the last he saw of Cuza.

Caleb emerged from the pond, shaking water from his fur. Darius and Damien approached, barking in frustration: the attackers were not all accounted for. They trotted back into the trees, where Doña Flóres had decapitated a vampire and was now sneezing and wiping her muzzle on the ground to get rid of the taste. Caleb checked the woods, finding no sign of their attackers. He did find another metal stick, next to the vampire whose head had been severed from his neck, as well as the wood and metal contraption that had fired those silver-tipped sticks. He dragged them, one at a time, to the pond and watched them disappear beneath the surface.

Darius and Damien barked to get his attention. He followed the pair down the path the led away from the clearing until they came to a wall of dust tinged with the unpleasant tang of car exhaust. Caleb howled in frustration, while the other two chased the retreating car fruitlessly, returning a few minutes later, panting and unsatisfied.

The three werewolves limped back to the clearing where Buck's lifeless body lay splayed on the grass. Doña Flóres had returned to Fang, licking his wounds and trying to comfort the whining Alpha. A howl rose from inside the old house, and Caleb barked permission for Bela to come out, Rudy trailing in his wake. The rest of the night, Caleb guarded the perimeter of the clearing with Darius and Damien, leaving him exhausted when the moon finally set.

* * *

SOPHIA WOKE, HEART STILL pounding, and fought the tangled sheets to sit up. Had she heard the rooster in a dream? She couldn't be sure, but she wasn't going back to sleep anytime soon. Struggling into her robe, she stumbled to the window and peered through the curtains into the back yard, rendered starkly black and white by the cold moon overhead. That dream of fire fountaining up and engulfing the chicken coop had seemed so real that she expected to see flames. As the dream faded, she thought that something wasn't right. Was the gate to the chicken wire enclosure around the coop closed? She should have closed it when she put the chickens in for the night. She was positive she had done so. Yet from her vantage point, the gate appeared slightly ajar. As she stared longer, she thought she could see a shape on the ground inside the enclosure. A predator? Perhaps she'd been too distracted to properly latch the gate, and something had slipped inside.

She crossed the dark kitchen, her way lit by shards of moonlight slanting across the floor. In the mudroom, she shoved her feet into a pair of boots. She felt the tingle of the ward that Caleb had set on the door. He had told her that he'd put wards on the house because he was worried about the werewolf biker gang causing trouble. But tonight, of all nights, she wouldn't have to worry about the Hellhounds. She closed her eyes for a few moments, calling to mind the procedure for making a temporary portal in the magical barrier.

Outside, she pulled her robe tighter, feeling hints of the cold, autumn bite that would arrive soon. In the back yard, no flashlight was need to see the chicken coop bathed in the brilliant moonlight. The gate to the fence-enclosed yard around the coop wasn't latched. She stepped inside and squatted next to the motionless body of the rooster. Dead, but still warm. She didn't see blood and feathers as she'd expect from a predator attack. Instead, the bent neck and twisted head told a different story: a person, not a fox or a weasel, had strangled the bird.

From inside the coop, the hens clucked nervously. Cautiously, she opened the door, peering in. Though too dark to see clearly, the hens didn't seem fearful as she cooed to them soothingly. No, whatever killed the rooster wasn't in the coop. She latched the door and crossed the enclosure, stepping around the body. There was nothing she could do about the poor, dead rooster until morning.

She was careful to latch the gate to the chicken yard, then turned with her back to the fence, heart pounding and skin prickling, and slowly scanned the deep shadows. At first, she saw nothing, and chided herself for being paranoid, until she caught a faint movement of darkness shifting in darkness. She pressed her back against the chicken wire as the air around her began to hum, softly at first and then growing louder, as if all the cicadas in town were suddenly wide awake.

"Well, well. Sophia Daigle," said the figure that swam out of the shadows and stepped into the cold, merciless moonlight.

* * *

CALEB YAWNED, TOOK IN a mouthful of smoke from the fire, and doubled over, coughing until his eyes watered. He turned his back on the fire, hands on his knees, aching for sleep, but knowing that sleep was a couple of hours away. There had been much to do after the werewolves returned to human form and confronted a horrible scene: a dead vampire, ripped apart by wolves, and one of the Hellhounds, the giant Buck, dead from a silver bullet through the heart.

For Rudy, it had been another loss, another adult ripped away, as the little boy had stared around the clearing in wide-eyed, wordless terror. Caleb had tried as gently as he could to explain that they'd chased away the bad people who had been there in the night. He hadn't been able to coax a single word out of Rudy, but had finally persuaded him to curl up in a blanket and sleep.

In his sleep-deprived state, Caleb had a hazy impression of the wolves chasing their attackers through the trees. And they had been vampires, which almost certainly meant that Cuza had led the hunting party. The wolves had only killed one vampire, one Caleb didn't recognize. The spent shell casings among the trees suggested that Cuza had three or four vampire allies. They'd escaped and would attack again, if Caleb didn't stop them.

Except for Bela and Rudy, the surviving werewolves had a variety of cuts, scrapes, and punctures. Fang had the worst wound, livid and swollen from the effects of the silver arrow that had pierced his shoulder.

Groggy and exhausted as they were, there had been a few things that needed doing. Buck's inert body had been carefully wrapped in a sheet, laid on an old door, and carried into the farmhouse. Everyone except Fang had gathered wood, and they'd started a roaring fire near the pond. Caleb had dragged the body of the unknown vampire and heaved it into the fire. A hot fire was the only way to be sure a vampire wouldn't return. Darius, Damien, and Bela had stood ready with buckets of water to douse wayward embers that escaped onto the grass.

Now, as the sun crested the trees and sparkled on the pond, Fang slept fitfully in one of the tents, while Caleb and Doña Flóres kept watch over the embers of the fire. The older boys huddled together near the motorcycles, murmuring about arcane matters of engines and gears and timing as a way to distract themselves from the reality of the morning after.

79

"What was I saying?" Caleb croaked, after he'd stood up and wiped his eyes. "Right. Fang's wound. Willow bark tea will help with the pain." He coughed to clear his throat, while Doña Flóres eyed him severely.

"Oh, sí, sí. I know about making such things. I can find what I need here," she said.

"But he'll need more than that. The wound won't heal if there's still silver in it," he explained. "Trust me on this. I've seen others of our kind wounded with silver. I know a poultice that might draw out the poison."

Doña Flóres fixed her hard, black eyes on him, fatigue etched on her face. He read interest instead of scorn in her expression, which was an improvement.

"I don't suppose you have any ginseng root? Or chamomile?" he asked, running over the recipe in his mind. "No? I have those. Collect some rose hips and yarrow root. I know you can find them in the woods around here. I'll put together the rest of the ingredients when I get home. Can you send someone to get them this afternoon?"

She nodded, suppressing a yawn, which made him yawn as well, though this time he fought down the urge to cough.

"Right, right. We need to get going," he mumbled, hoping that he'd be able to persuade Sophia not to kick him out yet. "Where is Rudy?"

"Do not worry," Doña Flóres crooned soothingly. "The pobrecito is our responsibility.

"No," he said, waking up as a sudden jolt of adrenaline tied his stomach in knots. "Fintonclyde and Sophia promised Rudy's grandfather that they'd take care of him."

"Estúpidos!" she spat. "They are not our kind, what do they know? The little one is ours now. That is how it has always been when a child is bitten by the pack."

"You can't take Rudy away from the only family that's left to him," Caleb insisted, raising his voice.

She glared at him for several long moments. Her stance shifted, suggesting she was too tired to argue further. "When Fang is better," she cautioned, "we will talk. He will not want to give the boy to your human friends."

"I will help take care of him," he promised in a gentler tone. "I raised Bela after he was bitten."

She stared at him for a long minute, as Caleb tensed, knowing he was too tired for a fight. Finally, she shook her head, clearly not pleased, and barked to Fang's sons across the clearing, "*Dónde está el niñito? Tráelo aquí.*"

Caleb took a deep breath as Damien disappeared into one of the tents. He emerged with a sleeping Rudy wrapped in a blanket. Caleb took the little boy and stumbled back to the Land Rover, calling over his shoulder for Bela.

After Bela had crawled into the back seat to join Rudy, Caleb started the engine, eager to get back to Sophia's house where they'd all be safe.

Chapter 9: German Engineering

EEEW. STRAWBERRY JAM," RUDY complained, lifting a corner of bread and peering inside as if it were a peanut butter and rat sandwich on the plate before him. "Sophia always makes them with grape jelly."

Bela saw Caleb's shoulders tighten, heard the knife clink on the counter when Caleb stopped making his own sandwich and turned around to face them, both hands gripping the edge of the counter. He attempted a soothing smile, but Bela wasn't fooled. He knew by the tautness in Caleb's jaw and the rigid lines of his knuckles on the counter that he was trying not to upset Rudy. The kid, in spite of his grumbling about the sandwich, was doing fine after their Night. Bela wasn't sure about Caleb.

"Are you going to eat that?" Bela asked, pointing at the unloved sandwich on Rudy's plate.

"No! I want grape jelly!" Rudy shouted, shoving the plate away and glaring up at Caleb. "And I want Sophia to make me a sandwich!"

"We need to let Sophia sleep for now." Caleb grimaced and ran a hand through his hair. He'd been checking on her every ten or fifteen minutes, becoming more anxious every time.

Looking at Caleb's ashen face made Bela's bones ache with all the sleep he'd missed. He'd been hoping for a long nap once they returned to Sophia's house, but that hadn't happened. Instead, he was full of raw, unfocused energy and ravenously hungry.

Caleb yawned, concluding, "Fine. Go find the jelly in the fridge and I'll make you another one."

A chair scraped the floor as Rudy rocketed across the kitchen toward the refrigerator. *The kid got more sleep than I did*, Bela thought as he reached across the table for Rudy's plate. He couldn't understand what Rudy was complaining about. Peanut butter was still an exotic food as far as Bela was concerned, and strawberry jam had been a rare treat back home.

The back door rattled, startling them all. Bela hastily put down the sandwich. Caleb sprinted across the kitchen and yanked open the door to the mudroom.

Bela heard a muffled snort of irritation as Caleb stepped back to admit Fintonclyde. The old man wore the same stained overalls and battered leather boots as when Bela had first met him. Long, wispy gray hair fell over his forehead, but didn't hide the angry glare he threw at Caleb.

"Well! Here you all are," Fintonclyde huffed.

"Yes," Caleb answered slowly. "What did you expect?"

"I had no idea what to expect, because I heard not one word from you yesterday. You were supposed to be on the island last night."

"Oh, that," Caleb said, turning his back on Fintonclyde and retreating toward his half-made sandwich on the counter. He called over his shoulder, "We were with the Hellhounds. I thought it would be a good chance to get to know them."

"You could have told me about it!" Fintonclyde stomped his big boots as he advanced toward Caleb. Dried flecks of mud littered the floor in the old man's wake.

"I don't have to check in with you like you're my camp counselor." Caleb pivoted to face the old man. "I had an opportunity to get to know them, and I took it."

"Without telling me!" Fintonclyde shook a finger at Caleb, his narrowed gray eyes hard and menacing.

"I'm trying to clean up your messes," Caleb countered, sounding calm, but tensing his shoulders as if ready for a fight. "The biggest mess being the Hellhounds, who are going to cause more trouble if they stay around here much longer."

In spite of Caleb's tight control, Bela smelled the anger swirling around him, could almost make out the roiling fog of rage sending tendrils through the room. Bela had a sudden vision of an adolescent Caleb, a boy not as controlled as the man Bela knew, having it out with Fintonclyde just the way Bela had often argued with his adoptive parents. He was starting to understand some of the stories that Caleb had told about his childhood and about why he had left Fintonclyde's island at fifteen.

"Endangering this young boy! How can you expose him to those—"

"You're no expert on how to raise a werewolf, no matter what you might think," Caleb said stiffly. "I'm not going to try to explain what we do on our Night, but Rudy was in no danger from the Hellhounds when the moon was full."

It was a different story after the sun came up, Bela thought, *and then there was the vampire attack*. How much was Caleb going to tell the irate old man? This could get interesting.

"They were okay, I guess," Rudy said uncertainly, clutching a large jar of grape jelly with both hands. The little boy's worried eyes bounced between Caleb's stony face and Fintonclyde's reddening visage.

Caleb smiled thinly and ruffled Rudy's hair. "They're not a bad bunch," he said absently. "You boys go outside for a bit, okay? Mr. Fintonclyde and I have some things to talk about."

Rudy thumped the jelly jar on the counter, wide eyes still on Caleb. As he passed the cookie jar, he snaked a hand inside, then scurried toward the door, clutching a couple of oatmeal cookies like talismans. Bela pushed his chair away from the table and stood, giving his abandoned sandwich a longing glance. As he ushered Rudy through the back door, the shouting resumed.

Rudy slipped through the gate and disappeared into the back yard, but Bela hung around the door, trying to make sense of the shouting from inside the kitchen. After a few minutes, Fintonclyde's voice rose to a crescendo, then Caleb growled something in a low tone that had an air of finality. Silence for a few heartbeats. The old man burst from the back door, long, gray beard flouncing as he clomped down the steps and crunched along the gravel driveway.

Bela flattened himself against the wall of the house until Fintonclyde had turned onto the street and disappeared from sight. After failing to find Rudy—the kid had hiding places that even Bela didn't know about—Bela drifted toward the garage. Maybe now was a good time to finish that clean-up project.

After fifteen minutes of poking through piles of junk and kicking boxes, perspiration beaded on his hair and slid down his cheek in uncomfortable rivulets. He pulled up his t-shirt to wipe his face, pushing sweaty ringlets away from his forehead. Opening both garage doors had not brought the stifling interior down to a comfortable temperature. Outside the sun shone fiercely and nary a leaf moved on the trees. For a boy raised in cool, dry mountain air, the sweltering summer wasn't something he'd get used to any time soon. But no matter how bad it felt in the garage, it was better than being in the house.

Having abandoned any pretense of cleaning, he was leafing through a motorcycle magazine when a battered pickup truck pulled into the driveway.

"Dude," Bela drawled, doing his best to sound like the teens he'd heard at the drive-in, as a familiar ginger-haired boy jumped down from the cab of the truck. "What's with the disguise?"

"Hey," Damien Fang called. Today he wasn't dressed like a biker; he'd traded boots, jeans, and leather vest for a pair of flipflops, denim cut-offs, and an "I ♥ Lobster" t-shirt. "I didn't think it'd be cool to bring the bike into town. Too many vampires on the loose, you know?"

"Yeah, can't be too careful," Bela said with a nod toward the rafters. "I already checked to make sure there's no bats up there."

The other boy gave a faint laugh at Bela's attempted humor, the encounter with vampires too fresh and too painful.

"Hot enough for you?" Damien asked, changing the subject.

"Listen, dog," Bela moaned, "this is the worst ever. I can't see why anybody'd come here for a vacation."

"Yeah, well, you should try living in Florida. That's why we always get outta there in summer, though coming here was hardly a vacation." Damien lapsed into silence, avoiding eye contact. The things neither of them wanted to talk about weighed down conversation like the thick, sticky air.

"Is Caleb around?" Damien resumed. "I'm supposed to get some herbs or something from him."

"For your father? How's he doing?"

"Better," Damien answered, shoving his hands in the front pockets of his cutoffs. "Doña Flóres sent us out into the woods to collect flowers and bark and dig up roots. She made this weird, nasty-smelling tea."

"Yeah, Caleb was always doing stuff like that for us back home."

Damien ran a hand through his ginger hair. "We've been in lots of fights, but nobody's ever shot at us with silver. I thought that was just a thing in movies."

"Up in the mountains, sometimes they'd go after us on our Night with silver bullets," Bela said.

"When you got attacked, did you ever, you know, lose anyone in your pack?" Damien tried to sound casual as he picked up the motorcycle magazine but didn't look at the pages.

Bela remembered Buck's inert body on the grass, lit by the early morning sun. After shaking off the transformation, he'd had the queasy feeling that something bad had happened on the Night, even before Caleb had told him about the attack.

"Well," Bela began reluctantly, "before I was in the pack, there was this one Night where the pack attacked a farm because the farmer had killed a family of wolves. I mean, not wolves like us but the other kind... I don't know the word in English."

"Yeah, I get it," Damien said, looking up from the magazine to stare at him.

"One of the pack was killed, because over there, the humans always keep silver bullets around, ready to shoot us. And then, after the sun came up, when the pack was, you know, tired, the farmer and his buddies came and killed another one of us. All that stuff mostly stopped after Caleb took over, because he talked the pack out of stealing chickens and sheep, and because he made all these wards so that we couldn't get at the farmers and the farmers couldn't wander into the packs' territory on our Night."

"Wards are magic, right?" Damien asked, tossing the magazine on the table. "I thought that was just in the movies, too."

"Not everyone can do it and those that can, keep quiet about it," Bela explained. "Sophia and Fintonclyde are really good, Caleb says. And not only wards. Need some extra light?" He held out a hand, palm facing up, and a ball of yellow light about two inches in diameter blossomed, floating in the air above his outstretched palm.

The older boy made a face, then gave a short laugh. "C'mon. How are you really doing that? I don't see any wires. There must be wires."

"No wires," Bela shot back, irritated at the laugh more than at the disbelief. With a quick flip of his hand, the ball of light disappeared. "It's easy to summon Fire, which is good if you need to stay warm. Or if someone attacks you, you can shoot flames at them."

"Yeah, let's see that," Damien said, lingering disbelief in his voice.

"I don't exactly want to start a fire with all this junk around," Bela said nervously, nodding toward the haphazardly piled cardboard boxes behind him and piles of greasy rags on the table. Wanting to impress the older boy, he concentrated his gaze on a wrench lying on top of the pile of tools. The rusty metal bar twitched and wobbled, softly clinking against other tools at first, then rose to hover six inches above the table.

"How the hell are you—" Damien exploded.

"Hey!" Bela cried as the wrench seesawed in the air and then fell on top of the magazine with a soft clunk. "Scare a guy, will you? It takes some concentration, you know. Back home we had this old canoe that I fixed up so that it would fly. Yeah, that was cool. And Caleb's better at, uhm, I guess you'd call it summoning Wind. He'd just fly over the mountains sometimes when he was in a hurry."

"Wow, pretty cool. And sorry I didn't believe you at first." Damien grinned sheepishly. "Now that I remember, that old man did something to us, sort of tied us up without ropes after… well, you know, after all that stuff happened back in June."

"Yeah, wards," Bela said. "I'm mostly good at breaking wards, which makes Caleb mad at me."

Damien laughed again, this time with Bela, and picked up the wrench, tapping it against his palm. "Maybe you could teach me?" he asked hesitantly.

"I can try," Bela said, adopting an air of nonchalance. "Caleb says we should have some ability because of, you know, the magic that lets us change. Next time we come out to your camp, okay? I shouldn't really be doing this stuff around here." He inclined his head toward the open garage doors and the street beyond.

"Cool! And I can show you how to ride a bike, maybe even that old German one, if we could get it running."

"Really?" Bela pictured himself riding a motorcycle in a black leather jacket, like the cool-looking guys in the magazine.

"You know," Damien said, latching onto Bela's excitement, "I asked my father about that bike. He said it might be worth twenty, thirty thousand dollars."

"Is that a lot of money?"

"Holy crap, yes!" Damien replied with a look that pegged Bela as a clueless country bumpkin. "If the bike was fixed up, I mean. I reckon we could do that, but we might have to scrounge some parts. Do you think Caleb would lend us money?"

"Maybe. He's got a lot of money in his—what is it? —his bank thingy," Bela answered tentatively.

"I've got time before I have to be back, so maybe we could bring it out here and take a look," Damien said, pointing to the back of the garage. He feigned a disinterest that barely concealed his eagerness to get another look at the mysterious German motorcycle.

"It's not going be easy," Bela warned as he faced the wall of junk that lay between them and the back of the garage.

He balanced a wooden rocking horse precariously on top of a broken chair, while Damien stacked cardboard boxes into a shaky-looking tower. They wrestled a defunct washing machine out of the way, clearing a path to the motorcycle, which leaned against the back wall, shrouded under a tarp.

"If we can get this to work, it'll be the only good thing to come out of this summer," Damien muttered as he pulled back the tarp to reveal the mysterious bike. "I wish we'd never come here."

Bela couldn't think of a reply, knowing how much the Hellhounds had lost: two of their pack members dead this summer and Damien's father recovering from a silver-tipped arrow through the shoulder. Last night, they had killed one of the vampires that had attacked them. From the amount of spent ammunition, they could tell that at least three vampires had survived the attack. Those vampires were still on the loose in Bar Harbor, and one of them was the clever, powerful, and nasty Cuza.

They were both sweating by the time they rolled the motorcycle to the front of the garage and parked it near the table piled with tools. Damien circled the bike, sliding his hands across the cracked leather seats reverently. He squatted next to the engine located beneath the seat, tugging at wires and blowing away dust.

"Looks like I'm going to need a hex-head, metric, of course," Damien stated casually as he stood up.

"I have no idea what you just said."

"Wrench," Damien said distractedly as he moved to the table, clinking the tools as he searched. "It's a German bike, so the tools have to be metric, but I bet you've got the right ones here."

"Oh, right, metric," Bela said, pretending he knew what the other boy was talking about.

"Aha!" Damien exclaimed, holding up a tool that looked like a lot of the other tools. Squatting next to the dull silver heart of the bike, he tugged with the wrench until, after some effort, it began to turn. "My father said to drain the carb and then check the fuel tank. The battery's probably a goner, but we might be able to revive it. After that, we could try to turn over the engine."

Damien stood, looked down at his fingers, which were already mottled with grease and dust. He wiped his hands on a rag and said, "See if you can find a pan or something for draining fuel."

Bela clattered through a cardboard box full of kitchen utensils, finding a battered aluminum pot that didn't seem to have any holes in the bottom. "How's this?"

"Great," Damien said, briefly looking up. He'd returned to the bike with more tools, which he'd spread out on the tarp. While he disconnected hoses and tugged on wires, he said in a tighter voice, "In our pack we do this thing when someone… dies. A big fire. I guess you'd call it a pyre. Anyway, we're going to do that for Buck." Damien paused apparently intent on tracing wires that snaked through the engine. "Yeah, today at sunset, if Caleb wants to come. I mean, you could come, too."

Bela settled himself on the garage floor, cross-legged next to Damien, and set the pot on the ground. He shivered, suddenly chilled in his sweat-soaked t-shirt by thoughts of pack members dying, and said, "You can ask Caleb, but I don't know if he wants to leave Sophia after what happened on the Night."

Damien nodded emphatically, not looking up from the pieces of engine arrayed around him. "Yeah, all those vampires attacking us."

"That wasn't the only thing going on," Bela said. "While you were fighting those stinking corpses in the woods, another one came here and bit Sophia. When we got back in the morning, tired and wanting to sleep, we couldn't find her in the house. Caleb was panicking, and then he saw her lying on the ground in the back yard. She had these bite marks on her neck and not from mosquitoes or anything. So now Caleb feels guilty for leaving her alone. Before we left, he put all these wards on the doors and windows, but she went outside in the middle of the night, and she hasn't been able to say why yet."

"So…" Damien pulled his eyes away from the engine to stare at Bela, swiping an arm across his sweaty forehead. "Is Sophia one of them, I mean, a vampire now?"

"What?" Bela asked, amazed at how little the Hellhound knew about the Undead. "No, it takes three bites. Each bite kind of makes you closer to being one."

"Whoa." Damien whistled through his teeth. "But even one bite would be… bad, right? It would freak me out if one of my pack got bitten."

"*We* don't have to worry about that. Caleb says that if one of them bites us, the magic kind of collides, and it makes the vampire sick, a little crazy. It's like that disease that dogs get by biting a squirrel or a skunk that's acting weird. I don't know the word in English, though."

"Rabies?"

"Yeah, I guess. Anyway, biting us is definitely something vampires avoid."

"What happens to us, if we get bitten?"

"Caleb always said it's way worse for the them than for us," Bela said. "Back home, all the vampires knew, so they'd never try."

Damien asked hesitantly, "Is she, Sophia I mean, okay now?"

"She's been passed out all day. Caleb checks her every ten minutes and worries a lot in between. That's one of the reasons why I had to get out of the house, dude. Too much guilt."

Bela's final word hung in the air. Damien turned his attention to a fist-sized piece of gray metal that resembled a heart with stubby tubes sticking out like veins and arteries. The silence, which had stretched into a few minutes, was broken by the crunch of tires on gravel and the sharp report of a slamming car door.

A large black car with heavily tinted windows had parked next to the pickup truck. Bela scrambled to his feet as two men in dark sunglasses approached, their shiny black shoes pounding the gravel as they neared the open garage door. Although he had never seen Western cowboy movies, he recognized the men's swagger, because even in the remote Transylvanian Alps, there were bandits or government officials who'd try to shake you down.

"This can't be good," he breathed.

Damien got to his feet, muttering, "Cops."

"Huh?" Bela scrambled up off the floor, too.

"Police. They look like police," Damien whispered out of the side of his mouth.

Both boys folded their arms and narrowed their eyes as the two men approached, looking like wannabe gangsters in their black suits and skinny black ties, swinging black faux-leather briefcases. The taller of the pair, an older man with wan skin and thinning pale hair, seemed oblivious to the stifling heat. His shorter partner's round face was framed with curly black hair and already shone with sweat.

Damien drew in a sharp breath when the older man slipped a hand under his jacket, but exhaled loudly when the man produced a laminated ID card, which he flicked at them for an instant before putting it away.

"Agent Hulstad," intoned the man, and with a microscopic twitch of his head toward the other man. "Agent Gallo." Then adopting the tone that adults often used to talk to small children or the hard of hearing, he said, "Well, well. Bela Muscatura, isn't it? How do you like Bar Harbor, Bela?"

"Staying out of trouble?" The shorter one, Agent Gallo, sneered while aggressively chomping on a wad of gum.

Bela regarded the pair stonily, but Damien nudged him, telegraphing that not answering might be worse than answering.

"Not much going on," Bela said, trying to sound nonchalant. "There's this what-do-you-call-it place, uhm, drive-in that has burgers and fries. Pretty good, I guess."

"What's that you're working on?" Agent Hulstad asked, tilting his chin toward the array of tools and parts spread on the tarp at their feet.

"Something we found in the garage," Bela muttered.

"A motorcycle," corrected Agent Hulstad. "Seen any other motorcycles around town?"

"Who's your friend, here?" snapped Agent Gallo.

"Danny Campbell," Damien replied smoothly. Bela suspected he must have lot of practice lying to the police.

"You know a lot about motorcycles?" the shorter agent inquired suspiciously.

"Well," Damien answered, drawing the word out so that it sounded like *Waaaaaaaaaahl*. "I've fixed lawnmowers before, so I reckon a motorcycle can't be that different."

"You from around here, kid?" Agent Gallo challenged, taking off his sunglasses and peering at Damien with small, flinty eyes. "You don't talk like you're from around here."

"My family's here on vacation," Damien said in a bored tone, "but it's, like, not cool hanging out with them. I met Bela at the drive-in, and he said he found this old bike, so I thought I'd take a look, see if I could get it to work. It's something to do, you know."

"Is that so?" the agent retorted. "Are you sure you don't know a little—or maybe a lot —about motorcycles?"

Damien tensed, and Bela had a sudden fear that the other boy would flee. He suspected that these agents wouldn't take that well, although the thought of pudgy Agent Gallo, sweating in his black suit while giving chase, provided fleeting amusement.

"Gallo, drop it. We've got other business," Agent Hulstad ordered, then addressing Bela, "Mr. O'Connor is here, I presume?"

Bela shrugged in response, suspecting that these creeps already knew the answer. Agent Hulstad turned away from the garage toward the house, but Agent Gallo lingered to put on his sunglasses, glaring at Damien as if it were the boy's fault that the interrogation had been cut short.

"Catch you later," he said, snapping his gum menacingly.

Damien stepped through the garage door into the driveway to watch the men march across the lawn and climb the steps to the front porch of the house. "Who were those guys?"

"Trouble," Bela moaned. "Caleb is not going to be happy."

Chapter 10: The Big Hangover

SOPHIA DREAMED OF FIRE, of screaming, of a familiar face with black pits for eyes. After waking, feverish and queasy, she stumbled to the bathroom and threw up.

Gripping the sides of the sink for support, she stared at her pale reflection in the mirror. Dark circles under her eyes stood out against the ashy whiteness of her cheeks, and her hair stuck out wildly. Did she have a hangover? She had no memory of drinking. And why had she been sleeping in her bathrobe?

She dragged herself down the hall that led to the kitchen, leaning on the wall for support. She braced herself in the doorway and wondered why the light hurt her eyes so much. Caleb sat hunched at the kitchen table, staring at his hands. A hazy aura floated around him. *Maybe because the light was all wrong?*

"Too bright," she mumbled.

Caleb turned to stare at her and gasped, which made that weird aura pulse around him. She shook her pounding head.

"What are you—" She took a step, meaning to cross to the table, but her legs buckled, and all she saw was the fast-approaching floor.

The next thing she remembered, she was seated at the table, alone. *Where was Caleb? Had it been a dream?* Suddenly a steaming mug appeared next to her.

"I made you some tea. Try it," he urged softly as he drew up a chair beside her.

"Why did you let me sleep so long? Have I been sick? And why is it so bright in here?"

"The tea will make you feel better," he insisted.

She put out a hand toward the tea, but missed the mug, because three cups swam in front of her eyes instead of one. Caleb took her hands in his and curled her fingers around the hot cup. Obediently, she lifted the mug in two hands and took a small sip.

"What's in this? Tastes funny and... sugar," she complained. "Don't like sugar in my tea."

"I put a few things in the tea to help you feel better. And the sugar is, well, because some of the things I added taste rather vile." He smiled.

It's a nice smile, she thought. *It makes that haze around his head wiggle and change color from yellowish to greenish, which can't be right. Maybe that's just sunlight through trees.*

"I don't feel so great," she confessed. The tea had burned as it went down, but she shivered nonetheless.

"Let me hold this for you." He took the mug from her as her hands began to shake violently. He brought it to her lips, and she took a few more sips. She wrinkled her nose at the smell, but kept drinking, feeling warmer with each swallow.

"Why are you staring at me? What happened?" she asked, pushing the tea away, which was having an effect in spite of the terrible taste. The pulsating light around Caleb had receded, and her eyes didn't hurt as much. "It's afternoon, right? Did I get the flu?"

"Not exactly, no." He hesitated. "Sleeping this long isn't unusual in your situation," he finished matter-of-factly.

"My what? What are you talking about?" Panic slithered into her gut.

"What's the last thing you remember?" he asked.

She put her head in her hands, covering her face because the light still hurt. "There was a fire... No, I dreamed there was a fire, but it was the rooster... The rooster crowed, except the rooster's dead." She pulled her hands away and turned her head to scan Caleb's worried face. "Did I dream that, too?"

"No, the rooster was... is dead," he answered gently. "You went outside in the middle of the night, didn't you?"

"Yes…" She tried to hold onto the memory, which fluttered like smoke from a fire, visible but insubstantial. "I heard something, a cry or a screech or… The moon was bright, but there was so much darkness and, in the shadows…" The memory dissolved, leaving nothing but darkness. "Did I fall and hit my head? Because I don't remember anything after that."

"Nothing?" he asked sharply. "You didn't see anyone when you went outside?"

She snatched at wisps of memory. Eyes, eyes that reflected nothing but sucked in all the light around them. Was that part of her dream? "No… I dreamed about someone, someone in the fire, but that wasn't real."

"Sophia, I think— No, I'm sure that you met a vampire when you went outside," Caleb said carefully, "and the reason that you don't feel well, the reason that you've been asleep for so long, is because the vampire bit you."

"What? No? I can't have slept that long. I've never… Bitten? You must be joking. You mean fang marks and all that?"

"That's precisely what I mean."

Her hand crept to her neck as he spoke.

"No, left side," he said sadly.

She gasped, as her fingers identified one raised bump and then another.

"Oh," she breathed after a minute's silence. "A vampire."

Saying the word made it real, although she had no memory, no memory except those black eyes in her dream.

And saying the word released a torrent from Caleb. "Oh, god, Sophia, I should have warned you. I should have warned you not to go outside, but I didn't want to scare you. I put wards on the doors and windows so that vampires couldn't get in. I was worried because when Bela and I went to the bank before the full moon I met, that is, I saw a vampire, a vampire I knew—an old, powerful one, trained in the Romanian sorcerer's tradition, and with no love for me. When the moon was full, vampires, including this old one, attacked us. We drove them off and I thought that was all of them, but when we came back here in the morning, we found you in the yard. There were more vampires, at least one, besides the ones that attacked us. This is all my fault. But it's going to be okay, because a vampire has to bite you three times to become… uhm…to change… You'll recover and everything will be okay. I promise. And I'm going to make sure this doesn't happen again. I mean, there are things I can do to protect—"

"Stop. You're making my head hurt." She waved her hand to silence him, confused and exhausted by his words. She concentrated on remembering what had happened, because not remembering scared her as much as the idea of being bitten. "I dreamed the chicken coop was on fire, but it wasn't. The dream seemed so real that I went outside… I must have done that."

"Did you see anyone when you went outside?" he asked again.

She shook her head. "There was someone in my dream… Maybe that was real…"

A sharp knock on the front door cut short her attempt to remember and made her head throb again.

Caleb frowned. "I showed Bela how to open the wards. He's usually so keen to break them, I can't believe he'd actually knock."

The rapping came again. He sighed wearily and got up. She took a sip of the tea, which tasted worse the colder it became, while he swept out to the front hall. She expected to hear Caleb haranguing the boy after the door opened, but instead heard an unfamiliar voice, speaking in low tones. Had the Hellhounds come calling?

Instead of leather-clad bikers, the two men in rumpled suits who trailed Caleb into the kitchen looked like salesmen, the kind that would sell you shady life insurance policies and then leave town in a hurry. Both men wore black suits, with black ties and white shirts, and carried official-looking briefcases.

Sophia remembered her time in Boston when, with her newly awarded culinary arts degree, she'd wanted to become a chef, but after working at several restaurants in lowly cook positions, the shiny object of her desire had tarnished due to fourteen-hour days, pressure from chefs for her to do them favors she didn't think they deserved, and behind-the-scenes blackmail in the big city. At one restaurant, the owner made regular payments to the local mafia, which were collected by a swarthy idiot barely out of his teens but dressed like Las Vegas. He would swagger into the kitchen to collect payment, filching food and expecting something on the side from the female staff. Sophia had been fired for telling off this sub-sub-lieutenant of the local crime family, which had hastened her decision to come back to Bar Harbor.

She thought of that mafia foot soldier as she appraised the shorter of the newly arrived pair, dark curly hair plastered with sweat around a plump, sallow face. The taller of the two, with his thinning, pale blond hair and washed-out blue eyes, looked the part of an insurance salesman.

"Mr. O'Connor," the tall man acknowledged with a nod of his head. "And you must be Ms. Daigle."

She pulled her bathrobe more tightly across her chest. Something about this man made her feel like a bug under a magnifying glass.

"I'm Agent Hulstad, and this is Agent Gallo," the newcomer continued. "Sorry to intrude, ma'am, but we have a few questions for Mr. O'Connor."

The other one, Agent Gallo, sauntered to the table, dropped his briefcase with a thud, and pulled a chair out, swinging it around and straddling it with his arms resting on the back. He snapped a wad of gum loudly as he waited for the other one, who was clearly his boss.

Agent Hulstad extracted a small notebook and ballpoint pen from his jacket pocket; he clicked the pen, the sound echoing in the quiet kitchen. Caleb seated himself next to her, his face impassive but his body tense.

"What's going on here?" she asked, trying to gather her scattered wits. "Some sort of interrogation? Who are you? This is my house, and I think I have a right to know."

With a show of irritation, Agent Hulstad drew from his jacket a laminated plastic card that had a small, blurry photograph and a seal with tiny writing that danced in front of her eyes before he abruptly put the badge away.

"I didn't catch the logo on your ID," Caleb said.

The tall one – Agent Hulstad – mumbled, "Extraordinary Alien Registry, Boston Field Office. Maybe Alexandru Arghezi mentioned our agency to you. He worked for us for many years as a consultant."

"Alexandru might have mentioned it," Caleb said coolly.

"We were alerted to unusual activity in Bar Harbor this summer by Mr. Fintonclyde," Hulstad continued. "We believe you can be of great assistance to us in our investigation, which we expect you will do gladly."

"And we thought you might need some help," Agent Gallo said with a thick Boston accent. "We help you, you help us, see?"

"I'm not aware that I need any help," Caleb replied, appearing confused and irritated.

"You were very busy in Bucharest," said Agent Hulstad with a thin-lipped smile, "where you applied to adopt that boy outside. You must know that there are many steps in the process, many hurdles that must be overcome. Paperwork, Mr. O'Connor, has a way of going astray, unless watched carefully." The man paused to curl his lips in a brief, mirthless grin. "We can help put in a good word with the right people."

"You don't want the kid to get sent home, do you?" Agent Gallo sneered.

"What do you mean?" Caleb asked.

"We don't like trouble, Mr. O'Connor," Agent Hulstad said. "We especially don't like trouble caused by what we call Extraordinary Aliens. And I think you know what I mean."

"Let's pretend I don't," Caleb said tensely.

Gallo chortled. "Give me a break, pal. We're talking about your furry friends, who've killed a couple of people already this summer."

"Allegedly," Caleb said, his fingers curling around the edge of the table. "But you'll have a hard time finding witnesses to prove it."

Hulstad, cleared his throat loudly with a warning glance to Gallo. "Ma'am? May I?" he asked in a flat tone as he pulled a chair from the table.

Sophia waved a hand and the tall agent sat down across from her, depositing his briefcase precisely on the floor with a sharp click.

"Part of our job is to keep tabs, as you might say, on a number of unusual individuals who could cause harm to ordinary citizens such as yourself. And if American citizens are threatened, we have a duty to intervene," Agent Hulstad addressed her calmly, ignoring the simmering feud between Caleb and his colleague. "We expect that you should be willing to cooperate with an ongoing investigation, considering what has already taken place in Bar Harbor. If you are not willing to help, we have other instruments, legal instruments, at our disposal."

"Might as well get this over with," Caleb conceded, relaxing his claw-like grip on the table slightly. "What do you want to know?"

"The moon was full last night," Agent Hulstad began.

"Yes, I did not fail to notice," Caleb said dryly.

"The local police have no reports of disturbances overnight. However, the Agency wants a full accounting of the movements of the so-called Hellhounds. What can you tell us about their whereabouts?"

"I got here a few days ago, and now I'm responsible for a pack of strangers?" Caleb asked sarcastically. "The furry ones are not what you should be worried about. What about the bitey ones? Vampires, that is. Don't you keep track of them, too?"

"Blood-feeding immortals. BFIs," Agent Hulstad tossed off in a monotone.

"Why aren't you looking for BFIs, which are a much, much bigger problem around here?"

"Hey, pal," Gallo piped up, jabbing a thick finger toward Caleb. "You don't get to tell us how to do our job, okay? Fact is that those Hellhounds have caused a helluva lot of trouble this summer."

Exasperated and finally pushed to speak, Sophia said, "Odd things have been happening for months, and we—Fintonclyde and I—thought there was at least one, uhm, BFI, likely more, in Bar Harbor since last year."

"We have interviewed Mr. Fintonclyde as part of this investigation. However, there have been no confirmed BFI attacks in Bar Harbor," Agent Hulstad noted. "Circumstantial evidence, perhaps. As my colleague so colorfully expressed, the Hellhounds were implicated in several deaths during the full moon in June."

"You won't find any reliable witnesses for that night in June," Caleb said hotly. "And I know, because Alexandru told me, that you're not allowed to take any action against 'aliens' unless you catch them in the act."

"And what about the aftereffects, huh?" Agent Gallo popped his gum in punctuation.

"Excuse me?" Caleb asked.

"We're hearing that people are still getting sick around town even a couple of months after that gang went nuts, so we figure it must be because of all that biting. We gotta investigate stuff like that."

Caleb blew out a long breath, his eyes darting between the two agents. "There are two aftereffects—if you want to call them that—of a werewolf bite. Those that don't die from the bite or the first transformation become werewolves. It's as simple as that. We know about Rudy, who survived the bite, and, believe me, if there had been another new werewolf in town for the past two months, you'd know it. If people are getting sick, it's not from werewolves."

Agent Hulstad flipped through his notebook, then stopped, giving a slight nod as he ran a finger along a particular page. "Information we received indicated that certain blood-borne illnesses can be attributed to the bite of the werewolf," the agent recited.

"As if you could get rabies from werewolves?" Caleb laughed harshly. "You really don't know anything about us, do you?"

"Hey," Agent Gallo growled, standing up, knuckles clenched on the back of the chair, and glaring down at Caleb. "You don't get to tell us how to do our job!"

Caleb shot back: "But there are vampires in Bar Harbor. People are in danger. Aren't you going to do anything about that?"

"Gallo, take it down a notch," Agent Hulstad warned. Turning to Caleb, he said blandly, "I am not sure what you expect us to do, Mr. O'Connor. There have been no confirmed BFI attacks in Bar Harbor."

"Well, in June," Sophia said, "there was a BFI that the Hellhounds, uhm, took care of. The body was burned—"

"Which is the only sane thing to do," Caleb finished.

"Right," Gallo retorted, settling back in the chair, but still breathing heavily. "No evidence. Now, your furry friends, there's plenty of evidence of them, but here's the funny thing: they haven't been seen in town for days. And whadaya know? They seem to have disappeared. Have they left town? We don't think so, and HQ is breathing down our necks to close this case. If that pack is still hanging around at the next full moon, causing trouble, we might have to bring in the SOG boys."

"The what?" Caleb asked sharply.

"Special Operations Group. Guys in camo and bulletproof vests that tidy things up." Agent Gallo smiled as he mimed shouldering a rifle and then stuttered in imitation of gunfire.

"Sophia?" Caleb implored. The agonized look on his face showed him torn between protecting her and confirming the shadowy vampire attacks. "Could you—would you mind showing these gentlemen the, uhm, evidence?"

She frowned, not comprehending at first. Caleb stared at her expectantly until she understood. Without speaking, she turned sideways in her chair, exposing the puncture marks on her neck.

Gallo whistled under his breath, although she had no idea what he was reacting to. Tiny dots? Raw, livid wounds?

Agent Hulstad grunted. "That's a possible BSI. We'll have to document it. Gallo, take a picture."

As the other agent reached for his briefcase, Caleb asked, "BSI?"

"Blood sucking incident," Hulstad replied without looking up from scratching in his notebook. "All BSIs have to be documented and reported to HQ."

"This woman was bitten by a vampire, and all you can think about is paperwork?" Caleb exclaimed.

Gallo heaved his briefcase onto the table, flipped the latches, and opened it. From inside he extracted a small camera, while Hulstad continued making notes, face impassive.

"Okay, okay," Gallo muttered as he maneuvered around the table to hover next to her. "Turn your head... more...a little more. There."

The flash from the camera, even out of the corners of her eyes, made bright flecks of light swim around the room. Reflexively, she covered the puncture marks with a hand, reluctant to share any more. Agent Gallo seemed satisfied and retreated.

"Ma'am?"

"Mmm?" She stared into Agent Hulstad's washed-out blue eyes as he regarded her clinically, like a body on a mortuary slab.

"Can you tell us where and when this incident occurred?"

She looked up, her eyes roaming across the ceiling. How could she know? It wasn't like a script or a story written in a book that she could recite. But if it were a book, then pages had been torn out and the remaining scraps weren't in the right order. She gathered together the shredded pages of memory and dragged her gaze back to the stony-faced man. "Last night I was here alone. I heard...something outside. I don't know what time, but the moon was high. I went out back and... I don't remember anything after that."

Hulstad clicked his tongue in disapproval, not pleased with her performance.

"When I returned this morning," Caleb quickly jumped in, "I found Sophia outside in the back yard, lying on the ground. She was in something of a coma state and didn't wake up until this afternoon, which isn't surprising. The first bite is usually the worst."

"Well, those marks are suggestive," Agent Hulstad said without looking up from his notetaking.

"Suggestive?" Caleb barked a laugh. "Have either of you ever dealt with vampires before? Because I've seen dozens of people bitten, and this is clearly the work of a vampire."

"Oh, and you know so much more than us." Agent Gallo sneered, tossing the camera back into his briefcase and slamming it shut.

"Six years in Romania," Caleb seethed between clenched teeth, white-knuckled as he gripped the edge of the table again, "working with Alexandru Arghezi—I think you've heard of him? —tracking down and killing vampires. Yes, I think I know more about vampires than you."

"Shut it, Gallo," Hulstad ordered. "It does seem credible that Ms. Daigle was bitten. That is evidence for one BFI in Bar Harbor. We will get the paperwork started."

"One?" Caleb laughed. "There are at least five other BFIs, including an old, dangerous one from Romania. I saw him in town before the full moon. If I know him, he'll have organized the locals and that can't be good."

Agent Hulstad knit his brows in concentration as he reached for his briefcase. He balanced the case on his knees while he opened it and then rifled through folders until he extracted one in particular.

"Dangerous BFI from Romania," the agent said to himself as he closed the briefcase and laid the folder on top. After opening it, he meticulously turned over pieces of paper one by one. "We had—Ah, here it is—a report last year of a possible ABE from Hungary or Romania who might have been headed for Maine."

"ABE?" Sophia asked.

"Alien bloodsucking émigré, ma'am," Hulstad replied, continuing to leaf through the folder. "The destination of this alleged ABE appeared to have been a ruined house in the area."

"Lilac House?" Caleb and Sophia said simultaneously.

"Yeah, we checked out that old wreck," Gallo put in. "No BFIs there neither."

"Now there's proof of a vampire!" Caleb insisted. "Not only did one bite Sophia last night, but I saw another one in town a couple of days ago. Look, I'll give you a deposition; I'll swear to what I saw, whatever you want."

"One BFI," Agent Hulstad said in clipped tones. "This BFI you allege knowing could have come to Ms. Daigle's house last night."

"No, because he was…" Caleb trailed off.

She watched him debating with himself about how much to reveal.

"Because this particular vampire, who calls himself Peter Brody by the way, attacked us last night. He had other vampires with him, three or four of them. It was a well-planned attack; they used silver bullets and silver-tipped arrows."

Caleb had the agents' attention now. Gallo had lost his sneer, and his mouth hung open. Hulstad's eyebrows went up. He pursed his lips before he began scratching quickly in his notebook.

Gallo recovered, asking, "Whadaya mean 'we'? You and that kid outside? You're telling us the two of you survived an attack by four or five BFIs?"

"We were with the Hellhounds," Caleb admitted reluctantly.

"Hah! So, you do know where those bikers are!" Gallo retorted. "Why didn't you say so before?"

"Mr. O'Connor," Agent Hulstad said, talking over his excitable associate. "You make serious allegations which could, if confirmed, change the nature of this investigation."

"Finally!" Caleb slapped his palms on the table.

"However, we will need proof," Hulstad finished.

Caleb took a deep breath before answering. "One of the Hellhounds was killed last night, and another took a silver arrow in the shoulder. We killed one of the vampires and drove off the rest of them."

Agent Hulstad flipped to a new page in his notebook and wrote diligently for nearly a minute. He looked up expectantly at Caleb, pen poised above the paper, and asked, "Can you provide us the location of this alleged attack as well as the whereabouts of the motorcycle gang? We will have to make a full investigation of the site and interview the Hellhounds."

Caleb glared back at him. Werewolf solidarity appeared to win out, and he evaded the question. "You wouldn't find much, just guns and a lot of silver bullets. And silver-tipped arrows."

"What happened to the inactivated BFI?"

"We burned it, of course," Caleb said. "You don't expect me to keep a vampire's body around, do you? You can't be stupid enough to think that would be a good idea."

"Hey, that's enough from you!" Gallo shouted. "Calling us stupid ain't going to make it any easier for you!"

"Agent Gallo, your outburst is not helping," the other agent said in a low tone. "And you, Mr. O'Connor, could be decidedly more helpful to our investigation. The more help you give us, the better we'll all get along, all right? For example, we can help speed up the adoption process for Bela Muscatura. It would be a shame if he were deported, because his paperwork got lost."

Caleb, shaking with rage, opened his mouth to speak, but Sophia laid a hand on his wrist. Caleb blew out a long breath, his eyes still trained on Agent Hulstad.

"Gentlemen," Caleb said through clenched teeth. "We want to be of help, and we will consider all that you've said. However, Sophia is recovering from a serious wound and needs rest."

Agent Gallo stood, scraping the chair loudly across the floor, his eyes locked on Caleb's. "We're staying at the Pines Motel. Drop in and see us, pal, before we come looking for you."

Chapter 11: Icebergs Astern

T HE FRIDAY LUNCH CROWD trickled into the Lobster Pot in ones and twos. Mickey's favorites were the regulars who came in early, skipping out on their jobs (if they had jobs) and staying all afternoon. Not that they bought a lot of alcohol. Some of those guys—and most of them were male—could nurse a single beer for hours. Other bartenders might have pressured them to drink more, but Mickey had other priorities.

This early in the day, the bar's main room had the hushed feeling of the waiting room of an office staffed by dodgy doctors or disbarred lawyers. Incandescent bulbs in dusty fixtures hung from the ceiling and didn't spread much light around the room. A few fingers of sunlight, alive with glowing dust motes, poked through the dark, musty curtains covering the high windows, the only way to know if it were night or day.

As yet, there were only three patrons. One man sat in a booth, reading a newspaper. Two of the regulars hunched over the bar: Dave, an unemployed sailmaker of about sixty, all sinews and bones with brown hair moving toward white the way color drains from a winter landscape; and Tom, a fifty-ish contractor with a stocky athletic build, now filling in around the midsection. Tom usually went back to work after stopping in for lunch, unlike Dave who often haunted the place from opening until closing.

Behind the bar, Mickey yawned, a human affectation that had transcended the Big Sleep, while listening to Dave ramble on about the boat he was restoring. Sensing a gap in the story, Mickey asked, "Did you find that thing, you know, that thing you needed?" This was usually sufficient to send Dave off on a tangent about how people were ripping him off, what with the outrageous prices they wanted for stuff.

Dave snorted, indignant about how people were ripping him off, and took a swig of beer. He set his half-empty bottle down sharply, grousing, "Fifty-five dollars, can you believe it? But I talked him down."

Mickey suppressed another yawn as he agreed that Dave had been mighty smart to avoid being taken for a sucker. He felt tired and listless after last night's romp in the woods. That final sprint through the damnable trees had been humiliating. Those wild dogs with glowing eyes had snapped at their heels as they tripped on roots and fought off branches. The Big Cheese hadn't bothered to show up this morning, leaving Mickey to get everything ready without even the useless Frenchie for help. Before opening the bar, he'd made another trip to the Jackson Laboratory, because the imperious Dr. Patel had so much more important stuff to do. He needed a jolt to wake up. He needed a drink of that good old cherry syrup.

"Hey, how 'bout some lunch?" Tom asked, looking up from drawings of some future construction project that he'd spread out on the bar in front of him.

"What?" Mickey's sluggish brain had been miles away. "Oh, right. What'll you have?"

"Fish and chips," Tom grunted.

Mickey ducked under the end of the bar and turned toward the kitchen door. Frenchie had better show up soon, because Mickey didn't fancy being a short-order cook as well as a bartender, especially today.

"Hey, how about a shrimp platter? You can put it on my tab," Dave called as Mickey disappeared through the swinging door.

The high-pitched buzz of fluorescent lights in the kitchen grated on his nerves. A battered commercial refrigerator-freezer occupied one end of the room. Large steel sinks punctured the adjoining counter, some of it now occupied by the new white laboratory freezer, looking too clean and too modern. Opposite the refrigerator squatted the gas-fired range, rarely used as their kind had little love of fire. Next to the range, under a soot-stained hood, the deep fryer reeked of the acrid odor of hot oil.

Dishes clattered as Frenchie sloshed them in the sink, with his back to the door and the hood of his jacket pulled over his head as usual.

"You're late," Mickey grumbled.

"I've been here for a while," Frenchie muttered without turning around.

"Sneaking through the old tunnel again, huh?" he asked.

"I don't like to come in through the bar," Frenchie whined, turning toward him, his face hidden in shadow. "Someone might recognize me, and I'm supposed to be dead."

"Yeah, well, your face is kinda recognizable," Mickey conceded. "Anyway, time to get to work. Need an order of fish and chips and a shrimp platter."

The Lobster Pot specialized in food that could go directly from the freezer to the deep fryer: fish and chips, battered shrimp, clam strips, chicken wings, mozzarella sticks. The customers came to drink, after all, and weren't fussy about food. The immortals running the bar cared little about that kind of food.

"Swell," Frenchie said, shuffling toward the freezer. He yanked open the door and thrust his arms in, searching through the inside while tendrils of mist floated around his shoulders. As Frenchie slammed the door shut, the hood fell away from his face, which looked suspiciously rosy.

"Feeding already? You know you're supposed to wait for the Boss to have at the customers," Mickey said with a sneer. "Though I could use a pick-me-up. Last night was rough."

"I'm glad I didn't go on that stupid mission in the woods." Frenchie smirked as he tossed assorted frozen items into the baskets perched above the sizzling oil.

"It was your boss's idea, so maybe you shouldn't call it stupid."

"Well, I had a mission of my own. A very successful mission." Frenchie giggled, flicking the baskets of frozen food, which hissed and spluttered as they dropped into the hot oil.

"Whadaya mean? You were just supposed to be doing surveillance," Mickey said, irritated and tired. He craved the tangy smell of fresh blood, but was stuck with the acrid stink of burning oil.

"Well," Frenchie said, the corners of his mouth turning up in a smile, "if something happens to come my way, why shouldn't I..."

"You moronic little maggot. You mean you were feeding on the mortal you were supposed to be watching? He's going to be pissed about that."

"Why is that?" Frenchie asked, unconcerned.

Mickey shuddered at the bald-faced stupidity standing there, grinning at him. "Evidence, you nimwit. You got rid of the evidence, right?"

"I couldn't do that to—" Frenchie jerked his head from side to side as panic swirled across his face, wiping away the smugness. "But they don't remember, you know that."

"So, you didn't," Mickey surmised. "We're trying to lay low, not attract attention, which means that" —he spoke slowly, as if giving a lesson to a small child— "afterward, you break the neck and you make it look like they was in car accident or jumped out the window or something."

"Puh-puh-please don't tell him," Frenchie pleaded, wringing his hands, an escalation of his usual histrionics.

"He's gonna find out one way or another," Mickey pointed out, shaking his head. "Better to get it over with now."

Right on cue, Cuza's voice could be heard in the main room.

"Speak o' the devil," Mickey tossed over his shoulder as he left Frenchie in the kitchen, still cringing.

Cuza stood next to the bar, talking to Tom, who was finishing his first beer of the day. The proprietor of the Lobster Pot, dressed in a crisp, charcoal-gray suit, looked ridiculously out of place in a basement dive bar. Vito and Donnie were conspicuously absent today. They'd had a hard run through the woods last night, although things could have gone worse. At least they'd found Donnie's hand, which had been ripped off by one of those nasty mongrels; that would speed up regeneration.

Some of that hot, fresh red gold would help, too. It certainly would, Mickey thought hungrily as he slipped behind the bar. He flicked a questioning glance toward Cuza, who nodded almost imperceptibly at Tom—*first meal of the day*—then cocked his head toward Dave—*your turn next.*

Mickey licked his lips and smiled.

Cuza clapped Tom on the back and sat next to him, hunching over the bar to look him in the eye. Mickey couldn't hear the low conversation, but the words weren't important. Their kind had more effective ways of persuasion than mere words.

"How about another beer?" called the lone man from the booth across the room.

Mickey pulled a beer from the cooler and slowly opened the bottle, his eyes following Tom as he stood, muttering something about visiting the Gents'. Cuza slipped out of the room behind the man a few moments later. Mickey ducked under the end of the bar and made his way toward the man seated in a booth by himself, scanning a newspaper.

"You've been in a few times," Mickey said, setting the bottle down and taking a seat opposite. "You want some lunch?"

The man appeared to be in his twenties, with brown hair and a bushy beard. He wore a Park Service uniform and had the ruddy face of someone who spent a lot of time outdoors. A healthy-looking guy, in other words, who might be worth chatting up.

Irritation flashed across the man's face as he folded his newspaper. "Why not? They decided to cut my hours to half-day on Fridays. Saving money, they say. A load of bull, I say. Anyway, what's good today?"

"Same old, same old," Mickey said. "Most people like the fish and chips, although I don't care much for fried food myself."

"Yeah, okay, that sounds good," the man concluded after taking a swig of beer, and then went back to reading the newspaper.

Mickey got up and crossed the room, thinking that recruiting the taciturn park ranger would take some work. Frenchie bumped through the swinging kitchen door, carrying a couple of plates, which he deposited on the bar, before scuttling back.

"Hey!" Mickey yelled to the retreating hooded figure. "Another order of fish and chips."

As he turned back to the bar, Dave caught his eye, inclining his head across the room and asking, "Who's that? I seen her around the place before. Kinda posh English accent. Not from around here, is she?"

Lady Agatha stood in front of the dusty velvet curtains that hung in the entryway, poised like an opera singer about to start an aria, waiting for the swelling of the orchestra.

"Oh, no," Mickey muttered.

He hurried toward her as her high heels clacked on the wood floor. Today she wore a flowery knee-length dress with a full skirt that swirled around her legs. The summery outfit was at odds with the narrowed eyes and face twisted in fury.

"Where—" she said through clenched teeth.

"Your Ladyship," he bubbled brightly, putting on a stiff smile. "We didn't expect to see you this early."

"—is he?" she finished, not deterred by his charm assault.

"You mean, the Boss?" he said disingenuously as he guided her to the end of the bar, as far away as possible from Dave, who stared at her in open-mouthed fascination. "Oh, he's around somewhere. Can I get you a G&T?"

"You know who I mean. Where is Guy? He did not return last night from your military-style campaign."

"Hey, no need to broadcast that to the whole room," Mickey murmured as he slipped behind the bar. "Let me make you a drink."

Lady Agatha tapped long, pastel-pink nails on the bar while Mickey focused all his attention on cutting up a lime, and then made a double gin and tonic. He was putting off the inevitable, but he rationalized to himself that Cuza should be the one to deliver the bad news.

"Guy and I, we are the only ones left after…" She trailed off, taking the drink that he handed her.

…after the last guy was torn apart by werewolves, he silently finished her sentence. He'd known her fellow refugees from the Titanic since the 1930s and thought they were worthless—but to her, they could do no wrong as long as they fawned over her with enough enthusiasm.

The party two months ago at the rented mansion by the sea had reminded Mickey of the old days: room after room of fashionably dressed people laughing, dancing, drinking. It would have been perfect, if the moon hadn't been full on the final night of the long weekend. The guests were New Yorkers, mostly mortals. On that night, Cuza had mingled discreetly in the high-ceilinged room that looked out on the ocean, no doubt carefully selecting his next meal, while Lady Agatha had surrounded herself with a crowd of admirers as she told amusing stories in her upper-class British accent, which captivated Americans like magic. Mickey had been ensconced in a dark corner of the room with a drunk young woman, someone's personal assistant, and had been about to suggest they go someplace more private where he could quietly slide his fangs into her neck, when he'd heard the sound of breaking glass: not the tinkle of someone dropping a champagne flute, but an ominous crunch as something large smashed through a French door. Then the screaming had started.

As he'd elbowed through densely packed partygoers, Mickey had glimpsed furry shapes punching through the crowd as people scrambled for any exit. Amid shouting, he'd heard snarling. He'd hoped they were only dogs, but he'd feared something much worse.

Mickey had found Lady Agatha and was urging her toward the nearest door when a snarling wolf burst through panicked party guests. The beast had sniffed the air and pointed its blood-smeared snout toward them, a good indication that this was no ordinary animal, but a werewolf on the hunt. As Mickey had pulled Lady Agatha away, the beast savaged one of her fellow refugees, who'd cried "Away, foul beast!" in a final gesture of misplaced chivalry.

Now seated at the bar, she swirled the glass pensively, rattling the ice. Her eyes unfocused as she sank into memory, musing, "It was a lark, really, sailing on that ship. So many parties, so much champagne, so many dark, shadowy places. We passed icebergs, and we thought them exotic and amusing, an entertainment that the captain had arranged for us. But that last night was utter madness. I hung on to them, wouldn't let them go until we all made it into a lifeboat. Now Guy is the only one left to me."

She clunked the glass down on the marble surface and said angrily, "Perhaps revenge is in order, but Cuza was insane to think he could just shoot them like ducks in a pond."

"Yeah." Mickey winced uncomfortably, glancing around to make sure that Dave hadn't heard her. "Those dogs, they're smarter than you'd think. Guy was great last night, though, a real trouper. He, er, yeah, wasn't as successful as he could've been."

"What does that mean?" she asked sharply.

"Well, maybe you better talk to the Boss…" He trailed off, not meeting her diamond-hard gaze.

Cuza entered from the short hall that led to the shadowy back rooms with an arm around Tom's shoulder. The Boss chatted animatedly, cheeks flushed and eyes glittering, while Tom stumbled and muttered in a lackluster tone about needing to get back to work.

Cuza chuckled. "Stay for one more. It is Friday, is it not?"

"Where is he?" Lady Agatha pounced like hawk spotting a baby bunny, her voice building to a gritty growl as she stabbed an arm toward Cuza.

"Mickey, get our friend another beer. On the house, because it is Friday," Cuza said smoothly. Still smiling, he turned to calmly appraise Lady Agatha, a slight narrowing of his eyes the only sign that he knew she was about to explode.

Tom shambled slowly across the room, eyes dull and unfocused. Mickey hurried from behind the bar, maneuvered Tom toward a stool, and gently pushed him down before fetching a beer.

"Tom? You okay, buddy?" Dave asked from the next stool.

"Fridays, you know?" Mickey laughed weakly, as he opened the bottle and slid it across the bar to an uncomprehending Tom.

As he reached over to fold the man's fingers around the bottle, Mickey caught sight of Cuza striding toward Lady Agatha, who radiated incandescent anger.

"Always nice to see you here. Did Mickey make you a drink?" Cuza purred.

"I told him not to go," she said, "but he was swayed by you and your gun-loving—"

"Dear Agatha, can we discuss this in private?" Cuza put a hand on her arm.

"Where is Guy?" she demanded, hopping off the stool and pushing his hand away. She glared up at him, shaking with rage.

"I shall explain, do not worry, but let us talk in the back where it is quiet." Extending his arm toward the hall, he flicked his wrist like a magician revealing the finale of a trick.

"No," she seethed, "you will tell me where Guy is *now* or you will not have a partner any more. Instead, you will have my lawyer, beavering away to dissolve our business arrangement and give me complete control of this bar."

"Agatha," Cuza murmured, dropping his voice and speaking in tones inaudible to Mickey.

"Hey, how 'bout another beer? How many times does a guy have to ask?" Dave's irritated voice punched through Mickey's scattered thoughts.

"Yeah, sure," Mickey mumbled, as he strained to hear the low conversion taking place at the end of the bar. He dragged another bottle up from below and woodenly opened it.

"Boy, she's steaming. What did he do to make her so mad?" Dave asked, reaching across the bar to take the beer from him.

"Oh, she's, er, that is, they're old friends and they got unfinished business," Mickey said, but was interrupted by a shriek from Lady Agatha.

"Huh, somebody die or something?" Dave asked, eyeing the woman who had switched from screaming to cursing.

"Or something," echoed Mickey faintly.

Lady Agatha regained enough composure to issue a warning in a dangerously flat tone: "He survived the greatest cruise ship disaster in history, only to be consumed as fodder for your idiotic desire for revenge. Let me remind you that when there are icebergs, you pay attention or you sink. I wonder whether you are paying attention."

She spun around, away from Cuza, her heels clicking a staccato beat as she headed for the entrance. She stopped, turned, and snapped her fingers at Mickey. "You will drive me home. Now!"

As he escorted Lady Agatha through the velvet-draped entrance, Mickey thought glumly that his prospects of getting a good meal today had sunk like the HMS *Titanic*.

Chapter 12: Bonfire Night

I can't find him," Caleb said as he entered the kitchen, Bela at his heels.

"Mmm?" Sophia gazed into the mug of tea before her, not meeting his eyes.

"Rudy," he explained. "It's time to go, and he's hiding. Any ideas?"

She lifted her head, trying to focus on him. Her unnaturally pale face and the dark smudges under her eyes worried Caleb. He'd seen many victims of the Undead, but none so close to him as Sophia.

After a moment she shook her head slowly and said, "He's a tricky one. Have you tried behind the chicken coop or the crawlspace under the back of the house?"

"We checked around the coop," Caleb said. "Bela, how about checking the crawlspace?"

Bela made a face, but left the kitchen, banging both the exterior door and the gate to the back yard sharply in protest.

"Feeling better?" Caleb asked.

She frowned, idly playing her fingers over the papery garlic bulbs heaped on the table before her.

"Better. My head doesn't hurt so much anymore," she said listlessly.

"Ah, that was from dehydration," Caleb said, not sure that naming a thing could make it hurt less.

"I've certainly drunk enough of your vile tea," she replied with a bit of her usual spark. She stared at the ceiling, lost in thought for a moment. "Yes, I am better, but you don't expect me to wear this garlic necklace, do you?"

"Only when you leave the house."

"Oh, come on," she scoffed, sitting up straighter. "Is that really going to protect me?"

"Garlic makes vampires weak and disoriented," Caleb said, "and they tend to avoid places, or people, where there's a lot of it, which might give you a head start on running away, at least."

Garlands of garlic or discrete cloves tucked into pockets were common in the mountainous regions of Romania, where he wouldn't have had to explain, because everyone knew the lore: knew what to do when bitten by a vampire, knew how to tell the first bite from the second bite, knew how to keep vampires from coming back. In the isolated village where Sophia had grown up, stories of vampires probably still lingered, but it had been fifty or sixty years since anyone had been bitten. In the town of Bar Harbor, vampires weren't on anyone's radar, even though that was where the Undead survivors of the Titanic had come ashore and set up a colony. *They didn't even need lifeboats*, he thought with a shudder.

"Humor me, okay?" He attempted a grin, not knowing if it would reassure her.

She stared at him, open-mouthed for a moment, and didn't seem convinced. "What about garlic in jars? That would be less messy to carry around," she said at last.

"Well… I suppose," he said, thinking that he'd have to keep working on her.

"I can always try to hit the vampire over the head with the jar," she said sourly.

Caleb cringed at the thought, but didn't have time to continue the lecture on vampire lore. Both he and Sophia were startled by a sudden pounding on the stairs leading up from the basement. The basement door smacked against the wall as Bela entered with Rudy behind him. Both boys had cobwebs in their hair, and Rudy's knees were covered with dirt.

"How did you get into the basement?" Sophia asked, rattled by the unexpected appearance.

"Rudy showed me how to get in there through a loose board in the crawlspace. It was a tight fit," Bela explained triumphantly, while the younger boy hid behind him. "I bet grown-ups couldn't get in through there."

"I thought I fixed that years ago," Sophia said, not sharing the boy's delight. "Well, it explains a lot about Rudy's mysterious disappearances and about why there are so many spiders in the basement."

"I'll fix it when we get back," Caleb said impatiently, "but now it's time to go."

"No! I don't want to go back there!" Rudy declared, shifting uncomfortably from foot to foot while eyeing the door to the basement as an exit route.

"We won't stay long," Caleb said.

"Why do I have to go?" Rudy whined, switching from truculence to self-pity.

Caleb squatted next to the little boy, explaining, "We're going to say goodbye to one of the Hellhounds. It's what we do when someone..."

Caleb's final unspoken word hung in the kitchen. He read varying degrees of unease and dread in the others' faces. He wasn't crazy about the idea either, but he'd run with the Hellhounds during their Night, which created ties between them that couldn't be ignored. He also had a strong suspicion that he'd need their help to "neutralize" the vampires.

"There's going to be a fire," Bela chimed in halfheartedly. "A really big fire. It'll be fun, sort of."

Caleb stood and picked up a set of keys from the table. Turning to Sophia, he asked. "Are you ready?"

"What? Me? No, I'll be fine here," she protested.

"No and no." Caleb pushed back. "What if the v-" — he glanced at Rudy, not willing to say the word— "visitor, unwelcome visitor, comes back? I don't want you to be alone tonight. You don't have to do this thing with the Hellhounds. You can wait in the car."

"What about the wards on my house? Aren't those going to keep out those unwelcome visitors? And what about this garlic necklace you insist I wear?" she asked, picking up the garlic bulbs strung roughly on twine.

"That might not be good enough, because—trust me on this—it's not a good idea for you to be alone," Caleb finished lamely.

"You don't think I can take care of myself, is that it?" she retorted, her eyes coming to life with a bit of fire. "Perhaps you've forgotten that I could usually beat you and Toby at your stupid magical duels. You might be better at wards; I'll give you that. But I can protect myself and, if necessary, defend myself."

Caleb thought back to Fintonclyde's library and remembered when his vampire knowledge had been limited to the contents of those old books. Of course, he and his friends had mostly giggled at the thought of stakes and garlic. The first time that things got real in Romania and he held up a garlic braid he'd just felt silly—like warding off a monster with a slice of pizza. He didn't know how to make Sophia take it all seriously, or to get her to understand that self-defense wasn't just about your powers, it was about knowing what your opponent was up to.

Maybe it was this half-mythological knowledge that had killed Toby and René. *René was fortunate*, he thought, *because he died quicky and innocently.* Toby had been tricked or coerced or seduced into abetting vampires, and Caleb understood now just how that might happen.

"Rudy, you can bring your Gameboy, if you want," Caleb said. "You and Bela go upstairs and get it."

"Aw, you always make me leave when you—" Bela objected.

"Now," Caleb ordered.

Both boys gave Caleb dark looks as they left the kitchen, although for different reasons.

"I know you're good at magic," Caleb said, sitting at the table across from her, "but after you've been bitten, you become... more susceptible to vampires."

"You're full of advice, aren't you?" She glared at him, unconvinced, and then pushed her chair away from the table. "But it all boils down to me being a prisoner in my own house while vampires lurk in the shadows trying to ambush me. And I don't know anything about them, only what you tell me."

Sophia got up, nearly knocking the chair over, and turned her back on him. She wrapped her arms tightly around her chest and seemed to be staring out the window into the back yard.

"Can I tell you a story?" Caleb asked quietly.

She held herself very still, but faint tremors shook her shoulders and rippled down her back. In anger or in fear? Caleb couldn't be sure.

When she didn't answer, he said, "I learned how to hunt vampires when they were at their most vulnerable: hiding or sleeping, if you can call what vampires do true sleep. But it was a couple of years before I ever saw a vampire with its victim, before I understood what goes on when…" He spread his hands on the table, palms down, and took a deep breath before continuing. "There was this one time when an old farmer, a friend of Alexandru's, asked him to look into some odd things that had been happening. Alexandru took me with him."

"This happened a lot to you in Romania, showing up at someone's house like exterminators looking for vampires instead of termites?" she asked, scowling when she turned around to face him.

"If you want to put it like that, yes," he answered defensively. "One of the farmer's grandchildren, a sixteen-year-old, had had fever and delirium a couple of times after the new moon that summer. That might not seem remarkable to most people, but vampires in Romania like to hunt at the new moon, when their old enemies, the werewolves, are less active. The boy had the bite marks that confirmed what Alexandru had suspected: he'd had already been bitten twice and had hidden that from his family."

Caleb watched her hand creep unconsciously to her neck, then continued, "After dusk we hid in the hayloft of the barn, where the boy had been sleeping for the summer. After he fell asleep, we heard a faint noise from above that grew louder until it sounded like chanting or singing. I couldn't tell you if there were words to the song, or if I only imagined words. At the time, I thought I understood it: a welcome release, an opening into another place that was dark, secret, and mysterious, the promise of something beyond what we would call life.

"And it called to the boy who moaned in response: in fear or pleasure, I can't be sure even now. A woman with long, dark hair and dead eyes stood at his feet, appearing so suddenly that at the time it seemed like magic. The boy sat up clumsily. His eyes opened, wild and disoriented, but he saw only the vampire. He lunged at her, shouting her name. I dragged him away, but he fought me viciously, trying to free himself. Alexandru had warned me, but I wasn't ready, not truly."

Sophia stepped closer and wrapped her fingers tightly around the back of the kitchen chair.

"Alexandru had come prepared. He had ways of incapacitating vampires, because he wanted to question her, to ask the same question he asked all the vampires we found. He was looking for his old enemy."

"The vampire you told those agents about?"

"Yes, him. There was a long history between those two." Caleb stopped, not wanting to reveal the reason Alexandru had pursued the vengeance that had eventually killed him.

"What about that vampire, the one who wanted the boy? Did you...?"

"Alexandru ended things," Caleb answered, slowly pulling himself out of memories and returning to the sunny kitchen. "The boy was—I don't have words for it—not in his right mind? He wanted the vampire with all his being. And the song she sang, it called to me, too, but not as much as to him. After each bite, it gets harder to resist the song. Eventually victims want to give themselves to the vampire so much that... That's why I'm afraid for you, if you're here by yourself. It's not that I think the wards are weak or the garlic won't work. But what if you throw away the garlic and open the wards?"

"The song," she said.

"The song," he echoed.

* * *

No one spoke as the Land Rover jiggled and shook its way down the bumpy dirt road. Sophia watched puffy clouds tinted with the pastel colors that advertised the coming sunset. They drifted above the trees in a slow, dreamlike parade. Eventually, Caleb slowed the vehicle and pulled into a large clearing where he parked in the shadow of a tumbledown house, part of an old farmstead. A battered pickup truck and a line of motorcycles were parked near the house. At the far side of the clearing, canvas tents had been pitched. The tall summer grass had been thoroughly trampled by both feet and tires, suggesting that the occupants of this makeshift camp had been there for a while.

"Here we are," Caleb said as he set the handbrake with a sharp creak. Although he took the keys from the ignition, he made no move to leave the car.

"Can I get out of now?" Bela asked from the back seat after a minute elapsed in silence.

Caleb grunted an assent. Bela tumbled out of the back, leaving the door hanging open, and ran toward the center of the clearing.

"You don't have to— I mean, this is something I need to do: a werewolf thing," Caleb said, jingling the keys while not meeting her eyes. "You and Rudy can stay in the car. There are blankets in the back, and you can sleep, if you're tired."

Sophia stared through the windshield without answering. The people in the camp looked like bikers in their matching black leather vests with identical logos on the backs. At the center of the clearing, a shallow pit, nine or ten feet in diameter had been circled with stones. Branches had been piled in the middle of the pit where two teenaged boys argued, while an older man sat nearby in a lawn chair and harangued them. A cloth sling wrapped around one shoulder hindered his movement as he gestured toward something in the circle with his good arm. The dispute seemed to be about the wood that had been laid inside the fire pit. Bela gravitated toward the boys, who were older by a few years. *Too young to be bikers*, she thought.

Caleb got out of the car, took the grocery bag from the back seat, and closed the doors. He cast a look at Sophia through the window, inclining his head in a silent question, and then gave her a brief shrug.

Sophia watched him stride confidently into the midst of the Hellhounds. He belonged with them in some indefinable way. He seemed taller and straighter, more comfortable in his own skin than the teenaged werewolf she remembered from long ago.

The heaviness in her limbs wasn't the fatigue she'd felt earlier. Was it fear? And what was she afraid of: a pack of werewolves or a gang of bikers or an old, unrecognizable friend? In any case, she was letting fear define her, confine her, and make decisions for her. And that was not right.

"Do you want to come with me?" Sophia asked, turning to look at Rudy, wrapped in blanket in the back seat. He shook his head wordlessly, gazing down at the video game in his lap as it beeped and trilled.

Come on, Sophia chided herself. *If you're going to get out, get out.* She opened the car door and struggled to free herself, belatedly realizing she was tangled in the seat belt. Fighting to keep her balance as she dropped from the Land Rover to the ground, she was determined not to look weak. As she walked, she concentrated on not tripping on the uneven hillocks of grass and tire ruts.

The argument about stacking firewood continued in the center of the clearing, but Caleb wasn't paying attention. He stood in serious conversation with a small, dark woman whose long black hair fell down her back in a single braid.

"This is my friend Sophia," Caleb said simply as she approached. "Sophia, this is Doña Flóres."

"How do you do?" Sophia said, unsure of the best way to address either a werewolf or a biker. Doña Flóres narrowed her eyes, looking her over without a word in return.

Caleb hastily said, "We were discussing poultices. Doña Flóres has a lot of experience with herbs and that sort of thing."

Silence ballooned to the point of awkwardness. Caleb smiled vaguely, looking as uncomfortable as Sophia felt, and was about to speak. Whatever he'd meant to say was cut short as one of the teenaged boys sauntered toward them with a practiced swagger. Under his backward baseball cap, long copper-colored hair brushed his shoulders.

"Sophia, this is Fang's son Darius," Caleb said.

"Oldest son," the boy replied smugly with a wink.

Was he flirting with her?

Caleb ignored the boy's attitude, thrusting the paper bag toward him. "I brought some food and something for your father."

"Beer!" Darius said enthusiastically after peering inside.

"For your father," Caleb scolded. "You're not old enough to drink, are you?"

Darius shot back a cheerful obscenity and turned away, arms around the bag.

"That's Damien, Darius's brother." Caleb pointed to the other teenaged biker who was now jabbering with Bela, both boys crouched next to one of the Hellhounds' bikes. Indicating an older man seated in a folding lawn chair near the fire pit, he said, "And that's Fang, the Alpha, I mean, the leader."

As they approached the pack leader, Darius threw his father a can of beer, which he caught with one hand. Fang's closely cropped hair and beard were ruddy, and his tan, weathered face told of a life spent in the sun and wind.

"Thought you didn't drink, Fido," Fang drawled, nimbly popping the tab on the beer can.

"It's for you. Painkiller." Caleb chuckled as he moved two lawn chairs closer to the pack leader, indicating Sophia should sit next to him.

"Not my first injury," Fang said. "First silver arrow, though."

Taking his time, the pack leader looked her up and down before he took a long pull of beer from the can. "So, you brought your old lady."

"What? No!" Caleb exclaimed sharply. "This is Sophia, a friend. I brought her because she was attacked by a vampire on our Night. I thought she'd be safer here than alone at home."

"More of those rotten cadavers?" The pack leader took another drink.

"As if this shitshow couldn't get worse."

Caleb cleared his throat, hesitated, then said, "Maybe it could. A couple of agents came to see me today. They were from—"

"I know those bastards," Fang growled. "What did they want?"

"Information. About werewolves," Caleb answered laconically. "It took an effort to get through to them that vampires are the real problem. We do have evidence of a vampire attack. They even took pictures."

"That's not going to be enough to get them off our backs, though," Fang said. "Not if they're like the assholes in Florida that come snooping around."

"Right. We have to find the vampires," Caleb insisted, "and we have to find them soon."

"Good luck with that," Fang answered. He drained the can, crumpled it with one hand and tossed it into the fire pit. "Soon as I can ride, we're out of here. Not hanging around any longer, especially not if those agents are around."

Doña Flóres approached them, appearing solemn and sad.

"It is time," she said softly, laying a hand on the pack leader's good shoulder and motioning to Darius and Damien with the other.

"Wait a minute. You can't leave town like that." Caleb said to Fang, but pitched his voice loud enough for Fang's sons to hear. "Don't you want to get back at the vampires that attacked us? You know the agents probably won't do anything."

"We gotta finish this," Darius growled, curling and uncurling his fingers into fists as he approached. "If I get my claws on those stinking, rotten hunks of—"

"Shut it!" Fang roared, standing up and glaring at his son. "This ain't our fight. Let Fido go after them. We've lost too much already."

Darius ducked his head, looking down at his feet. Sophia saw from the boy's tense frame and balled fists that he didn't agree with his father.

Fang nodded to Doña Flóres, animosity and anger draining from his face. "It's time." He addressed Caleb: "You and your boy gonna help?"

Caleb folded his arms and inclined his head in assent. The argument had ended for now, but Caleb didn't appear willing to concede, only delay.

Caleb and Bela followed the boys into the farmhouse. After a few minutes, they emerged carrying an old door; Caleb and Fang's sons each balanced a corner at shoulder height, while Bela, shorter than the others, gripped a corner with hands raised awkwardly above his shoulders. On top of the door lay a large body wrapped in a white sheet. Sophia wished she'd thought to ask Caleb the dead werewolf's name.

No one spoke as they trudged to the edge of the stone-lined pit, where they set the door on the ground. Darius and Damien lifted the shrouded corpse at the feet and shoulders, stepping carefully over stone and branch to lay it gently in the center of the circle. Twigs and tinder snapped as the body came to rest.

Fang and Doña Flóres joined the others at the edge of the stone ring. After a long silence, the pack leader grunted softly to himself, clumsily took off a leather armband and tossed it on top of the shroud. He nodded to the other Hellhounds. Each of them in turn threw something into the shallow pit: Doña Flóres, a shiny, metallic object, a piece of jewelry perhaps; Darius, his baseball cap; and Damien, a book.

Fang nodded to Darius, who picked up a plastic fuel can and sauntered around the ring, splashing kerosene on the shroud and the wood beneath the body. When he'd finished soaking the wood, Caleb, Bela and Fang's sons gathered long branches that had been stacked outside the pit and set them upright, forming a teepee. No one spoke. No one argued. The sun had dipped below the horizon. What had been a gentle, silent breeze now forlornly rattled the leaves of the trees. The chill creeping up her arms told Sophia that the night would be colder.

Fang looked at Damien, who lifted a long stick wrapped with cloth at one end. His brother poured a measure of kerosene on the cloth, then took a lighter from his pocket and struck a flame. The tip of the makeshift torch whooshed into a small fireball. Damien walked slowly around the ring of stones, stopping every so often to thrust the torch into the logs. Flames bloomed, merging and lengthening, like a time-lapse movie of a field of flowers bursting open and reaching for the sun.

Fang gazed into the pyre, seeing something tangible in the pulsing tongues of flame and the pale white smoke that threaded through the upright branches to be swallowed by the darkening sky. The pack leader closed his eyes and howled. The other Hellhounds joined him, a chorus of pain and frustration and loss.

The flames morphed from red to orange to yellow, roaring like a gathering storm, crackling like the Fourth of July. Sophia gasped at the waves of heat pouring from the fire. She hastily pulled her chair further back from the fire pit. As she settled in, Rudy materialized suddenly next to her, the flickering firelight reflected in his wide, unblinking eyes.

Without a word, the little boy climbed into her lap. She opened her mouth to protest as she shifted her weight uncomfortably. Rudy threw his arms around her neck, and she felt the pulse of his breathing as he settled his cheek into the hollow of her collarbone. She raised her hands and gingerly patted his back. Did Rudy know that his mother had been cremated? Did he know that his grandfather had taken her ashes back to Germany? She wasn't always sure if the boy heard what she told him. How much had he understood of what had happened this summer?

Embers darted through the air like fireflies. In the center of the pyre, flames licked the blackening shroud. The heart of the fire was almost too bright to look at, but Sophia could make out a dark figure at the center like a giant slumbering bear. The stench of burning hair and flesh made her gag. All of a sudden, she wanted to hide under a blanket in the Land Rover.

She watched the firelit faces of the Hellhounds as orange tongues of flame wobbled in the wind and pushed upward, like hands grasping for something out of reach. The pack occasionally murmured to one another or told stories and jokes. The stories were all unfamiliar to her; the jokes' punchlines, which sometimes resulted in cascades of laughter, made no sense.

Damien and Darius poked the fire with long sticks and added more wood from time to time. Caleb and Bela stood at some distance from the stone circle and chased down glowing embers, stomping on them or dowsing them with water from buckets.

Rudy became restless, wriggled out of her lap, and hopped to the ground. He ran to Bela and helped stomp on embers, now laughing at a new game. She marveled at how easily the little boy's mood could swing from anxious terror to giddy delirium.

She didn't know how long she watched the fire, losing herself in the chaotic wobble of the flames, but when she rose from the chair, she was stiff and sore from the rough fabric strips and aluminum frame that had been digging into her legs. She stretched, then drifted toward Caleb, who stood ten or twelve feet away from the fire, his body half tinted with orange light and half in shadow. When he turned to look at her, she saw a face she almost didn't recognize. There was pain there, which was familiar, but there was also a flinty hardness that wasn't.

Caleb tilted his head toward the sky. She followed his gaze upward. As the brightness of the fire faded from her vision, she saw that the scattered clouds had gone, leaving the sky above clear and dark.

"You studied astronomy," she murmured. "What do you see up there?"

"Hmm. Maybe not what you'd think," Caleb said, gesturing toward the gibbous waning moon that hovered just above the treetops. "The Wolf sees only her harsh, unblinking stare, but humans see the stars and planets, too; they make up stories that live in the constellations; they watch the sky, cataloguing and learning. When I can see the stars, I know I'm human."

What do I see up there? she wondered. For her, the starry sky meant summer and freedom and friends. Growing up in the tiny village of Tribulation, she hadn't often gone outside to look at the stars, because there were chores and too many relatives and sometimes the need to hide from her abusive father. During summers spent in Fintonclyde's camp for odd and exceptional children, she'd learned about the constellations and the movement of planets and had discovered the simple pleasure of staring at the faint ribbon of the Milky Way. Now, as she gazed upward, she might almost dive into the twinkling lights to swim among alien suns, to escape the too-familiar earth.

"Here," came a voice softly in her ear. Warm breath tickled her neck as a scratchy wool blanket dropped over her shoulders.

She'd lost track of time, of her body, of the fire. She shivered, as cold as if she'd jumped into an ice-crusted winter pond. Cold, white moonlight bathed the clearing. How long had she been star-gazing?

An arm circled her waist, drawing her closer to the dying fire. Slowly, the ice drained from her veins. Caleb guided her to a chair. She sat, pulling the blanket tightly about her chest. He squatted next to her, one hand on the arm of the chair. His face, grim and unrecognizable, dissolved into that of the boy she'd known as a child, like an optical illusion that puzzles and frustrates, until the trick is suddenly plain to see.

"I'm sorry," he said quietly. "I should have known you'd get chilled when the fire died down. It won't be much longer now, then I'll take you home."

Wordlessly, she took his hand, and felt an electric jolt when he squeezed hers in return.

In the center of the fire pit, the charred corpse was surrounded by glowing coals, pulsing like an ancient alphabet that might hold the secrets of the universe, if only she could decipher the letters. Next to her, Rudy huddled underneath a blanket in another folding chair, while Fang and Doña Flóres sat several feet away, heads together in a low conversation. Bela and the Fang sons had disappeared to the shadowy edges of the clearing.

"We've got to be going," Caleb called to Fang, who jerked his head up as Caleb approached.

Doña Flóres got up from the chair and walked toward Rudy. She leaned over and whispered something to the boy. Rudy poked his head from under the blanket. Fang stood, and then strode toward Caleb until they were almost nose-to-nose.

"But the boy stays here," Fang said flatly.

"Okay, good that you want to be responsible," Caleb countered, "but we've got this."

"The pack will take him," Doña Flóres declared matter-of-factly. "That is how it has always been."

"What? He'll just disappear into some rundown trailer park in Florida, and that's the end of it?" Caleb shot back, starting to get angry. "I do have experience raising a kid who's been bitten and lost his family."

Darius, Damien, and Bela had drifted in from the dark recesses of the camp, attracted by conflict like moths to a flame.

"Our doing, our responsibility. That's how it is," Fang rumbled in a menacing tone.

Rudy stared open-mouthed, his gaze bouncing between Caleb and Fang, who were facing off in front of his chair. The harsh light from the nearly full moon hardened their faces into grotesque masks.

"You think biting him gives you the right to own him, like a puppy from the pound?" Caleb snapped.

Tempers flared like a fuel-soaked rag, and Sophia lost track of the words. Bela, hands balled in fists, defended Caleb, while Darius shouted over him. Doña Flóres let out a long tirade in Spanish, gesticulating angrily at Caleb. Damien was the only one of the Hellhounds not fighting Caleb and Bela, trying instead to calm down his pack. They ignored him, except for Darius, who cuffed his brother on the head.

Rudy looked from face to face, eyes wide, mouth agape and lower lip trembling. Sophia was the only one to notice him slip out of the chair and flee from the brawling werewolves. She pushed herself out of her seat, though her stiff legs screamed in protest, and followed him. She found him sitting on the ground with his hands wrapped around his knees, leaning against the front tire of the Land Rover. She knelt stiffly on the lumpy ground and touched his shoulder, not knowing if she was being comforting or creepy.

"I want to go home," Rudy mumbled, his face buried in his knees.

Sophia had no answer for the little boy, who began to cry, quietly at first, then with rough, shuddering sobs. She watched and waited silently, while her heart broke.

Eventually the crying subsided, and he whispered, "I miss her."

She sucked in a deep breath, as if a lungful of air could give her the wisdom to help this grieving, broken boy. Exhaling, she said, "I didn't know your mother, but your grandfather told me about her. She was an amazing person, and she loved you very much. I promised your grandfather that I'd take care of you so that you'd grow up and make her proud of you." Sophia gently smoothed Rudy's hair, which was tangled and wild from sleeping under the blanket. "Caleb wants to help, too. He knows what it's like to… to be special the way you are."

"I don't have to go with them?" Rudy sniffled and then ran the back of his hand under his dripping nose.

"What?"

"That lady, she said I have to go with them."

"She said that? No, you don't have to listen to her. You're staying with me."

"Caleb, too?" he asked with a quaver in his voice. "You won't make him go away?"

She barely remembered the hard words she'd had for Caleb before the full moon, which seemed like months ago, instead of two days ago. "No, Caleb's not going away," she said.

In the center of the clearing, the shouting continued. Sophia wondered whether anyone had noticed that the little boy over whom they were fighting was missing. She slowly got to her feet. "It's past my bedtime and yours, too."

The little boy looked up and nodded solemnly.

"You get in the back, okay?" Sophia said, opening one of the Land Rover's rear doors. She helped him scramble onto the back seat. "I'm going to go get Caleb and Bela. Then we'll go home."

After quietly closing the door, she strode toward the shouting match, which showed no sign of winding down. She wondered how werewolves settled fights when they were human.

The harsh moonlight washed out colors so that the scene before her could have been from an old, black-and-white Western movie. Caleb and Fang stood a few feet apart, while Bela and the other Hellhounds formed a circle around them. From the tense postures and hard words, this could be the moment in the saloon fight right before a chair was smashed over someone's head.

"Stop it!" Sophia yelled, stepping in between Caleb and Fang. Uncharacteristically bold, she pushed them apart. Doña Flóres made a grab for her arm, but Sophia twisted out of her reach. Into the silence that followed her audacious and unexpected behavior, she pointed to Caleb, then to Bela.

"We are going home. Now," she ordered.

"We're not done here!" Caleb rounded on her with a fury she'd never seen directed at her before.

Sophia faltered for a moment at the sight of the hard angles of his face, transformed by the moonlight into a grotesque black-and-white caricature. But she had a wounded little boy to protect.

"Done enough," she said firmly, meeting his unblinking gaze with one of her own.

Caleb's hard expression softened slightly, puzzlement creeping in around the edges. He snapped his head around to glare at Fang.

"I'll be back to finish this—" Caleb insisted, but was drowned out by Fang.

"Don't bother! We're done here, Fido. I don't need to hear any more of your whiny yapping."

Caleb clenched his hands into fists, holding his body rigid. The grimness of his expression had Sophia worried that he might knock her over in an attempt to get to the pack leader. She took a deep breath, clamped both hands around Caleb's arm, and pulled him away from the angry Hellhounds. Fang and Darius continued to call after them, but she ignored the naked insults and profanity.

"What do you think you're doing?" Caleb said in a low voice once they reached the Land Rover.

Sophia released his arm and slumped against the front of the truck. "I know what I'm doing," she gasped, fighting to catch her breath. "Get in and drive or give me the keys."

Bela trotted up, accompanied by Damien. The two boys were having a rapid, whispered conversation about when Damien could sneak into town and work on the German motorcycle.

"Come on, Bela," Sophia snapped as she yanked on the front passenger door and climbed inside.

Caleb started the engine and flicked on the headlights, which froze Damien and Bela in the sudden bright light. The Land Rover turned around jerkily, and Bela dashed to catch up. After Bela had swung himself into the back seat, Caleb nosed the truck toward the dirt track leading away from the clearing and accelerated.

As they bounced along the rutted road, Caleb turned to her, more puzzled than angry, and asked, "What was that all about? I could have sorted it out with them."

"I'm not so sure," she said. "We can't wait for the next full moon for you to settle things like werewolves, and I didn't see you making much progress resolving anything like humans."

"What do you know about—" Caleb said with exasperation, then checked himself. With forced calm he continued, "I can't let the Hellhounds take Rudy, you know that. He's scared of them, and they're not fit to take care of him. Now I'm going to have to find a way to get him back from them."

Bela laughed from the back seat. "The joke's on them, because Rudy's right here."

Chapter 13: Mystery Illness

HAVE YOU EVER SEEN a dragon?" Rudy asked, pushing fried egg around the plate with a fork. Two days after the altercation at the Hellhounds' camp, and the little boy still hadn't regained his appetite, but Bela had a knack for distracting Rudy enough to make him forget his fears for short periods of time.

"From a distance," Bela said, buttering a piece of toast while standing at the kitchen counter. "And I found that dragon's skull back home."

Rudy turned his eyes toward Caleb, who sat across the kitchen table from him, gazing into the dregs of his tea. He'd been mired in private thoughts, going over the local gossip he'd picked up over the last several days and paying little attention to the conversation around him. Now he looked up to see Rudy's eyes sparkling with curiosity.

"I've been close to one a couple of times," Caleb answered distractedly.

"Huh," Sophia snorted from beside him, while she sorted through the Monday-morning mail. "What about the time you and Toby rode that dragon over Southwest Harbor?"

"Yes," Caleb began slowly. "But it didn't end well. And we never told Fintonclyde, because… well, we just didn't."

"You two must have really made that one mad." Sophia smirked. "It's only this summer that Fintonclyde finally coaxed another dragon back to the island."

"You never told me about any of that!" Bela said, slathering strawberry jam on his toast.

"As I said, it didn't end well. And we could have been killed when we flew low over the town: fried in power lines or impaled on a boat mast. Honestly, you shouldn't mess with dragons."

A crestfallen Bela, having crammed the toast into his mouth, mumbled, "Yeah, right. Can we go outside? Rudy's going to show me how to ride that board with wheels that I found in the garage."

"Skateboard, dummy," Rudy corrected with a laugh.

"That old thing? I thought I got rid of it." Sophia frowned as she slit open an envelope with a finger. "Okay, but stay on our street and watch out for cars and don't hit any pedestrians and maybe you should wear a helmet. I think there's one in the garage."

"And clear your plates!" Caleb called as both boys headed for the door.

After a certain amount of grumbling, the boys deposited their breakfast dishes in the sink and then boiled through the door, eager to be gone.

Caleb cleared the remaining dishes from the table. As he began to run hot water into the sink, Sophia glanced up from the piles of mail before her.

"You don't have to," she said. "I do have a dishwasher."

"There are only a few dishes, not enough to run that thing. Besides, if I'm not useful, you might decide to kick me out."

"I didn't mean that, what I said before," Sophia stammered, her face reddening.

Caleb looked down at the sink, concentrating on soaping dishes, buying time to gather his thoughts. Her declaration before the full moon had stung him more than he'd admitted to himself at the time and, he realized now, he'd been weighed down by the possibility that she'd decide to order him out of her house again.

"Rudy was pretty excited to give Bela skateboard lessons," Caleb commented, attempting to change the subject.

"He's opened up a lot since you got here. I didn't seem to get through to him before. I mean, nothing I did…" Sophia said, shaking her head.

Caleb glanced over his shoulder, noting the misery on her face. "It just takes time," he said softly. "And the Night, I mean the full moon, probably helped. Rudy knows he has a family now. Not that we could ever entirely fill the hole left by his mother's death."

"Even the Hellhounds?" Sophia laughed nervously.

"In a way, yes," Caleb answered thoughtfully. "I can't explain this very well, but having a pack, any pack, makes a difference." He thought about the joy he'd felt running through the mountains for the first time with Pack Six, despite the abuse he'd endured from its dimwitted leader.

"About the Hellhounds, do you think they'll try to… try to take Rudy again?"

"I don't know." Caleb considered this as he rinsed plates and set them in the rack. "Rudy certainly doesn't want that, but I'm not sure Fang's on board. I'm going to have to have another talk with him."

"Talk or dogfight?" Sophia asked with a worried edge to her voice.

Caleb didn't want to go into werewolf relations with her, but he thought Fang would see reason eventually. He needed the Hellhounds on his side if he was going to eliminate Cuza and his gang, although he didn't know how he was going to accomplish that yet. He finished washing and drying the dishes in silence, while Sophia pulled letters and bills from envelopes and stacked them separately from junk mail.

"What did happen that night with the dragon?" she asked.

Caleb set a fresh mug of tea on the table and took a seat next to her. Glancing at the pile of papers, he asked, "Is that Tom's estimate?"

"You're trying to distract me," she said with mock severity. "Come on: spill it."

"We were idiots," Caleb said with a smile. "Or I was an idiot to listen to Toby. You know how it was: he'd talk me into doing stupid stuff, though he seemed to come out on top most of the time."

"Most of the time," Sophia said in a small voice.

Except that last time, Caleb thought as his smile faded. *He went charging into Lilac House six years ago, and I wasn't there.*

The air in the kitchen stilled, and the only sound was the relentless ticking of the grandfather clock from the front hall. Ghosts crept into the silence between them: a dark-haired boy in a cracked leather jacket, hands jammed into the pockets of his jeans, who grinned at them with malicious humor; and a smaller boy, his scarred face bravely twisted into a smile as he gazed up at the friend he idolized.

Caleb snatched the estimate from the top of the pile and studied it. "The renovations are going to be pretty cheap, unless I've forgotten how much things cost in the last six years."

"What?" Sophia blinked, shook her head, and looked around the room as if she'd been teleported from another time and place. Slowly, her eyes focused, and she took the piece of paper from Caleb. "Hmm. No, that's not right. Look, he's left the labor cost out of the total."

"When Tom was here the other day, did he seem different to you?" Caleb asked.

Sophia bit her lip and gazed up at the ceiling for a moment, then shrugged. "A bit off, I guess. I mean, he usually cracks jokes and makes really bad puns. And Trudy had to remind him twice about finishing the estimate."

"It's more than that," Caleb said. "Trudy said he's been sick for a month and so anemic he needed a blood transfusion."

"So? He's feeling a bit under the weather, and he can't do math right." Sophia didn't appear concerned as she laid the paper back on the table.

"When Trudy told me about Tom being sick, I didn't pay a lot of attention to it, but people in town are talking about this mystery illness, the same one the agents were telling us about. It's some kind of flu that makes people tired and not themselves, and it's locals catching it, not tourists."

"That is a bit odd," Sophia said, "because usually it's the tourists infecting the townies."

Caleb nodded. "Tom was the first one I heard about, but there's at least a dozen more people who've got this flu, and one of them died. Trudy hasn't been sick, but some of Tom's friends have. It makes me think there's something weird about the way this disease spreads, if Tom's been sick for a month and hasn't given it to his wife. I haven't checked up on all the people who're sick, but Tom and his friends have at least one thing in common: they're all regulars at the Lobster Pot."

"That place on Main Street? What about it?"

"Did I mention that I saw Cuza signing the papers to buy the whole building? It was the day after I got here, when Bela and I went to the bank. Oh, and the former owner of the building was the one who died from this mystery illness."

"And Cuza is…?"

He blew out a frustrated breath and said, "The vampire from Romania that I thought I destroyed last year, only I didn't. He's the one I told the agents about. Didn't I mention his name?"

"There were a few things you forgot to mention," she said acidly. Her eyes slid away from his, and she picked up the estimate again, twitching the paper without reading it. She sighed. "I guess it wouldn't have mattered."

He took a slurp of tea while asking himself if he believed that was true.

He'd known there could be danger if Cuza had recognized him, and he'd protected the house as best he could. But he'd been thinking of himself as the target, not Sophia. Could he have prevented the vampire attack if he'd told her more?

"I don't blame you for what happened, though. I was stupid to go outside that night." She gave him a brief smile before her lips compressed into a hard line and her brow crinkled anxiously.

Caleb closed his eyes, both hands squeezing the mug. His presence had made her a target for vampires and had thrown her into the middle of his fight with the Hellhounds. Maybe she'd been right when she'd told him to get a motel room.

"But I'm scared, Caleb," she said quietly after a pause. "I'm scared to fall asleep at night. I'm scared to go outside by myself, even to the mailbox or the chicken coop, and I— I don't want to live like this." She wiped a knuckle under her eyes to draw away tears. "So, we'd better figure out what the vampires are up to and stop them, right?"

"You don't have to—I mean, I'm the one who needs to…fix this," Caleb said, fearing there was little comfort in his words.

"Doing something, anything, is better than hiding under the covers," Sophia said with a smile that was bright but brittle. "What about Fintonclyde? Maybe he'd know if it's some weird illness connected with vampires."

Caleb dismissed the idea sourly. "Trudy asked me that, too, but he won't be much help. He claimed to know all about vampires when we were young, but he held back a lot of what he knew or fed us half-truths. And I haven't seen evidence that he's learned much more since then."

"Don't be so hard on him," she said. "He fought against the original Undead inhabitants of Lilac House back in the forties. That speaks to some knowledge of vampires."

"With help from Alexandru Arghezi," Caleb countered, "who knew more about vampires than anyone I've ever met."

"Sure, sure," Sophia said, "but Fintonclyde has a good memory and a large library. And he does want to help."

"I suppose that not all of his books on vampires are utter rubbish," Caleb conceded. "There might be a few in his library that could be useful."

"The boys could use an outing," she mused. "And I'll bet the dragon eggs that Fintonclyde's been fussing over all summer have hatched by now."

Chapter 14: Drive, She Said

BEHIND THE SOUNDS OF chirping crickets and croaking frogs, snatches of conversations leaked out of the hotel windows. Alone in front of the entrance to the grand old building, Mickey lost himself in the back-and-forth rhythm of the chamois cloth as he polished the hood of Lady Agatha's Rolls Royce. The sun had departed hours ago. The lamps flanking the hotel's entrance lit the wide porch and threw a half-circle of light on the cobblestone driveway. The lack of other illumination didn't bother Mickey; he had excellent night vision and had done this chore for long enough that he could make the car shine perfectly on a dark, moonless night.

As he polished the chrome grille, he could almost believe it was the 1930s again. The old car didn't seem out of place parked in front of a hotel that had been built around the turn of the century. He longed for that grander, more graceful past, for a time when he'd understood the order of things. He had fled chaos and confusion in Romania to find a place among Bar Harbor's high-society immortals, but the good times had gone south the night his brother Alexandru had killed or driven away most of the inhabitants of his comfortable world. Then, after years of hibernation, he'd found himself in a nightmare being run by Cuza, the creature that he least wanted to meet ever again. *Why can't it go back to the way it was?* he thought bitterly.

"Young man! Young man!" A peevish voice cut through the silence.

Mickey looked up with mild curiosity to see a well-dressed couple in their sixties approaching the hotel's entrance. A woman in a conservatively cut, dark green velvet dress with a small battering ram of a purse over one arm marched ahead of a man dressed in a pale tweed suit. The man stopped short, while his companion noisily clomped up the steps of the porch.

"Come along," she commanded. "We're going to be late."

"Is that what I think it is? It can't be!" The man goggled in wonder.

"Come *on!*" the woman said, frowning down at him from the top of the short flight of steps.

"Go in without me," the man said irritably, not taking his eyes from the car. Toward the car, he adopted a reverential tone. "A Phantom! I haven't seen one of this vintage for a long time. A 1929?"

"1930," Mickey answered, continuing to polish the grille.

The man peered inside the passenger compartment, eyed the shiny black wheel covers, and patted the car as if he didn't believe it was real.

"Pity it's so dark. I'd love to see under the hood," he said, gazing longingly. "Three-speed or four-speed transmission?"

Mickey had to think about this. He knew how to keep the old car running, he knew how to drive it, but he didn't bother much with what things were called. "Three."

"Ah, yes! This was one of the ones made here in the US, not in the UK."

"If you say so, mister," he muttered.

Newly arrived in America in 1935, Mickey had wanted to make himself useful at Lilac House and had started hanging around with the old codger who took care of the cars, but could no longer see well enough to drive them. He'd never seen such machines back in the old country, but he soon learned how to service and drive the various vehicles in Her Ladyship's collection. He'd looked sharp in a black chauffeur's uniform. Lady Agatha, who had an eye for pretty boys, had taken to him. Little remained from those times except a few rusting old clunkers and the 1930 Rolls Royce Phantom.

"Is this your car?" the man asked critically.

"I'm only the driver." Mickey turned his back on the man, hoping he would go away.

"You tell the owner that I'd like to buy this beauty," the man announced, slapping his palm on the hood of the car for emphasis.

"My employer won't part with it," Mickey called over his shoulder. "You're wasting your time, mister."

The man persisted, thrusting a pale calling card under his nose. "I'll make it worth his while."

"Her while," Mickey corrected as he took the card. "She won't sell. Too sentimental."

"You see?" the woman called. "You are wasting your time *and mine.*"

The man gave an exaggerated sigh and, as he joined his wife under the portico. "You give her my card, boy. She'll want to talk to me!"

"Yeah, sure."

As the couple disappeared through the carved oak front door, he let the card fall to the ground and applied the chamois cloth to the fingerprints the man had thoughtlessly left on the hood.

"Are they gone?" came a hoarse whisper from a large rhododendron bush.

"Death and damnation!" Mickey gave a shout at the sound. "What are you doing in the shrubbery, Frenchie? Hunting squirrels?"

The familiar hooded figure emerged, rattling leaves while pushing branches away from his face. Frenchie crossed the driveway cautiously, darting his head toward the hotel.

"N-n-n-no," Frenchie stuttered. "I just don't want to be recognized, you know?"

"Right! Like someone at this fancy hotel is going to know who you are?"

"Why do you bother with an old car like this?" Frenchie jeered at him. "There's plenty better new ones around."

"Don't touch the car!" Mickey snapped. "You don't know nothing about cars, so shut up about it. What are you doing here anyway? Aren't you supposed to be working at the bar?"

Frenchie did his annoying hand-wringing and sniveled, "The Boss, he kinda got mad at me, uhm, because of what happened at the full moon. He wants me to...uhm..."

"—eliminate the evidence," Mickey finished with a satisfied grin. "Didn't I tell you?"

"I need a place to hide. Please?" Frenchie pleaded, sidling up to him and whispering in his ear. "He said I should get of his sight and not come back until I... until I fixed my, uhm, problem, and if I didn't, he'd cut my head off and throw me into a fire. Do you think he'd do that? Really?"

"Well," Mickey began, thinking about Cuza's vendetta against the Ar-ghezi family: corrupting his brother's wife, Ana Maria, then fifty years later killing his brother and even murdering his harmless, elderly aunt in Bucharest. His aunt's only crime had been possessing the letter to his family that Mircea had written decades before when he'd arrived in Maine. "You should stay away from the Boss for now. I gotta think that at some point he's going to need someone to run errands or wash dishes, then he might forget how mad he is."

"H-h-how long will that be?" Frenchie stammered, his cratered face twitching seismically.

"Dunno. Maybe a week," Mickey said thoughtfully, taking pleasure in Frenchie's distress after all the bootlicking the little weasel had done to suck up to Cuza. "Or two."

"No!" Frenchie wailed, pawing at his jacket. "Can I go back with you to Lilac House? There's room, right? I mean, now that Guy is... not around anymore."

He pushed Frenchie away, stepping around him, then making a show of ignoring him as he applied himself to polishing the hood ornament.

"First, you ain't supposed to talk about Lilac House. Even Cuza doesn't know about Her Ladyship's hideaway," he said gruffly. "Second, Her Ladyship likes her privacy, which means she ain't going to tolerate the likes of you."

"Wh-wh-what about the garage," Frenchie spluttered, "with that trapdoor into the old tunnel. Where you and I first met, remember?"

Mickey couldn't forget the tunnel where Frenchie had stumbled on him six years ago. He'd lain hidden there for decades after Lilac House had been magically locked tight with Lady Agatha and the others trapped inside. Even though he'd escaped the magical battle by dashing into the smugglers' tunnels, he'd been alone and scared with all of his compatriots sealed up or destroyed, and with his own brother leading the effort to rid the town of immortals. The best plan he could come up with was to hibernate in an improvised coffin made of empty whisky crates. He didn't know how long he'd been there when he was roused by a bleeding mortal stumbling into his ad hoc crypt, but he sure knew he was hungry. That clueless kid, scraped up and oozing from his clumsy attempts to explore the tunnels, had proved impossible to resist. A foolish move, in hindsight. Frenchie was his greatest mistake.

"I remember the tunnels," Mickey said sourly, moving away and taking a sudden interest in polishing the side mirror.

"Please, please?" Frenchie persisted, following him like a poorly trained puppy. "I don't want to go back to that cellar. It's damp and disgusting and too close to the Lobster Pot. What if he sees me?"

"What, that old cellar where they used to store hooch back in the day? The one under Kelly's Drugstore?"

"Yeah." Frenchie scowled, wrapping his arms around his chest protectively. "Is there any place in Bar Harbor where you and your pals didn't stash illegal liquor?"

"Not a lotta places." Mickey smiled at the memory of happier times. "Look, you ain't coming near Lilac House. Hey, maybe you should leave town. I don't think you have much of a future with the Boss, even if you do make up with him."

"I can't," moaned Frenchie, pacing the driveway in agitation. "I've got things to do, unfinished business. I mean, I got plans, too, you know."

"You could get yourself out of this mess by getting rid of that mortal you bit last week. He might forgive you quicker that way," Mickey suggested.

"What? No! I can't do that." Frenchie rolled his eyes, shaking his head from side to side like a wind-up toy.

"Still can't stand the sight of you-know-what? You're the most pathetic immortal I've ever seen."

"Yeah, that's it. It's the b-b-blood," Frenchie agreed quickly, his head bobbing spastically. "You know me, I'll probably make a mess of it. You can help me! Will you help me? Please? Please?"

Mickey laughed. "Not out of the goodness of my heart. You gotta make it worth my while."

"I can help you with the car," Frenchie exclaimed, snatching the cloth from Mickey's hand.

"Stop that! You're gonna mess it up!" Mickey yelled as Frenchie tried to polish the hood. The twit was likely to leave more fingerprints than he erased.

"I could… I could tend bar for you," Frenchie proposed. He'd stopped trying to polish the car and was corkscrewing the cloth into a tight cylinder between his hands.

"Not likely. Oh, gimme that!" Mickey pulled the now-ropelike chamois cloth away from Frenchie's frantic hands. "First, one of the locals might recognize you, and second, I like working the bar. It reminds me of the old days, before *he* showed up."

Turning away, Mickey squinted at the hood of the car, looking for fingerprints.

"Can I please, please, please hide out at the garage?" Frenchie's voice crackled with anxiety. "Maybe there's something else I can do—"

The front door of the hotel opened, spilling a wide river of light onto the driveway. From inside, Mickey heard Lady Agatha's trilling laugh. He spun around to face the hotel's façade as Frenchie darted back into the rhododendron.

The heavy scent of roses preceded Lady Agatha. She stepped onto the wide porch, her arm linked with that of a middle-aged man in an expensive suit.

"Let us take a long, slow drive along the coast," she purred as the pair trod the short set of steps and then strolled across the driveway.

Her companion gawped. "This is yours? You said you had an old car, but…" Untangling himself from her, the man began a slow circuit around the Rolls. To Mickey, it was Her Ladyship's car, nothing more than that, but mortals seemed incomprehensibly drawn to a past they could not remember.

"Been in the family for ages, you know how it is," Lady Agatha rejoined lightly. "And it still drives like a dream, you'll see."

Mickey eagerly opened the rear passenger compartment, standing at attention by the door. They were sure to feast tonight.

"Did I see you talking to that odious little rat?" she whispered to him as her eyes hungrily followed the man who circled the car, while commenting to himself about this and that detail.

"Who? Frenchie?" Mickey asked nonchalantly.

"Yes. What was he doing here? Is Cuza spying on me?"

"Oh, he dropped by to snivel a bit," Mickey said with a smirk. "But I don't think he's going to be reporting back to the Big Cheese, not this time."

Chapter 15: The Amulet

J UST A LITTLE HIGHER," Bela called down, "then we'll be able to see."
Below him, Rudy whimpered. Bela, hooking an arm over a branch, twisted his body to look at the little boy hugging the tree trunk like a shipwrecked sailor clutching flotsam. Fifteen feet below, the yellow Lab whined and circled the base of the pine tree.

"C'mon, kid. You wanted to see the dragons, didn't you?"

"Yes, but, but…" Rudy quavered. "I didn't know we'd have to climb so high. My mom never lets me climb trees."

"Okay, okay, I'm coming down," Bela said. He found it hard to believe that the little boy had never climbed a tree. He'd been scrambling up trees and scaling rock faces since he was younger than Rudy.

The rocky clifftop cave where the baby dragons allegedly sheltered was only about a hundred feet away from the stand of pine trees, but it was as close as they were going to get, because Bela couldn't figure out how to get through the wards that formed a magical fence around the Reserve, Fintonclyde's collection of unusual and exotic creatures from all over the world.

That morning Caleb had taken him, Rudy, and Sophia to Dragonshead Island, the isolated spot off the coast where Caleb had spent his childhood with Fintonclyde and his magical menagerie. Bela had heard Caleb complain for years about how he couldn't wait to get off the island, but to his eyes, Fintonclyde's large, rambling house and tidy barnyard were palatial compared to the small, drafty cabin that belonged to the pack back home. The best part had been when the old man had taken them all into the Reserve.

They watched the billdads splash in shallow water, catching wriggling, silver fish in their beaks. The ashanti, a barnacle-encrusted lobster the size of a pony, crawled out of an ocean pool to talk to Sophia in a crackly, creaking voice. As they wandered the Reserve, the ghuls, doglike creatures with a sharply pointed noses and intelligent eyes, crooned to them in understandable English about how lonely they were and how much they wanted to play. Fintonclyde warned them not to pay attention to their pleas, as the ghuls wanted to eat them if they could. The napping manticore, sprawled across a large rock, had opened one eye sleepily, growled at them, then gone back to sleep. However, the old man wouldn't let them get close to the dragon's cave on top of the cliff, explaining that the eggs had recently hatched and the mother dragon would protect the little dragons with fire if they got too close.

Bela and Rudy had chased the more harmless creatures and peppered the old man with questions, while Caleb had been impatient and withdrawn. Something was eating at him, Bela knew from experience. Caleb had been relieved when Fintonclyde had suggested they go back to the cabin to make a batch of brownies.

Fintonclyde's cabin was boring, full of musty old books packed into tottery shelves stacked to the ceiling. Once the brownies were in the oven, the grownups had huddled over stacks of books, talking about stuff that had happened years ago. They hadn't noticed the two boys and the dog slipping outside.

"Nothing to be scared of," Bela said when he reached the place where Rudy sat astride a branch, eyes closed with arms tightly wrapped around the trunk. Below, the dog barked out concern for her humans. "I'm going to show you where to put your hands and feet, okay? I won't let you fall, don't worry."

As he coaxed the younger boy up with step-by-step guidance about each move, sometimes cupping a hand to give him a boost up, he realized how hard the climb was for Rudy. His arms and legs weren't as long as Bela's, and he couldn't reach some of the handholds that Bela could. After many long minutes, Bela found a high enough spot where Rudy could sit safely on a branch. Bela settled himself nearby and got out the brass spyglass, which he'd found at Sophia's house.

"Can you see the cave now?" Bela asked, gesturing toward the shadowy place near the top of the cliff as he adjusted the little telescope.

"Yeah, I think so. It's so far away, though," Rudy said, his voice fading as the wind whooshed through the branches.

"Ever use one of these?" he asked, leaning carefully toward Rudy and handing him the spyglass. "You should be able to see the cave. Keep one hand on the branch, though."

Rudy's hand shook as he grasped the spyglass and raised it to one eye. "But where are the baby dragons?"

"You have to be patient," Bela counseled, knowing that patience had never been one of his virtues, if he had any virtues at all.

"Look!" Rudy cried, pointing up into the lead-colored sky.

He followed the little boy's arm and spied a dark speck, barely visible against the roiling, gray clouds.

"Dragon!" both boys yelled together. As they watched, the tiny speck grew into a V-shape, becoming larger as it flew in circles, ever closer to the cliff top. The dragon's white belly and the nearly translucent wings made her hard to see against the overcast sky, but when she dipped her wings to spiral down to earth, they could see the brownish-gray of her back.

The dragon held a large, silvery fish in her talons, which she dropped just before landing. The huge wings folded as the she touched down, letting out a loud screech. Two little heads poked out of the cave mouth; two little dragons waddled outside, their mouths wobbling open, although from such a distance their cries were faint. The dragonets had large heads and stubby back legs, which meant that they fell over a few times in their haste to get to the fish.

"Funny looking," Rudy giggled as the baby dragons enthusiastically ripped into their snack, while their mother looked on, nudging them to finish.

"See? I told you we'd see dragons," Bela crowed triumphantly, retrieving the spyglass from Rudy.

"Can we get down now?" Rudy fretted. "It's scary."

Bela wasn't pleased either by the way the top of the pine tree bent farther with each gust of wind, though he wasn't going to admit that. He quashed his nervousness, trying to sound calm as he said, "I'll go down first, so I can help you, okay? I won't let you fall, don't worry."

He braced himself with his legs, anchoring his feet between the trunk and branches, while using his hands to make footholds for Rudy. As he slowly coaxed Rudy down, the dog barked impatiently.

"Almost there. Sit here and wait for me to get down," Bela ordered, indicating the lowest branch, which was about five feet about the ground. After Rudy settled there, Bela jumped to the ground.

"That was fun!" Rudy shrieked and launched himself from the branch.

Bela stretched out his arms to catch the boy, but the dog bounded into him and he tripped, losing his balance and tumbling to the ground, while Rudy crash-landed with a sharp wail, as if the breath had been knocked out of him.

Bela crawled toward the little boy, who lay curled on his side, unmoving, and shook him gently, muttering, "No, no, no."

After a few moments, which seemed like hours, Rudy opened his eyes, looking around wildly. The dog whined and nudged his chest with her nose.

"Are you hurt?" Bela asked, pushing the dog away.

"Yes. I mean, no!" Rudy sobbed, rolling to a sitting position, knees drawn into his chest. "Everything's all wrong and nothing's ever going to be right again."

"That's not true. I mean, maybe it seems like that now," Bela said, frantic to sound soothing as he inspected the little boy critically, hoping no bones were broken.

"Those people from the woods, they want to take me away, but all I want is my mom back." Rudy moaned, his face becoming red and blotchy.

"They're not going to take you," Bela promised bravely.

"How do you know? You can't stop them. It's the law," Rudy sobbed.

"Huh?" Bela was taken aback, unsure of how to respond. "Who said that? What do you mean?"

Rudy cried and cried, unable to get out meaningful words. "The p… the po-po…" He drew a deep breath, rubbing his eyes, as Bela patted his back without speaking.

"The police," Rudy managed at least. "They were here. They're going to give me to the mean lady."

"Huh?" Bela started to laugh, then checked himself. "Is that what she told you?"

Rudy nodded miserably.

"She's lying. Those agents weren't here for you. It's because of me."

Rudy looked up hopefully. "Really?"

Bela settled himself cross-legged on the ground so that Rudy could see him. "Caleb had to work hard to get me out of Romania. When I got bitten, my parents left me in the woods and Pack Six took me in. I don't know where my parents went after that, but Caleb had to prove he hadn't kidnapped me. Of course, we couldn't tell anyone we were part of a pack. The agents helped him get me out, but in exchange for something… I'm not sure what. Information about vampires, maybe, but Caleb won't talk to me about it."

The dog pushed between the two boys and licked Rudy's tear-stained face, which made the little boy smile fleetingly. "You promise you won't let them take me?"

"I won't let them. And Caleb won't let them. He's good at that. After he found me in the woods, I was his son. And you're my brother."

"I'd like to have a brother." Rudy sniffled, wiping the back of his hand under his leaking nose.

"You can't tell anyone, though," Bela cautioned. "What we are, I mean." He stopped, almost ready to blurt out *because most people are afraid of us and that makes them hate us.* Instead, he said, "Because we can do amazing stuff, and regular people would get jealous."

"Like what?"

"We're really strong and sometimes we can see smells, like another color or something. I'm not explaining that last thing well," he said as he helped Rudy to his feet and then brushed pine needles off his back. "But after a while, you'll see."

* * *

CALEB SNAPPED THE BOOK shut and tossed it onto the haphazard pile at one end of the long table. Beside him, Sophia toiled over another stack of books, while Fintonclyde made tea in the kitchen.

The central room of the cabin was large and many-sided, with floor-to-ceiling bookshelves anywhere there wasn't a door or a window. The shape of the room defied any simple geometry. Over the years, additions made to the cabin had lopped off parts of the main room and added odd-shaped alcoves as bedrooms or storerooms.

A long wooden table dominated the room's center. With the rounded Art Deco carvings on its sides and thick legs, it might have come from the boardroom of an early-century robber baron and then fallen into a Great

Depression of dents and scratches. Although the table seated twelve, it functioned as Fintonclyde's desk and horizontal filing system. Meals were usually taken on the rough wood-plank table in the kitchen.

Up among the sooty beams of the high ceiling floated blobs of light, held aloft by magic, swaying gently in a faint current. Fintonclyde only lit the kerosene lamps if visitors to the cabin might be unsettled by the untethered, glowing puffballs. The dancing lights had always soothed Caleb, while the smell of soot and kerosene from the lamps had made him nauseous.

"Nothing I don't already know," Caleb said with disgust, reluctantly reaching for another book. As he'd suspected, Fintonclyde's library contained little new vampire lore.

"I haven't found anything similar to Tom's symptoms in these books on curses and magical maladies," Sophia admitted, closing the book before her. "At least I got better after the bite. Whatever's happening to Tom, he doesn't seem to be recovering."

Caleb scowled and pushed the stack of books to the far side of the table. "It has to be related to vampires taking over the Lobster Pot. I went back to the bank to ask about Peter Brody, as Cuza calls himself. He's been hanging around the bar for a couple of months, becoming pals with the previous owner, who died mysteriously. Then Cuza showed up at the bank with a signed contract for the sale. Too much coincidence."

"Maybe Cuza has a vampire associate with abilities we don't understand," she speculated. "Perhaps one of the vampires from Lilac House."

Fintonclyde emerged from the kitchen holding a large tray with a teapot, mismatched mugs, a pitcher of milk, a sugar bowl, and a plate of brownies that smelled richly of chocolate.

"What do you know about the vampires that were at Lilac House?" Caleb snapped, frustrated by his fruitless search. "You or Alexandru must have known something about them before you attacked in 1942."

Fintonclyde abandoned the tray on the end of the table closest to the kitchen and settled into a chair. Sophia rose and began arranging the tea things on the table.

"Let me see," the old man murmured, pulling on his bristly, gray beard as if that would improve his memory. "The elders of Tribulation had known about the Undead inhabiting Lilac House for decades. During Prohibition, the vampires smuggled liquor from Canada, which attracted the living and the Undead. The mansion had become synonymous with decadence, and the parties didn't end with the repeal in 1933. By the late thirties, the number of Undead increased as vampires fled the turmoil in Europe. Sophia's great-grandfather, Old Daigle, thought something should be done to rein in the vampires, but the rest of the magical community chose to ignore them, since the Undead mostly preyed on transient partygoers and not on the residents of Tribulation. Alexandru became our ally, convinced that his brother was at Lilac House, and the three of us planned an assault.

"There were old, powerful vampires there, some of them adept at magic. Let me think… Lady Agatha Pilkington, an English vampire hundreds of years old, who had allegedly sailed on the Titanic and escaped to America when it sank by walking under the water to shore. She always surrounded herself with young men, or men who looked young. She was the *grande dame* and hostess at Lilac House, although the whiskey smuggling operation was run by a vampire from New York City. Hmm. There was a Hungarian vampire, can't recall the name, and Alexandru had some history with her, which he never made clear to me.

"When we attacked the house, they put up a fight. In the end, we destroyed many of the Undead, but never accounted for Lady Agatha or Mircea Arghezi, if he was ever there. I wanted to burn the house down, but Alexandru argued against it. Perhaps he was afraid that his brother was still inside. In the end, we created powerful wards around the house to trap any vampires that might be hiding there. We never expected boys like Toby and René to be able to break those wards decades later. I've often wondered if they had help."

"And by that you mean that Toby was working for the vampires. How can you believe that?" Caleb growled, pushing himself up from his chair and away from the table.

Sophia, trying to guide the conversation back to more neutral territory, quickly observed, "Those were all European or American vampires, then. We know what happens when they bite, but there's something different going on in Bar Harbor now."

Caleb paced the perimeter of the room, weaving around upholstered armchairs, straight-backed wooden chairs, and small tables that were tucked under windows or nestled next to bookshelves.

Sophia continued, "We were hoping for evidence of something more exotic, a vampire with unusual powers who had escaped from Lilac House when Toby and René… when the house burned down."

"Clearly a powerful vampire corrupted Toby." Fintonclyde nodded emphatically. "How else can we explain his behavior that night?"

"How dare you!" Caleb exclaimed, turning to glare at the old man. "Toby had faults, I won't deny that, but corrupted by vampires? That's not even remotely possible. He might have started the fire, though, because vampires wouldn't have done that. If they're afraid of anything other than a stake through the heart, it's fire."

"Maybe René started the fire," Sophia mused quietly, peeking inside the teapot, as if that would make the tea steep faster.

"Why would you think that?" Fintonclyde asked in a neutral tone, regarding her with his deep-set eyes beneath bushy gray eyebrows.

"René was always terrified of fire," Caleb said. "It stands to reason after what happened to him as a child."

"He was obsessed with fire, certainly," she said, drawing out the words. She gazed up at the dancing lights near the ceiling and then looked directly at Fintonclyde. "I promised him I wouldn't tell, but I guess it doesn't matter now. He tried to burn down my house once. Well, my chicken coop really."

"When was this?" Caleb asked.

"It must have been the spring of 1984. You were away at college, and I was living in Bar Harbor. René wanted to get out of Tribulation. I can't blame him for wanting to leave that backward village full of—" She shook her head to clear away memories that Caleb suspected were painful. "Anyway, he stayed with me while he looked for a job in town, but I didn't want him staying with me for the whole summer." She hesitated, chewing on her lip. "I think sometimes he used to sneak into the house, when I wasn't there. I can't prove it, but…"

"He did have a crush on you," Caleb said, smiling at the memory of René's clumsy attempts to hide his feelings for Sophia. Toby teased him about it sometimes, making René blush and stammer that, of course, they were all just good friends.

"But this was, I don't know, creepier." She tried to smile, but could only grimace. "Anyway, he ended up getting a job as a clerk at the drugstore on Main Street and found a room to rent somewhere."

Caleb remembered that old drugstore: black-and-white tiled floor; tall, crowded shelves lining one wall; and the long lunch counter opposite. The enormous mirror behind the counter had made the place seem huge in his childhood memories.

"One night when he was staying with me, the rooster woke me up long before daybreak," she continued. "That rooster, he was as regular as an alarm clock. I went outside to see what was wrong. I thought maybe a raccoon or a fox was making trouble in the yard.

"Instead of an animal, there was René, standing in front of flames that rose above his head. Maybe there was some magic involved. The fire was getting dangerously close to the chicken coop. I called out his name, but he didn't move. I ran to him and shook him. He had a glassy-eyed look, and the fire seemed to be burning in his eyes, too. I knew it was only a reflection, but it scared me.

"He finally woke up from his trance and recognized me. He confessed that he didn't know what he was doing; he'd wake up in the middle of the night and there would be a fire and he didn't know how it started. He begged me not to tell anyone, especially not Toby, and he promised to stop."

"I can't say that I am surprised," Fintonclyde ruminated. He reached across the table to pour himself tea. As he stirred milk into the mug, he said, "I have long suspected that he started the fire that burned down his family's house and gave him those scars, although his parents always denied it."

Caleb took a seat next to Sophia, absentmindedly reaching for the cup of tea she had poured him. "So, it *is* possible that René started the fire at Lilac House," he said.

"There might have been more going on at Lilac House that night," the old man conceded grudgingly. "I have something I want to show you."

Fintonclyde's chair squeaked across the floor as he pushed away from the table. He stood, surveying the room, then drifted from one bookshelf to another, mumbling to himself.

"Ah, here it is," Fintonclyde clucked, stretching his arms to retrieve an object from a high shelf. He blew a thick layer of dust from the lid of a dented cookie tin before setting it on the table.

"We found this in the ruins after the fire," Fintonclyde said as he pried off the rusty lid and reached inside. He held up a chain from which dangled a circular piece of metal blackened with soot and warped from heat.

Both Caleb's and Sophia's eyes widened in recognition.

"As you'll remember, René's parents gave him this to protect him from fire," Fintonclyde said. "But I doubt it was intended to protect him from *starting* fires. The magic is long gone, in any case."

Sophia gasped. "That's all you found of René? I never heard about this at Toby's trial."

"Of course not," Caleb said with a sneer. "The so-called Elders of Tribulation weren't interested in actual evidence, because they already *knew* Toby was guilty." He stood up with clenched fists, knuckles resting on the table, arms held taut.

"Caleb, calm yourself," Fintonclyde cautioned in the tone he'd used on Caleb as a child.

"You're not my guardian anymore," he shot back, irritated by the proprietary note in the old man's voice. "I'm twenty-five, not ten. I don't need your permission to be angry, and if I'm not civilized enough for you, that's my problem, not yours."

Silence spread through the room, like a bomb that had exploded in reverse, sucking in all sound. Caleb, to his surprise, saw the old man flinch at his words.

"Of course," Sophia murmured, lightly brushing a hand across Caleb's white-knuckled fist. "But what about the amulet?"

Caleb pulled in a lungful of air and slowly exhaled before continuing. "I've seen that amulet since René died. When I was in Romania, I got lost in a cave and met a leptothrix."

"Gadzooks!" interrupted Fintonclyde. "Did you really meet a leptothrix? I am amazed you survived."

"Wait a minute," she put in. "What are we talking about here?"

"A leptothrix is a sort of a ghost," Caleb explained. "Supposedly of someone strong who died with ambitions unfulfilled. In the Transylvanian Alps, they were probably victims of one of the many massacres of the past: Hungarians, Russians, or homegrown Communists. It's all the same up there."

"According to accounts I've read, the leptothrix feeds off the courage and ambition of its victims," said Fintonclyde. "It is usually no more than an hour before they have taken everything from a man: his memories, his strength, his hopes and dreams—

"—twisting everything he loves into something he hates," Caleb finished. "Worse, the leptothrix lures its victim by taking on weirdly warped forms of the victim's friends or family."

Caleb left the table, unable to remain still, fleeing to the dark recesses of the room and away from the lights clustered in the center. The remembered smells of that cramped, dark cave in Romania flooded his senses: mold, bat guano, faint traces of werewolves.

"The leptothrix took the form of people I knew," Caleb said. He closed his eyes and turned away from the others. The vision of Toby that he'd seen in the cave took his breath away even years later. How elated he had been until he realized that the sneering, taunting boy before him was an apparition and not his best friend.

He opened his eyes, directing his gaze upward to the lights bobbing in and out of the beams. Haltingly, he continued, "It showed me a vision of René: a burned, decaying corpse and around its neck was that amulet. I've wondered whether that vision was something pulled out of my mind by the leptothrix or something that really happened." He returned to the table and picked up the amulet, running his fingers over the warped metal.

"That, my boy, is one of the many mysteries of that terrible night," Fintonclyde said, reaching into the tin, "but there are other puzzling facts, which may be connected. We found this outside the house, far enough to be out of the fire. I am sure you recognize it."

Fintonclyde pulled out a lump of navy-blue wool with a few flecks of ash lodged in the weave. Sophia gasped as if she'd seen René's ghost instead of his old knit cap.

"Yes," the old man said, "it was René's, and it does not appear to have been touched by the fire. For a long time, I thought that perhaps René lost it before he and Toby broke into the house."

Caleb held out a hand to Fintonclyde and took the hat from him. A door slammed in the kitchen, and the sound of pounding feet heralded the boys' return.

"Brownies!" Rudy yelled as he rushed in, colliding with the table to stop himself, and then thrust a hand toward the plate.

"How did you get so dirty?" Sophia scolded. "Have you washed your hands? No, I see not."

"But brownies," Rudy whined.

"Back into the kitchen and wash those hands," Caleb said absently, looking up briefly from his study of René's old cap.

Bela, standing in the door between the kitchen and the main room, had to dodge out of the little boy's way.

Caleb held the cap up to his nose and closed his eyes for a few moments. He murmured, "This was close to the fire, probably in the burning house.

I smell mostly soot. And there is something else... faint." His eyes opened wide, and he gasped, "Cadavru!"

"*Ce pusca mea?*" Bela shot back.

"Language, Bela," Caleb cautioned.

The boy switched to English, saying, "Are you kidding me? A vampire?"

All was silent in the room, until Fintonclyde asked, "Are you sure?"

"I guess you don't know how many vampires Caleb has hunted and killed," lectured Bela as he sidled up to the table and snatched a brownie from the plate. "If he says it was a vampire, it was a vampire."

"Doesn't this confirm Toby's story about that night?" Sophia jumped up from her chair, hands on hips, and glared fiercely at Fintonclyde. "That a vampire was attacking René in the house, and Toby fought with it, accidentally starting the fire?"

"Not conclusively," the old man said cautiously. "He could have chased René away and…"

"What? Started a fire for fun?" she shot back. "How can you continue to believe something so ridiculous? For years I couldn't think about that night, because thinking about Toby was too painful, so I shut it all away, but Caleb's made me remember how brave and good Toby was, and how he'd be the last person in the world to go along with vampires. Oh, I know the Tribunal liked the fantasy well enough. Toby's absolute guilt let them believe that everything burned up and there weren't any vampires on the loose. Now we know better, don't we?"

"Let's talk about facts," Fintonclyde retorted, his gray eyes glittering and his expression stony. "Alexandru and I created the wards around Lilac House, and Toby could not have broken them without assistance. You both know that when Toby wanted something, he'd use whatever was at hand. And he did not always show the best judgement. Maybe he thought he could trick a powerful vampire into helping him break the wards, then double-cross it. You cannot think René would have been any help, can you?"

Caleb sank into a chair, turning the knit cap over and over in his hands. He imagined René tagging along with Toby on that night, pestering him with questions and taking the answers as gospel truth, as usual. "The poor kid wouldn't have stood a chance against vampires," he murmured to himself.

Silence filled the room, punctuated by Rudy's yip of satisfaction at grabbing a brownie before zipping back to the kitchen.

Finally, Sophia asked, "No trace of René other than the amulet was ever found in the ruins of the house, right? I mean, no bones or anything?"

Fintonclyde sighed, stirring his cooling tea with a spoon. "You saw what was left of the house after the fire. It's a wonder we even found the amulet."

"I guess you're right," Sophia answered, staring up into the rafters and slowly rubbing her neck.

Chapter 16: Meet Me in the Crypt

FOG PLAYED PEEKABOO GAMES with the pine trees, making them vanish and then reappear. The nearby tall, straight trunks seemed solid, but distant trees faded into the relentless gray. Fine particles of mist clung to Caleb's hair, coalescing into drops of water that ran down his neck. The fog and the thick carpet of pine needles deadened their footfalls as they picked their way through the trees.

"Are you sure you know where this house is?" Bela grumbled, breaking the silence. "Because we've been walking for a while, and all I see are trees, when I can see anything."

"The fog will burn off when the sun comes up," Caleb called over his shoulder.

"That's another thing— Ow! Stupid tree!"

He turned to see Bela right himself after stumbling over a twisted nest of knobby roots. He held out a hand, but the boy batted it away.

"Come on, then. We're not far, I think," Caleb said as he resumed walking. He had doubts about bringing Bela on this excursion, but he needed backup or, at least, someone to run for help if things didn't go well. Sophia had wanted to come, but he'd been opposed, arguing that because she'd been bitten once, it would only take another two bites to rip her away from the world of the living into that twilight place where the Undead existed. After a long discussion, which had devolved into a spiky, tense silence, he'd convinced her to stay on the island with Fintonclyde. This caused much delight for Rudy, who adored the old man's dog.

"Why couldn't we do this later, when we could actually see where we're going?" Bela asked, limping more than usual to catch up.

"I thought you wanted to learn how to hunt vampires," Caleb said. "Vampires, even the old ones that can stand sunlight, sleep during the day if they can. Old habits, maybe. So, early morning is the best time to find them."

Even in Romania, he'd never attempted anything this insane, but Sophia had insisted that he needed allies. He'd argued against her proposed mission, but she'd worn him down. Eventually, he'd admitted that allies would be useful. But he was a vampire hunter, not a vampire negotiator.

As they walked out of the shelter of the trees, the wind gusted. Beneath their feet, the carpet of pine needles gave way to tall grass, heavy with the burden of morning dew, soaking his pants from the knees down. The dark gray wall of a building suddenly materialized out of the mist.

"I thought you said everything burned down."

"Not the garage. I guess it's far enough from the main house that the fire didn't touch it," Caleb explained.

Their feet crunched on gravel as they neared the structure. Dark patches of moss splotched the wooden siding and ran up the brick chimney to their right. Caleb approached a door in the side of the building, motioning for Bela to be quiet as he carefully twisted an old doorknob and then pulled. The door opened about a hand's width with a sharp snap followed by the creaking of rusty hinges; he smelled the unpleasant tang of gasoline and, underneath, odors of dust, grease, mold, and vampire. Listening intently for a few moments, he heard nothing from inside and wrenched the groaning door open farther. Bela crowded beside him in the doorway. Caleb made out large shapes in the dim interior, which had room for at least four vehicles. Stray light from the brightening morning leaked inside the interior and glinted on the well-polished body of the closest car.

"Yesterday, when I looked the place over, I saw that" —Caleb gestured to the shiny antique before them— "pulling out. The driver got out, shut the big garage door, and then drove away. There was at least one person in the back of the car. I couldn't see clearly, because I was hiding in the trees. The car's back now, meaning that at least two vampires are around here somewhere."

"You think they're in here?" Bela asked. "Because I can smell vampire under all the other stink."

Stepping into the garage, Bela conjured a ball of light that floated above his upturned palm, throwing shadows that danced on the high ceiling overhead. Light twinkled on the polished black body of the car closest to them.

"No, they're probably somewhere in the ruins of the house," Caleb said in a low voice, "but keep quiet anyway."

"Ugh! This place is worse than Sophia's garage," Bela whispered as he moved into the depths of the interior, cursing as he stumbled over objects in his path.

Caleb stayed in the doorway, arms folded, unwilling to enter further. One end of the garage, opposite the big roll-up doors, held cluttered piles of tools and the hulking forms of machines for metal-working. Dimly, he made out a set of stairs that led to an upper story, which might have once been lodging for servants at the old mansion. The cavernous space had an unpleasant, unlived-in smell mixed with the reek of an internal combustion engine. No self-respecting vampire would consider this an acceptable place to rest his or her Undead bones.

Bela's magical light cast shadows on the far wall as he examined the carcass of an ancient pickup truck, which was missing its hood and covered in scabrous rust. Beyond that, Caleb could make out the frame of another car in worse shape than the truck. The nearby Rolls Royce, on the other hand, had been well taken care of. Somebody loved that old car.

"So, why can't we just wait for them to come out of wherever they're hiding and get into the car?" Bela asked, returning to his side.

"I'd prefer not to confront vampires like that."

"You think they'd bite first and ask questions later?"

"Biting us won't work," Caleb dismissed. "I suspect they know what happens."

"But they might attack anyway," Bela pointed out. "Try to tear off our arms or something. Remember Vlad Alpha had that scar from where one hit him with a tree limb."

Caleb pressed on, undeterred. "If they're in the ruins of the house, then they're probably, uhm, resting now. I want to get the jump on them, like Alexandru and I used to do. The Undead are slow immediately after they've been wakened."

He gave Bela a push outside, shutting the door behind him, glad to be free of the unpleasant stench.

"And why are you so sure we're going to find them in a burned-down house?" Bela asked.

"It's like this," Caleb began as if constructing a mathematical proof. "Fintonclyde and Alexandru attacked Lilac House in 1942. They killed some of the vampires, but couldn't account for all of them. They thought some might still be hiding inside, but couldn't find them, so they put wards around the whole house. Toby must have broken the wards six years ago, and then there was the fire that—" Caleb looked away from Bela and into the gray mist that surrounded them, still not able to assemble all the puzzle pieces.

"Well?" Bela asked impatiently.

Caleb cleared his throat, unsure of how long he'd been lost in the fog of the past. "Fintonclyde says that after the fire, there were hints of vampires in town. Therefore, we can assume that one or more vampires had a well-concealed hiding place here, probably underground, because vampires like dark, cool places and because there's not much left aboveground. Come on, let's check out the ruins."

Caleb turned right, cutting in front of the large wooden doors at the front of the garage and heading toward an overgrown hedge, a dark line of evergreen bushes bristling like the carcass of a huge woolly caterpillar in an advanced state of decay. Harsh winters had carved holes in the original bushes where enterprising saplings poked through. Large old maples, sooty sentinels with partially blackened trunks, leaned above the hedge.

Past the end of the hedge, a weedy meadow extended several hundred feet before dissolving into a rocky cliff to which a few gnarled pines clung. The mist had thinned, although the sun remained largely hidden by a fog bank out at sea. Occasional glimmers of the red disk shone through shifting clouds. Unseen waves crashed in the cove below where, according to Sophia, lay the entrance to an old smugglers' tunnel that ran through the cliff and terminated in the garage. Turning their backs to the ocean, they passed a large gazebo with a roof that had collapsed and fallen into the interior, not from fire, as far as Caleb could see, but from decades of decay.

"That doesn't look so big," Bela said as the ruined house came into view.

One corner of the house had been almost completely gutted by fire, with little left but fallen, charred beams and a tall brick chimney. The other corner must have held a conservatory, but now all that remained was the twisted metal that had anchored the glass, reminding Caleb of the greenhouse at Castle Arghezi, which had come to a similar end. Remnants of a granite façade in the middle of the building had resisted the fire better.

From the base of the remaining wall, a broad stone terrace met the grass and weeds in a series of steps. A dry fountain filled with oak leaves sat in the meadow that had once been a lawn. Stone benches crouched amid the long grass and summer wildflowers.

"This is the back of the house. The fire seems to have been more intense here, because the ground floor is all that's left." Caleb gestured to taller walls on the far side of the ruin. "It looks bigger from the front, where some of the second story survived."

French doors had once been set in the outer walls, but now the wide, empty doorways gaped at them like mouths frozen in mid-scream, the frames showing blistered paint and rotten wood underneath. Hinges hung forlornly, separated from doors that must lie somewhere beyond in the lumpy, charred wreckage. The jumbled interior, smelling of damp, moldering leaves and a hint of charcoal, was bounded by the remains of the exterior stone walls. Tall brick chimneys pointed skyward. Autumns past had blown oak and maple leaves inside, lapping up to blackened, fallen beams, chunks of the stone façade, and the wreckage of furniture like waves on a beach. Few traces of interior walls were visible, while in some places saplings and wildflowers poked up through the rot amid twisted metal objects: the arms of an old-fashioned chandelier, the base of a lamp, and other unrecognizable shapes.

"What a mess! How do you expect to find anything in here?" Bela shook his head as they stepped inside.

"Sophia said there was a basement under the kitchen." Caleb pointed to his left, dismayed by the amount of decay and disorder. "Of course, she was here six years ago, right after the fire."

"Things have gone downhill since then," Bela observed.

Caleb picked his way carefully in the direction of a large, iron stove tilted to one side, suggesting that the underlying floor was no longer solid. His boots squelched as he prodded the floor ahead of him with a long, brass rod he'd found jutting out of a burned and decaying pile of curtains covered in wet leaves.

"Whoa!" Bela exclaimed as a hole appeared, and the muck dislodged by Caleb's probe slid into darkness with a squishy sound.

"This might be what Sophia was talking about," Caleb speculated, peering into the murky opening. He conjured balls of light, sending them down into the darkness. The flickering light illuminated stairs, a descending series of simple wood planks.

"I'm not going down there!" Bela protested, slowly squelching through the muck until he stood next to Caleb.

"Where's your sense of adventure?" Caleb asked as he used the brass rod to clear away debris. "Okay, fine, stay up here and keep an eye out for vampires."

Caleb cautiously put one foot on the top step, testing to see if it would hold his weight. He advanced down slowly: one step after another. When the fifth step split under his foot, he steadied himself by flinging out an arm to grasp the step above. Pulling himself to a sitting position, he felt slick ooze from the stairs soaking through his jeans.

"Caleb? Caleb!" Bela's panicked voice burst from above.

"Nothing's broken," he called, "except the stairs."

From where he sat, he could see the outlines of shelves containing glass jars and wooden barrels, some still upright, while other shelves were broken and slanted further down into darkness. Millipedes scurried away, burrowing into damp piles of ooze as he illuminated more of the cellar by sending light into dark corners. The still air below had the faintly sulfurous odor of rotting vegetation. Judging from the smell and the condition of the stairs, no one had been down in this cellar for many years. Grunting in frustration, he pushed himself up the stairs backward, one step at a time, until he could get on his feet.

"That was a bust," he said, wiping his hands on his jeans. "But the vampires must be here somewhere."

"A secret passage?" Bela mused. "That would be cool, but there's not much left standing, except the chimneys."

Caleb turned, slowly surveying the ruined house around them. The sun had finally pierced the fog, throwing reddish light onto the blackened front wall. He circled the ruins of what had once been a grand staircase, now an island of detritus in a sea of muck, looking for a door or opening that might lead under the house, but the furniture skeletons, charred floorboards, and slate roof tiles heaped on top of the staircase hadn't been disturbed in years.

"Hey! It's a tower, like the one in the castle!" Bela's voice echoed on the surviving walls. He pointed to the northwest corner of the ruin, where the outer stone wall bowed out, curving to form a two-story tower that had once anchored that corner of the house.

The tower's upper story was only partially destroyed. What remained of the second story looked like a mangled dollhouse: a jumble of furniture and roof beams rested on what remained of the upper floor. A few shards of glass still glimmered in the window casements.

Bela's feet thudded on stone as the boy approached a blackened grand piano that squatted near a wide stone fireplace set into the tower's outer wall. The piano's once-polished exterior had bubbled and warped, while the ivory keys had been consumed, making the front of the piano look like the toothless maw of a beggar.

Caleb carefully followed, noting that the floor beneath his feet felt more solid than the peaty layers of composting leaves in other parts of the ruin. As Bela peered into the interior of the piano, Caleb squatted down, brushing away a thin layer of muddy leaves, revealing slabs of gray slate that had been cut into closely fitting squares. He rapped on the stone with his knuckles thoughtfully.

"There might be something under here," Caleb commented as he stood up.

Bela turned toward him, sniffing the air. "Do you smell that? It's like flowers, maybe roses."

"Someone's been here," Caleb concluded. "I don't see footprints, but with all the old leaves, it would be hard to see tracks." He also caught the faint scent of roses mingled with the smell of rotting leaves. *More complex than roses*, he thought, *more like perfume*. And twined around those smells: *vampire*.

"Maybe there's a secret passage in there," Bela proposed, stepping in front of the fireplace. The boy knelt before the hearth, peering up into the chimney. "Aha! What about this?"

Caleb stood next to Bela as the boy thrust a hand up into the area above the hearth and yanked at something that made a rusty creaking noise. Then, with a soft thud, a wet lump dropped from above.

"That's the lever for the flue damper."

"Yeah, I can see that," Bela grumbled as he sat back on his heels, brushing soggy leaves out of his hair. A dead swallow had dropped out of the flue and rested in a nest of old leaves on the hearth. "But what's this other lever for?"

Caleb knelt beside Bela. "Is there a second flue?"

"Nope," Bela countered as he peered up into chimney. "So maybe there *is* a secret passage behind the fireplace."

"This doesn't look like it's been disturbed in years, except for that mess you dislodged from the chimney," Caleb murmured, inspecting the interior. "But let's see what this does. Move over."

He nudged Bela aside and craned his neck to get a good look at the second metal rod, which wasn't as rusty as the other one. Bela scrambled to his feet, standing to one side as Caleb raised his arms and wrapped both hands around the lever.

"This is tough to move, whatever it does," Caleb observed. With effort, he forced the metal rod to one side. Rotating his head to peer into the dark corners, he said, "That didn't do a thing. No secret passage here."

"Uhm, there's something you should see," Bela said from behind him. "Turn around, but don't step back too far."

The stone slab on the floor directly behind him had tilted up slightly at one end, revealing a two-inch gap. As they knelt next to the opening, Caleb whispered, "You were right about a secret passage."

He stared at the thin line of darkness that almost certainly led to the vampires' lair, wondering again if this was going to work. Vampires had no reason to trust werewolves, or vice versa. Once he'd trusted a vampire and believed her when she'd said she could change. *Had he been a fool to trust her? Had he learned nothing?*

"So, are we doing this?" Bela called, his tone suggesting that he'd been trying to get Caleb's attention for some time.

"Right," Caleb muttered through gritted teeth, chasing away unpleasant memories. "We don't know if this is the only entrance, so be ready to get out fast if there's trouble."

"But I want to help. How do you expect me to learn if I run away?" Bela complained.

Caleb held up a hand. "We don't know how many vampires are down there or how they'll react. If things go wrong, I need you to send the signal to Fintonclyde and Sophia. Do you remember how to do that?"

With a frown, the boy reached for a small leather bag, the strap slung across his chest. He pulled out a brass cylinder, four inches long and two inches in diameter, examining the cap at one end quizzically. "I pull this off and that sends a message?"

"Don't hold it too close to your face and remember to be clear of the building, under the sky, otherwise the energy will be attenuated too much." Seeing Bela's expression, Caleb tried again, this time in the most basic terms. "The magic gets scattered."

"Right, the magic gets scattered," Bela echoed unenthusiastically, tucking the cylinder back into the bag.

"Here goes," Caleb said, blowing out a long breath as he stuck his fingers into the opening and grabbed the edge of the slab.

They were both surprised when the slate square swung upward easily, as if on a well-balanced hinge, to reveal the metal steps of a spiral staircase disappearing into darkness.

"Wait until I get to the bottom. I'll give a signal if it's okay to come down," he said softly to Bela.

Caleb rose and put a boot on the top step, feeling patterned wrought iron through his sole. With one hand on the central metal pole of the staircase, he carefully tested each step before descending slowly to let his eyes adjust to the darkness below.

As he went lower, the stink of rotting vegetation faded, replaced by a musty smell. The air was still and stuffy, making him think there wasn't another opening. Vampires wouldn't miss the lack of fresh air. He didn't detect the ammonia odor of nesting bats, another indication that there wasn't a second opening in the chamber through which the creatures could come and go.

The smell of a vampire was something he could not mistake even in his nasally dulled human form. He'd walked or crawled into many dark caves in the mountains of Romania, had felt the thrill of anticipation as the smell of vampire grew stronger. The cloying, rose-scented perfume they'd encountered aboveground also grew stronger, which brought him back to memories of another vampire, of *her*. They'd been lovers in Romania, as impossible as it now seemed for a werewolf and a vampire to find common ground, much less love.

Caleb stumbled as his foot encountered a solid floor instead of the next step. The scuff of his boot on smooth stone seemed extraordinarily loud. He stiffened, straining to catch any sound, knowing that above him Bela would be getting anxious. As he stood listening, his eyes adjusted to the room around him in which the only illumination fell from above. He was in a stone-lined chamber with a vaulted ceiling about twenty feet above him. On his left side was a wall about a foot from the staircase. To his right, a wide, curved arch led into darkness, a gaping maw like the mouth of a ravenous giant in an old fairy tale. Fifteen feet directly in front of him was another arch of the same shape and size, though better illuminated.

Through the opening, he saw the faint outline of a pale oblong shape, like a table or a box or a coffin.

After several minutes, he'd detected no sounds; the cool air of the chamber felt surprisingly dry and completely still. He tapped his palm softly on the metal pole at the center of the staircase—*one, two, three*—signaling to Bela. The boy's descending footfalls rang like a bell, making Caleb wonder how much noise he'd made on the stairs.

He placed a hand on the wall to his left. The stones were well shaped and fitted together tightly, tokens of good workmanship, and were cool to his touch, slightly damp, but not wet. The chamber must be well sealed from the rotting ruin above. He moved aside as Bela came down the final step, laying a hand heavily on the boy's shoulder.

Cupping a hand around Bela's ear, he whispered, "See that arch to the right? Your job is to watch it. Make sure nothing comes through, but don't go in there. Got that?"

Bela nodded. Caleb reached into the leather bag the boy carried, closing his hand around a fist-shaped lump of rock, the sunstone that he and Alexandru had used to incapacitate vampires during their hunts.

Caleb extracted the stone, patting Bela on the back. Fingers trailing along the near wall, he trod softly until he stood in the archway. A pale stone box, about three feet high and eight feet long, rested on the floor. A second object of the same size and shape could be seen on its far side. Beyond that, the light was too dim to make out details.

This second coffin—he couldn't think of these as anything else—had a smooth stone top, but the nearest one was open, and inside the outline of a body dressed in dark clothing was visible. *This is old-school vampire*, he marveled, remembering the caves, attics, and barns where he'd uncovered the Undead during his years of vampire hunting in Romania.

He halted a few feet from the prone figure. *Now or never*, he thought, holding out his arm.

"*Helios!*" he commanded sharply, focusing his mind on the magical stone resting in his outstretched hand, seeing the light in his mind first before it burst from his palm.

A dazzling radiance, bright as noon on a cloudless day, emanated from the lump of stone. The rays fell on a dark-haired boy dressed in black, who appeared to be not much older than Bela, and who stirred fitfully as if in the throes of a bad dream. When the boy opened his eyes, the sunstone's merciless glare laid bare the pale face and glinted off curly dark hair, but the black eyes drank in light like holes in the fabric of the universe.

"Mircea Arghezi?" Caleb recognized the face he'd seen almost every day for over seventy months, the face that had looked out at him from a frame in the portrait gallery of Castle Arghezi, the face unchanged by the decades.

The vampire sat up, running a hand through his black curls, then snarled, "Mircea Arghezi is gone!"

"You look just like his portrait," Caleb said.

"Name's Mickey," he replied sullenly, shielding his eyes with a hand. "And I know who you are: Caleb O'Connor, the one who's got Cuza so hot and bothered."

"So, you're working for Cuza," Caleb said.

Mickey gripped the sides of the coffin and pushed himself up, then swung his legs over one side. He stood, the stone coffin between them.

"With him, not *for* him!" The vampire's face contorted as he squinted in the blazing light. "D'you need so much light? I mean, are you looking for some kind of confession here? Jeez, it's like being hauled in by the cops."

"I'm here to talk. That's all," Caleb said. Softening slightly, he pointed to an iron lamp mounted on the wall at the head of the coffin. "Can you light that?"

Wordlessly, Mickey shuffled to the lamp. He extracted a box of wooden matches from a pocket, struck a light, and snaked a shaking hand into the interior of the lamp. A candle flame sputtered to life, barely visible in the harsh light of the sunstone.

Caleb closed his fingers around the stone, concentrating on its invisible heart until the bright light ebbed and winked out. Suddenly the chamber seemed impossibly dark. As his eyes adjusted, Caleb heard a strangled cry. He pivoted to see Bela twitching, half in shadow, with something like a collar around his neck. No, not a collar, but pale fingers ending in long, pink lacquered nails wrapped tightly around the boy's windpipe. Bela stumbled forward into the archway, being choked by a blonde woman wearing a pink, floral dressing gown and bulky carpet slippers.

"What have we here?" she said in a crisp British accent, shaking the boy. "Someone needs to learn manners. A bite might settle you down, or perhaps I could break your neck?"

"Yeah, go ahead and bite me," Bela rasped, his hands pawing at the chokehold. "If you like the taste of werewolf."

"By the Darkness!" the woman exclaimed, yanking her hands away in disgust.

Caleb put an arm around Bela, who had doubled over coughing. "You all right?" he murmured.

"Fine," Bela replied weakly. "I guess we found them, huh?"

"This is an outrage!" the woman cried, sweeping into the candlelit chamber and focusing her ire on Mickey. "How did you let this happen? Are you not meant to be guarding me from ruffians, thieves, and...werewolves?"

"Lady Agatha Pilkington?" Caleb asked, turning to face her.

The woman ignored him, not meeting his eye as she adjusted her dressing gown. She could have been a Hollywood starlet from the 1940s—blonde, shoulder-length ringlets framing a pale, heart-shaped face--except for eyes darker than night.

Mickey cleared his throat, staring down at his feet, then looked up with a smile as insincere as someone trying to sell shoes to snakes. "Lady Agatha, may I present Caleb O'Connor and his, er, companion."

"Bela," the boy coughed, leaning against the side of the arch and massaging his neck.

"I apologize for the sudden entrance," Caleb said, "but I need to talk to you, just talk."

"A letter of introduction and a calling card would have been more appropriate," she retorted while picking imaginary lint from the sleeve of her robe.

"Cuza's told us all about you," Mickey said, eyeing him venomously, "how you offed a lot of us in Romania, including Ana Maria! Don't try to deny it, you bastard!"

"A sweetheart back in the old country?" Lady Agatha tutted. "Old history, really. Aren't you overreacting?"

"She was—" Mickey spluttered, hot anger tempered by Agatha's sharp reminder of the icy coldness of the Undead. "She was my *naşă*."

"Godmother?" Caleb translated doubtfully.

"In English, we would say my *angel*," Lady Agatha murmured.

Mickey sat heavily on the stone coffin lid behind him. "When your *naşă* is gone, it hits you hard. Maybe it's like that for you dogs with the one that bit you."

"We don't remember such things when we're changed. Often, we never know the one who bit us," Caleb said.

"Sometimes you do," Bela put in. "Sometimes you're bitten by a vicious moron like I was. But it's cool. My mom ripped his throat out last year."

Lady Agatha made a sour face, but Mickey didn't appear to notice Bela's reminder of the savagery of werewolves.

"I wanted to take care of her, but what did I know at sixteen?" Mickey mused, then silently stared into his lap for several moments. "I was only a boy, and I'd never been farther from home than the village, but when my brother brought her home… I hated my brother for the way he treated her. And then *he* came to the castle, and everything went wrong."

Caleb tried to imagine Ana Maria alive as a young bride. When he'd met her, she'd called herself Lamia and had been a vampire for more than sixty years. She'd traveled the world and had tried to make a different life for herself.

"She talked about you, when…" Caleb halted, not finding the words for their bitter parting. "One of her biggest regrets was what she did to you. If she could change one thing in her past, she said she'd have told you to run away, to take your mother and get out of the castle before it was too late."

"You destroyed her." Mickey jerked his head up and fixed his dark, soulless eyes on Caleb.

"I ended things for her," Caleb quietly admitted. "I begged her, told her there had to be another way. She tried hard, so very hard, to become something different, to free herself from—" His throat constricted, the words strangled by the memory of staring into Lamia's bottomless black eyes while she wordlessly pushed the piece of wood toward him that would pierce her heart, ending her pain forever. "Lamia—that's who I knew her as—wanted to, tried to become a different person, to manage her need for human blood, but she failed too many times to want to go on."

"What rot!" snapped Lady Agatha. "We are who we are. We cannot give it up any more than you can stop rampaging under the full moon!"

"Right!" Bela chimed in. "Maybe you can talk some sense into him. He thinks he can change the world by being some kind of superhero."

"Thanks for that vote of confidence," Caleb said to Bela. "As I said, Lady Agatha, I wanted to talk with you. My methods were unconventional—"

"Uncouth!" Lady Agatha interrupted.

"But I wanted to avoid running into Cuza," Caleb finished.

"That worm! I shall never allow him to set foot here." She dismissed the idea with a toss of her blonde curls.

"Oh, that's good. I mean, good to know. I didn't know if you were working for him on whatever's he's doing at the Lobster Pot," Caleb said hesitantly, teetering like a tightrope walker in a high wind trying to keep from tumbling down.

"Work for him? Hah!" She laughed harshly. "He should be working for me, since I am the legal owner of that building. His little scheme has some merits, I'll admit, but it's a bit too modern for me. The old ways are so much more refined and civilized."

"Killing humans, you mean," Caleb prompted.

"It's not as if werewolves never kill," she said haughtily. "The bodies keep piling up, don't they?"

"Werewolves have been killed, too!" Bela interrupted, his hands twitching for a fight. "Just last week you killed one!"

"Don't pin that on us, junior," Mickey snapped. "That was our dear pal Guy. A terrific shot, but it didn't save him."

"Yeah, his head was ripped right off," Bela said with satisfaction.

Lady Agatha cried out, "Savage curs! Invading my—"

Mickey cut her off, jabbing a finger at Bela and shouting, "Oh, you like tearing us apart, do you? And you wonder why we tried to kill your doggie pals?"

"'Cause you're disgusting dead things—"

"Enough!" Caleb yelled, clamping a hand around Bela's arm to keep the boy from springing across the stone coffin at the vampires. "I said I came to talk, just talk. Can we all take a deep breath—okay, not you two since you don't actually breathe—and talk?"

Bela's breathing slowed. The two vampires glared at Caleb with hard, stony expressions. He released his grip on the boy's arm. *Some progress*, he thought.

Taking advantage of the momentary lapse in hostilities, Caleb guessed, "Hunting werewolves with silver bullets was all Cuza's idea, right? He's the one who put your friend in harm's way."

"And let's face it, werewolves are going to go after vampires. It's like putting dry tinder and a lit match together," Bela said with a wicked grin.

"And here you are." Mickey sneered, coming around the sarcophagus to stand menacingly in front of Caleb.

"When the moon is full, he means," Caleb added hastily, putting a hand up placatingly. "Cuza is a menace to humans, to werewolves, and to you."

Lady Agatha pursed her lips and patted her curls. "Things were better before he arrived, that is true. If one is careful, one can avoid undue attention and unnecessary casualties. A little seduction goes a long way."

"What about that guy at the big party who actually *wanted* to be bitten?" Mickey laughed. "He even said he'd pay for the experience. Crazy New Yorker."

"That was rather singular," Lady Agatha replied thoughtfully. "I might have taken him up on the offer, if those dogs hadn't burst in."

Bela nodded his head approvingly. Mickey tensed at the mention of werewolves shredding vampires.

"What about this scheme of Cuza's you mentioned?" Caleb asked quickly. He wondered how long he could he could keep the lid on the simmering feud between Mickey and Bela.

Casually examining her long, painted nails, Lady Agatha scoffed, "For months he talked about his grand plan to free us, he said, from the need to hunt, but it turned out to be…oh, I don't know… boring, really. No sport, no challenge."

"How does it work, this grand plan?" Caleb asked, cautiously perching on the edge of a sarcophagus.

"There's this scientist Cuza recruited, *Doctor Patel*," Mickey began, relaxing slightly.

"Recruited?" Caleb asked. "You mean, the way vampires recruit?"

"Yeah. The Doc loves the immortality thing, always talking about how she can work all night and write more papers than anyone else." Mickey laughed, revealing a decided distaste for this Dr. Patel. "She works at that Jackson Lab where she does experiments with mice or something like that. Dunno much about it except she makes this stuff that's gotta be kept in a special icebox. We inject it into the drunks so they don't mind being drained."

Caleb's mouth hung open as he tried to wrap his mind around this weird tale. "And after three bites…?"

"That's the point, I guess," Mickey said. "They come back week after week, a little jab and that's it. We bite 'em and send 'em on their way."

"People in town are starting to notice that something funny's going on, and it won't be long before they connect it to the Lobster Pot," Caleb said.

Mickey shot a glance at Lady Agatha, who nodded thoughtfully.

"What do you expect me to do about it?" she asked icily.

"He's got to be stopped, before—"

"Stopped? Like stake-through-the-heart stopped?" Mickey interrupted. "Maybe we think he's crazy and a jerk besides, but that don't mean we want to see him offed. Too many of us have gone down already."

"Fifty years ago," Caleb said through gritted teeth, "you attracted too much attention. Certain people noticed and" —he waved an arm at the crypt around him— "this is all that's left of Lilac House."

"Are you threatening me, Mr. O'Connor?" Lady Agatha asked tartly as she crossed the chamber to stand next to Mickey.

"I'm asking for your *help*," Caleb said slowly, the words tasting bitter in his mouth. Could vampires be trusted? "You don't seem to want Cuza around any more than I do. If we teamed up..."

"Trust a werewolf? I believe I have heard enough. Go!"

Caleb stood up, hesitating as if the still, heavy air of the chamber had trapped him like a bug in amber. Both vampires gave him flinty-eyed stares. He took a step backward, then another. He heard Bela's boots scraping the floor behind him, then the ringing of the boy's feet on the metal staircase.

Walking slowly without turning away from the two grim faces, Caleb crossed the chamber to the stairs. Gripping the metal railing, he swung himself onto the first step. Only when he'd taken several steps up did he turn his back on the vampires.

"Mickey," called Lady Agatha behind Caleb's retreating back, "I do think you should secure a supply of silver bullets... for the next time we have unannounced guests."

Chapter 17: Breaking and Entering

ALEB AND HIS FRIENDS had practiced magic during those long-ago summers on Fintonclyde's island, when the old man had taught them to make wards and to call forth the Elementals: Fire, Earth, Wind, and Water. Toby had excelled at summoning Wind, gliding like a surfer above the choppy Atlantic waters as he whooped with joy or, when he'd been able to cobble together a sailboat, zipping across the bay, even when the ocean was becalmed. Caleb had watched more than he'd tried, and when he had attempted to summon Wind, he'd often ended up falling into the water or crashing painfully to the ground.

The morning after Caleb's first full moon in the Transylvanian Alps, he'd met a local werewolf, both of them shivering in the cold, thin mountain air. Trying out his new Romanian vocabulary, he'd learned that he was miles away from Castle Arghezi, where he'd left his clothing and shoes before moonrise. Caleb hadn't wanted to walk back to the castle naked and barefoot. More than that, he knew now, he'd wanted to impress the local werewolf with his magical skills. Maybe because the bone-tired weariness had prevented his addled brain from telling him he couldn't, or because the Wolf within him knew that he had to succeed, he'd summoned Wind and floated away in a semi-dignified way. Once he was out of sight of the other werewolf, the spell had failed and Caleb had tumbled to the ground, but he'd known that he could do it. Over the next six years, harnessing the Elements had become second-nature as a way to navigate the wild, trackless mountains.

Using those skills in the pre-dawn morning, Caleb silently floated above the Jackson Laboratory. He saw only a few cars in the parking lots below. He hoped that any sleep-deprived scientists who'd been working all night were too tired to look out the windows.

The previous day, Caleb had done "research," which meant lurking in coffee shops with ears pricked for mentions of genetics and DNA sequencing. Posing as a postdoc interviewing for a position at the lab, he'd asked about the best researchers to work for and the ones to avoid. That last line of questioning often led to a certain Dr. Patel, the one mentioned by Mickey. By repeating this process over several hours in the spots frequented by scientists (drinking a frightening amount of coffee in the process), Caleb had narrowed down the location of Dr. Patel's building.

From above, the building was a long, narrow rectangle with a flat roof in two levels; the higher level was like a separate building that ran the length of the roof, housing all the equipment needed to move air through the ductwork. Parallel pipes stuck up from the highest part of the roof like a giant comb, though he knew them to be the exhausts for the many fume hoods of the laboratories inside. He gently landed on the lower level of the roof near a door in the side of the equipment enclosure.

Caleb smiled to himself when he found the door locked. Had he expected breaking in to be easy? A little light shone red on the numeric keypad affixed to the wall next to the door. During his brief time in graduate school, he had, on certain occasions, wanted to get into a locked lab. Old-fashioned mechanical locks usually yielded to a handy set of master keys, but electronic locks could be coaxed to open with a bit of magic.

In the dim pre-dawn light the numbers on the keys were indistinct, but that wouldn't matter. He touched the keypad lightly, focusing his mind on summoning Fire, but on a very, very small scale, more like summoning Electrons. Although it wouldn't do to take the analogy too far. In the past, when he'd tried to reconcile magic and physics, it had made his head ache. After several attempts to call up the correct spell, the light on the keypad blinked from red to green, and the lock gave a satisfying click.

Once inside, Caleb threaded his way around noisy fans and the network of insulated ducts that snaked through the enclosed space until he found a stairway down to the floors that held the laboratories. He had no idea which of the myriad of labs belonged to the Undead scientist, but he could walk the halls impersonating a clueless post-doc until he found someone to ask.

On the other side of the window, a woman mechanically pipetted dose after dose of liquid into tiny tubes arrayed in a rack before her. Fascinated, Caleb timed her, marveling at how each operation took precisely six seconds as if controlled by an unseen overseer. Her blonde hair had been pulled back, wild tendrils escaping to frame a thin, pale face. The bone-white skin and dark circles under her eyes made him wonder if he'd found the mysterious Undead scientist on the first try. Or maybe there was more than one vampire in the Jackson Lab.

He rapped on the window, making her jump and squirt an aliquot of the mysterious liquid on the counter. She was clearly irritated when he stuck his head in the door of the laboratory and hesitantly said, "Sorry to disturb you. Do you know where I can find Dr. Patel's lab?"

The pale blonde researcher frowned at his question, remaining silent for long enough that he worried she didn't speak English.

"Dr. Nina Patel?" he asked again, channeling the emotional state of a newbie post-doc, adrift in the sea of labs.

"Her? Her lab's in the basement," said the researcher, speaking English with an upper Midwestern twang and showing as little affection for the vampire scientist as the other Jax denizens he'd questioned over coffee.

"Oh, great. Thanks. Sorry to have bothered you," he said. "Uhm, can I help with anything?"

She shook her head from side to side, giving him a withering look that suggested the most helpful thing would be a time machine erasing his existence.

Once safely inside the lab's basement corridor, he'd expected to succumb to comfortable flashbacks of grad school, but the basement of the world's biggest mouse genetics lab contained nothing like the Van de Graaf generators and the smell of pump oil that he remembered from MIT's Infinite Corridor. The overpowering odor of scared, sick, and crowded mice made his skin prickle with goosebumps, and there was another smell, too, one that made him instinctively want to run, something that yelled DANGER. It was all he could do not to howl, and only by talking quietly to himself was he able to work through the anxiety and keep walking.

The corridor was flanked on either side by glass-windowed laboratories, where tubes and bottles rocked, shook, and spun in a variety of machines. Here and there was a mouse cage or a dead mouse on a benchtop, waiting to be dissected.

He suddenly remembered the source of the scary smell and had to fight to keep from laughing out loud. He'd overheard some of the mouse researchers talking about studying the fear response… using coyote urine. If he recalled correctly, they were arguing about whether or not it had to be reagent-grade coyote urine.

Reagent-grade coyote smelled a lot like any other coyote, but reassured, he pressed onward until the corridor made a left turn and stopped at a solid metal door. A plaque next to the door identified it as Dr. Patel's laboratory. He couldn't see in, but he could hear someone in there puttering around.

After a few moments spent wondering if using magic would give him away, he tried the knob and found the door unlocked. Caleb entered, and immediately had to fight the urge to sneeze. The assault on his nose reminded him of college chemistry lab. Benches topped with shiny black counters formed a U-shaped area in the center of the room. The counters held clusters of bottles, some with printed labels and some hand-labeled. More bottles crowded the shelves above the counters. Caleb recognized a scale and a centrifuge, but other pieces of equipment baffled him. The room's only occupant was a dark-skinned woman with black hair drawn back in a ponytail, wearing a bleached white lab coat and lavender rubber gloves. She stared intently at a row of tiny tubes in a metal rack on the counter as she injected clear liquid, faintly pink in color, into one after the other with a micropipette. She didn't notice him for a long moment.

"Don't interrupt me," she muttered, continuing to count, "…ninety-three, ninety-four, ninety-five, ninety-six." She expelled the plastic pipette tip into the garbage can and turned to face him. "Who are you?" she wondered idly, making some notations in the notebook under her elbow.

"Well," he said, hoping to be sufficiently vague, "I'm new."

Snapping shut all the lids on what seemed to be ninety-six little plastic tubes, she retorted, "Oh, right. A post-doc?"

Now Caleb's old memories came crowding in, as he shifted mental gears to retrieve a lexicon that he thought he'd never need again. "Right, the behaviorist. I'm studying fear—got a truckload of coyote urine waiting out there."

"Great," she responded sarcastically. "Look, I'm not a behaviorist, so I can't really help you much. Have you been to HR to get your badge?"

"Well, I tried, but… uhm… the person was out with the flu. They said to come back later." He rolled a lab stool over to her bench and sat down.

"Hmm. Seems to be going around," she commented unsympathetically, continuing to write in the notebook.

"Is it?" He tried to give her a knowing look, but she wasn't paying attention. "Say… what do you work on?"

She wrapped the rack of tubes slowly and carefully in aluminum foil, not meeting his eye or acknowledging his presence until she had taken the rack to a large upright freezer and placed it inside. Then she came back to the bench, pulled up her own stool, and faced him.

"I work on longevity. Or, if you prefer, immortality," she said with casual haughtiness.

"I hate that term," he scoffed. "No one truly lives forever."

She raised an eyebrow. "Oh really? What if I told you we could stop the processes of cell death?"

"Being a re-animated corpse is not the same thing as being alive," he shot back before he could help himself.

"So…" She chuckled slightly as she stripped off the purple gloves and tossed them into the garbage can. She got up from her seat and began unbuttoning her lab coat, which she then hung on a peg alongside a row of others. "I gather you believe in—what do you call it—the `Undead'?"

Caleb recognized the scientist's arrogant need to impress a lowly postdoc. Wondering how far he could push her, he flashed a knowing smile and said, "I grew up around here. I know what goes on."

"Oh, you do, do you?" She spun around, taking a few steps toward to him. "Hmm. What if I told you that the director of this institute was interested in those questions and that certain government agencies are willing to provide funding?"

"And you're going to figure this out by using mice?"

"There are mouse models for everything," she explained, stepping over to the wall, which was plastered with a floor-to-ceiling poster called JAX MICE. Hundreds of tiny rodents bared their teeth or contorted in seizures or reared on their hind legs in hundreds of brightly colored squares labeled with vivid names: Shaker, Waddler, Pirouette, Twitcher, and even Annoying. "Some of these mutant mice occur spontaneously. Others are carefully constructed by knocking out or inserting a specific gene."

"I see: Chompy, the vampire mouse?"

The hand pointing to the mouse poster dropped to her side as she slapped her thigh in exasperation. "That's not how it works. You know nothing about how a vampire's bite works."

Maybe not, he thought, *but I know exactly how a scientist's mind works.* "No one can know," he replied with the frostiest scorn he could muster. "It's impossible to define. It's the realm of magic, not science."

"That's wrong," she interrupted, before he had even stopped talking.

He had her exactly where he wanted her. "Is it?" he murmured in a tone of naïve curiosity.

"The mouse model for a bite has been around for decades. What you call the 'Undead' are not dead at all. They are alive."

"I don't believe that," he challenged.

"Why not? It moves, it thinks, it eats, why isn't it alive?"

Because it smells like death to a wolf's nose was not a good answer, he knew. *Because I'd feel bad if, after all these years, I'd been killing people* was even worse.

"Because… because something that cannot die is not alive," he tried lamely. "Death is a part of life, as much so as breathing… and the Undead don't have to do either."

"Ah, so you've heard the cave story," she purred in condescending amusement. "I suppose you've heard that it takes three bites to make someone a vampire because the entire blood volume has to be drained and the victim killed."

"Yes, of course."

"Well, that's wrong. *Totally* wrong. Think about it just a little," she said to the wall, then turned back to face him. "You don't need to be bitten three times in quick succession. It could be months apart, plenty of time for blood to regenerate. You also don't need to be completely drained. I called that the '30% drain' theory, and it's just incorrect. Even with three tiny sips the victim will still convert."

"So, you made a mouse that turns into a vampire after you bite it three times? That's almost as ridiculous as the mice doing the biting. Who's draining the mice? You?"

She tilted her head at him with exaggerated patience, returning to her bench and reaching for the box of purple gloves from which she slowly and deliberately extracted a pair, pulling them tightly over her fingers. Caleb thought she might go back to her pipetting and ignore him, but instead she reached down into a cabinet and brought out a device.

It was mounted on a breadboard, that much was familiar to him. But instead of lenses and beam-splitters, it had some kind of little mouse-sized cradle. A couple of syringes with needles and a tiny IV dripper were set up on each side of the cradle.

And at the rear of the cradle, mounted to a manual translation stage, was a pair of fangs.

Not cleaned up, reagent-grade fangs, either. These were stained, slightly cracked, well-used teeth pulled out of some hapless vampire's head. He wondered how she'd acquired those. Not from a lab supply catalog.

"I have been scientifically studying the precise number of bites that it takes to turn someone," she began in a pedantic tone with an underlay of sarcasm. "You might be surprised at this. The three-bite rule is just a general rule. But we don't often pay attention to the ones who don't convert after three bites, because they just die. The question is: is it possible to get bitten three or four or more times without converting or dying?"

"I haven't heard of it," he said with scorn.

"Well," she declared smugly, "it happens. There are a few people who are outliers. They can be bitten and bitten and they never turn. Oddly enough" —she flashed him a scary smile— "one of these happens to be the Research Director of this institute."

He didn't want to interrupt her, but couldn't help the exclamation of surprise that escaped from his lips. This story was getting weirder by the minute.

"Uh-huh, that's right. Maybe that's why he has managed to live here safely for so long? Though the local vampires have made a point of not biting the scientists. Mostly they hibernate through the winter, when there would be nothing to feed on except the researchers." She fiddled with the setscrews on her fanged apparatus, smiling faintly. "Anyway, getting the director's blood was fairly easy in my position, in the guise of a 'negative control.' And it turns out that his blood transfers whatever resistance he has to others. His serum will do it, too. One injection and a mouse, or a person, can be bitten as many times as I can count without either death or conversion."

"Have you found the reason?"

"Not yet," she muttered, seeming to grow agitated, almost fevered. "I will, though, I *will*. Then we will be able to choose who converts and who doesn't, without having to carefully avoid multiple bites. For now, we can just use the serum. Of course, my supply is limited. Eventually the director will get suspicious and stop donating. Thus, I need to find the secret…"

She bent over her apparatus, cradling it lovingly, then placed it back into its drawer.

"Let me get this straight," he said. "You're trying to make it so the people in town can be bitten over and over without becoming vampires. Is this merely to make it easier for vampires to feed? Or do you all want to stop hibernating and prowl the town all winter?"

"You can't know this," she said quietly, looking Caleb in the eye as if seeing him for the first time. "In fact, you know entirely too much."

Caleb stared back at her without blinking. She didn't like that. Flustered, she broke away from his gaze, her eyes darting wildly without apparent focus. When she turned her soulless eyes back to him, her lips curled in a smile.

The close air in the lab began to hum softly, not like a centrifuge or some other scientific instrument, but with the alluring buzz of the vampire's song. Clearly, she'd had enough of the clueless post-doc and meant to wipe his memories clean or worse.

When Caleb didn't respond to her attempt to ensnare his mind, she moved closer to him, her smooth forehead crinkling in concentration. In a flash, he knew what she intended to do next.

He grimaced as she sank her fangs into his neck, taking one for the team since he knew she wasn't going to like what she tasted.

The violence of her reaction was still a surprise. After no more than a taste she sprang back, clutching her throat and foaming at the mouth. She collapsed forward onto the bench, but not before Caleb reached over and pulled away the lab notebook.

He felt woozy and tingly, unable to feel his fingers and toes for a few minutes. But he was still upright, unlike the Undead scientist who had slumped off the counter and lay twitching on the floor.

Shaking off the numbness, he opened the freezer and took the foil-wrapped packet. Whatever he did with it, it would at least not serve to turn more residents of Bar Harbor into blood slaves for vampires.

Chapter 18: Gambit

A FEW SPACES REMAINED IN the motel's parking lot, which was packed with out-of-state cars. On this hot, sticky August afternoon, the swimming pool was packed, too. Squealing children splashed water, teenagers sulked, and parents gossiped on plastic chairs set far enough back to avoid the occasional sprays that fountained upward. The long one-story building curved around the parking lot like a crooked arm scooping up the asphalt. A low-angled roof shaded the concrete walkway between the parking lot and the building. Each room had a window, flanked by faux wooden shutters incapable of thwarting a nor'easter, and under the window sat a pair of white plastic chairs with a little table in between.

The heat from the pavement soaked into Caleb's feet as he left the shade of the namesakes that loomed over the Pines Motel. Was the asphalt buckling in the heat or was he starting to hallucinate from fatigue? Sweat trickled uncomfortably down the middle of his back, and he felt relief when he reached the shaded walkway in front of the rooms, although the air was just as humid and hot. The lone occupant of the motel's long line of plastic chairs wore a black suit and a skinny black tie, shoulders hunched over a chessboard on the table before him.

As Caleb approached, Agent Hulstad carefully lifted a black pawn, then brought it down near the center of the board. The agent looked up, his ice-blue eyes registering mild surprise.

"Mr. O'Connor," he drawled in his flat Midwestern accent. His age could have been anywhere between forty and sixty, given the white-blond hair and pale skin. A thin sheen of sweat covered his forehead, and he didn't seem to notice the rivulets dripping down the side of his face. "Do you play chess?"

"What?" Caleb asked. The question knocked him out of the carefully cultivated calmness he'd constructed on his walk to the motel. "I used to play with a friend, but he always beat me."

"Pity," the agent answered laconically. "I get tired of playing myself."

Caleb cleared his throat. "And Agent Gallo isn't much of an opponent, I'll bet."

Agent Hulstad twitched one corner of his thin-lipped grimace. "What do you recommend here?"

Caleb's exhausted mind drifted back to long winter nights in the library of Castle Arghezi, to games played in the flickering light from the large stone fireplace, to the grim visage of Alexandru on the other side of the board as he plotted Caleb's destruction.

"White could distract that black pawn in the middle with the knight," he suggested hesitantly.

"You're suggesting the King's Bishop Gambit?"

"Is that what it's called?"

"Hmm," the agent murmured, staring intently at the chess board for a moment. "Are you sure you don't want to play white?"

"No! I mean, yes, I'm sure," Caleb spluttered. "There have been, uhm, developments, and I came by to tell you…"

"The Hellhounds have left the area?" the agent asked mildly, eyes still fixed on the board in front of him. "Is that what you've come to tell me?"

"What? No. I mean, there's something else," Caleb answered testily, sitting heavily on the chair opposite the chess board and settling the paper grocery bag he'd brought with him on his lap. "It's Cuza."

"Who?"

Caleb waited until a pair of teenaged girls, wrapped in towels and giggling to one another, had passed in front of them heading for the pool, then said quietly, "Peter Brody, the vampire that I told you about, the one from Romania."

"Ah," Agent Hulstad said, extracting a slim notebook from an inner pocket of his jacket and flipping through the pages. "We have investigated

Mr. Brody. He arrived in Bar Harbor approximately November of last year claiming to be Hungarian, although we've found no evidence of that and no evidence of his entry into the US. The timing is suspicious, certainly. Brody could be the ABE that we had a report about last fall."

"Exactly!" Caleb said. "This Peter Brody went by the name Cuza in Romania, where he was responsible for the death of Alexandru Arghezi, among other things. I was there. I saw it. And now he's—"

"One moment, Mr. O'Connor," Hulstad interrupted as he pulled a ballpoint pen from his front jacket pocket, clicked it authoritatively, and wrote doggedly for a moment. "This Brody, or Cuza as you call him, is the BFI you encountered last week?"

"Yes!" Caleb exclaimed, frustrated by the agent's snail-like pace. "I saw him in the bank where he was signing papers to buy a building on Main Street, which has a bar in the basement—the Lobster Pot—that's a local hangout. A couple of the regulars at the bar have come down with that mystery illness, which is not caused by werewolves, by the way. And I have proof that—"

"Well, look who it is," crowed a voice from behind Caleb.

He turned to see the junior of the two agents looming over him. Agent Gallo didn't sport the black jacket and skinny tie today. The sleeves of his white dress shirt had been rolled up to his elbows and his paunchy middle pushed the shirt out over his black pants. In one hand, he carried a couple of large cardboard pizza boxes and, in the other, a plastic grocery bag bulging with soda bottles.

"Did our furry buddy come to spill the beans?" Agent Gallo mocked, his pudgy, grinning face gleaming with sweat.

Why don't you just call me Fido and get it over with? Caleb thought irritably.

"Pull up a chair, Gallo," Agent Hulstad ordered. "This citizen has some information for us."

Agent Gallo dropped the plastic bag on the concrete with a thud and dragged a chair across the walkway, angling it next to his partner. He thumped into the seat, balancing pizza boxes on his lap.

"You want a piece?" Gallo grunted, lifting the lid of the top box. "Pepperoni or Hawaiian."

"No, thank you," Agent Hulstad replied primly. "Mr. O'Connor has been telling me about a bar."

"The Lobster Pot," Caleb corrected.

"These cutesy names just kill me," Gallo chortled before cramming the end of a folded pizza slice into his mouth.

"It's a bar on Main Street," Caleb continued. "We're pretty sure it's being run by vampires."

"Hmm," Agent Hulstad said, scribbling in his notebook. "This might pose a threat to the public."

"Threat!" Caleb's laugh had an edge of hysteria. "The vampires, the ones running the bar, have been giving people doses of a serum, a drug, and it makes them immune to multiple vampire bites. They get sick, like the flu, but don't become vampires, which means the vampires keep feeding on them."

"Wait a sec," Agent Gallo interrupted, screwing up his face in concentration. "Don't it take three bites to turn someone?"

"Usually, yes, but Cuza, he's your ABE, teamed up with a scientist from the Jax to make this drug, so that the vampires can keep biting people."

"Jax?" Agent Hulstad asked, head still bent over his notebook.

"The Jackson Laboratory, a place in town where they do experiments with mice, trying to cure cancer and other things. Cuza recruited a scientist from the lab, who created this drug that they've been using on the regulars at the bar. I've been reading her lab notebook and… Look, I don't want to get hung up on the details. This serum they've been using on people sometimes has fatal side effects. It's only a matter of time before else someone dies."

"This is a remarkable tale," Hulstad said, while Gallo guffawed. "Can you offer any proof?"

Caleb gripped the top of the grocery bag in his lap. He'd unconsciously worried the paper so much that it felt like cloth under his fingers. He opened the bag and extracted the dark brown notebook, "Jackson Laboratory" stamped in gold letters on the cover.

"This is a record," Caleb said, displaying the notebook, "of how this scientist developed and tested the drug."

"How did you obtain this evidence?" Agent Hulstad asked suspiciously.

"I walked right into her lab," Caleb answered with mock cheerfulness, "and she was eager to tell me about her wonderful plan."

Agent Gallo thrust a greasy hand at the notebook, but Caleb pulled it back. Hastily, he tucked the book into the bag, then extracted a sheaf of papers, bound with a rubber band.

"Here's a photocopy. Study it all you want, gentlemen," he said, handing it to Hulstad with a sidelong glance at Gallo. "The conclusion will be that vampires have found an insidious method to prey on the citizens of Bar Harbor."

"This scientist," Agent Hulstad began, frowning as he paged through the photocopied notebook, looking for her name.

"Dr. Nina Patel," Caleb filled in.

"You allege that she is a BFI?"

"I have the bite marks to prove it," he retorted with grim satisfaction, turning his head to show the puncture marks on his neck. "Do you want to take a picture?"

Agent Gallo whistled under his breath, and the older agent, scribbling again in his small notebook, asked matter-of-factly, "Really? When was this?"

"Early this morning, eight or nine hours ago," Caleb said, though he felt as if several sleepless days might have passed since she had sunk her fangs into his neck, based on the heaviness in his limbs and the pounding in his head.

"Huh," Gallo grunted suspiciously. "You recovered pretty fast."

Caleb rubbed his aching temples with his fingers. "We 'furries' aren't much affected by vampire bites, it seems. However, I can't say the same for the ones doing the biting."

"Care to elaborate, Mr. O'Connor?" Hulstad inquired, looking up from his notes.

"Let's just say that you probably won't be able to take a statement from Dr. Patel. When I left her lab, she was lying on the floor foaming at the mouth."

The older agent gave him a penetrating stare.

"It wasn't my idea for her to bite me," Caleb pointed out.

Agent Hulstad cleared his throat. "You cannot expect us to take your word for any of this without verification, Mr. O'Connor. We'll have to interview the alleged victims, take medical histories, that sort of thing."

Caleb massaged the back of his neck, rolling his head until something popped. He hadn't expected it would be this hard to convince the agents. Maybe he was too tired or too much affected by the bite to think clearly.

"Okay, start with Tom Matthews. He's got the mystery illness and so do some of his buddies."

While Caleb gave them Tom's address and phone number, a mini-van pulled into one of the few remaining parking spaces, next to the agents' black sedan. The van's windshield, front grille, and license plate were spattered with constellations of dead bugs. Doors popped open, almost simultaneously, disgorging father, mother, a bored teenaged girl muttering about the interminable car ride, and a six- or seven-year-old girl clutching a stuffed giraffe. Inside the van, a toddler wailed as the mother made hushing noises. The young girl wandered in the direction of the swimming pool, until her father snatched her from the path of another car that was cruising the lot in search of a parking space. The mother brought out the squirming toddler, while the father piled luggage on the pavement.

"It's the week before Labor Day, and Bar Harbor is full of tourists," Caleb said softly between clenched teeth. He gestured toward the van with his head, willing to bend the truth in order to get the agents to take him seriously. "See that family? Which of them will it be? I'd put my money on the older girl: likely to wander away from the others, likely to fall prey to our charming friends, likely to be found (if she's found at all) white as a ghost and drained of blood. That's what's going to happen, if you don't help me stop them. Do you want that on your conscience? Do you want that on your service record?"

Gallo started to rise, the pizza boxes sliding to his feet as his face darkened in anger. The older agent clamped one hand around his forearm, forcing him to stay seated.

"If this Brody or Cuza is confirmed as dangerous to the public," Agent Hulstad assured stonily, "we can request backup from Special Operations."

"You mean the guys with the bulletproof vests?" Caleb asked, buoyed by the memory of Agent Gallo's description of the gun-toting squad at their previous meeting. "When can you get them up here?"

"It is Friday afternoon and after the close of the work week in Washington, unfortunately," Hulstad answered, shaking his head. "In any case, we will have to provide documentation to HQ before any action can be taken."

"What about shutting down that bar?" Caleb seethed, feeling anger flush up his neck and wash over his face. "Cuza and his gang are just going to keep feeding unless something is done to stop them and soon. Look, can't you arrest them?"

"If there is sufficient evidence, we can bring suspects in for questioning," Agent Hulstad said.

"Sufficient evidence? What does that even mean?" Caleb shouted, gripping the flimsy arms of the plastic chair. "Don't you understand? We have to stop them now!"

Agent Hulstad ignored Caleb, turning his attention to his partner. "Gallo, do you remember that bar in Boston where one too many drained corpses turned up? We couldn't catch the BFI in the act, but we did get the place shut down."

"Duffy's Tavern," Gallo said as he retrieved the pizza boxes from the sidewalk. "Yeah, that might work here."

"How long is all this going to take?" Caleb asked, exasperated. "Because if I have to go into that bar myself, I will."

"Furry vigilante, huh?" Agent Gallo guffawed.

"Maybe you could get me a bulletproof vest," Caleb said, warming to the idea of storming the Lobster Pot. "The vampires have guns and silver bullets, which are not healthy for werewolves."

"You think we'd give you one?" Gallo retorted. "That's government property, pal."

"There might be a way we could provide you with protective equipment," Agent Hulstad mused. "We are always seeking to hire contractors, trusted contractors, who can support our mission."

"And that means?" Caleb asked warily.

"You clearly know a lot about Extraordinary Aliens, which could be of use to the Agency. We are in need of a subject matter expert since the tragic loss of Professor Arghezi."

Caleb narrowed his eyes, scrutinizing the impassive agent. "So, I help you and you help me? Is that it?"

"Precisely, Mr. O'Connor," Agent Hulstad said with the grimace that passed for a smile on his stony face. "A bit of paperwork: a non-disclosure agreement, ethics training, getting you on the payroll. What do you say?"

"Is that the same deal you had with Alexandru?" Caleb asked suspiciously.

"Professor Arghezi was enormously helpful to the Agency. He advised us on the more difficult cases and trained our field officers."

"You mean, he taught you how to spot werewolves so you could spy on us. I'll bet there's a file on *me* somewhere. I'll bet Fintonclyde used to send in reports on me," Caleb growled, exhausted and feeling the way he did right before the full moon: wanting to snap someone's head off.

"That information is classified," Agent Hulstad replied icily. "As you know, we are not authorized to take direct action except in certain circumstances in which citizens are in immediate danger. Training is essential for field agents to be able to recognize—"

"—and neutralize," interrupted Gallo.

"—certain dangerous actors," Hulstad continued smoothly.

"Werewolves, you mean," Caleb said hotly.

"And BFIs, Mr. O'Connor."

"What about *neutralizing* the BFIs in town before anyone else gets hurt?" Caleb exclaimed, rising out of the chair in agitation.

"We take your allegations seriously, and we will act on them, make no mistake," Agent Hulstad answered blandly, tucking his notebook back into an inner jacket pocket. "We appreciate your willingness to volunteer information. It speaks highly of you. And, please, consider our offer."

Caleb stared openmouthed, both hands gripping the top of the much-worn paper bag that held the notebook. Anger ricocheted inside him like a pinball in an arcade game gone crazy. Jaws clenched to keep from yelling, he muttered, "I ask for help and what I get are conditions and more paperwork, but it all amounts to blackmail. No, thanks."

Agent Gallo snickered at his retreating back as Caleb stumbled across the parking lot, sick from frustration and lack of sleep. There had to be another way.

Chapter 19: Hair of the Dog

'MON, TWO MORE STEPS," Mickey wheedled, hauling the Doc's twitching body along the alley. A single spotlight feebly illuminated the cracked pavement at his feet. He kept one eye on Main Street, but it was late and he didn't detect any movement. That was one less thing to worry about, and he had plenty to concern him already.

"Weaheeuhih?" the scientist mumbled thickly. Her swollen tongue flopped to one side of her mouth, like a garden slug trying to crawl away and hide.

As Mickey had feared, being the courier for the Doc had become his regular job in the last week and a half. He'd convinced her to give him a badge so that he could let himself into the building in the evenings, when fewer of the staff were around. This evening, he'd found her lying on the floor, twitching and moaning with dried foam flecking her puffy, mottled cheeks. She'd been conscious, but not coherent. Those scientists did weird stuff in that laboratory, but immortals should have been immune. Shouldn't they? Not knowing what else to do, he'd hauled her to a more or less upright position and dragged her out of the lab, because if someone found her there, questions would get asked—questions that might lead to an inquiry into the odd behavior of some of the regulars at the Lobster Pot.

Mickey figured she was Cuza's problem, not his.

He had an arm around her waist and hooked one of her arms over his shoulder. She was taller than him by a few inches, and her feet dragged on the worn steps as they descended the stairs—*thud-thud-thud*— into the basement, then scraped softly across the wood floor of the short entry hall that led to the main room.

The scientist twitched as the heavy velvet drapes that marked the entrance brushed across her cheeks. Even the normally dim light seemed bright after the dark entry hall. Conversations hushed. The clacking of pool balls ceased. Eyes turned toward them.

Her head lolled to one side as she peered at the room through puffy lids, mumbling, "Wuthaheh? Eheeowthooee?"

She spasmed and her arm slid off his shoulder, causing her body to slump toward the floor. Mickey heaved her upward, clamping a hand around one of her wrists and draping her arm around his shoulder again.

"Hey! Don't go bringing drunks into a bar!" called someone who thought himself witty.

Not pleased with the attention, Mickey muttered, "Found her in the parking lot. Musta been a hit and run or something. Taking her to the back room for a lie down."

Anyone who believed that story was probably already drunk, which Mickey was counting on. The blotchy face, dark skin mottled with ashy gray patches, and sharp cheekbones swallowed by swollen flesh looked nothing like the aftermath of a car crash.

Vito, tonight's bartender, gave him a quizzical look, which Mickey ignored. Across the room, Cuza stood joking with two men shooting pool, but his jaw tightened at the sight of his pet scientist bloated and flopping around like a fish on a beach.

Mickey turned into the hall that led to the office and bathrooms, relieved once he was out of the noisy, smoke-filled main room. The Doc continued to jerk as his pace slowed to turn a corner, and he struggled to keep from losing his grip on her.

Mickey would have breathed a sigh of relief, if he had breathed at all, upon entering the tiny office that held little else besides a wooden chair and a massive oak desk, covered with hillocks of bills, account books, and other papers. He eased her into a seated slump, propping her up by hooking her elbows around the arms of the chair. He tried to swing the door shut, but Cuza burst in, slamming him against the wall.

"What did you DO?!"

"Whoa, whoa, *whoa!*" Mickey answered, closing the door firmly. "This ain't my fault, Boss. She was like this when I found her."

"Where?" demanded Cuza, grabbing the lapel of his jacket.

"In her lab," Mickey said, unclenching Cuza's fingers and pushing him as far away as possible in the confines of the small, cluttered room. "I went up there to do a pick-up, like I been doing all week, and I found her lying there on the floor. I never seen one of us act like this. Think it's the weird stuff they do at that place?"

Cuza lifted one of the scientist's eyelids and peered at her pupil. Letting his hand fall, he laughed bitterly. "Werewolf. This happens sometimes in the old country when our kind are careless. You must know this."

"Hey, I didn't stick around long enough back there to tangle with were-wolves and, until this summer, we didn't have none of them dogs around here," Mickey retorted hotly, neglecting to mention his recent coffin-side encounter at Lilac House. Wanting to change the subject, he asked, "This always happen when we bite one of them?"

"The new ones do not know and" —Cuza gestured disdainfully at the bloated, twitching form in the chair— "this is the result."

"After the mess this summer, we knew there were a lot of dogs in town. You could've warned the Doc," Mickey said just to needle Cuza. Lady Agatha probably knew the aftereffects of a bite, judging by her reaction to the werewolf she'd attempted to choke in the crypt, but the newly Undead scientist had been ignorant of the danger posed by sinking her fangs into the wrong neck.

"She is all the time in her lab! Why do I need to warn?" Cuza objected, evading responsibility as usual.

Mickey sat on the edge of the desk, crossing his arms, wanting to be as far away from the infected scientist as possible in case a werewolf-bite was contagious. "Is the Doc going to snap out of it?"

"Some die, others do not, but if the screaming becomes too much… Sometimes we—how do you say?"

"Put them out of their misery?" Mickey suggested uneasily, not liking the idea of immortals putting down other immortals.

"Yes, yes," Cuza replied thoughtfully. "But some come back to us like that boy at the castle. You must remember."

"No, of course, I don't." Mickey scowled in irritation. Cuza persisted in the belief that Mickey had been in the band that had driven the remaining mortal members of the Arghezi family from the castle and dwelt there for decades.

"No? I chain him in the cellar until he stops screaming and hitting and breaking things."

"Like a lunatic?" Mickey interrupted, chortling at the lunar reference, which Cuza did not find amusing. "And how long did that take?"

"Days, weeks… I do not remember," Cuza said distractedly, gazing at the once-beautiful face of Nina Patel, her sharp cheekbones and arched brows submerged in a puffy, wrecked landscape.

"Gotta go," Mickey said, easing himself off the desk and attempting to squeeze past Cuza, who stood stroking his chin, lost in thought. "Her Ladyship's expecting me and…"

Cuza slapped the scientist's cheek, demanding, "Who did this?"

She squinted up at him through swollen lids, eyes attempting to focus on the sharp planes of Cuza's angry face. Flinging her arms out to the sides of the chair, she managed to push herself up out of her near-comatose slump.

"Poth-hoc," she began, trying to talk around her engorged tongue. Then, after swallowing, she mumbled thickly, "Eew ooh muth."

"Lupeni, again," said Cuza angrily. "Caleb O'Connor, as he calls himself, has done this!"

Obviously, it had been O'Connor: Mickey had told him her name and where she worked. Did he feel sorry about that? Not remotely. But he did wonder if the werewolf had taken anything, as he tried to recall the situation in her lab. He'd been so preoccupied with her bizarre condition that he hadn't bothered to look around.

She slumped back into the chair, eyes closed and head lolling to one side like a discarded rag doll. Cuza slapped her face again, which elicited only incoherent moaning. Then, as if reading Mickey's mind, Cuza spun around to face him, demanding, "Was anything missing from the lab?"

"Er, didn't check," he admitted. "Too busy trying to get the Doc out of there without raising suspicion."

"You must go back. What if this dog has stolen from us?"

"Like I said, Lady Agatha…" Mickey muttered as he stretched an arm toward the door handle like a drowning man reaching for a lifeboat.

Cuza clamped a hand around his wrist, shoving his other hand against Mickey's chest to flatten him against the wall. "You will go now, and you will bring me more serum and her notebook."

Mickey drank in the naked hatred written across Cuza's contorted face, openly broadcasting what Mickey had suspected: Cuza had meant to wipe out the entire Arghezi family from his first visit to the castle decades ago. The pretense of Romanian comradery—*Remember the good times back in the old country?* —had fallen away to reveal a long-concealed vendetta against his family for reasons Mickey couldn't fathom. Right now, the reasons didn't matter.

"Agatha will not protect you," Cuza whispered, a malicious smile playing across his face, "because I will hunt you down, *Mircea Arghezi*, last of the Arghezi family. I will hunt you down and destroy you, no matter where you run. Do you understand?"

Mickey nodded mutely and fled.

* * *

ONLY A FEW REGULARS remained at the bar by the time Mickey returned empty-handed from the Jackson Lab. Cuza's piercing shriek of frustration combined with the incoherent moaning of the Doc, who had been restrained in the office, cemented the Lobster Pot's reputation as the most haunted place in Bar Harbor.

Chapter 20: Easy, Rider

"LOOK! IT'S BELA!" RUDY hung out of the Land Rover's window, pointing to the approaching figure emerging from a roiling cloud of dust.

Caleb swerved the truck toward the encroaching bushes to avoid the motorcycle, which chugged past them, coughing and misfiring. The Land Rover shuddered to a halt, tree branches scraping metal and pushing up against the windshield like nosy onlookers at a gruesome accident. In the rearview mirror, he saw the rider, face obscured by goggles and a bandana around nose and mouth, fishtail and clumsily turn the bike around. The motorcycle that pulled alongside the idling Land Rover was nothing like the big black-and-chrome Harley Davidsons that the Hellhounds rode. So different, but so familiar.

Caleb closed his eyes, breathing in dust and listening to the recognizable rumble of the engine as he remembered another boy astride that bike. Toby had spent the summer of his seventeenth year bringing it back to life. He'd begged, pleaded and cajoled Sophia's aunt to let him restore the Zündapp, which Sophia's late uncle had brought back from Germany after the war. Caleb had tagged along on Toby's trips to junkyards all over New England in search of needed parts. Along the way, Toby had made friends with a network of grizzled old motorcycle enthusiasts, who had supplied tips, tricks, and timeless wisdom. Dozens of scavenged parts later, the engine had roared to life and hit the pavement.

Sophia, sitting beside Caleb in the front seat, stared into her lap, knotting her hands restlessly, fingers in motion. What memories did the sight and sound of the motorcycle conjure for her?

"We got it working!" Bela shouted after pulling down the bandana and pushing the goggles up on his head. The stripe of dust under each eye made him look like a raccoon.

"I can see that," Caleb called out. "Where's your helmet? That was one of the conditions, remember?"

"On roads, sure, but this is just dirt." Bela punctuated his casual defiance by revving the engine.

Caleb grunted noncommittally as he backed the Land Rover out of the bushes and into the middle of the dirt track.

Bela snugged the goggles back on his face, pulled up the bandana, and revved the engine. With a brief wave of one hand, he zoomed away toward the camp.

Rudy's eyes were filled with envy as he stuck his head between the front seats and cried excitedly, "I want to learn how to ride!"

"You definitely have to wear a helmet," Sophia cautioned, the unwelcome voice of reason.

Caleb extended an arm and gently pushed him back into his seat, saying only, "Roll up the window."

Reluctantly, Rudy obeyed as the dust plume from the departing motorcycle drifted into the Land Rover, making Caleb sneeze. Watching the hazy, swirling cloud dissipate as the bike receded, Caleb wondered if it had been wise to let Damien spend several days in Sophia's garage, disassembling and cleaning the motorcycle while Bela had attached himself, leechlike, to the older boy. After failing to get the engine started, Damien had asked if he could take the bike and Bela back to their camp, where his father would know what to do about the engine and Bela could learn how to ride. Sophia, de facto owner of the Zündapp, had been worn down by the boys' entreaties, allowing Damien to roll the bike into the back of the pickup truck with the promise that it would be working soon. Bela had been delighted; Caleb, less so.

When Caleb pulled the Land Rover into the Hellhounds' camp, Damien and Bela stood on either side of the German motorcycle talking about timing and valves and other things Caleb vaguely remembered. He'd been surprised and pleased at how quickly Bela had developed a friendship with Damien. There hadn't been any kids his age in their Romanian pack and those in the village wouldn't have anything to do with a werewolf.

The dilapidated farm house still verged on slumping into a heap of rubble, but the Hellhounds' camp had changed since his last visit. Jumbled crates and black plastic garbage bags sat near the Army surplus tents, lending an air of transience to the area. Shouting came from inside one of the tents as items were tossed through the open flap: clothing, beer cans, packaging, wads of paper. Damien's older brother Darius sorted the accumulation outside the tent, looking displeased with his job as trash collector, and carried armloads of paper and plastic to his father, who stood beside a battered 55-gallon metal drum. Flames poked above the rim, dancing in the early afternoon breeze.

Caleb brought the Land Rover to a stop, killed the engine, and jerked the hand brake, which responded with a sharp, groaning creak. He stared at the steering wheel, attempting to collect his scattered thoughts.

"I'm sorry to drag you out here," he said, turning to face Sophia. "I need to talk to Fang, but the vampires… You couldn't stay at home alone." He shook his head ruefully. "If there were any other way, I'd—I don't know what I'd do, to tell the truth."

Sophia laid her fingers lightly on one of his hands, which gripped the steering wheel with white-knuckled tightness.

"You need to stop apologizing, for one thing," she said tartly, regarding him with more warmth than her words implied. She squeezed his hand briefly, flashing a grim smile before withdrawing her hand. "Get out there and talk or bark or whatever you need to do. I think it's better if Rudy and I stay in the car, though."

"Right," Caleb said, loosening his grip on the wheel.

From the back seat, Caleb retrieved the foil-wrapped packet on which shiny beads of water had condensed during their journey. He stepped out, but before closing the door, he said, "Lock the doors, okay? I won't be long."

Caleb stood for a moment next to the truck, taking in the scene in the broad clearing. Darius ambled over to the pair of boys fixated on the motorcycle. Caleb watched Bela stiffen, losing the casual air of comradeship, and then laugh too hard at Darius's jokes, pretending not to be hurt by teasing from the older boy, who had an aura of coolness, a bravado that reminded him of Toby. Caleb remembered how other boys had treated Toby, who always seemed to be the coolest guy in the room. Caleb ached for his adopted son, but Bela would have to figure some things out for himself.

"Didn't know if I'd see you before we left," Fang commented casually as Caleb joined him next to the burn barrel. The pack leader, dressed in a faded Harley Davidson t-shirt and jeans, wasn't wearing a sling today, but his left arm still moved stiffly.

"You're not leaving right away, are you?" Caleb asked. The Hellhounds hadn't been the world's best allies, but he'd take whatever he could get at this point.

"Long past time to get out of here." Fang grunted, reaching down for a can of beer perched on a lawn chair at his side. "You want a beer?"

"No. No, thanks."

"Suit yourself." Fang tipped the can into his mouth. After draining the last of the beer, he crushed the can with one hand and tossed it into the fire.

"You don't look like you can ride yet," Caleb observed.

"Maybe not," Fang conceded, "but I'll drive the truck, if I have to. Just waiting to sell Buck's bike. I got a buyer scraping together the cash, says he'll have it in a day or two. Then we ride."

"So, a day or two," Caleb said as he went through vampire-hunting scenarios in his head. "I've got some news for you, too, but first, can I toss something into the fire?"

"What you got there?" Fang asked, eyeing the foil-wrapped package that Caleb gripped with both hands, the water on its surface starting to evaporate from the heat of the fire.

"It's a long story."

"I got time," Fang said. "Pull up a chair, while I get another beer. You sure you don't want one?"

Caleb refused the beer and the chair. He removed the foil to reveal the rack with its matrix of tiny, stoppered vials, each the size of his pinky, each containing a pale, pink liquid. Then he began the tale: "There's a bar on Main Street…"

The thread of the story wandered, as Caleb had to explain about Cuza and the three-bite rule and the Jackson Lab. Halfway through the telling, Doña Flóres arrived, which forced him to go back to the beginning. Finally, at the end of the tale, Caleb held the rack above the barrel and turned it upside-down so that the vials spilled into the fire, clinking against one another as they fell, then hissing and spitting as they broke open.

"That's the magic stuff that makes people immune to vampires?" Fang asked, wrinkling his nose at the coppery stench rising from the fire.

"According to the vampire scientist, it's not magic, it's science," Caleb said, realizing too late that the Hellhounds wouldn't get his weak attempt at humor.

"You take this science away from the vampires. What will they do?" asked Doña Flóres, crossing her arms and regarding him shrewdly through narrowed eyes.

"They won't be giving the stuff to the locals anymore, won't be making them sick," Caleb said as he stared into the flames.

Doña Flóres shook her head, admonishing him. "Los cadáveres must feed, no? They will not stop."

"You're right: the vampires will just go on biting. That's why I could really use your help," Caleb said, turning to face cold stares from Fang and Doña Flóres. "I tried to get help from those agents, but they said it would be days before they can do all the paperwork. That might be too late."

"Agents!" Fang's face hardened in anger and his hands balled into fists. He let out a string of curses, before stomping across the clearing toward the German bike where Bela and Damien laughed at a story Darius was recounting. Caleb couldn't make out all the words, but the ones he did hear mostly consisted of profanity.

Caleb started to go after the pack leader, but Doña Flóres dug her fingers painfully into his arm to stop him.

"Wait," she cautioned. "He is too angry to talk."

"I know these agents are frustrating to deal with. Okay, they seem like idiots a lot of the time, but they might be able to help," Caleb said, trying to shake off her viselike grip.

"This is first time for you with *esos cabrónes*? They are bad men," she said hotly.

"Maybe the ones down in Florida are bad," Caleb began, but she cut him off.

"They threaten us, they spy on us, and worse," Doña Flóres hinted, her voice dropping to a low, rasping whisper. "The agents, they kill Fang's wife. He cannot forget this."

"They what?" Caleb turned to look at Fang, who appeared calmer than when he'd stormed off. While Damien explained something to Bela by tracing cables on the bike, Fang had pulled Darius away from the other two boys, speaking too quietly for Caleb to hear. Darius stood close to his father, nodding his head. Seeing them together like that gave Caleb a pang of unease, though he couldn't say precisely why.

Doña Flóres shot a narrow-eyed stare at Fang, too, then continued, "Eight years ago. It is the Howling. We have a score to settle with some others."

"The local agents got wind of this meetup with the other pack?"

"Sí. We are far from houses, people, roads, but they say we are danger to the public," Doña Flóres spat. "They come with guns."

"Silver bullets?"

"Estúpidos! No, they are not smart. They try to shoot us, but the bullets do not kill us. They fire guns everywhere, maybe they are scared, maybe they are fools. Fang's wife, she waits in the truck, because she is not wolf."

"Sweet Selene," Caleb exhaled softly.

Doña Flóres nodded grimly and wrapped her thin arms tightly across her chest. Caleb didn't need to hear the details to picture agents panicking and firing wildly, not knowing or caring about what they would euphemistically call "collateral damage." A hot flush washed over his face and his stomach knotted as he thought back to Romania where the local farmers—who had an ample supply of silver bullets—had tried several times to exterminate the werewolves, and where Alexandru Arghezi had sided with the farmers. Was he wrong to think the situation would be any better in America?

"Werewolves have to stick together. Fang must understand that," Caleb said quietly, after breathing in and out a few times to control the anger boiling inside. He glanced reflexively over at the pack leader, who'd returned to Damien and Bela, haranguing them about some piece of motorcycle minutia. Darius had vanished, which amplified Caleb's unease.

"How many have you lost?" Doña Flóres seethed, pursing her lips and then answering her own question: "None! Our pack, our family, is never the same after this summer. We leave before we lose more. There is no more to discuss."

A flash of movement at the edge of Caleb's vision dragged him away from her words. He quickly pivoted to see Darius at the rear of the Land Rover, fiddling with the handle of the back door.

"Hey!" Caleb shouted, sprinting toward the truck.

Darius had forced open the door and had dived into the back by the time Caleb arrived. Rudy's muffled shriek came from inside. Caleb pounded on the window to get Sophia to unlock the door, but her attention was on the back seat where Darius wrestled with Rudy.

Front and rear passenger-side doors flew open at the same time. Darius emerged with both arms around the flailing and writhing little boy. Sophia closed on the pair as soon as she shot out of the front seat.

"Let him go!" she shouted, her words barely audible above Rudy's incoherent shrieks.

Sophia backed Darius against the side of the Land Rover by kicking and pummeling him wherever she could, while Rudy scratched at his face and squirmed in his grip.

Caleb rounded the front of the truck, but was forced to a halt when Fang and Doña Flóres, on either side of him, seized his arms hard enough to yank him backwards.

"Not so fast, Fido," Fang growled in Caleb's ear. "This doesn't have to be hard. In fact, it's simple. The kid belongs with his own kind: that's us. We're leaving and he's going with us."

"Can't you see? He doesn't want that," Caleb answered through clenched teeth as he lunged forward, trying to break the grip of the other two werewolves.

"He is a child. He does not know what he wants," Doña Flóres said sharply.

Rudy wriggled out of Darius's arms and scrambled onto the roof of the Land Rover, where he got shakily to his feet.

"Come back, you little—" Darius yelled, thrusting long arms up toward Rudy, who backed away from him.

"No!" Rudy sobbed, tears running down his blotchy red cheeks. "You can't make me!"

Rudy stumbled backward to escape Darius's long arms and groping fingers. Bela ran to the Land Rover and tried to pull the older boy away, but he was shoved roughly to the ground. Darius thrust an arm across the roof and took a swipe at Rudy's foot.

"Get away!" Rudy yelled, dancing backward to avoid the grasping hand. "Get—"

Rudy's words dissolved into an incoherent screech as he took another backward step, lost his balance, and tumbled off the roof.

Growls and screams evaporated, leaving a heavy silence punctuated by Darius pounding on the roof. Caleb shook off his stunned captors and sprinted to the rear of the Land Rover, where Sophia knelt next to Rudy's limp, sprawled body. The boy was breathing, Caleb noticed as he went down on the uneven, rutted ground. He gently lifted one of Rudy's eyelids, then lightly probed arms and legs for obvious fractures.

"No broken bones that I can see," Caleb murmured.

Sophia exhaled loudly with relief. Bela and the Hellhounds clustered around the fallen boy. Caleb carefully picked Rudy up, cradling the boy's head next to his chest.

"Is he—is he going to be all right?" Bela asked shakily.

"He's got a concussion, but no obvious broken bones," Caleb answered grimly. "We won't know more until he wakes up. Fortunately, we heal faster than most people."

The Hellhounds offered no resistance as Caleb shouldered his way through them, bearing Rudy in his arms.

"We're going to take Rudy back with us," Caleb said, turning to glare at Fang. "I don't expect more interference from you."

"He's just a kid and he doesn't know—" Fang protested.

"What more do you want?" Caleb shot back harshly. "A neon-sign? A billboard-sized message? Rudy doesn't want to be here with you, and that's putting it mildly."

Fang tensed and opened his mouth to object, but Doña Flóres tugged at his sleeve and whispered in his ear. He listened intently for a few moments, then shook his head slowly.

"The kid has to be raised right, not by humans." Fang glared at Sophia. "So, you better watch it, and we're gonna check up on the kid."

Caleb nodded curtly to Fang as he called to Sophia: "Can you settle Rudy in the back?"

She climbed into the back seat and held out her arms to take the boy from Caleb. She carefully nestled Rudy in her lap before slamming the door with stormy glances toward the Hellhounds.

Caleb grabbed Bela's arm and dragged the boy away from the group of bikers. "We're leaving. All of us and right now. If you're going to ride that motorcycle back to town, wear a helmet. Otherwise, you might as well leave it here."

Bela's eyes danced between the Hellhounds and Rudy in the back seat of the Land Rover. Caleb wondered where Bela's loyalties lay.

"Yeah, helmet," Bela mumbled on his way toward the German motor-cycle.

Caleb climbed wearily into the driver's seat. The adrenaline buzz was draining away, leaving his limbs sluggish and rendering his thoughts scattered. After starting the engine, he looked over his shoulder at Sophia who stroked Rudy's hair and murmured to the unconscious boy.

"Ready?" he asked, shifting into reverse.

"Let's go home," she said softly.

* * *

CALEB DIVIDED HIS ATTENTION between the narrow dirt road ahead and the rearview mirror in which he could keep track of Sophia, holding Rudy on her lap in the back seat, and Bela, trailing behind the Land Rover on the motorcycle. He half expected to see more than one dust plume behind them, but the Hellhounds hadn't followed. One less thing to worry about, and he had plenty of others.

His anxiety slowed time and distorted distance. The mile and a half from the Hellhounds camp to the paved road seemed more like ten. Turning onto pavement brought him scant relief, although the teeth-rattling bouncing stopped and the Land Rover's creaks and groans grew a lot quieter. He worried more about Bela, especially once they were on the state highway leading to town where traffic was heavier. He'd been crazy to let Bela learn to ride that bike, and even crazier to think he'd be able to get any help from the Hellhounds without consequences.

Rudy moaned in the back seat. Caleb's eyes snapped to the rearview mirror. The little boy slowly lifted his head from Sophia's lap, blinking owlishly at his surroundings with an unfocused stare. Caleb took a large gulp of air, the tightness in his chest melting away, as if a heavy weight had been lifted.

"Head hurts," the little boy whimpered, wriggling himself into a sitting position.

"Don't try to talk. Stay still," Sophia murmured as she stroked Rudy's black hair, which was streaked with dirt and peppered with dried grass.

"He was chasing me and... and..." The boy's eyes went wide as returning memories pushed him to panic.

"Hush," she said. "You hit your head, and you've got a big lump to show for it, but you're going to be okay. It's all going to be okay."

"Where's Bela?" Rudy squeaked, frantically jerking his head to scan the inside of the Land Rover. "Did they get him?"

"Bela's right behind us on the motorcycle," Caleb said. "We're all going home."

"You'll be headed for the bath and then to bed," Sophia added. "I'll bet you'll want to sleep for a while."

Rudy blurted out: "But what if those people chase us? What if they come at night?"

"Caleb made a deal with them," Sophia said, her eyes meeting Caleb's in the rearview mirror. "You're going to live with us, but if the Hellhounds behave themselves, they're allowed to visit sometimes. Isn't that right?"

Caleb barked out a laugh, partly at Sophia's sing-song delivery and partly to release the tension bottled inside him.

"Well," Rudy said thoughtfully as he snuggled against Sophia's side, "if they can be nice, I guess that's okay."

"If they come around, I'll make sure of that," Caleb stated loudly, then, almost to himself, he muttered, "Though I doubt we'll be seeing them again."

"And you were counting on their help, weren't you?" Sophia asked.

"What an idiot I was," Caleb said ruefully. Did he expect werewolf solidarity? It wasn't as if his Romanian pack had always been united and willing to help him.

"Maybe the agents will come through," Sophia offered, though her tone didn't suggest confidence.

"But do I want their help?" Caleb said, shaking his head. "They said they could call in some special squad with guns, but could I trust them to get it right? Maybe I should just charge into the Lobster Pot, and take out Cuza. I've rammed a stake through his heart once, and I can do it again."

"But you don't know how many vampires are in there. Can you take them on all by yourself?"

"I don't know, but I have to try! Otherwise, people are going to start dying," Caleb fretted. He knew Doña Flóres was right: vampires would keep being vampires, whether or not they had the serum. And desperate vampires were an even greater danger to the human population of Bar Harbor

"What about Fintonclyde?" she suggested hesitantly. "He taught us all magic when we were kids, and he's fought vampires before."

"Where was he when Toby needed help?" Caleb growled. "What was it he said when we went out there? 'Clearly a powerful vampire corrupted Toby.' That's rubbish! No, I'm not asking him for help."

"What other choice do you have, Caleb?" she asked quietly.

Chapter 21: In Need of Repair

ALEB TIED UP THE boat, a skiff borrowed from an acquaintance of Sophia's. Weak sunlight filtered through thick gray clouds and a stiff wind tugged at his oilskin jacket, making him wish he'd worn a wool cap. No shadow accompanied him as he placed a foot on the rough wood planking of the little dock, which creaked and shifted underneath him.

Earlier in the week, when he'd brought Sophia and the boys to the island, he'd been preoccupied by the mystery illness and concerned with keeping Bela and Rudy, neither of whom had ever been on a boat before, from tumbling into the water. All these distractions had kept him from noticing the condition of the old dock. As a child, he'd sanded, scrubbed and oiled the planking yearly, repaired loose boards, and scraped barnacles from the pilings. None of these tasks had been done since he left, he thought as he trod carefully on the warped wood, avoiding the gaps from missing planks. The dock rocked under his feet, and the barnacle-crusted pilings leaned like drunken sailors. Stepping off the swaying mass, he felt an unexpected sense of relief as his boots crunched on the stony beach.

He tugged the hood of his jacket over his head and then trudged along the path that wound up a rocky slope. Cresting the banked side of the cove brought him to the flat headland where, several hundred feet distant, lay the cabin and outbuildings. The large barn loomed over the two other buildings, Fintonclyde's cabin and the Bunkhouse, as they'd called the rough dormitory for residents of the old man's summer camps. A thin stream of smoke, flattened by the wind, trailed from the cabin's chimney, the only sign of habitation.

Caleb could have traveled back in time, so little had changed about the scene in front of him. An apparition from the past bounded across the headland toward him, skidding to a halt at his feet and barking wildly. Caleb squatted to rub the yellow Lab's ears. The dog licked his face in return, happy to see him. The wiggling, excited animal looked exactly like one of the dogs of his childhood, although he knew it was one of her offspring.

"Let's go find the old man," he said reluctantly, standing with a hand resting on the dog's back.

The yellow Lab paced next to him as he plodded toward the little farm. As they neared the barn, the dog gave a bark and dashed through its open door, returning accompanied by Fintonclyde, clad in the usual denim overalls and big mud-crusted rubber boots. As he stepped out of the barn, the wind pulled at his beard, tugging at trapped wisps of straw.

"Well, this is an unexpected surprise," Fintonclyde said pleasantly. "Are Sophia and the boys here, too?"

"I came alone," Caleb ground out reluctantly, shaking his head. Sophia had urged him to seek help, but now that he was here, he wondered if coming had been a good idea, especially as it meant leaving Sophia with just Bela for protection. She'd told him that she would be fine. There were wards on the house, but the wards hadn't stopped the first attack.

"I assume you did not come all the way out here to help me muck out the goat pens, mmm?" Fintonclyde asked, narrowing his eyes and regarding Caleb more cautiously. Receiving no reply, he continued, "Why don't you go make us some tea while I clean up."

Fifteen minutes later, Caleb stood at the cabin's kitchen window, hands gripping the edge of the battered metal sink, gazing at a clump of pine trees thirty or forty feet away. The trees twisted and bent in the wind, branches darting back and forth like fencers toying with unseen opponents. Behind him on the scarred wooden table, the tea steeped in its pot, but he felt too restless to sit. The recent past was consisted largely of drinking endless cups of tea during conversations that went nowhere.

"You're out of milk," Caleb commented, turning away from the window as the old man entered the kitchen looking slightly cleaner and without straw in his hair.

"I haven't had time to milk the goats, but I don't suppose you want to help with that either," Fintonclyde said mildly as he searched the cupboards and rattled the drawers, returning to the table with condensed milk and a can opener.

As Fintonclyde sat and poured himself tea from the pot, Caleb remained leaning against the sink, arms folded tightly across his chest. The only sound in the kitchen was the clinking of metal on metal as the old man punctured the can.

"Your dock is falling apart," he noted.

"Yes, that has not escaped my notice," Fintonclyde replied, tipping a stream of milk into his mug. "It will have to be fixed, if there is a summer camp next year."

"If? Are you giving up on the borderline juvenile delinquents and the magic lessons?"

The old man sighed as he stirred milk into his tea. "Funding cuts from the state have reduced the number of under-privileged campers, and now that Tribulation has electricity and telephone service, only a few of the children are interested in learning magic. Most are more interested in those beeping boxes—what do they call them?"

"Video games?"

"Yes, whatever that means." Fintonclyde pushed his chair noisily away from the table and crossed to a set of open shelves on one side of the kitchen, returning with a box of gingersnaps.

"Have a cookie," he said, thumping the box on the table.

"I'm amazed you kept the summer camps going after I left," Caleb said, ignoring the offer and digging his fingers into his upper arms. "Didn't you start those camps just to find playmates for your pet wolf?" That came out nastier than he'd intended; he averted his eyes from the distress on Fintonclyde's face.

"Yes, I did start them to bring other children to the island."

"Juvenile delinquents, mostly," Caleb said dryly as he shifted his gaze back to the old man, who still looked uncomfortable. "I learned how to get beaten up by bigger kids."

"But you met Toby," Fintonclyde said, staring down into the mug as he dunked a cookie in his tea. "And later, you made friends with Sophia and René."

"Sophia actually stood up to the other kids from Tribulation, who were horrified at having to do magic lessons with a werewolf," he noted grimly.

"And what about poor René?" Fintonclyde asked, popping the cookie into his mouth, then washing it down with a noisy slurp of tea.

Caleb turned away from the interior of the kitchen, shifting his gaze back to the jittering pine trees outside. Poor René, indeed: picked on by the other kids from Tribulation because of the grotesque scars on his face; Toby's grinning, goofy sidekick; ready for whatever adventures their fearless leader decided on, although not always strong enough or smart enough to see them through. Caleb knew what it was like to be shunned and ridiculed and perhaps that was why he'd always tried to give René hints when they were studying or helped him catch up with the rest of their friends as they raced through the back alleys after pulling some prank. As they grew older, though, René seemed to lag farther and farther behind them in abilities: a loyal friend, but one who needed a lot of coaching even for performing simple magic.

"The other day," Caleb said, turning slowly to face Fintonclyde, "you said that Toby couldn't have broken the wards at Lilac House on his own, but what about René? He could have helped Toby."

"René?" Fintonclyde tilted his head to one side and stared up at the ceiling. "That seems unlikely. Two people would have been needed to break the wards, because that's the way Alexandru and I created them. Supposing Toby had known that, he could have used René's help, but it's more likely that he had help from a powerful vampire--because on his own, Toby wouldn't have known about such advanced magic."

"I—" Caleb started, not able to form coherent words as a swirling cyclone of memories engulfed him. "I think I hear the dog outside."

Caleb fled the kitchen, dodging boots, crates, and tools in the mudroom, and stepped outside into unexpected late afternoon sunshine. The wind had calmed: the branches of the pines barely fluttered, and a breeze whispered faintly in the trees. Leaning against the side of the cabin, he dug the heels of his hands into his tightly closed eyes and remembered the last time he'd spoken to Toby.

"Hey, Dog Boy, what took you so long to answer the phone?"

"I'm studying. I have finals coming up, just after...you know."

"Aw, you don't need to study—you never did. That's why they let you into that school after all. Anyway, you gotta come up here this weekend. You can't stay down in Cambridge, locked in your apartment."

"But finals start next week—"

"And here's the coolest thing: You gotta come help us. 'Cause we did it, we got in."

"Got in where? Not—"

"Lilac House, yeah, we did it. Well, sort of."

"Toby, are you crazier than I think you are? Nobody has—does—I mean, it's not—If anyone finds out..."

"You worry too much. We were fine. Okay, René was pretty much a wuss, like he always is, but me and Sophia—"

"Wait a second, Toby. Sophia went with you?"

"She's better than me at undoing wards—not as good as you though, and that's why you have to come up this weekend. She says she won't go back."

"She's smart, smarter than you sometimes. I wish you'd listen to her."

"But we were really close, and it would be so cool if we could figure out the wards to get into the main house. No one's ever done that."

"You mean no one's ever lived to tell about it. Toby, you can't—"

"Sure, I can, Dog Boy, but it'd be easier if you helped me. The wards on that house were really solid, you know? I tried every which way to break them. You're good with wards, so you gotta come help me."

"Finals, I've got finals. I'll come up after exams are over. And then I'll be there all summer, I promise."

"Yeah. Right. You used to be fun, you know that?"

"Hmm. You say they're different from what we're used to. How?"

"They almost feel like Fintonclyde made them, but it's like there's something else there and I can't break through."

"Fintonclyde's been around there forever, so it's weird that there's a strong ward that he didn't make, but... maybe he teamed up with someone else on this one."

"So? What good does that do me?"

"Maybe if more than one person made the ward, then—"

"Hey, that's right! I guess MIT hasn't totally messed up your brain, Dog Boy. Listen, I gotta go. See you when I see you, okay?"

The dog trotted up, clamoring for his attention with an anxious bark. Caleb slid down to a crouch, letting the Lab lick his hand. He threw his arms around her neck, transported back a decade or more by the smells of the barnyard and of unwashed dog.

"Trixie," he addressed the dog seriously, holding her head in both hands. "Rudy says that's your name, in spite of what Fintonclyde thinks. Is that right?"

The dog sat back on her haunches, cocked her head, and gave an affirmative bark.

"Let's go inside," he said, getting to his feet while the dog happily waved her tail.

Inside the kitchen, Fintonclyde hadn't moved from his seat, but looked up when Caleb entered. Trixie excitedly greeted the old man, pushing her nose into his lap.

"That jar on the counter, next to the flour cannister," Fintonclyde said with a wave of his arm.

"Since when do you give treats to dogs?" Caleb asked, as he opened a large mason jar filled with colorful, vaguely bone-shaped biscuits and tossed one into Trixie's open maw. "You used to tell me it wasn't good to pamper dogs."

Slightly chagrined, Fintonclyde mumbled, "These new dog treats are supposed to clean their teeth and have vitamins."

Caleb shook his head. Even humans could learn new tricks. He picked up the pot to pour himself tea, but noticed how cold it had grown. Crossing to the stove, he lit one of the burners.

"I figured out a lot about warding from some of your books," Caleb admitted, "but I'd never tried out more advanced spells myself until I went to Romania."

"Alexandru was better than anyone I've ever known," Fintonclyde said with uncharacteristic admiration.

Caleb stared into the flames dancing under the old, dented kettle. "You know, even though René wasn't great at magic, he could have been the one to… to help Toby break the wards."

The hiss of steam grew louder, but the conversation died while he waited for the kettle's high-pitched whistle. After the water boiled, Caleb carried the kettle to the table and carefully poured steaming water into the teapot.

Fintonclyde didn't stir until Caleb had seated himself at the table, the tea pot between them, then he said, "Since your last visit, I have searched my memories of that time, horrible as it was. Perhaps I misjudged the events that…"

"That led to Toby's execution?"

The old man huddled protectively over his mug and sighed. "And that drove you away."

"You're not the only one at fault," Caleb said gruffly. "I would have left eventually. I had to get out and see the world. It was going to happen one way or another."

"You haven't said much about Romania," Fintonclyde said, peering at Caleb from under bushy gray eyebrows. "Did you find what you were looking for there?"

"I met others like me," Caleb said haltingly. "It wasn't always—I mean, it was different than I imagined."

How could he explain to a human what it felt like to run with a pack after spending every full moon of his childhood alone? He did not have clear memories of those Nights when the moon was full, but he knew the Wolf at a level deeper than memories, knew that in Romania the Wolf had run free with others of his kind. He also knew that on some Nights the Wolf had savagely fought other packs or defended himself and his pack from gun-toting humans with silver ammunition. When not in wolf form, he'd fought with his pack members as often as they'd worked together. Yet for all the bickering, they were a family, the only family he could remember.

"You weren't the first," Fintonclyde said cryptically.

"Here on the island?" Caleb was stunned as the old man nodded gently. "There were other werewolves before me?"

"One," Fintonclyde replied uncomfortably.

"Why didn't you tell me?"

The old man took a sudden interest in the teapot, raising the lid to peer inside. His hand shook as he poured a shimmying stream of liquid into his mug.

Setting the pot back on the table with a thump, Fintonclyde regained some of the bossiness that Caleb remembered from his childhood, insisting, "You were far too young and wouldn't have understood. And it was all in the past, in any case."

"I'm not a child anymore!" Caleb snapped, then, after drawing in a deep breath to calm himself, he said, "And I know a lot more about werewolves than I did back then."

Fintonclyde blinked at him owlishly. "Yes, I suppose you are correct on both counts."

After adding milk to his mug, taking a loud slurp of tea, and rooting around in the box of cookies, Fintonclyde tugged his beard and stared into space, a familiar ritual when the old man was stalling for time. Caleb clenched his jaw and tried very hard not to shout at him to get on with it.

"I came to Dragonshead Island when I was about your age," Fintonclyde began at last. "Before that, I traveled here and there, learning languages and lore, seeking out shamans and healers."

Caleb poured tea and reached for the tin of milk, fearing that he was in for a long, wandering tale. On another occasion, perhaps he'd have been more interested as Fintonclyde rarely talked about the time before he came to the island and, when he had, he often told conflicting stories. Now, however, Caleb felt the need to get back to Sophia as the afternoon waned.

"What brought me here was a dragon's egg," Fintonclyde continued. "It's an interesting story about how I came by that egg, and then I carried it with me for—"

Caleb laid a hand on Fintonclyde's arm, seething with the effort of keeping his voice level. "Another time? You were going to tell me about the werewolf."

"So I was, so I was," the old man agreed reluctantly.

Caleb reached into the box of cookies until his fingers closed around several gingersnaps. He popped one into his mouth, crunching loudly to move the story along.

"It was the summer of 1938—no, 1939, because that was the year that the ghul had a litter of pups—that a cousin of Old Daigle's, a logger from the north country, brought us a werewolf that he'd caught outside his camp when the moon was full. The boy, seven or eight years old, was dressed in filthy rags and had long, matted hair. Well, you know how the local magical community regarded werewolves—"

"—as little more than animals," Caleb finished, remembering the harsh looks from the inhabitants of Tribulation on the few occasions that Fintonclyde had taken him there. The Romanians in the remote mountain village hadn't been much better, although he felt pride at slightly improving human-werewolf relations during his time there.

"It was worse back then, I'm afraid," Fintonclyde said regretfully. "Old Daigle had me build a cage for the... boy. A wooden crate didn't work, because he destroyed it in short order, so I welded together iron bars to make an enclosure that we kept in the barn. During the day, the boy could go out and run with the dogs, but at night...the cage. And when the moon was full, the howling was..."

Caleb stared in horror at the old man's pale face. He tried to form a coherent question, but only spluttered, "Why didn't— How could you?"

"I didn't know. I didn't know," Fintonclyde said softly, throwing him a look that pleaded for forgiveness. "Old Daigle and the others from Tribulation all thought the boy was little better than an animal, a wild dog. And I— I believed them."

"What changed your mind?" Caleb's fist closed around a gingersnap. He crushed it and let the crumbs fall onto the table.

"The boy couldn't be controlled nor did we think he understood us. He never spoke an intelligible word that I can recall. After he killed a chicken and hurt one of the farm dogs, Old Daigle locked him in the cage most of the time and…" The old man faltered, dropping his head into his hands, the next words coming out in a whisper. "The boy refused to eat, snarled at us, and threw any food we gave him back at us. He grew weaker until…until one morning, he didn't move. His body was cold." Fintonclyde shuddered, digging his fingers into his hair. "In the cage I found hidden under the blankets— I found drawings that the boy had made with bits of charcoal on stolen scraps of paper. The drawings were… the drawings were of trees and dogs and… my face, a good likeness. And he had written words, copied from feed sacks and newspapers."

Caleb said quietly, "The boy was no animal." Tears ran down his cheeks.

"When I had the chance with you," the old man murmured, not meeting Caleb's eyes, "I wanted to make it right… but I can never undo what was done to that boy."

Caleb pushed his chair back, the legs groaning and scraping the wood floor, and turned away from the table. He leaned against the sink, one hand gripping the edge, the other tapping softly in an echo of his pounding heart.

The dog barked and scratched at the door. The kitchen had dimmed and outside the sunlight had drained away, rendering the pine trees as brooding shapes against the brighter sky. Caleb looked around in confusion, realizing that the afternoon light had faded because the sun had gone. How long had he been standing there? Stiffly, he shrugged his shoulders to throw off the ache in his back.

After Trixie gave another sharp yip, Caleb let her outside. When he returned to the kitchen, he stood behind a chair, leaning on its back as he wondered again why had he come back to the island. He blew out a long breath through pursed lips, letting the sound die away in the silent kitchen.

"Some things have happened," Caleb said when he could form words again, "and I could use your help."

Chapter 22: You Belong with Me

WHERE IS CALEB?" SOPHIA murmured to herself.

Outside the kitchen, the gloom of early evening was swallowing the back yard. At the table, the boys huddled over the Game Boy as Rudy showed Bela how to play a game involving collecting magical objects while battling evil, as far as she could tell. She knew they were oblivious now, but would be ravenously hungry soon. And she was out of bread and milk and a lot more besides, because she'd mostly been a prisoner in her own house, save for yesterday's disastrous visit with the Hellhounds followed by a couple of hours in the Emergency Room to make sure that Rudy didn't have any fractures after his fall.

"Well, I can't wait," she announced loudly, rattling a set of keys. "Come on, boys. I need to go to the store."

"Can't we stay here?" pleaded Rudy, pulling himself away from the blinking display.

Before Sophia could answer, Bela jumped to his feet and said, "Nope. We all have to go. Orders from Caleb."

Sophia smiled at Bela's eagerness, but wondered if he'd be much help in case of attack. At least, his werewolf senses might provide some warning.

"I could use help picking out ice cream," she answered, slinging her purse over one shoulder.

"Ice cream?" Rudy scrambled to his feet, the game forgotten.

She ushered them out the door, musing on how well bribery worked on eight-year-olds when commands didn't. They piled into the Land Rover because, although the store was only a few blocks away, filling her empty larder would require more grocery bags than she wanted to carry.

Taking Bela to an American grocery store, even the small one in central Bar Harbor, took five times longer than a normal shopping trip as she patiently answered questions about exotic produce—*Bananas, what are those? Is a watermelon full of water? Why aren't lemons called 'yellows' if oranges are called 'oranges'?*—and introduced Bela to the mysteries behind the ranks of glass doors in the freezer aisles: neat little boxes and colorful plastic bags holding too many different foods for her to explain. Meanwhile, Rudy prowled the aisles, tossing things into the shopping cart when she wasn't looking. She spent more time putting back the boxes of brightly colored, sugar-filled cereal and bags of candy.

At the wall of ice cream in the freezer section, Rudy excitedly named each flavor to a puzzled Bela, who understood chocolate and knew strawberries, but wasn't sure how they got the fruit into those boxes. More exotic flavors, like Rocky Road, took longer to explain. In the end, she bought a half-gallon of Neapolitan ice cream to give Bela three flavors to try.

By the time she pulled the Land Rover into the garage, the streetlights had come on and both boys were grumbling about empty bellies, lobbying for ice cream first. She opened the back of the vehicle, marshalling her ravenous, complaining helpers to carry groceries into the house.

"Here, Rudy," she said, holding out the watermelon. "Bela, can you take this bag?"

Bela wrapped his arms around the paper bag she handed him, peering inside critically. "Where's the ice cream?" he asked.

"Nice try," Sophia said, hefting the remaining two bags, as she struggled to close the truck's rear door, "but I've got it here."

"But when we get inside, we can have ice cream!" Rudy said happily, as he took a few staggering steps toward the house, shifting the watermelon in his arms to balance himself.

"I want to try that melon-thingy," Bela called, chasing after him. "Don't drop it!"

Sophia hurried to keep up with the two boys, distracted by their bickering and her growing hunger. Her mind jumped ahead to what she could quickly make for dinner before they staged a revolt and stormed the freezer.

"Okay, Bela," she said, when they stood before the door at the side of the house, "why don't you undo the ward so we can get in?"

Bela gave her a look half-grateful and half-nervous. She nodded encouragement. The boy had an aching need to prove himself, and Caleb didn't give him many opportunities. Bela briefly closed his eyes, brows furrowed in concentration for several seconds. He raised an arm and traced the outline of the door in the air. The edges of the door glimmered unevenly with a faint blue light, and then the whole door pulsed briefly with the same nearly ultraviolet glow.

"After you," Bela said, holding the door open, a small, satisfied smile on his face.

In the kitchen, Sophia tossed the keys on the table and began putting groceries away.

"Can we have some ice cream now? Please, please?" Rudy asked predictably, after watching the carton disappear into the freezer.

"Hmm? No, I'm going to make dinner first," she answered, while looking around for something she expected to see. "I must have left my purse out in the car. I'll be back in a minute, and then I'll start cooking."

Sophia grabbed the keys, realizing that she hadn't locked the car or the garage door, as she'd promised Caleb.

"I'm going with you," Bela said, shadowing her on the way to the door. "Caleb said not to leave you alone."

"Right, let's go," she said, then called over her shoulder to Rudy, "No ice cream while I'm gone, but you can have one cookie before dinner. Okay? Just one."

Outside, few hints of dusk remained in the darkening sky, and the evening cricket orchestra had begun to play. A streetlight shone on the back of the Land Rover, although the rest of the truck lay in the shadows of the garage's dark interior. After opening the car door, she didn't see her purse on the back seat where she'd left it. She conjured a ball of light to probe the dim recesses under the front seats, catching a glimpse of her canvas shoulder bag under the driver's seat. She reached under, tugging on her purse, which felt heavier than usual. She remembered then that she'd bought an extra-large jar of chopped garlic and had tucked it inside, thinking that would make Caleb feel better. She slung the purse over one shoulder and closed the car door.

"Something's not right," Bela called uneasily from the garage entrance.

"What is it?" she asked, turning toward him.

"Something smells wrong..." Bela's face, half-lit by light from the street, contorted with an anxious frown. "Like vampire wrong."

The sound started as the whirring of wings. Behind Bela, the air shimmered like heat rising from the desert floor, quickly becoming opaque and solidifying into a human form with a soft sigh like air rushing out of a leak.

Sophia gasped. The figure that had materialized, wearing dirty jeans and a gray hoodie, was terrifyingly familiar.

Bela whirled around with a wordless shout and lunged at the vampire. With reflexes quicker than a human's, the vampire rushed forward, grabbing Bela's shirt and pinning him against the outer wall of the garage. Bela punched and kicked, but the vampire didn't loosen his grip, shaking the flailing boy like a rag doll. Sophia heard a dull thud as the back of Bela's head smacked into the siding. The boy gave one grunt of pain before crumpling into unconsciousness.

"Stop!" Sophia screamed as the vampire turned toward her, hooded face deeply shadowed.

She tried to run, but her sluggish body slowed like a spent wind-up toy, while a buzzing sound swelled around her. The air itself vibrated like a sad, lonely harmonica. She listened, couldn't stop listening, was mesmerized. There was a tune, not a melody exactly…if only she kept listening, she might work it out.

"Don't hurt him," was all she could croak, the breath driven from her lungs.

With a shrug, the vampire released his hands from Bela, who slid down the wall, then flopped into a heap on the driveway. The vampire pushed off his hood. His black eyes trapped her like a wasp in amber.

"Hello, Sophia," said René Cousineau. "Let's go for a ride."

* * *

SHE WAS LYING ON a thin mattress or a blanket. The fabric felt damp, as if she'd been sweating through a fever dream, but she shivered from the cold, clammy air that sucked away her warmth. She forced herself up on her elbows and then pushed her body into a sitting position. Wrapping her arms around her knees, she pulled them to her chest to stop the shaking as waves of nausea overtook her.

Sometime later, she opened her eyes; she'd stopped shivering and the world no longer spun around her. To her left, a light hung in the air. Sun? Her fuzzy mind worked slowly to process what her senses reported. Not sun, fire. The hazy nimbus around the light hurt her eyes. She knew when she'd seen these weird auras before. She raised a trembling hand to her neck and her fingers contacted sticky ooze. She didn't need to look to know that it was blood, her blood.

Forcing her eyes to focus, she told herself that she'd been through this once before, and she embraced the woozy weirdness as something that would pass eventually. Did it take as long to recover from the second bite as from the first? This wasn't a question that she'd wanted to raise with Caleb.

More time passed. How much, she couldn't say, but she had the feeling she'd been staring at the light for minutes... or hours?

Take stock, she told herself. *You're going to feel better and, when you do, you need to figure out what happened.*

Start with the light, glowing like a fat yellow carrot in a bowl: the globe of a lamp... a kerosene lamp? The lamp dangled from a bare metal pipe that ran above her, disappearing into darkness. She was in a cellar, looking up at water pipes. Her confused mind triumphed at the realization.

To her right, she felt the contours of a stone wall, cold and slick with moisture. Behind her, rough-planked wood met the stone foundation, forming the corner where she sat.

She extended her left arm, brushing a hand along cold, damp dirt. Her exploring fingers felt the fabric of her purse, and she wanted to weep with joy at finding something familiar. Closing her hand around the strap, she dragged the canvas bag to her side. She was breathing hard after she wrestled the strap over her head and across her chest. Another small triumph, which required resting until the shaking went away.

To the left of the lamp, a thick wooden support, like a square tree trunk, ran up into the dim recesses of overhead beams. A few feet beyond that, the dark shape of a bear reared up on its hind legs. She blinked, realizing that couldn't be right. Next to the wall sat an old-fashioned black cast-iron furnace with rounded metal curves and pipes poking from its sides like arms. Beyond the furnace, a shovel leaned against the side of a shadowy coal bin.

Other senses returned. The cellar smelled damp and musty: a sickly-sweet odor of mold mixed with decay. Small animals had died here, and she did not want to find any of them. She heard no other sounds, except for the faint hiss of the lantern and her ragged breathing.

But someone had brought her here. Or she had come willingly?

What had Caleb said? *After each bite, it gets harder to resist the song. Eventually victims want to give themselves to the vampire.*

She concentrated on memories as murky as the dim corners of the cellar around her. She had realized who'd attacked her after they'd pieced together the events of six years ago. Had part of her known after the first bite? She had dreamed about him, hadn't she? But it had been more than a dream that night under the full moon. She hadn't resisted then and, foolishly, she'd thought she could resist if it happened again.

Fear shot through her belly and flowed into her veins, dissipating the paralysis in her arms and legs. Pushing her back upward in an attempt to stand, she scraped along small pieces of metal attached to the wall. She turned, hands on the stone foundation for balance, to find hinges marking the edge of door with a metal latch. She jiggled and pulled, which moved the door a little. Something on the other side held it tightly shut, a padlock perhaps from the *bump-bump-bump* noise when she rattled the latch.

Turning away from the door, she staggered across the small cellar, and stumbled into the furnace, scraping a palm against metal. *Great*, she thought, inspecting the ragged line of blood on her hand, *vampires won't be able to resist me now.* She sucked on her palm to stop the bleeding.

From opposite the lantern, she heard a rattling sound. Leaning against the cold shell of the furnace, she made out a flight of steps descending into the cellar. Weak light from outside trickled down the steps as a set of storm doors were opened from above with a groan from rusted metal hinges. Was there anything she could use as a weapon? As weak as she felt, the shovel standing on the other side of the furnace might have been miles away. Groping inside the purse slung across her chest, she felt nothing useful, except perhaps the jar of garlic.

Shoes slapped the stone steps. Then a figure emerged into the light wearing dirty jeans and a gray hoodie pulled over his head. He thudded on the cellar floor, face in shadow. As he stepped toward the empty mattress in the corner, he pushed the hood from his head, revealing the scarred face of her old friend René. Oddly he didn't have that weird aura around him, the one she'd seen around Caleb after the first bite.

"Sophia?" he called, his body jerking oddly as he turned to scan the cellar.

She shuddered involuntarily, lurching away from the furnace to collide with the wall.

"There you are," he said slyly, breaking into the least reassuring smile she'd ever seen. "I brought this for you. It gets cold down here, I think."

She stared at the plaid wool blanket in his outstretched arm, open-mouthed, for several thudding heartbeats, then croaked, "What? You don't know?"

"Cold doesn't bother me so much now." He laughed weakly, advancing to stand between her and the lantern.

She shook her head, sliding along the wood-planked wall away from him, not trusting herself to step into the open without falling.

"Here. You take it," he insisted petulantly and threw the blanket at her feet: the culmination of a humanitarian mission for which she should be grateful.

As she edged away from him, the kerosene lantern lit the side of his face. He looked exactly as she remembered, except that the familiar navy-blue cap no longer covered his missing right ear. As a child, she'd become accustomed to the lunar landscape of René's face: the scars from the fire that had destroyed his family's home and killed his younger sister. She'd felt sorry for him then and had stood up for him when other children had taunted him. No matter how young he looked, he wasn't a boy any more, with those empty eyes sunken into his scarred cheeks.

No, don't look at his eyes, she cautioned herself as her hands found the rough metal of the rusty and useless door latch.

"Aren't you happy to see me, Sophia?" he crooned softly, the song hiding under his words like a shark just beneath the ocean's surface. "I missed you. You were away for a while, but now you're back and I... I can't wait much longer. But he's back, too, isn't he?"

Don't look into his eyes. Don't look into his eyes. Don't look into his eyes.

"Who?" she whispered, stalling.

"Caleb, of course. Why did he come back? He should never have come back," René concluded with a petulant whine. "But that's not going to matter soon."

"Why not?" she stuttered as he took a step toward her.

"Because... you'll see."

She risked a glance at his face on which hunger warred with anguish. Fighting to turn her head and look away again, she could only grind her teeth in frustration as her treacherous body refused to obey.

He smiled, stretching out a hand and stroking her cheek. "Oh, it doesn't hurt or anything. You just wake up and... things are different."

"After..." She faltered.

"After the third bite," he finished with satisfaction.

He was close now, though she couldn't feel warmth or hear breathing. That strange humming rose around her, making the air dance and buzz, as something alien drilled beneath her skin and crept into her mind. A sudden strangling claustrophobia began to crush her chest like a giant fist.

"How—" she gasped, fighting to get air into her struggling lungs. With great effort, she forced herself to look away from him, though her head wanted to turn and gaze into those soulless eyes. "How did you become… like that?" she rasped as words died in her throat.

"Remember when we found the smuggler's tunnels, the ones that went from that cove up to Lilac House?" he answered, moving closer and stroking her neck.

"T-T-Toby took us there on a b-b-boat he b-b-borrowed." She flinched, tightly shutting her eyes, but that didn't prevent him from invading her mind.

"You remember," he said, his fingers now playing across the fresh puncture marks on her neck. "I was exploring those tunnels, while you and Toby were, I dunno, somewhere else, and I woke up this vampire, who did what we do in those situations."

His tongue caressed her neck. Part of her yearned for teeth to sink into her flesh and end the terror, but another part screamed inside her head that she needed to run away. Now.

"So, that was it?" she ground out between clenched teeth.

"No, of course not," he answered, pulling away from her, shaking his head. "That's not how it works at all."

She risked a glance at his face, which betrayed irritation.

"This vampire, he wanted to get into the house, but I didn't know how, so he made me come back and bring Toby. If Toby could get into the house, then he promised me that I could be like him forever."

"So, all you had to do was dare Toby to break the wards around the house," she said, slipping away from him by sidling a few inches along the wall.

"Well, that was easy." He chuckled, coming closer again. "Toby could never resist a dare. And when he did break the wards, there were vampires inside the house, lots of them. Toby tried to fight, but he didn't stand a chance."

The triumphant note in René's voice sickened her. She turned disgust into a shield, expelling the lethargy that had crept into her muscles and her mind, and feebly shoved one hand into his chest to push him away.

"You killed Toby," she breathed. She wanted to scream, but could only manage a weak gasp.

"Not me," René replied smoothly, clamping a hand around one of her wrists and pulling her closer. "I heard it was the Tribunal that executed him" —he gripped her jaw with his other hand, forcing her to face him— "for helping the vampires."

His eyes, blacker than jet, doors into another world, held her like a fly in a spider's web. His smile revealed pointy canines glinting in the lamplight. Sophia slipped beneath the surface of consciousness as the light around her dimmed and the buzzing filled her head.

"Hey, Frenchie! You in there?"

René flicked his head in the direction of the voice, which came from outside the cellar. "Not now," he moaned, releasing his hand from her face. "What does he want?"

Sophia slumped, freed from the vampire's spell as his eyes were drawn to the stairs that led out of the basement. Shoving her down onto the mattress, he said quietly, "Don't say a word. Not a single word."

She opened her mouth, but found her throat constricted painfully when she tried to scream. Her hands clutched at her neck, in a futile effort to shake off the weird paralysis.

"I know you're in there, Frenchie. Do I have to drag you out?" From outside, someone called to René, almost certainly another vampire. One had been enough trouble, but she didn't know if she could resist a pair of them.

"Okay, okay," he answered, turning away from her and scuffling up the stairs. "Not so loud."

She tried again to scream, but to her dismay she still couldn't utter a sound even after he'd gone. Though silenced, she could move. She got to her feet shakily, leaning on the wall for support. Outside she heard an argument in progress.

"What do you want, Mickey? I'm kinda busy right now," René said churlishly.

"Really? Whatcha got down there?"

"Nothing, nothing. That was a little joke." René tittered nervously.

She pushed away from the wall, stumbling a few feet until she could throw her arms around the thick wooden support in the middle of the cellar. She remembered the old coal chute in the basement of her aunt's house. Once upon a time, she'd been able to evade her cousins during hide-and-seek games by wriggling up the dusty chute.

"Really?" Mickey, the other vampire, asked skeptically. "Anyway, the Boss sent me to find you."

"Oh, you're working for him now, are you?" René said with a high-pitched giggle.

"No!" Mickey shot back. "It's just that, well, Her Ladyship thinks anything we can do to get him to leave town… Never mind that. The Boss says you gotta come."

"Why? What does he want? He doesn't know where I am, does he?" René's words jangled with panic.

"Don't worry, I didn't give you away," Mickey reassured him. "And no self-respecting vampire would consider this a place to rest. I mean, I been down there back in the day. Does it still have rats?"

"No!" René protested. "Well, I think I got rid of all of them."

Sophia focused on the old coal bin four or five feet away, one part of her mind still on the conversation. One, two, three steps, and then she clutched the edge of the bin. She closed her eyes and concentrated on breathing.

"Proves my point," Mickey said. "Listen, some stuff happened and the Boss says he needs your help."

"What stuff?" René asked suspiciously. "Maybe he's just saying that so he can get back at me."

"Look, I don't got all night, so let me lay it out for you. The Doc is kinda out of it, because she…" Mickey hesitated. "Well, she, er, she bit a werewolf."

Sophia peered into the shadowy coal bin. Dim light filtered through a dirty, rectangular window set in the top of the wall; the window had iron bars on the outside. The furnace hadn't been used in decades, and there hadn't been a coal chute for decades, either.

"What?" René asked.

"Yeah, your old pal Caleb O'Connor. He got into her lab somehow and…"

"Serves him right," René said gleefully.

"Oh, no, you don't understand. Biting one of them makes you sick, really sick, like when dogs get rabies. I don't know what it does to werewolves, but Lady Agatha says it's worse for us."

She turned away from the coal bin and scanned the cellar, hoping in the lanternlight to see something she could use as a weapon, because the stairs were the only way out. Her fingers closed around the handle of the shovel next to the coal bin

"Is there a cure or a vaccine?" René asked, becoming agitated.

"*Back in the old country*," Mickey said sarcastically, "the Boss would chain them in the dungeon until they got better or he got tired of their screaming, but there's a little problem with that. Caleb O'Connor stole all the Doc's doses *and* that notebook where she writes all her recipes or formulas or whatnot. For a couple of days, she was raving mad, but Lady Agatha told the Boss to give her a lot of extra blood."

"Did it work?"

Sophia gripped the shovel's handle with both hands. She fought to hold it upright as she made her way across the cellar toward the bottom of the stairs, wincing at the noise when the shovel slipped and the metal tip scraped dirt.

"Sort of," Mickey said. "We had to sacrifice good ol' Dave. Yeah, he took one for the team. The Doc still looks like crap, but she's coherent more of the time. And, boy, is she mad about that notebook. The Boss figures you can tell him where this Sophia lives and that'll lead him to Caleb O'Connor."

"Sophia?" René squeaked. "No. I can't do that! I was just about to leave town. Didn't you tell me I should get out of town? We're— I mean, I'm leaving tonight. Yeah, that's right."

She rested when she reached the first step with a giddy sense of accomplishment for having made it this far. Six or seven more steps? She could do this! She carefully balanced the shovel while adjusting her shoulder bag to rest in the small of her back. She gripped the shaft of the shovel in both hands like a battering ram, preparing to ascend.

"We?" Mickey asked. "I know you don't got no friends but me. But you really had a thing for this Sophia. You didn't do what I think you did, did you?"

With each step Sophia took, her legs wobbled less and her confidence increased. At the top of the stairs, daring not to breathe too loudly, she poked her head through the open storm doors. She spied two sets of legs in the dimly lit area behind the building that had been her prison. The two arguing vampires stood a few feet from the top of the stairs on a paved area, grass growing through cracked asphalt.

"I don't know what you're talking about!" René shook his head in denial. "I told you, I'm leaving town. That's all."

"What's down in that cellar?" Mickey asked suspiciously. "Maybe I'd better check."

"NO!" René shrieked as Sophia staggered from the top step onto the pavement, swinging the shovel in a rough, shaky arc. It flew out of her feeble grip, knocking into the vampires' ankles, then clanging uselessly on the ground.

René, his mouth in a round "O" of surprise, stared up at her from the ground where he'd fallen. The other vampire looked like a boy of about Bela's age with the same curly black hair and thin frame, but he hurled curses at her more appropriate for a grizzled old sailor than a teenager.

Panting from exertion, Sophia willed her leaden legs to move. She lurched past the surprised pair, trying to run but only managing to stumble ten feet before she fell to her knees, her bag clunking on the ground beside her.

René struggled to his feet, pushing away the shovel, which struck Mickey on one of his legs. Another torrent of cursing ensued.

"Please, Sophia!" René pleaded as bore down on her. "You don't understand. You and I will be together. Forever."

Thrusting a hand into her bag, desperate for anything that could be used as a weapon, her fingers closed around the jar of garlic. Deciding that it might be more useful as a projectile than anything else, she lobbed it at René, now looming over her. Instead of connecting with the vampire's midsection as she'd hoped, her puny attempt sent the jar crashing to his feet, where it shattered on the pavement.

The sharp tang of garlic filled Sophia's nostrils. She wrinkled her nose and tried not to sneeze, but the vampires reacted more strongly.

"My eyes! I can't see!" René wailed, bent over with his hands on his knees.

Mickey eyes went wide at the cloud of toxic vapor coming for him. He looked down in horror at the splattered blobs of chopped garlic on his shoes and stumbled, falling backward onto the pavement.

Sophia scrambled to her feet, not sure how long the garlic bomb would delay pursuit. She lurched into a dimly lit alley. Breathing heavily, she jerked her head from side to side. The ends of the alley seemed impossibly far away.

She turned left and managed a stumbling run, wanting to put as much distance as she could between her and the groaning vampires. Hulking, unfamiliar shapes of parked cars huddled along the sides of the alley. She passed a dark crevice between two buildings, then doubled back. Nothing was visible in the blackness, but something tickled her memory. With a quick glance into the alley to check for pursuers, she entered the passageway, trailing her hand along one wall. She was several feet from the alley when she ran into a large metal object blocking the passage. Her hands made out the boxy hood and peculiar recessed front grille of the Land Rover. She fell against the hood, never so glad to see the old heap.

She heard René stagger into the alley and call her name piteously. But she felt no pity, only a crazy exhilaration at still being alive.

She forced her shaking fingers around the handle of the driver's door, praying to whatever gods might protect her against vampires. Some deity heard her desperate plea, because the door cracked open: unlocked! Summoning strength that she didn't know she had, she pulled on the door and fell into the seat. *What if the keys weren't here?* She could try to barricade herself inside, but the vampires might be able to break in.

"Sophia, please," René pleaded, throwing his body heavily across the hood of the truck. "You belong with me!"

In response, she locked the door. The vampire's eyes were fixed on her, but his face was twisted with panic. She didn't think he'd be able to mesmerize her now. Her hand reached around the steering column, feeling a fresh jolt of energy as her fingers touched the keys.

"Get out. Get away," she said through clenched teeth, not caring if he could hear her.

The engine started. She put the transmission into first gear. The Land Rover jumped and almost stalled as she nosed out of the narrow passage, while the moaning vampire held onto the side of the truck. Once in the alley, she cranked the steering wheel and revved the engine. As the truck lurched between parked cars, René fell to the ground. She made it to the end of the alley where she recognized landmarks; she wasn't far from home. In the rearview mirror, she had one last glimpse of her old childhood friend crumpled on the ground.

Chapter 23: The Price of Protection

EET POUNDING. STAIRS. FEET slapping. Bare floor. From behind.

Caleb jerked his head up. His neck cracked sharply and his shoulders spasmed from the sudden motion as he twisted in the chair.

Rudy stood in the doorway, his face screwed up with worry.

Caleb wondered what he looked like to the little boy: bleary-eyed and unshaven with wild hair, a hostile expression on his face in an unconscious response to being dragged up from the depths of sleep. Seeing Rudy's distress, he forced a smile.

"Mmm. What time is it?"

"Breakfast time?" Rudy answered warily.

Caleb pushed himself to stand, his back and shoulders screaming from being folded into the hard kitchen chair for too long, his fuzzy mind reeling from too little sleep. Sunlight slanted in through the kitchen windows. He shuffled across the room and squinted at the numbers on the stove's digital clock. 7:38. Four hours of sleep? Maybe?

With a sudden stab of last night's terror, Caleb remembered finding Bela crumpled in a heap on the driveway with a goose egg on the back of his head. His panic had grown as he'd walked the streets and back alleys of Bar Harbor, desperate for any sign of Sophia or the missing Land Rover. Far worse had been admitting defeat after his search had turned up nothing.

He'd returned to the house around one in the morning to find Bela and Rudy asleep in the living room. Rudy hadn't stirred when Caleb had carried him to bed, but Bela had startled awake, confused and panicky. He had soothed the boy with hollow words of reassurance, but that had been enough to induce Bela to sleep. Then he'd paced the kitchen, going over and over in his mind where he'd searched and what he'd missed, telling himself that when morning came, he'd find her.

A little after two, the familiar sound of the Land Rover's engine had yanked him out of a miserable meditation on the consequences of his failures. He'd run outside as the truck pulled into the driveway, Sophia alone at the wheel. The relief had hit him like a punch to the gut; he'd doubled over, hands gripping his legs to keep from falling down, while gasping with relief.

After making her drink the herbal concoction that she hated, he'd been able to coax her to sleep around three. She hadn't been coherent, but she'd been sure about the identity of her abductor. The bite mark on her neck had needed no explanation. Other details, such as where she'd been held or why Mickey had arrived unexpectedly, would have to wait.

"Sophia always cooks breakfast," Rudy insisted, suddenly appearing at Caleb's side and staring up at him with the unsaid question written across his face like a newspaper headline in 48-point type: *Where's Sophia?*

Caleb blinked. Hadn't Rudy been on the other side of the kitchen? Had he lost time?

He squatted to look into the boy's anxious eyes and put a hand on his shoulder. "Sophia's sleeping now. She got... lost last night and didn't feel well when she came back. But she's okay. She needs rest, is all."

Rudy nodded solemnly at the reassurance, which was more or less true. The boy had already been through so much. Caleb wanted to spare him the added pain of knowing that Sophia, the person who had promised to take care of him, had been kidnapped by a vampire.

"Right. Let's make breakfast," Caleb said with forced cheerfulness, standing and running a hand through his unruly hair.

"I know how to cook bacon," Rudy said hesitantly. "Sophia showed me."

"Okay. Get the bacon out of the fridge." Caleb yawned as he reached for a cast-iron frying pan hanging on the rack above the range.

He settled the pan on a burner, carefully adjusting the flame underneath. After setting a plate on the counter next to the stove, he ripped sheets of paper towel to layer on the plate, silently counting out *one-two-three*. Too tired to talk, he pulled a piece of bacon from the package and carefully placed it in the pan, gesturing for Rudy to do the same.

Hissing turned to sizzling. Rudy poked the bacon with a fork as he peered over the edge of the frying pan. Caleb watched the boy for a few minutes to make sure he had things under control, while his mind drifted and his stomach rumbled at the aroma filling the kitchen. Rudy had wandered off into fantasy land: he talked to the bacon as he prodded sizzling pieces, telling one strip to stay away from its neighbor, asking another if it was ready to turn over.

Caleb set a mug on the counter and fumbled with the tea canister, prying the lid off after several tries. His head throbbed and his gut ached. Lack of sleep, combined with anxiety, churned inside him like an oozing, corrosive sludge. The lightheaded relief at Sophia's return last night had come crashing down, replaced by the realization of how close he'd come to losing her forever, and of how he'd put Bela in danger by blithely assuming that a fourteen-year-old with no experience could defend himself against a vampire. He needed a plan, he needed help, and he needed his head to stop pounding.

A cup of tea wasn't going to be enough, he thought as he extracted a tea bag and flipped it into the mug. As he filled the kettle from the sink, he heard feet pounding down the stairs. Caleb turned, holding the kettle in one hand. Bela stood in the doorway, a fearful frown on his face as his gaze swept over the Sophia-less kitchen.

Putting the kettle on the counter with a clunk, Caleb crossed the room, while from the stove, Rudy piped up, "Bela! I'm cooking bacon!"

Bela smiled weakly, raising a hand in a tentative salute. After Rudy turned his attention back to the pan, Bela asked hesitantly, "Did she... is she?"

"She came home, and she's going to be okay."

Bela plunged his hands into the pockets of his jeans as words spilled out like air rushing from a popped balloon. "I'm sorry, so sorry. You told me to protect her and... I tried, I really did, but he was stronger than me—"

Caleb placed his hands on Bela's shoulders. "I told you last night, it's not your fault. You've never had to deal with a" —he turned his head quickly to the kitchen behind him, where Rudy was again engrossed in his cooking project— "with one of them before."

"Did she get...?" Bela said, flicking an anxious gaze at Caleb.

"Yes," Caleb hissed, holding up his palms up like he was pushing away thoughts he didn't want to think and words he didn't want to speak.

"Well? Did she know who it was?" Bela asked loudly.

"Keep your voice down," Caleb whispered. He wasn't ready to speak the name that he'd heard from Sophia's lips last night as she'd rambled incoherently. At first, he'd thought that her vampire-addled mind had confused dreams of their dead friend with her attacker, but when she'd told Caleb how René had laughed at the great joke of tricking Toby, pieces clicked into place like the final twist of a Rubik's cube. As Caleb had paced the kitchen in the wee hours of the morning, he'd agonized over all the clues he'd seen but not understood, both when they were kids and since he'd been back. They all pointed to the truth that René, their bumbling, tag-along childhood friend, had joined the Undead.

"We'll talk about this later, okay?" Caleb said wearily, giving Bela's shoulder a squeeze intended to be reassuring.

Bela nodded, dropping his head to avoid meeting Caleb's eyes.

"Right," Caleb said, letting his hand fall from Bela's shoulder. "Do you want to make pancakes? I know I've showed you how."

"Yeah, sure," Bela mumbled without much enthusiasm, but as eager for a change of subject as Caleb.

Bela emerged after searching the refrigerator carrying a carton of eggs with a stick of butter balanced on top and cradling a quart bottle of milk in his other arm. Caleb found the rest of the ingredients, set them on the counter, and then put the griddle on the range.

After coaching Bela on how to make the batter, Caleb settled at the table with his hands cradled around a mug. He'd only taken a few sips when there was a knock at the front door.

"We expecting someone?" Bela called.

Caleb rose, puzzled. "Fintonclyde is coming over today, but it's too early for him to be on the mainland."

His apprehension grew as he reached the big oak door. He focused his mind on releasing the magical ward that protected the entrance before cracking the door open by a few inches.

Agent Hulstad stood on the front porch, clad as always in a black suit, crisp white shirt, and skinny black tie. Instead of his black briefcase, under one arm he carried a large package wrapped in brown paper and tied with string. Morning sunshine behind the agent gave him a halo, so that he looked like a stained-glass saint bearing a holy relic.

"Rough night, Mr. O'Connor?"

"Tired, just tired." He made himself yawn for the effect. "What can I do for you?"

"I have some news, and this," the agent said, indicating the package under his arm.

"You might as well come in," Caleb said, swinging the front door open and gesturing for the man to step into the hall. While Agent Hulstad set his package on a small table near the door, Caleb silently restored the ward.

Metal clanged on the kitchen floor, followed by loud swearing in Romanian.

"Do you want some breakfast?" Caleb yawned, this time genuinely and ignored Bela's outburst. "Or tea?"

"Tea would be acceptable," the agent replied.

"This way," Caleb said, pointing to the door into the kitchen at the other end of the hall.

Bela, waving a spatula in the air, popped his head above the counter of the kitchen island. The boy eyed the agent suspiciously. "Nothing to worry about. Just lost a pancake."

"Have a seat," Caleb offered, gesturing to the chairs around the kitchen table.

He filled the kettle again, tossed a teabag in another mug, and wondered about the reason for this early visit from the agent while he waited for the water to boil.

At the kettle's whistle, he poured water in the second mug and carried it to the table. "Milk? Sugar?"

"Milk, thank you," Agent Hulstad said politely in his unsmiling way.

"Where's your partner this morning?" Caleb asked, placing the bottle on the table, to make conversation more than anything else.

"Surveillance."

"Ah," Caleb answered noncommittally, choosing a chair across the table from the agent as if they were about to begin a game of chess.

"And he has the task of liaising with the local Health Department," Hulstad said, pouring milk into his tea. "We are requesting that they close down the Lobster Pot."

"Oh? For what reason?"

"They will find one, Mr. O'Connor. In my experience, once you start looking in the dark corners of a kitchen, you can always find sufficient code violations, no matter how fancy the place. And you've given us reason to understand that the Lobster Pot is not a fancy place."

"Hardly. They serve beer and fried everything, according to Tom's wife," Caleb said with a laugh.

Rudy slowly approached the table, hands gripping either side of a plate mounded high with bacon and set the plate down like he was serving breakfast to royalty. Caleb's stomach rumbled. He realized that the last thing he'd eaten was a gingersnap yesterday afternoon. Unable to resist the warm, greasy strips, he snatched one.

"Good job, Rudy," Caleb mumbled with his mouth full.

"Don't eat all the bacon," Rudy said, fretfully eyeing Hulstad as if the thin, taciturn agent were likely to gobble up the entire plateful. "We have to save some for Sophia... for when she wakes up."

"Good point," Caleb said, getting up from the table. "Why don't you help me set the table. Get knives and forks, okay?"

While Rudy carefully counted the flatware, Caleb took plates from a high kitchen cupboard. As he arrayed them on the table, he leaned close to Agent Hulstad, murmuring, "There have been other developments."

"Yes, there have been. An extremely suspicious death for one—"

"Want some?" Caleb interrupted, as he plucked another strip of bacon from the pile. Extremely suspicious deaths were best discussed out of earshot of the two boys. The agent shook his head. Using the bacon as a pointer, Caleb gestured at the doorway leading into the hall.

"Last night, there was another... incident," Caleb said to the agent as they left the kitchen. "Sophia was kidnapped by a vampire and..." His mouth felt dry, and his voice failed him for a moment. Through the doorway, he heard Rudy chattering to Bela as he finished cooking pancakes.

"Miss Daigle? Did she survive?" Agent Hulstad asked in a matter-of-fact tone as he extracted the little notebook from his jacket.

"Did she...survive?" Caleb repeated faintly.

Agent Hulstad stared at him expectantly, pen hovering above the page.

"Oh, I see what you..." Caleb tried to pick up the thread of the conversation, wondering if he had lost track of time again. "Yes, she escaped. She made it back here. But not before she was bitten a second time."

"Your Mr. Brody had a busy weekend," the agent commented, scribbling notes.

"Cuza? No, it wasn't Cuza the first time *or* the second time," Caleb said, the rising anger at René's betrayal focusing his scattered mind. "The vampire that bit Sophia was an old friend of ours who... It's a long story. But what do you mean by 'Mr. Brody had a busy weekend'? The vampires got someone else?"

Agent Hulstad, who didn't have a spontaneous bone in his body, flipped through a few pages in his notebook before reciting: "Body found on Main Street yesterday evening, neck broken. David Alroy, 63, unemployed, known to have spent most days at the Lobster Pot. Too much damage to the neck to identify puncture marks, but Mr. Alroy was missing a great deal of blood."

"Cuza's not being subtle anymore," Caleb said.

"I have come to that conclusion as well, Mr. O'Connor."

Caleb paced the hall while gnawing on the bacon. He'd warned them this would happen. Now someone was dead, left on display by Cuza to taunt them. Would it have happened if he hadn't taken away the notebook and the serum?

He turned to face the agent and asked, "What are you— What are we going to do about it?"

"We have confirmed that the SOG can be here by tomorrow or the day after."

"Uhm, SOG?"

"Special Operations Group. We discussed this with you on Friday."

"Right. Right. I remember." Caleb stumbled through the memories of a weekend in which so much had happened that he might as well have had that chat with the agents a month ago. "And you're going to close down the Lobster Pot so that the regulars won't become vampire fodder. What about the rest of the town?"

"Agent Gallo and I will keep the Lobster Pot under surveillance until backup arrives. After that, we'll have the resources for an assault, if needed," Hulstad replied. "We could use your help in this, Mr. O'Connor."

"Help with surveillance or assault?" Caleb asked, confused.

"Descriptions of the BFIs would be more useful," the agent replied reproachfully, pen poised over paper.

Caleb readily described Cuza and René, but not the others. He had a suspicion, perhaps no more than a desperate hope, that Lady Agatha might be persuaded to help him. She had made it clear that she wanted nothing to do with Cuza.

"There were a few more with Cuza, the night they attacked us," Caleb explained, "but only the wolves saw them. I think you'll agree that wolves are not reliable witnesses."

"Hmm," the agent murmured, not looking up from his notes.

"What's in there?" Caleb asked, pointing to the paper-wrapped package.

Agent Hulstad gave him a narrow-eyed stare for a few moments before reluctantly putting away his notebook. He pulled on the string around the package, causing the brown paper to open like a flower. Inside lay a black dome-shaped lump, dull like an enormous sooty beetle. Caleb cocked his head at the object, not understanding what it was until the agent held it up.

"A vest," Caleb said, light dawning.

"More specifically, a Level Three vest," Hulstad explained in his toneless manner, "which should be protection against a shotgun blast or even a .44 Magnum bullet, but not armor-piercing rounds."

"How about an arrow?"

"You're joking," the agent said mirthlessly.

"I wish I were. One of the Hellhounds was killed with a silver-tipped arrow," Caleb said, not able to keep the bitterness from his voice. After wiping his greasy hands on his jeans, he took the vest, viewing it from several angles, then running a finger across the strange black material. "I thought you said you weren't getting gear until those special operations guys showed up."

"Correct. This is my vest, which I could loan you, provided—"

"Provided I work for you," Caleb finished.

"I believe there will be mutual benefit to an arrangement," the agent said smoothly. "We could use help from someone with your knowledge of Extraordinary Aliens. And you have no love for BFIs."

The vest offered protection, but also obligations that Caleb wasn't sure he wanted. He gingerly set it down. "I help you find werewolves so that you can—what was the word you used the other day? —neutralize them? Because I can't be part of that. I can't be part of what you did to the Hellhounds."

"We have done nothing to the Hellhounds since they've been in Maine," Agent Hulstad replied blandly.

"What about what happened in Florida eight years ago? A bystander, a *human* bystander, was killed at the full moon, probably by that special operations bunch," he countered, folding his arms as he took a step back from the agent.

"Ah, that incident. That was regrettable," Hulstad said, as if he were talking about some minor bureaucratic slip-up.

"You keep lists of all the werewolves in America, don't you?" Caleb growled, not satisfied that the Agency had the best interests of his kind at heart.

"I will remind you that the name of our agency is the Registry," Agent Hulstad said. "We also keep lists of BFIs, all the ones *we know about*. Every year there are deaths that appear to be the work of BFIs, likely the ones that we *don't know about*. We're betting that you can help us find them."

"Hey!" Bela shouted from the kitchen. "Pancakes are getting cold."

"In a minute," Caleb called back, twisting his head in the direction of the kitchen. He massaged his neck with one hand while rocking his head from side to side in an attempt to stop the sharp pain lancing down his spine. "You spy on all these werewolves—"

"We prefer to say that we register them."

"Whatever," Caleb said, rolling his shoulders to dispel the pain. "You don't like it when they, uhm, do what werewolves do, and sometimes you might overreact, like you did in Florida."

The agent started to object, but Caleb held up a hand. "Hear me out. You want me to teach your agents to recognize vampires and werewolves. Fine. I can do that and help you hunt vampires. But what if I could work with the werewolves directly? Back in Romania, I showed the local packs how to stay away from humans at the full moon by..." He wasn't willing to talk about the magical wards he'd created in the mountains to maintain a safe separation. "...by finding special places for them. Anyway, what if I did that here?"

"Train werewolves?" Agent Hulstad asked skeptically.

"We're not dogs, you know," he shot back. "I mean, more like educate werewolves."

"An unusual proposal, Mr. O'Connor," the agent said as he placed the black vest on the paper, carefully wrapped it, and then re-tied the string. "I'd have to run it by HQ, see what they think."

"Well, what do *you* think?"

"It has some merit," Hulstad conceded. "I've been with the Agency for almost twenty years, and I've seen things go wrong, like the incident in Florida, that might have been prevented. Give me some time to talk to

Washington about your idea. In the meantime, consider the vest to be a loan."

The agent patted the paper-wrapped package and quirked his mouth into the closest thing to a smile that Caleb had ever observed on his stony face.

Caleb smiled back and said, "Pancakes? They're getting cold."

Chapter 24: Until Further Notice

LARGE GLASS WINDOWS FLANKED the salon entrance on Main Street, allowing passersby to glimpse wealthy women getting perms and pedicures, and above the door, a broad awning proclaimed *Chez Mimi* in script featuring an excess of curlicues. Around the back, though, a weathered door in need of painting was considerably less chic. A blonde with dark roots and gnawed fingernails leaned against the door, smoking and staring absently down the alley, but when Mickey approached, she gave him an annoyed glare as if he'd interrupted deep thoughts on the nature of the universe.

She exhaled a cloud of smoke at him and said, "What do you want? Delivery or something?"

"Lady Agatha? Mind if I go in?" Mickey asked, sidestepping the smoke. Just because he didn't breathe, didn't mean he liked cigarette smoke in his face.

"Sure," she said with a bored shrug.

He edged around her through the door, stepping up a half-flight of stairs into a shelf-lined storeroom full of towels, plastic bottles filled with mysterious goop, and gaudily colored boxes featuring pictures of pouty women with long, glowing hair. From the salon's main room, he heard the high-pitched chatter of women's voices and smelled a panoply of odors: perfume, soap, acrid chemicals, and mortals, so many mortals, which put his senses on high alert.

He planted himself in the doorway to the salon's main room; women in pastel pink smocks rested underneath bulbous hair dryers or sat in chairs, while other women curled, painted or snipped hair. Everywhere were mirrors, surrounded by hundreds of tiny lightbulbs. And mirrors were not vampires' friends. He spotted Lady Agatha seated near the rear of the shop, both hands resting on a metal tray, while a woman with brassy red curls carefully painted her long nails a shade of purple that he knew, from years of listening to the mind-numbing ins-and-outs of fashion, to be mulberry.

As he sidled across the room, Lady Agatha glanced at him, frowning. "What are you doing here? I didn't expect you for hours. Aren't you working today?"

"Er, not exactly, Your Ladyship," he mumbled, knowing that the sharp-eared ladies around him would spread gossip like a high wind spreads a wildfire. "Something's come up and I need to talk to you."

"Can't it wait? I'm having lunch with Mrs. Winchell," she said, nodding her head toward an elderly woman dozing under a hair dryer, "and her nephew, who's up from New York for the week. Handsome, single, and rich, she tells me. And he has a yacht."

The manicurist giggled.

"Great. Sounds great. But I need to talk to you," he said urgently. "In private."

"If you must," Lady Agatha said with a long-suffering look at the manicurist.

Mickey gratefully fled through the storeroom and out the back door, as Lady Agatha laughed, confiding to the manicurist that her driver must have something to tell her about oil changes or tires or something else terribly dull. He balled his fists into the pockets of his leather jacket and paced the alley.

"Well? What is so terribly important?" Lady Agatha demanded when she emerged, high heels clacking down the steps. Over a flowery dress in shades of purple, she wore a pink smock embroidered with more of that curlicue-infested writing that gave a guy a headache.

"Jeez, that place gives me the creeps. All those mirrors? Don't people in there notice they can't see your reflection?"

"Pfff!" She waved a hand dismissively. "I merely convince them otherwise."

He looked both ways along the alley, making sure they were alone, before saying, "I parked the car behind the bar after I dropped you off, thinking I was going to do a shift, but it was closed."

"Closed? What do you mean?" She stepped into the alley, a tiny furrow appearing on her normally smooth brow.

"I mean closed like there was a sign on the door saying 'Closed Until Further Notice by Order of the Health Department.'"

"The *what?*"

"Some government thing, I guess. It had an official-looking seal, anyhow."

She crossed her arms and stared at him through narrowed eyes. "The government? Like those faceless men who used to raid the bars back in the day?"

"Not sure, but the Boss hasn't been real, er, discreet the last couple of days," he said, dropping his voice lower. "Poor old Dave got dumped outside like a dead bird on the sidewalk. People notice stuff like that. I think the Boss is losing it, you want my opinion."

"I won't disagree, but you pushed him over the edge by telling that werewolf where to find the scientist."

"How was I supposed to know that O'Connor would show up at her lab and take her stuff? Or that she'd be stupid enough to bite him?" Mickey fought down irritation. They'd had this argument already. Lady Agatha had put two and two together when Cuza had asked her advice on the possibility of a quick "cure" for the Doc.

She inspected her newly painted nails for a moment. "Hmm. Perhaps Cuza will take the hint and leave Bar Harbor."

"The Boss, he's got a thing for vengeance. Don't I know it," Mickey said sourly. "And he ain't going quietly."

"I suppose this werewolf might take care of our problem for us," she mused.

"And if he don't?" Mickey countered. "We could go hibernate for a few years, but O'Connor might come looking for us. He knows how to get into the crypt."

"Most vexing." Lady Agatha waved a hand in the air, like batting away an annoying insect. "And none of my gentlemen here to protect me."

Mickey knew better than to observe that the "gentlemen," like Guy de Mornay, had been useless in her defense.

"Your Ladyship, maybe it ain't my place to say this, but we gotta take out Cuza." He gazed down at his boots. Silence, which stretched for an agonizing minute, prompted him to glance up quickly to see if she was going to yell at him.

"This business," she began, knitting her brows. "I should never have agreed to any of it: buying the building, running that bar, and the science experiment that has gone horribly wrong. There are times when one of us endangers others of our kind and we must take action to eliminate the danger. Do you understand me?"

"Er, taking out Cuza?"

"Crude, but accurate," she said, tapping long mulberry-colored nails against an arm. "Sometimes one must contemplate…"

"What?" he asked, both horrified and curious. The thought of finishing off one of their kind made him queasy, although this was Cuza they were talking about.

"St. Florian's Fire," she murmured obliquely, then shook her head with regret or maybe distaste. "This is not something that I relish undertaking without allies."

"Caleb O'Connor?" he put forth hesitantly. "If we can trust him?"

She considered this, a finger resting on her chin. "Although he is a were-wolf, perhaps he is someone with whom one could negotiate. Certainly, more rational than Cuza." She snapped her fingers and ordered, "Pick me up after lunch at the Harborside and we shall talk further."

Lady Agatha turned in a swirl of pink and purple and disappeared back into the salon.

* * *

"Thinking about getting a tat?"

"Huh?" Mickey whirled around to face a burly man in a tank top with bright yellow hair cut into a Mohawk and well-muscled arms covered with tattoos.

"These are only some of our designs," the man gestured to the pictures pinned up on the wall. "We do custom ones, too."

"Just looking at your, er, designs, because my friend, she… she wants to get a tattoo, but she's too scared to come in, so I told her I'd check it out."

"That's cool, man. We ink all kinds of people. And we sell ice cream," the man added with a grin. "Helps bring in the families, you know? Give the kiddies something to do while mom's getting that butterfly tattoo she always wanted."

Right on cue, a woman in her early thirties, sunburned and exasperated, herded three children into the shop, all clamoring for ice cream.

Ignoring them, Mickey directed his gaze across the street at the Haddock Building, a squat, two-story structure with dark brown weathered siding, except for the two large windows bordered by cream-colored wooden trim on the ground floor shop. A rainbow-colored riot of kites hung over the shop windows and fluttered in the slight breeze.

From his vantage point, he could see into the alley running from Main Street to the back of the building. Behind the building, an old garage leaned in the shade of an ancient maple, overgrown bushes crowding its sides and tickling its sagging roof. The garage's siding, once white, had lost so much paint that the remaining streaks looked like snow blowing sideways in a blizzard. The battered roll-up door to the garage had several panels missing. Anyone could try to crawl in, and the raccoons and foxes probably did. But the old garage was so full of junk that a human would find it hard to squeeze in that way. Around the back there was another door, smaller and locked, that provided entry into the dim, stuffy interior and access to a trap door in the floor, which dropped into a Prohibition-era tunnel that led straight to the kitchen of the Lobster Pot. When the feds raided the old speakeasy, patrons had needed an escape route that would keep them from embarrassment and out of jail. Frenchie favored the old tunnel, owing to his paranoia about being recognized. Or maybe he enjoyed sneaking around in the dark.

The garage was of little concern to Mickey. He fixed his eyes on the front of the Rolls Royce visible between the building and the ruined garage. The car was right where he'd left it after depositing Lady Agatha at the salon. Except now a fat guy with dark sunglasses and a black suit was leaning against the hood and eating an Italian sandwich, a cigar-shaped bun stuffed with meat and cheese, oil dripping out with each bite.

Mickey strolled across the shop to the counter where the part-time tattoo artist was mashing a scoop of ice cream into a waffle cone.

"Hey! Who's that guy across the street? The one with the black suit," Mickey asked.

"Beats me. I only seen him this morning," the man said, handing a triple-decker cone to an eager little girl. "You want my opinion, he looks like a cop."

"Yeah. He sure does," Mickey said absently, heading for the door as he donned his sunglasses.

Black Suit finished his sandwich, balled up the wrapper, and tossed it under the car. *What about all the oil you dripped on my hood?* Mickey thought angrily as the guy extracted a paper napkin from a jacket pocket and wiped his hands. The goon strolled down the alley, turned onto Main Street, and disappeared into McCarthy's, a convenience store that sold cigarettes, soda pop, and candy.

Out on the sidewalk, Mickey slipped from one gaggle of tourists to another, crossing the street a block away from the Haddock Building. He looped behind nearby buildings to approach the decrepit garage from a back alley. He tried not to rattle the bushes too much as he made his way to the front, where he sheltered behind the trunk of the large maple, scanning the area around the Rolls for any movement. No one seemed to be nearby. This was his chance.

"Psst!"

Mickey started back, bumping against the warped wooden siding of the garage.

"Where'd you come from?" he whispered sharply at the sight of Frenchie, face hidden inside his hood, hands jammed into the pockets of his jeans, which still stank faintly of garlic. *Did Frenchie have any other clothes?* he wondered, and then thought better of it, not wanting to know the answer.

"Oh, been hanging around here," Frenchie mumbled, trying to sound nonchalant, like hiding out in bushes was a regular thing for him.

"Cuza kick you out after you gave him what he wanted?"

Frenchie nodded jerkily, a familiar whine in his voice as he asked, "Last night, you didn't tell him about her, did you?"

"I don't work for the guy and I don't have to tell him nothing. But it was a really stupid move, kidnapping that girl."

"But now she's in more danger!" Frenchie said with a moan.

"More danger than you biting her for the third time?"

"Yeah!" Frenchie bleated, pacing around a small circle in the shade of the maple, head bowed. "I was going to free her so we could be together, but Cuza, he made me tell him where she lives and he's going to send Vito and Donnie to her house to—" He stuck a fist into his mouth, stifling a scream.

Mickey yanked Frenchie behind the shelter of the wide trunk, nervous that Black Suit would reappear. "Listen, this girlfriend of yours, did she buy into your plan? 'Cause she didn't look sold on it last night when she threw that garlic at us, which was a mess, by the way. I was lucky to get that stuff off my boots."

"Uhm, not yet, but once she sees what it's like to be one of us, it'll be okay," Frenchie whispered.

"If she survives the Change. You think about that?"

Frenchie's eyes went wide.

"Not everyone survives the third bite. Jeez, you're so dumb." That started Frenchie shaking like a marionette controlled by a drunken puppeteer.

"Stop that!" Mickey said and slapped the quaking face with the back of his hand. "Tell me about the guy who was watching the building just now. Ever seen him before?"

Frenchie slumped against the garage with arms wrapped around his chest. When he finally spoke, he'd regained a bit of self-control, although he mumbled at his feet without making eye contact. "Okay, I was hanging out here, just watching the place, 'cause I didn't know what I should do. Should I try to talk to Cuza again, should I go back to Sophia's—"

"Cut to the chase, will you?" Mickey snapped.

"There were two of them in those black suits. They got here around opening time with a third man, not dressed like them, just a regular-looking guy carrying a clipboard. They went into the Lobster Pot and came out about fifteen minutes later. The one with the clipboard taped a paper on the door. One of the guys in black suits has been hanging around since then. I didn't see what they put on the door. I was too scared to go look."

"Health Department notice, saying the place is closed. Looks official. The Boss really screwed this up," Mickey said. "Where's the other suit? I only saw that fat guy dripping stuff all over my car."

Frenchie looked up, a nervous twitch his only response.

"Okay, beat it," Mickey ordered. "I gotta get the car and I don't need you making a scene about it."

"What am I going to do?" Frenchie wailed, pawing at Mickey's jacket.

"First, you're going to take your hands off me, then you're going to keep your voice down," Mickey said, pushing him away. "Look, the Boss don't care about your girl. The only thing he wants is that notebook of the Doc's. He thinks O'Connor has it at her house. You get that book for the Boss, and you'll be right with him. He'll stop paying attention to your girl and you can snatch her, which is still a dumb idea, by the way." He smirked. "But you know we can't go into a house unless we're invited in."

"What? That's stupid!" Frenchie squeaked. "We go into the Lobster Pot all the time."

"The bar sort of belongs to us, so it don't matter. But if it's someone's house, you have to get an invite, otherwise you can't cross the threshold."

"What about windows? Or holes in the wall?"

"Death and damnation! It's old magic, and I ain't got no rulebook. Now beat it."

He swung around, away from the shaking Frenchie, to scan the alley and the area behind the building. Empty. He casually strolled out of the shadows.

Look at the mess that ape left on the hood! he grumbled to himself as he crossed in front of the Rolls. He wanted to stop and clean it off, but he thought better of it. As he stood next to the car, key in the lock, he sensed cigarette smoke and knew he wasn't alone.

Unlocking the door unhurriedly, knowing that cops sensed fear the way vampires sensed blood, he slipped inside, locked the door, and then made a show of carefully fitting the key into the ignition. Black Suit rapped on the window, his knuckles leaving oily smears while his mouth moved.

Mickey tapped one ear: *Can't hear you, pal.*

The other man scowled and made a circular motion with one hand: *Roll down the window, you jerk.*

Looking up in exaggerated exasperation, Mickey rolled the window down an inch. The guy managed to blow cigarette smoke inside the car before he started giving Mickey the third degree.

"This your car?"

"No." Stony silence, then he said with a weak grin, "I ain't stealing it, if that's what you mean. This car belongs to my employer, a very rich lady who is expecting me to pick her up, and I'm already late."

"You know anything about this place?" Black Suit asked, inclining his head slightly toward the back of the building.

"I know this is a good place to park," Mickey answered with a calculated mix of boredom and irritation. "Don't nobody bother the car if I leave it here."

"You haven't seen any funny stuff going on here?" The guy had to shout through the tiny opening, sweat dripping down his forehead.

"Nope. I gotta go, mister. I told you, my employer is going to be pissed if I'm late."

"Too bad. You're not going anywhere until you answer my questions."

A cop, all right, but not one of the locals, Mickey thought. This guy was more like the G-men that had come snooping around if you made your own hooch or ran a bookie operation. What had Cuza done to attract this much attention?

Mickey pushed the sunglasses up on his head, putting on his innocent face, and said, "You look familiar. Haven't I seen you somewhere before?"

"I'm asking the questions here!"

"No, no, something about your face," he said, rolling the window down all the way. "Or maybe it's the sunglasses, but I swear you look just like a guy I met in Boston a few years back. No, wait, Charlestown. There's this place—what's it called?—Sal's? Sally's? I don't exactly—"

The guy yanked off his sunglasses, growling, "Shut it! I said I'm asking the questions!"

A slow smile crept across Mickey's face as he hummed softly, focusing an unblinking stare on Black Suit's dark, piggy eyes. "Look at me. That's right..."

The man's jaw went slack and his face morphed into a lumpy potato with a curly mop of black hair. Mickey contemplated chomping on the guy, but thought better of it. Black Suit had a partner who could show up any time now.

"You work for the feds?" Mickey asked, his eyes not leaving the other man's.

Black Suit nodded slowly, like he was dragging his head through molasses.

"What's up with closing the bar? You looking for something or somebody?"

"Brody. Watching the place until backup gets here," the man replied in a dull monotone, his eyes glazed over.

Backup. Mickey had heard about the raids on the speakeasies from the old-timers. Backup meant a horde of G-men breaking into the bar, looking for Cuza. He didn't want to be anywhere near the Lobster Pot when that happened.

"You didn't see me, you got that?" Another slow nod from the mesmerized man. "You walked to Main Street and when you came back, the car was gone. Now repeat that back to me."

"I walked to Main Street," Black Suit echoed in a flat voice. "When I came back, the car was gone."

"Now, take a step back," Mickey droned slowly and deliberately. "Now take another… another…" Black Suit bumped against a covered metal trash barrel next to the building. Mickey continued in the same monotone, "Sit on that trash can. Right. You're going to take a nap, because you are so, so sleepy."

The guy was snoring before Mickey turned the engine over and shifted the Rolls into first gear.

Chapter 25: Interludes Over Drinks

YOU WANT ANOTHER ONE?"

"Huh?" Mickey jerked his head up in confusion.

The bartender in front of him critically inspected a wine glass before hanging it on a rack overhead. Harborside's dimly lit, silent lounge didn't open for another hour, but the bartender didn't mind Mickey's presence, because he knew that Lady Agatha was a frequent customer and tipped well.

"Yeah, whatever," Mickey mumbled, pushing the empty glass across the bar. He'd been nursing a shot of whisky for the last hour and hadn't noticed that his glass was empty.

"Lucky for you I got some decent rye," the bartender said, as he refilled the glass. "They want to turn this place into a fancy wine bar. You know the markups they're charging on wine? It's criminal."

Mickey grunted an answer and sank back into an uneasy reverie, vaguely aware of the sounds of glasses clinking in the background. He was navigating a narrow, twisty road at high speed, while being chased by enemies. *Who to trust?* His kind weren't generally loyal or honorable, but you stuck by them because they were your kind and because everyone else was against you. Immortals had no love for werewolves, but this Caleb O'Connor, the first werewolf Mickey had ever met, didn't seem like the crazed stake-wielder that Cuza had made him out to be. And Cuza, who'd been his mentor a long time ago, harbored a long-simmering hatred and desire for vengeance on the Arghezi family. *Who was an enemy and who was an ally?*

"Can I get you anything, Miss?"

Mickey wobbled on the bar stool, yanked out of his inner maelstrom.

"Perhaps a Perrier?" came a voice from behind him.

After the bartender poured the softly hissing drink, Mickey handed it to Lady Agatha as he tried to clear his head. She slipped a bill from her purse, sliding it across the bar with a smile. Crooking a finger at Mickey, she strolled toward a small table in the darkest corner of the lounge.

"I had a delightful lunch," she began, settling into a chair. "And a dinner invitation for this evening. After that, I expect we shall have a long drive along the coast, and you know what that means."

"Yeah, right," he answered mechanically without the excitement he normally felt when Her Ladyship lined up a new victim.

"Do sit down," she said, glaring up at him. "You are hovering, and I do not like hovering."

"Listen, I gotta tell you about some stuff," Mickey said, folding himself into a chair. He paused at the approach of the bartender, who set his neglected whisky glass on the table. After the man retreated to the bar, Mickey continued in a low voice, "When I went back to get the car, this guy was watching the building: black suit, sunglasses. He was a fed."

"A what?"

"You know, a G-man, like in the old days when those guys would come into town looking for illegal hooch. Anyhow, Frenchie told me about how a pair of these feds shut the bar down."

"Frenchie? What was that little maggot doing there?"

"Hanging around in the bushes, as usual. He's jumped up about this girl that he's been sweet on since they were kids and now he wants to make her one of us."

Lady Agatha waved a hand dismissively.

"Yeah, I know. This girl don't want to cross over, if you get my meaning. I tried to tell him, but Frenchie won't hear none of it."

"I fail to see how this is relevant to the problem at hand," she said, irritation lurking beneath a cultivated air of boredom.

"That dog O'Connor is staying with this girl, and he's probably stashed the Doc's notebook at her house. I'm betting Cuza will get his goons to grab it or maybe grab the girl and bargain for it."

"And if he kills O'Connor in the process, that might make life simpler," she said thoughtfully.

"But those G-men, they got what they call backup on the way."

"Backup?"

"I didn't get much of an explanation, but I think it means a lot more feds, maybe a raid on the bar, like in the old days."

She inspected her polished nails before looking at him with a mischievous smile. "Perhaps they will eliminate Cuza. Life would be much simpler that way."

"Er, Your Ladyship, you own that building. And the feds are gonna ask questions," he said uncomfortably.

"I shall tell them that I am a silly woman with money to invest who was charmed by that scoundrel Peter Brody." She took a sip of her drink, frowning. "Hmm. I wonder if this werewolf was sincere about an alliance when he forced his way into the crypt."

"I don't think O'Connor has sold us out, if that's what you mean. That guy who was watching the building, he didn't know me from Adam, just asked if I knew about any funny stuff going on there. I figure if O'Connor was going to blab to the feds, he'd have told them what I looked like."

"Then for the present, let us keep our werewolf liaison to ourselves."

"And?" he asked nervously. "We can't hide out for long, unless you want to load up the trunk with gold bars and get out of town. Even then, they're gonna know what the car looks like."

"I suppose I must make the attempt to dissuade Cuza from his insane and dangerous course," Lady Agatha concluded without much enthusiasm.

"And if he ain't persuaded? Are we going to take him out?"

"Please, do not be so crude. First, I shall try to reason with him. Do not laugh. An attempt must be made."

"And then we take him out?"

* * *

"NOT THIS AGAIN!" SOPHIA wrinkled her nose as Caleb set a steaming mug of vile-tasting tea on the table beside her.

Caleb settled into one of the weathered Adirondack chairs at the edge of the large grassy area between the chicken coop and the vegetable garden, where Rudy and Bela tussled with Trixie the yellow Lab.

"Afraid so," Caleb said with a chuckle, which her fed her irritation.

Fintonclyde, seated on Sophia's other side, patted her hand and observed blandly, "You've been through a lot and need to get your strength back."

Easy for him to say, she thought testily. *He doesn't know what it's like to be bitten by a vampire.*

She'd only been awake for an hour, but she didn't feel as wooly-headed and strange as she had after the first bite. But then she hadn't realized that she'd been bitten, but this time she knew. Last night, she had gazed into that dark country that was not death, but wasn't life either. Was this the Purgatory of her Catholic upbringing or something else? She didn't have much time to ponder theological questions, because as soon as she'd awoken, Caleb and Fintonclyde had thrown question after question at her. At least if she drank Caleb's tea, she didn't have to answer more questions. She lifted the mug with both hands, blowing across the steaming surface to delay the moment when she'd have to take a sip.

"How does this fellow Mickey fit into the picture?" Fintonclyde asked, worrying the details of Sophia's vampire adventure like a dog with a bone.

"I'm not sure," Caleb replied, frowning. "He made it clear to us that he wasn't working for Cuza, and yet... What was it he said, Sophia?"

"He'd been sent to get René by someone..." She sipped the tea, trying not to make a sour face as she sorted through the tattered scraps of last night's memories. "I don't remember exactly, but I don't think he said Cuza."

"Mickey wasn't too crazy about Cuza," Bela added, flopping down in the grass at their feet. "And that Lady Agatha, she called him a worm."

"True. Neither of them gave the impression that they'd do Cuza's bidding. There may be other vampires involved, though," Caleb said.

"Good thing Mickey showed up last night, 'cause that gave you time to think up a way to escape," Bela said to her with an awed appreciation that she found touching.

Caleb gave her a warm smile, saying, "And escaping from vampires is not so easily done."

She took another sip of tea, hoping Caleb wouldn't notice that her hands were trembling. The memory of René's huge black eyes and the leer on his scarred face as he got closer and closer to her neck haunted her. But far worse than the face of her Undead friend was the knowledge that part of her had wanted to surrender to him, to cross over into that dark country. Only part of her. Another part had resisted.

Setting the mug down, she said, "René made me mad, talking so casually about how he'd got Toby killed. And when I was angry, I didn't feel so—I don't know—paralyzed?"

"Perhaps a strong emotion like anger can neutralize the song of the vampire for a short time," Caleb said. "Although I wouldn't count on this working again, if you find yourself face-to-face with René."

"You didn't have any trouble resisting that scientist at the Jackson Lab," she said, eager to move the conversation away from her vampire ordeal.

"Or those two down in the crypt," Bela added. "And what about your girlfriend back home?"

Caleb reddened, throwing an irritated glance at Bela.

Delighting in Caleb's discomfort, the boy continued, "Caleb had a vampire girlfr—"

"I met a lot of vampires in Romania," Caleb interrupted, "and none of them were able to mesmerize me. I don't think their powers work on werewolves."

A vampire girlfriend? She gave him a sidelong glance.

"You won't have to worry about René," Caleb said gruffly. "We've strengthened the wards on the windows and doors."

"I hung garlic on all the windows!" Bela piped up.

"I've nailed up that loose board in the crawlspace," Caleb continued, "which isn't going to make Rudy happy, and put screens on the attic vents."

"The attic vents?" she asked.

"Places where a bat might try to fly in," Caleb explained. "Starting tonight, we'll be taking shifts patrolling the house. You'll be safe as long as you stay inside."

"A prisoner in my own house, is that it?" she said angrily. She should be more grateful, she knew. She should be kinder, but at the moment she felt too scared and too tired for gratitude or kindness.

Caleb sat silently brooding without answering her. Trixie dropped a slime-covered tennis ball flecked with mud and grass at Bela's feet. The boy ruffled the panting dog's fur, and then threw the ball hard enough to bang against the fence surrounding the chickens, who clucked loudly, swirling around one another in consternation.

"C'mon, Bela! Let's play tug-o-war," Rudy pleaded.

Bela seemed more interested in the grownups' talk of vampires than playing, but didn't have the chance to answer Rudy's plea. The sound of a rattling tap on the gate diverted everyone's attention. Jumping up, Caleb sprinted across the lawn, accompanied by the dog's excited barking.

"May I come in?" The flat voice of Agent Hulstad came from the other side of the gate.

Sophia swiveled her head as the tall, pale agent advanced across the lawn toward her. After offering his chair to Hulstad, Caleb remained standing, arms folded tensely.

"Ms. Daigle, you appear well today," the agent said, sitting beside her.

"All because of this lovely tea that Caleb makes me drink," Sophia said, pretending for Caleb's sake that her insides weren't a quivering mass of jelly.

"Any news?" Caleb asked.

"I have confirmation that the SOG will arrive in Bar Harbor tomorrow midday. As for the situation on the ground here" —Agent Hulstad flicked through the pages of the familiar little notebook— "we entered the Lobster Pot at 11:05 this morning, accompanied by a representative from the Health Department. Inside were two employees of the bar, Mr. Rizzo and Mr. Mancuso, and one patron, Mr. Emerson. Neither employee knew the whereabouts of Mr. Brody."

"They're not going to tell you," Caleb scoffed. "If they're working at the bar, they're probably vampires."

The agent coughed in irritation. "I will continue, if I may. The kitchen was inspected; sundry irregularities and code violations were noted. A suspension order was served. We departed."

"Did you search the whole bar?" Caleb asked. "There might be places where Cuza could have been hiding."

"Our writ extended only to inspection of the kitchen," the agent intoned. "We departed at 11:27. At that time, Agent Gallo commenced surveillance of the Haddock Building, while I proceeded here to watch Ms. Daigle's house. Agent Gallo subsequently reported that at 11:49, a black Rolls Royce of antique vintage pulled into the lot behind the building. The car was parked there until approximately 12:30 P.M. Agent Gallo did not witness the departure of the car as he was patrolling the other side of the building—"

"A big black car?" Bela interrupted. "That's—"

"Weren't you going to play tug-of-war with Rudy?" Caleb asked sharply.

"Yeah! You said!" Rudy insisted, planting himself next to Bela and glaring down at him.

"Fine," Bela said with a snort, giving Caleb a disgusted look as he got up from the grass.

"What Bela was going to say," Caleb continued smoothly, "is that we've seen that old Rolls parked around town."

The agent jotted a note, before continuing: "As I was saying, Agent Gallo could not provide a description of the driver nor any passengers of said automobile."

"Doesn't that seem suspicious to you?" Sophia asked hesitantly, remembering how René had rendered her mute with a single command when she'd been under his spell.

"In what way?" Agent Hulstad bristled.

"I'm not saying Agent Gallo was doing a bad job," she said slowly. "I'm suggesting that maybe he was influenced to not remember. I can tell you that vampires mess with people's minds, wipe out their memories, or, in some cases, plant false ones."

"Ah!" Fintonclyde said brightly. "That is not limited to vampires."

She glared at the old man, while discreetly mashing her foot on top of his. Now was not the time for a discourse on other magical means of altering memories.

"It is possible," Caleb said, "that Agent Gallo encountered a vampire who made him forget the driver of that car."

"Interesting," Agent Hulstad murmured, scribbling away.

"I'm not sure it's a good idea to leave Gallo there on his own. It might be better to have two of you there, if you see what I mean."

"Ms. Daigle's house also requires surveillance," the agent objected.

"We have it well in hand," Fintonclyde said cheerfully.

Sophia hoped he was right.

* * *

WINGS OVER BAR HARBOR, the store that occupied the ground floor of the Haddock Building, teemed with kites hanging from the high ceiling like a comic-book version of a natural history museum: instead of pterodactyls and whale skeletons, there were leering dragons, undulating cobras, and giant rainbow-colored butterflies floating on invisible threads. The dense shelving that crowded the walls held packaged kites plus all the other standard tourist fodder.

The proprietor of the kite store, a plump and sunburned man in his mid-forties, stood behind the counter, helping an older couple who had a grandchild in tow. The boy, six- or seven-years-old, pointed excitedly to one kite after another, unable to make up his mind.

The woman looked up and made a sour face. "Ugh! Was that a bat?"

"Heh-heh, no," the proprietor said. "The kites wobble a bit in the breeze,

I expect. They do that sometimes. Will you excuse me? I need to check something."

He scuttled from behind the counter and through a doorway leading into the back of the store.

"Oh!" the proprietor gasped upon seeing Mickey and Lady Agatha, the latter patting her blonde curls back into place. "Mrs. Pilkington, I didn't hear you come in. Is there a problem? Rent's not due for another two weeks."

"We need to speak with Mr. Brody downstairs on a small matter, nothing to concern you," Lady Agatha purred in her most charming upper-class accent.

"Not to worry," Mickey said, twirling a key chain around a finger and nodding toward a door on one side of the room.

Lady Agatha smiled, fixing an unblinking stare on the man. "Take care of your business, and we will take care of ours. Good day."

The man nodded woodenly, did a one-hundred-eighty-degree shuffle, and beat it back to the front of the store. After the man's footsteps had faded, Mickey unlocked the door and held it open, but hesitated.

"I should go first," he insisted, gesturing to the dimly lit stairwell, a Prohibition-era relic from the days when the ground floor had been a supper club with access to the speakeasy below.

"Really! Do you imagine I need protection from Cuza?" Lady Agatha asked.

"No, Your Ladyship," he replied hastily, unwilling to voice the possibility of ambush below. "But there's another door at the bottom that's tricky to open."

Mickey walked carefully down the stairwell, standing at the bottom to listen for movement on the other side of the door before opening it. He scanned the empty, silent kitchen which, for once, did not smell like hot, rancid oil.

Lady Agatha pushed past him impatiently, heading for the swinging door between the kitchen and the main room. She made a grand entrance, surveying the room like an actress waiting for applause. He crept in after her and slipped behind the bar out of habit.

Nina Patel sat on a bar stool, scribbling on a yellow legal pad. Three days after biting the werewolf, the puffiness on the Doc's face had receded, leaving greenish-yellow blotches on her cheeks and forehead. Around her, sheets of yellow paper covered with writing had piled up like fallen leaves underneath an oak tree.

"You!" Nina Patel cried, scattering sheets of paper like an autumn gust of wind.

"I wish I could say you were looking better, dear," Lady Agatha addressed the scientist in a syrupy tone.

Cuza's head jerked up from the pool table just as he'd been lining up a shot. The tip of the pool cue ripped into the felt of the table and a ball jumped, cracking loudly when it hit the floor, followed by the noisy clatter of the abandoned cue.

"Lady Agatha, how nice," Cuza said through clenched teeth. "Please, sit down. Have a drink."

"Tell me what is 'nice' about the present situation," she shot back, arching her eyebrows.

"Mickey! Make the lady a drink!" Cuza ordered imperiously.

Mickey leaned his elbows on the bar top and glared, even less willing than usual to take orders.

Lady Agatha tsked dismissively. "I do not think that you will be serving drinks anytime soon. I am informed that you have been closed by the Health Department."

"That? A trifle, a misunderstanding. Do not concern yourself with that," Cuza replied with a broad smile, a smile that didn't extend to his tight, narrowed eyes. "I speak with the right people and it will be fixed."

"Think you can bribe or bully your way out of this like in the old country?" Mickey sneered. "You got the feds on your tail, and they ain't so easy to bully."

Cuza dropped his smile for an instant, looking uncharacteristically baffled.

"Federal agents," Mickey said slowly and carefully, "from I-don't-know-where. But that don't matter. There's a guy watching the place right now, and they've got more coming."

"Feds!" Nina Patel giggled, her twitchy eyes darting around the room.

"They complain that our kitchen is not clean. That is all," Cuza said.

"A pretext, obviously," Lady Agatha observed. "They are interested in more than the kitchen."

"Like poor old Hal, there." Mickey pointed to the comatose bar patron lying on the bench of one of the booths with his head lolling against the wall. "I guess you're saving him as a snack for the Doc, and then you'll dump the body, like you did with Dave. I get the feeling these feds are looking for immortals. And if you leave more dead bodies around this town, it'll be like a trail of bread crumbs."

"What Mickey so colorfully expressed," Lady Agatha said, "is what I have been saying for some time: you have drawn far too much attention to us and there will be consequences."

"I'll fix everything!" the Doc slurred drunkenly, patting the pile of notes before her as if rewarding a dog for good behavior. "Just need that one little thing, that little ol' notebook, then everything will be right as rain."

Cuza didn't appear concerned by the ravings of his pet scientist; instead, he insisted, "We will get the book from Caleb O'Connor and the plan will proceed. I have defeated this dog before and I will do it again."

"Where? In Romania? That's a laugh, Boss." Mickey snickered. "You left the old country, tail between your legs, because of O'Connor. And when you tried killing him and his doggy pals here, it didn't work so well."

"Mircea Arghezi!" Cuza roared, lunging at him across the solid oak bar.

Mickey stepped back out of reach of the other's long arms. Cuza rounded the corner of the bar, only to be stopped by Lady Agatha. She thrust herself in his path, holding a hand up, palm out, and then pushed his chest. She merely tapped Cuza, but something about the gesture brought him up short. He fumed, arms held rigidly at his sides as if they were bound with invisible chains. Mickey knew Her Ladyship could wield magic, as his brother Alexandru had done, and he wondered if she had just worked a spell.

"Enough!" Lady Agatha cried. "I want no more of your schemes, your plans, your bullying, which have utterly failed, except to attract attention from the wrong sorts. I provided the money to buy this building. You are a threat to my investment."

"It is Caleb O'Connor who is the threat!" Cuza insisted, jaw clenched.

"A threat to you," she said icily. "I can see none to myself, except to be caught up in your ill-considered schemes. After all, I have not tried to assassinate werewolves nor have I left bodies lying about for the authorities to find."

"Your threats cannot harm me," Cuza said, regaining a bit of the old swagger. "Go back to the shadows, if that is what you want."

"Cannot harm you?" She laughed, mildly amused.

She flicked her wrists, unleashing a writhing column of fire that shot from her cupped hands and singed the old fishing nets that hung from the ceiling. Mickey wrinkled his nose at the smell of burning rope. Nina Patel shrieked, clutching pieces of paper to her chest like a mother hen shielding her chicks. Cuza stumbled backward, eyes wide at the pulsing flame.

"Careful we don't burn the place down," Mickey muttered.

With a toss of her blonde curls, Lady Agatha extinguished the magical fire. Cuza regained his composure, slicking back his hair with one hand as he glared at her coldly.

"You do not need my help? Then you do not need to be in *my* bar," she said grimly. "As I seem to have a soft spot for you, dear Cuza, I shall give you twenty-four hours to leave these premises."

"What? How can you?" Cuza spluttered, losing whatever composure he'd tried to regain.

"She owns the building, Boss," Mickey said, ducking under the counter at the end of the bar so that he could hold the kitchen door for Lady Agatha. As the door swung shut behind them, Mickey heard a long string of curses in Romanian.

Chapter 26: Bats in the Basement

ICK-TICK-TICK. The steady beat of the grandfather clock in the front hall echoed through the empty rooms. During the day, other sounds filled the house: dishes clattering in the kitchen or the gabbling of Rudy and Bela, who didn't know the meaning of quiet voices. With everyone else asleep, only the ticking of the clock filled the intervals between Caleb's footfalls as he patrolled the entirety of the first floor. Occasionally he climbed the stairs to the second floor where Fintonclyde and the boys slept, though he was reasonably sure that Trixie, who had snuggled in with Rudy, would wake if there were intruders upstairs.

Caleb had prepared himself as best he could: Agent Hulstad's body armor, several wooden stakes in his back pocket, and, draped around his neck, the garlic that Sophia had refused to wear.

He heard a faint noise that might have come from the kitchen, but, standing in the center of the large empty room, he saw nothing out of the ordinary and heard only the steady beat of the clock. Odd. Wondering if Sophia had woken, Caleb passed through the kitchen to the short hall on its other side. He stood at her door, which was open a few finger-widths, straining his ears until he heard the sounds of gentle, regular breathing.

She deserved to sleep peacefully. She'd been preyed upon by a vampire and bitten twice, and yet she'd been strong enough to escape from the second attack. She'd been tough when they were kids, too, earning his respect and admiration from the time he was twelve. Growing up, he and Toby and René had all been in love with her, but of course she'd fallen for Toby, the leader of their little gang. Caleb had accepted that he and René could never compete with Toby. But René had felt differently and apparently his resentment had festered undetected.

More noises interrupted his thoughts. The faint sounds of bumping, scuffling, and voices came from the basement. Could Rudy or Bela be wandering around? No, he would have heard them pounding down the stairs from the second floor.

He stole across the kitchen as silently as he could and halted at the door to the basement. From below, he heard a crash accompanied by the sound of breaking glass.

Slowly, he turned the old brass knob and cracked the door open. No lights were visible, but he heard movement: wood creaking and something slapping against a wall. He opened the door wider. Light from the kitchen behind him spilled down the stairs. His shadow fractured into puzzle pieces on the steps. He placed his feet carefully on the wooden stairs, mindful of the creaking. As he descended, a familiar scent made his nose wrinkle in disgust. Vampire!

At the bottom of the stairs, he withdrew the flashlight that he'd stuck in a back pocket, clicking it on. The beam swung to his left, playing over the hot water heater and the furnace, then straight ahead to illuminate shelves that held jars of preserves and stacks of paper goods. Light glinted off shards of glass amid an oozy blob of blueberry jam on the floor. To his right, the beam appeared to strobe on a peculiar object twisting and squirming. The wriggling, upside-down figure was suspended from a rope looped around its ankles; its wrists were bound, and a swath of shiny gray duct tape was plastered across its mouth. From any angle, he would have recognized the scarred cheeks and misshapen ear of René Cousineau.

As the flashlight lit up his face, René whimpered, but Caleb wasn't in a hurry to free his Undead childhood friend from this bizarre confinement until he knew who or what else was hiding in the basement. Someone had done this to René. After clicking the overhead lights on from the switch at the bottom of the stairs, he slowly scanned the basement's dark corners.

From behind, he heard a rustling, then a soft sighing whoosh. Pivoting, he saw a broad-chested, dark-haired man on his left. *Of course!* There was another vampire in the basement who'd hidden by transforming himself into a bat.

The flashlight slipped from his fingers, ringing as it bounced on the concrete floor. Slowly, he withdrew a wooden stake from a back pocket and stepped toward the vampire. Oddly, it stared at him placidly without reacting. Too late to turn around, he heard footsteps from behind. A metal bar slammed into his head and his mind exploded like a firecracker before dissolving into darkness.

* * *

CALEB PULLED HIMSELF UP to a sitting position, his head pounding. Bracing himself against a wave of nausea, he flattened his palms against a chilly floor. Cold, damp air filled his lungs. His body felt heavy and sluggish, not only because of the stiff body armor he wore beneath a baggy sweater. The sticky lump he felt on the back of his head told another story. He'd been expecting vampires brandishing guns and silver bullets, not wielding crowbars.

Somewhere off to his right came the sound of flapping or slapping. He turned his head too fast, making his vision blur. Something dangled from a beam. Odd, almost like a giant bat, albeit one trussed up with duct tape.

Before him plain, wooden stairs led up to... where? Squinting, he saw lights from above, from the kitchen, which meant that he was in the basement. Vertigo nearly overwhelmed him as he pulled himself upright, leaning on the stair railing for support. From above, he heard heavy footfalls crossing the floor, too heavy to be one of the boys and without Fintonclyde's characteristic clomping gait.

Far away, a door slammed as Caleb swayed, unable to summon the strength to mount the stairs. Nearby, the dangling not-a-bat thumped against the wall. Muzzily, he remembered who had been hung upside down.

Time slipped sideways. In what seemed like the blink of an eye, the dog bounded down the stairs, followed by Bela, Rudy and Fintonclyde bringing up the rear. Caleb fought to keep his balance as the dog collided with him, barking madly at the suspended figure hanging in the corner.

"Take him down and bring him into the kitchen," Caleb rasped, his head clearing as he pulled himself up the stairs.

He lurched across the kitchen, fighting off another wave of nausea, and skidded to a stop at the open door to Sophia's room. He caught his breath, clinging to the door jamb, while he peered inside at the tangle of sheets and blankets on the empty bed. Gone. And not just gone: taken, because of his failure to protect the house, to protect her.

He turned away from the deserted room, only staggering slightly on his way down the hall. He leaned against the doorway at the entrance to the kitchen and gingerly touched the back of his head. His fingers felt dried blood matted in his hair and a tender lump underneath.

Caleb heard the *bump-bump-bump* of something heavy being dragged up the stairs. Bela, barefoot and dressed in plaid pajamas, emerged from the basement door, hauling a writhing René by his wrists. Fintonclyde clomped up the stairs, wearing a long, graying night shirt and his heavy leather boots. Between the two of them, they carried the trussed vampire like a pig being dragged to a spit, although the main course at a pig roast didn't usually squirm to get free. Rudy, also in his pajamas, hesitantly peeked out of the doorway as the dog burst into the kitchen, dancing around the vampire and barking angrily at the Undead threat to her people.

René's wide eyes cast about the room, no longer the watery blue that Caleb remembered, but perfectly black orbs that didn't reflect light. His old friend was wearing dirty sneakers, jeans, and a stained gray hoodie over a dark t-shirt. He could have been a hobo or a college kid after a night of partying, except for those eyes.

"You're not getting away this time!" Bela yelled, resisting René's attempts to throw him off balance by knocking his head against Bela's legs.

Caleb crossed the kitchen, steadier on his feet than before, and pulled a chair away from the table. He and Bela lifted the struggling vampire by his shoulders and pushed him down into the chair.

"Help me tie him up," Caleb ordered to Bela, as hot anger solidified into icy rage.

"Yeah, that'll make it easier to put a stake through his heart," Bela said as he untied the rope still attached to René's ankles.

René tried to shove a knee into Bela's face. Caleb clamped both hands on René's shoulders, forcing him down, while Bela looped the rope across the vampire's chest and tied him securely to the chair. Caleb flicked a glance at Fintonclyde who stood rigid with arms folded tightly, glaring at the scar-faced vampire. Maybe the old man finally believed in René's betrayal of his best friend.

After Bela had tied a secure knot, Caleb ripped the duct tape from the vampire's mouth. He took a step back, looking René over clinically. He sensed a vibration in the air, a faint buzzing like an annoying swarm of gnats.

"Nice try, but that doesn't work on us," Caleb said. "Let's have a talk about why you're here and how you got into the basement."

René fixed his black eyes on Caleb's with thin-lipped grimness and rocked the chair, trying to loosen the rope around his chest or perhaps knock the chair over sideways.

"I'll make him talk!" Bela yelled, waving a fist menacingly at their prisoner.

"Punching a vampire isn't going to get us very far," Caleb said, putting a hand on Bela's chest. He took off the garlic necklace that had failed to protect him earlier and looped it over René's head. The vampire shuddered and whimpered, but didn't say a word.

Bela reached behind Caleb and pulled one of the stakes from his back pocket. The boy held up the slender piece of wood by the blunt end a few inches from René's nose. It was about eight inches long and the tip was very sharp.

"Oh, look. What's this?" Bela jeered. "Caleb's finished off a lot of vampires with these."

What do you call the opposite of a poker face? Caleb wondered as he watched René calculate his odds, then shift his expression from truculent to compliant.

"Why don't we start again," Caleb said, taking the stake from Bela and tapping it lightly against his palm. "How did you get into the basement and who tied you up?"

"C-C-Caleb," René stuttered, smiling weakly as he always had when trying to talk his way out of trouble.

"Answer his questions," Fintonclyde ordered gruffly, just as he'd done when they were children.

"Oh, Mr. Fintonclyde, sir," René said as if he'd only now noticed the old man. "Well, sometimes I would get into the basement, before I... when I was, you know, not immortal. But never when Sophia was home! Sometimes I'd just come in to look around at things. Yeah, there's this place where I used to, you know, get in."

"Through the crawlspace under the back of the house," Caleb prompted, wondering why he hadn't noticed that René was a creepy stalker when they were teenagers.

"Right, right," René answered with vigorous nodding. "Sophia fixed it, I guess, because I've been watching the house for the last couple of days, and I saw that boy" —René lifted his taped hands to point at Rudy who sat on the floor with one arm wrapped around the dog's neck— "go into the crawlspace and then come out complaining that he couldn't get through anymore. But I thought maybe I could still get in that way, 'cause it's not like a threshold if you make a hole in the wall, right?"

"Evidently not," Caleb said, filing that piece of information away for later.

René giggled, apparently pleased with his own cleverness, and continued, "So, I found a crowbar and pried up a couple of boards. It made a pretty small hole, but not too small for a bat to crawl through."

"And then you and your vampire buddies snuck in—" Caleb began.

"No!" The horrorstruck expression on René's face appeared genuine. "Vito and Donnie, they must have been watching the house, too. And they sort of followed me in."

"Why did they tie you up like some giant fly in a spider's web?" Bela asked.

"I was coming to warn you, and they tried to stop me. See, I was worried about Sophia, so that's why I came, to try to protect her and also to warn you—"

Caleb silenced him, saying, "Too late. Sophia's gone."

"No!" René wailed, jerking and writhing hard enough to make the chair legs thump on the floor. "They're going to hurt her, maybe kill her! You have to stop them!"

"And why should I believe you? You were the one who tricked Toby into freeing vampires from Lilac House. He trusted you, and we all know what happened to him."

"Caleb, I swear, I never wanted any of this to happen."

"You betrayed Toby," Fintonclyde rumbled, his face cold and hard as a glacier. "I suppose you didn't want that to happen either?"

"No, of course not!" Rene twitched his head from side to side. "But you don't know what it's like when a vampire tries to make you do stuff. You can't— You just can't resist."

"Sophia managed to resist you," Bela spat, then switched to a long string of curses in Romanian.

"Sophia! Yeah! We have to save her!" René bleated, his gaze darting from one stony face to another. "All they want is that book you stole. That's what they told me."

"They? Aren't you all working for Cuza?" Caleb asked.

"Not me! I want to save Sophia!"

"You want to turn her into a vampire, you sheep-stealing piece of—" Bela said.

"Evidence suggests you don't have Sophia's best interests at heart," Caleb cut in. "Where have they taken her?"

"Probably the Lobster Pot. That's where Cuza is, I mean was, the last time I saw him," René blurted out, eager to be helpful. "You just have to give him that book, then he'll let her go, I swear."

"There's nothing you could swear on that would make me believe you," Caleb said flatly.

"How many vampires does Cuza have working for him?" Fintonclyde demanded.

"Those two that tied me up, Vito and Donnie," René answered, eager to please. "And there's that Dr. Patel, but she's not right in the head, so maybe she doesn't count."

"Three, maybe four, total. We can take them!" Bela said eagerly.

Caleb shook his head, pacing the kitchen in a large circle with René at its center. Cuza could mesmerize Sophia, forcing her to break the wards and let him and his vampire stooges into the house. She was like a key that would open the locks and throw the doors wide open. According to Agent Hulstad, the Special Operations squad would show up in another twelve hours, giving Caleb enough help if he wanted to protect the house and lay siege to the Lobster Pot. Could he afford to wait that long? If the vampires attacked, it would be tonight.

Coming face-to-face with the René, Caleb said, "All right. Tell Cuza we'll trade the notebook for Sophia. I don't want to meet him in the Lobster Pot, though. There are too many possibilities for ambush in a basement. We need someplace above ground, more open, if we're going to do a trade."

"What about Oceanside?" Bela suggested. "The drive-in's got a big parking lot and that open space with picnic tables on the other side."

"The drive-in res-tau-rant," Fintonclyde said, pronouncing the syllables slowly as if speaking a foreign tongue. "It is open on three sides, as I recall, but with thick vegetation behind the parking area. Hmm, there are worse places."

"Not a bad choice." Caleb nodded. "Although there'll always be treachery when vampires are involved, no matter what place we choose." He squinted at the glowing blue digits on the stove clock as he juggled times and calculated probabilities. "It's twelve-forty now. Let's say... three. Tell

Cuza to meet me in the parking lot at three A.M. Just him, no one else. He brings Sophia, I see she hasn't been harmed, and he gets the notebook. You got that?"

"Three. Oceanside." René nodded jerkily, then balked. "I don't think he's ever—"

"You're going to tell him where it is," Caleb explained slowly. He slipped the wooden stake back into his pocket while his mind bounded ahead to tactics and defenses and allies. "And you'll do this because you say you want to help Sophia."

"Yeah, help her become a vampire," Bela derided.

Caleb ripped the duct tape from René's wrists and then untied the rope binding his chest. René got to his feet unsteadily, weak from the effects of the garlic necklace. Caleb dragged him across the kitchen to the mudroom. He opened the outer door, but didn't let go of René's arm.

Caleb looked directly into the soulless black eyes without flinching and said softly, "If you betray me to Cuza, you'll be signing Sophia's death warrant. And if you betray me, I will make it my life's work to hunt you down and destroy you."

"Of course, Caleb, of course," René said with a weak and unconvincing smile.

Caleb released René's arm, lifted off the string of garlic bulbs, and pushed him out the door. After the sound of footsteps faded, Caleb returned to the kitchen.

"I don't understand why you think we can trust René," Fintonclyde said with a cold anger that Caleb remembered from his childhood.

"Or Cuza," Bela growled with anger that ran hotter.

"I fully expect a trap," Caleb said, tossing the garlic on the table. "That's why we're going to need some help."

"I can help!" Bela said. "I can do magic. Well, some. And I'm not afraid of vampires."

"Me, too!" Rudy cried from the floor, where he had his arms thrown around the dog as if clutching a life preserver. "I want to help rescue Sophia!"

"You boys need to stay here and guard the house," Caleb said curtly. "In fact, you should be upstairs, Rudy. It's long past your bedtime."

"No, please!" The little boy started to sniffle.

"Okay, just a little longer," Caleb promised even as he wondered if it was healthy for Rudy to hear the nitty-gritty details of an attack on the vampires from which neither he nor Sophia might return, but sending him upstairs to sit alone in his bed—for he doubted Rudy would be able to sleep—wouldn't be good for him either.

Turning to lock eyes with Fintonclyde, Caleb said, "We know Cuza won't come alone. He's got two vampires on his side. I'm not counting Nina Patel. She's worthless because of the bite, according to René."

"Do you think he'll bring Sophia unharmed?" Fintonclyde asked.

"He'll bring her apparently unharmed, but don't forget that she'll be easily mesmerized by a vampire as powerful as Cuza. She might not act like herself." *She might try to harm me or harm herself,* Caleb thought but didn't say aloud. No need to tell them, Rudy in particular, about how vampires could twist humans under their thrall.

"Let's think about Cuza's advantages," Caleb began, pacing the kitchen again as he collected his thoughts. "He's got Sophia and will threaten to kill her."

"What if he tries to make her into a vampire?" Rudy asked in a quavering voice.

Caleb knelt down next to Rudy, putting a hand on the boy's shoulder. "That's not going to happen."

Rudy fought back tears and frowned anxiously.

"I've got a plan and we're going to get her back," Caleb said firmly, desperately wanting to believe those words. He wouldn't—couldn't—lose Sophia to Cuza.

Caleb stood up, giving Rudy's head an affectionate pat, and then took a seat at the kitchen table. "Okay, back to Cuza's assets. He's got two other vampires, who are big and tough. The one I saw was big, at least. They're probably the ones we chased through the woods on our Night. I rate them as muscle, not brains. They're around if Cuza needs someone to tackle me to the ground."

"Or shoot you with a silver bullet," Bela reminded him.

"Right. That's another advantage. They have guns and silver bullets. We took away some of their guns, but probably not all of them. Finally, there's magic. Last summer, Cuza used powerful Elemental magic in the fight at the castle."

"Which will he try first, guns or magic?" Fintonclyde asked, as he sat down opposite.

"Magic," Caleb answered quickly. "He'll want to destroy me with his own hands, if he can. The others will be backup."

"Speaking of backup," Fintonclyde said, "can the agents be of any help?"

"Good question. Let's talk about our advantages. You and I can both do magic, and it likely will come down to a magical battle. The agents are allies, insofar as they want to eliminate the vampires, but they don't have much to offer us until backup arrives around noon tomorrow—later today, I mean."

"Yeah, what about those special soldiers?" Bela asked, sitting next to Caleb. "Those agents told us about all the guns they have. You could wait for them to show up. Why pick three this morning?"

"Meeting somewhere in the open is safer," Caleb said, trying to sound rational. "At that time of the morning, the stretch of the road by Oceanside will be deserted. Less chance of harming bystanders, if there's a fight."

"The witching hour," Fintonclyde intoned solemnly, "when the veil between life and death is thinnest, when spirits can travel between worlds, and when magic is at its most powerful. Although" —the old man's eyes glinted beneath his thick eyebrows— "some call it the hour of the wolf."

"Whoa!" Rudy exclaimed.

"That, too," Caleb muttered, reluctant to admit that his real reason for picking the hour was to distract Cuza, before he could use Sophia to gain entrance to the house. Better to strike first against the vampires—and soon.

"Let's get back to allies. The agents won't be much help tonight. We ought to tell them what we're planning, I guess. We might need their help later for mopping up, and if we're open with them, maybe they'll go easier on werewolves in the future."

"The Hellhounds!" Bela yelled, slapping his palms face down on the table. "They're allies!"

"If they're still around. Fang said they were leaving town."

"Damien wouldn't leave without telling me," Bela insisted.

"Even if they haven't left town, Fang doesn't want to get involved," Caleb said, pushing away unpleasant memories of his final encounter with the Hellhounds.

"Damien and Darius don't believe that," Bela said. "They'll fight. Maybe those agents aren't worth much in a fight, but the Hellhounds would kick some butt."

"No. Fang made it clear we can't count on them," Caleb said, more forcefully than before. He pushed his chair back with a squeak, getting up to rummage in kitchen drawers for a pencil, then snatched a shopping list stuck to the refrigerator.

"Let's think about the layout at Oceanside," he said, laying the blank side of the shopping list on the table.

He sketched the building, parking lot, and the locations of picnic tables and large trees with corrections from Bela, who'd spent time there with Damien, gorging on burgers and ice cream. Rudy timidly approached the edge of the table, his eyes fixed on the crude drawing.

"I'm thinking it has to be in the parking lot." Caleb plunged ahead, tapping pencil on paper. "The other side of the building has too many obstacles and places to hide: trees and picnic tables. I want to make the call on where we meet, which means we have to get there first. I'm pretty sure Cuza will show up at the last minute, because he'll be overconfident and he'll want to make an entrance."

"You don't believe he will come alone?" Fintonclyde asked.

Caleb shook his head. "We won't see them, but his henchmen will be there. He might even bring Nina Patel—"

"Why trade away the notebook?" Bela interrupted. "That's crazy! Cuza doesn't just want that book, he wants to kill you."

"I'm not going to give up the notebook, if I can help it," Caleb said, "but we need to get Cuza out in the open to rescue Sophia. You've always been good at weather magic, Fintonclyde. If things get out of hand and I need some cover for a fast escape, can you conjure up a real pea souper?"

"Hmm. Time is short, but I believe I can do that." Fintonclyde stroked his beard and gave Caleb a nod.

"Then let's get moving," Caleb said, striding to the refrigerator. He yanked open the door, and pulled the notebook from under a pile of garlic in the vegetable bin. He tucked the book into the back waistband of his jeans, then patted his back pocket to make sure it still held several wooden stakes.

"You go wake up the agents," Caleb said to Fintonclyde, as he plucked the car keys from a peg near the back door. "I've got something I need to do, then I'll meet you at Oceanside and we'll get into position."

"What about me?" Bela asked angrily.

"And me!" Rudy squeaked.

"You two stay here and watch the house," Caleb ordered. "And we'll be back before you know it."

He tried to put a confident edge on his words, although he might as well be running through a minefield blindfolded. *Having a plan, any plan, was better than waiting to be attacked by Cuza.*

Chapter 27: The Witching Hour

HE SLEEPING TOWN SLID past her. From inside the dim interior of the car, she gazed out at empty streets, darkened store fronts, and houses lit by lonely street lights. *How had she come here?* A jumble of images faded in and out like flotsam from a shipwreck bobbing up and then sinking beneath the waves.

Sophia was in a car and she wasn't alone, wedged in the back seat between the man with the terrifying face and the woman who mumbled to herself, and whose hands and feet twitched spasmodically. *Was this a bad dream?* She couldn't make herself wake up, no matter how hard she tried.

If this were a dream, the man to her right featured prominently. His slick dark hair, haughty face, and eyes that were doors into another universe, a hall of mirrors that, instead of reflecting, sucked up all the light. Staring into those eyes, into that place, she'd known that she could cross over into that dark country so, so easily.

In the front seats, Sophia made out the dim silhouettes of two men. Past their heads and shoulders, she saw the headlights flick across a ribbon of empty road in which bushes and trees appeared suddenly and then vanished. The man in the front passenger seat half-turned toward the back, part of his face lit by the faint glow of the instrument panel. She remembered that face, remembered two grim men staring down at her with hard, dark eyes, and then a hand clamped over her mouth as she struggled in bed.

"This isn't a dream, is it?" Sophia asked, choking on the words as rising panic sent an acidic jolt into her throat.

"We go to see Caleb," the man seated next to her murmured in heavily accented English, stroking her cheek with his fingers. "You want him, do you not?"

The air around Sophia hissed like a familiar song playing on a distant radio. The man, his face wrapped in shadow, continued to caress her cheek. She moaned with desire and felt ashamed for doing so.

"You will be with him soon," the man continued softly. "Everything will be fine."

Sophia nodded. Everything was going to be fine.

"There is something you must do, small thing, then you will be together."

Sophia caught the faint glimmer of a smile from the man beside her. There was something she had to do when she saw Caleb. She couldn't remember what it was, but that didn't matter as long as she was with Caleb. Everything was going to be fine. The molecules in the air softly hummed: *fine, fine, fine, fine.*

"This is the place," said the man in the front passenger seat, with a heavy New York accent.

"This is the entrance to the... What is the word?"

"Parking lot, Boss. The only entrance, I think."

"Block it."

As the driver turned the car to the right, the woman next to her shuddered and asked in a panicked voice, "Is this the lab? I have to get to the lab!"

"Soon, soon," crooned the man on Sophia's other side. "We have a small errand to make."

The car's headlights swept across a vacant parking lot fringed with trees. The beams washed over wavy, buckled asphalt with grass and weeds poking out of cracks. The scene reminded her of camera footage from a submarine probing the undersea depths. And in the center, like a statue from a submerged temple still upright on the ocean floor, stood Caleb. Sophia squirmed to see through the window as the car turned away from Caleb, coming to rest across the entrance to the parking lot.

"Kill the engine, Boss?"

"Yes. Turn off the lights. We are creatures of the night, are we not?" The man chuckled. "You two stay in the car. Do not let the doctor leave until I give the signal."

The man to Sophia's right opened the door and stepped out of the car. He wore a black suit, the creases of his trousers razor-sharp, a dark gray shirt buttoned to the collar, and slick black leather shoes. He held out a hand to Sophia as if she were descending from a horse-drawn carriage in an earlier century. Warm, damp air filled her lungs. Crickets chirped, ignorant and unconcerned about the affairs of vampires, werewolves, or humans. The man gripped her forearm tightly as she swung her legs out and onto the ground. Her bare feet encountered pavement rough with small stones. She looked down, surprised to see that she was wearing her bathrobe, but it didn't feel right. A heavy object in one of the pockets bumped against her leg as the man pulled her along. She stumbled, stubbing her toe on a rock, but he paid no attention to her cry of pain as he dragged her in his wake.

No moon shone on the vacant parking lot. A distant streetlight provided scant illumination. As Sophia's eyes adjusted to the poorly lit scene, she saw an open expanse surrounded by trees and bushes, fireflies twinkling at the margins. Caleb wore a bulky sweater and stood about fifteen feet away, his arms crossed arms and a steely expression on his face.

Caleb was so close. She had to get to him, and then everything would be fine.

While she twisted ineffectually, trying to free herself, the man laughed harshly and said something in a foreign language.

"Speak English," Caleb said impassively. "It's impolite to exclude Sophia from the conversation."

"Ah, your Sophia," the man said pleasantly, although he didn't relax the painful grip around her upper arm. "As you see, she is not harmed."

"I'll be the judge of that," Caleb said. He reached an arm behind his back, and then held up a dark-colored notebook with pale lettering on the front cover.

Sophia frowned at the sight of the book. It was important, because… Her mind darted frantically, snatching at memories that flitted like the fireflies. Caleb had stolen the book, though she couldn't recall why or from whom. And the book was important to someone… to the vampire Cuza, she suddenly remembered, to the vampire that now gripped her arm and kept her from Caleb. But the book didn't matter. Everything would be fine, if only she could get to Caleb.

Cuza lazily raised his other arm, and Sophia heard car doors opening and closing, and then the sound of running feet.

"I told you to come alone, but I see you didn't stick to that," Caleb observed neutrally.

"If you came alone, you are a fool," Cuza said with a sly, malicious smile.

Her two thuggish kidnappers came to stand behind Cuza, while the woman from the car skidded to a stop when she spied Caleb. Motes of comprehension flickered in Sophia's woozy brain: this was Dr. Patel, the creator of the serum that had sickened the regulars at the bar, the vampire scientist who'd bitten Caleb.

"Thief!" Dr. Patel shrieked, struggling against the restraining arm that Cuza had flung in front of her.

"This is the book?" Cuza asked the scientist.

"Looks like it," she answered, eyeing it hungrily, "but I have to see inside to be sure."

"I toss the book on the ground, and you let Sophia go," Caleb proposed.

Cuza nodded. Caleb threw the book in front of him, so that it landed with a soft *plop* halfway between him and the vampires. Immediately, Dr. Patel lunged forward, went down on her knees to scoop up the book, and started frantically turning pages.

"Mine!" the scientist cried triumphantly, clutching the book to her chest. Then she jumped up, mumbling to herself, "Get to the lab. Have to get to the lab."

Dr. Patel stumbled past Cuza. Her shape faded into the surrounding darkness, but her mad, triumphant laughter lingered.

"Donnie! Catch her, you idiot!" Cuza barked to one of his thugs.

Heavy footfalls sounded behind Sophia while she squirmed in Cuza's grip. *She had to get to Caleb!*

Cuza laughed and let her go. She stumbled forward, so eager to close the gap separating her from Caleb that she collided with him, breathing heavily. He didn't look happy to see her as he held her chin with one hand, forcing her face upward.

There was something she was forgetting, something she needed to do.

Her eyes darted downward. One of her hands moved. She watched in fascinated horror as the hand slipped into a bathrobe pocket. The fingers encountered cold metal before closing around bumpy leather ridges. She grasped the handle, raised the silver knife, and slammed the blade into Caleb's breast.

* * *

CALEB COLLAPSED, PULLING SOPHIA down on top of his chest. He wanted to throw his arms around her and keep her safe, but the situation was light years away from being safe. Instead, he groaned, letting his arms fall limply to his sides.

"Caleb! Oh! What have I done?" she cried, staring at the knife in her hand.

He looked up into her wide, panicked eyes. Although her pupils were dilated, her eyes had lost the gauzy film that he'd seen before in humans who were mesmerized by a vampire.

"The bushes. Behind me. Fintonclyde," he whispered, keeping his body as still as possible. "Go. Now."

Sophia shivered at the sound of approaching footsteps. Moving slowly and deliberately, Cuza seemed in no hurry to reach them.

"No! I can't leave you!" she gasped, fear, panic, and confusion all flashing across her face.

"You! Get up!" Cuza ordered, halting a few feet from them.

Slowly she withdrew into a crouch at Caleb's side, still gripping the knife.

"Very good work, my dear, but I must be certain," Cuza said tenderly to Sophia, and then, in a harsher tone, he called over his shoulder, "Vito, shoot him."

"No!" Sophia screamed. She sprang toward Cuza, driving the silver knife through one of his black leather shoes.

Cuza howled from surprise, not pain, because, of course, he'd heal from that stab almost immediately. Caleb saw the vampire bend over and yank out the knife, which clinked on the pavement after he tossed it aside.

Sophia got to her feet as Cuza roared at his henchman, "Do not let her escape!"

Caleb remained motionless, though his stomach knotted and his arms and legs tingled with the desire to fight. He heard bare feet slapping asphalt and then, her cry of pain. If he could get the vampires to focus on Sophia, he could attack them when they weren't expecting it. Just play dead a little longer.

Through half-closed eyes, he watched a big, burly vampire drag Sophia as she tried to twist out of the grip of his meaty hands. She squirmed and kicked, but it had as much effect as fighting a brick wall.

"Sophia," Cuza sang, stretching the word out so that it radiated into the darkness and returned, amplified and more complex.

As his night vision adjusted, Caleb made out the two vampires: one tall and thin, the other broad and bulky, with a captive Sophia in between them. But he saw more: the song of the vampire, its tendrils swirling around

Sophia's head as its insidious hum intensified. Maybe the witching hour gave form and substance to magic that was otherwise invisible.

Caleb scrambled to his feet, his plan of playing dead ripped to shreds. He lunged toward Cuza, but didn't reach him.

"Aieeeeee!" A banshee wail erupted from the trees to Caleb's left, drowning out Sophia's moans as she slipped under the vampire's spell. René burst into view, like a heat-seeking missile with Cuza as his target. He pushed aside a stunned Caleb, knocking him to the ground.

"You can't! You can't! She's mine!" René screamed as he collided with Cuza's back and jumped up. He flung his arms around Cuza's shoulders and hung on like a housecat trying to subdue a lion. Vito tossed Sophia aside like a ragdoll and lumbered over help his boss. René had one arm looped around Cuza, trying in vain to break his neck. Though no match for the other two vampires in strength, René had manic intensity on his side. His wildly flailing legs made it difficult for Vito or Cuza to lay a hand on him.

Sophia had fallen to the ground. Gulping ragged breaths, she crawled away from the vampires on hands and knees.

"Get out of here!" Caleb called to her as he clambered to his feet.

She stood shakily, nodded to him, then broke into a stumbling run. As she vanished into the bushes, Caleb caught a glimpse of movement. Fintonclyde, his gray beard barely visible against dark foliage, waved a hand. Caleb nodded, then turned his attention back to the melee.

Vito had finally succeeded in pulling René from Cuza's back and threw him to the ground. The burly henchman planted a large booted foot on René's ribcage. Cuza pivoted, brushing the shoulders of his suit jacket and straightening his lapels.

"You!" Cuza sneered down at a squirming René. "You do not deserve to be immortal."

"You didn't mind before," René shot back, "because I spied on Lady Agatha for you and ran all your stupid errands. I deserve something in return!"

"Deserve? Yes, you deserve a quick end," Cuza said with a half-smile. Snapping his fingers, he nodded to Vito. "Rip his head off."

René shuddered, becoming still for a moment, then he held his hands up stiffly. Twin bolts of fire lanced up from his open palms and converged on Vito's chest. The vampire stumbled backward, beating on the flames sprouting from the front of his jacket.

"Good one, René," Caleb muttered to himself, impressed at how much his old friend had improved over the past six years.

"Is that the best you can do? I am better," Cuza said with a laugh, stretching out both arms toward René, who lay at his feet.

Flames sprang up from the asphalt around René, swiftly growing into a ring of fire. René, wide-eyed and frantic, couldn't break through the magical flames. As flames rose to several feet in height, the asphalt softened and oozed. René screamed, arms over his head in a futile attempt to shield himself.

Caleb backed away from the intense heat, but couldn't avert his eyes from the sight of his former friend in agony. For six years, he'd felt sorry for the clumsy, awkward kid who'd been dragged down by Toby's misguided assault on Lilac House—or so he'd believed.

The screaming stopped. Cuza flicked a hand casually and the flames went out with a sound like someone extinguishing a candle. A blackened, disfigured body lay curled in a fetal position. Caleb stared, aghast but unable to look away, as René's remains were reduced to a white powdery ash that collapsed with a soft sigh.

"Hey, Boss," Vito said hesitantly. "Something's up."

Caleb smelled the fog before he saw it, thick with the unpleasant tang of dead things washed up on the shore. What was Fintonclyde thinking? This was too soon. The fog was supposed to be a last-ditch effort if the fight with the vampires took a turn for the worse. The heavy, wet mist rolled along the parking lot from behind him, snuggling against the asphalt like a blanket.

Cuza swiveled his head in surprise as the creeping fog swirled above his knees and hissed faintly as it oozed over the smoldering remains.

Caleb tensed, knowing he'd hesitated for too long. Cuza turned to face him, contemptuously regarding him with empty black eyes, and parted his sneering lips to speak. There was nothing Caleb wanted to hear from him. He concentrated on making a ward--a solid, nearly invisible wall that gave off a faint blue glow as it wrapped itself around Cuza.

"Your magic cannot hold me!" Cuza taunted, even as the magical fence constricted, pinning his arms to his side.

Caleb couldn't squeeze the breath out of a creature that didn't breathe, but he could immobilize Cuza long enough to tackle Vito. He didn't want to take on two vampires at once unless he had help, which was not forthcoming. Fintonclyde was at least fifty feet behind him in the bushes. The original plan had been for the old man to guard Sophia while Caleb fought

Cuza. But that plan had also counted on other allies who were nowhere in sight, if they were coming at all.

"Shoot him!" Cuza screamed, squirming in the magical bonds.

Caleb reached for his back pocket. His fingers snagged on the bottom of his sweater as he tugged out a wooden stake. There was a flash of metal visible through the thickening fog as Vito produced a revolver from his jacket.

Great idea, Caleb thought, *bringing a stake to a gunfight.*

Vito fired. *Bam-bam-bam.* Caleb dodged sideways, reeling backward as one of the bullets slammed into his chest. He forced himself to remain upright, flicking a gaze down at the ragged hole in his sweater. Right over his heart. Vito was a very good shot. Holding back a sneeze at the acrid smell of spent powder and burnt wool, Caleb stepped toward his attacker.

"What is this devilry?" Cuza raged, still bound by magic. "Shoot him more! Shoot him in the head!"

The mist had risen to shoulder height as Vito looked at his gun, confused as to why the silver bullets hadn't felled the werewolf.

"This devilry is called body armor," Caleb called, forcing himself to smile as he took another step toward the vampires, because he knew how much it would annoy Cuza, even though his chest throbbed and his ribs ached with every breath. The vest had saved him from a silver bullet through the heart, but the impact had probably broken a few ribs.

As Vito raised the revolver, Caleb dropped to a crouch and rolled, barreling into the vampire's knees. Bam-bam-bam. The shots went wild as Caleb knocked Vito onto his back. He raised the stake in his hand and leaned in before Vito could get up. From behind, he heard a wordless shout of triumph from Cuza.

Vito clamped one meaty hand around Caleb's wrist, attempting to deflect the stake headed for his heart, while waving the revolver with the other. The gun was probably empty, but Vito could still crack his skull with it.

A sudden whistling sound from behind was Caleb's only warning that Cuza had freed himself. A blast of air slammed into Caleb's back, knocking him sideways. He pulled himself to his feet, his bruised and battered ribs protesting. He glimpsed Cuza's satisfied sneer through jagged holes in the thickening fog.

Before Cuza could marshal another magical attack, Caleb summoned Fire. Flaming, incandescent balls whistled through the air. Cuza deflected the barrage with a wave of his arm, creating a turbulent gust that battered Caleb and pushed Vito back to the ground as he tried to stand.

"You didn't defeat me before. What makes you think you can do it now?" Caleb called, knowing Cuza couldn't resist a well-placed taunt. And he needed to catch his breath.

"You learned a few tricks from Arghezi, you miserable dog, but he is not here to help you." Cuza spat out the words, no longer amused. "You make a small fire, but can you stop this?"

Cuza raised his arms like a symphony conductor, pointed his hands at Caleb's feet, and a ring of fire sprang up, similar to what had engulfed René. Caleb, who was better at magic than his late childhood friend, summoned Water by concentrating the droplets of mist into a swirling cyclone above him. A micro-downpour pummeled his head and shoulders. Water hit the pavement, dousing the flames. Caleb flicked a hand casually. The rain ceased. The sound of hot, hissing pavement was all that remained of the magical fire.

Thick mist filled in the gaps made by wind, fire, and rain. The ill-timed fog hadn't been as helpful as Caleb had hoped. The vampires couldn't locate him for another attack, but he couldn't see them either.

Cuza yelled, "Get him!"

Caleb took several steps to his left. He heard Vito patting his clothing and mumbling, "Musta left my ammo in the car." He very much hoped that Vito had run out of ammunition.

A throbbing bass rumble grew from faint to chest-rattling. Caleb saw a pearly patch of light in the fog off to his left, which resolved into three hazy beams that created ghostly outlines of trees and picnic tables. The explosive thrum of motorcycle engines crescendoed as Darius and Damien burst through the fog, whooping with teenage exuberance. Caleb gasped at the rider of the third motorcycle: Bela gripping the handlebars and, he noticed with grim satisfaction, wearing a helmet.

Out of the corner of his eye, Caleb saw Vito lumbering toward him like a runaway train. Too late to dodge, Caleb hit the ground as the vampire slammed into him. His face scraped against the rough asphalt as Vito hauled him to his feet, holding him by the back of his sweater like a puppy who'd done something wrong.

"I got—" Vito started, but stopped to gape at the motorcycle that thrust itself in his path.

"Hey! Look what we found!" Darius shouted, inching the bike toward Vito. A large man-sized lump dressed in black was slung across the were-wolf's knees. Darius tilted the bike to one side and a headless body slumped to the ground at Vito's feet.

Vito released him, and Caleb took a few lurching steps, fighting to stay on his feet. Blood oozed down one cheek where he'd been dragged across pavement.

"What'd you do to Donnie?" roared Vito, showing remarkable vampire solidarity, but little imagination.

Darius laughed. "Found this creep chasing a girl down the road."

"Turns out it was a nasty, stinking, rotten corpse," Damien called out as a spherical object arced upward and landed next to the body with a thud. Under a tangled mop of black hair, the severed head wore an expression of surprise.

"You—" Cuza turned toward the pair of Hellhounds, as he lapsed into a stream of Romanian invective.

Cuza flung out his arms, and lances of fire shot toward the motorcycles. Darius gunned his engine, let out the clutch, and fishtailed out of reach of the flames. Vito, preferring muscle to magic, lunged at the motorcycle like a grizzly bear attacking a hiker.

"Catch me if you can!" Darius laughed, speeding off into the dark with Vito in pursuit.

Damien aimed his headlight at Cuza. For an instant, the vampire stood frozen, bloodless white skin and dark suit, but just when it looked like the Hellhound was going to run him down, the vampire vanished. Confused, Damien turned his motorcycle back to where Cuza had been standing.

"He's turned into a bat," Caleb gasped hoarsely. "I'll deal with him. Go help your brother catch the other one."

"Right!" Damien shouted and sped toward the sound of his brother's engine.

As the rumble of the Hellhounds receded, Caleb turned angrily to the remaining motorcycle. "Bela! What—"

"You didn't believe me about the Hellhounds, but they came!" Bela gushed, idling the motorcycle and planting his feet on the ground. "And we got one of the vampires!"

Caleb heard the sound of feet slapping asphalt to his left. Sophia materialized from the mist, her hair flying wildly around her head as she twisted to scan the thinning fog.

"What's… going… on?" she asked, panting and holding her side.

"You shouldn't be here!" Caleb cried angrily as he searched for signs of a flapping black shape.

"Couldn't see through all the fog," she said. "I saw all the lights and—Bela? Where's Rudy? You didn't leave him home alone, did you?"

"Nah, he's with Fang—"

"What?" Caleb and Sophia shouted in unison.

Any explanation from Bela was cut short by the rapid whir of wings, followed by a whoosh as Cuza materialized in human form next to the motorcycle and casually kicked it with enough force that steel and chrome crashed to the ground, pinning Bela underneath.

"Another dog riding a motorcycle? You are breeding them faster than I can kill them." Cuza sneered. "Shall I dash his brains out or make a grand fire?"

"He's just a kid! Let him go!" Caleb shouted. "Fight me instead, you coward."

He took a step closer to Cuza, hoping that he'd distract the vampire before he attacked Bela again or noticed Sophia. But Cuza give Sophia a broad smile that showed off his canines in the pearly light of the motorcycle's headlamp.

"Ah, Sophia," Cuza said in a menacing voice. "Come to me."

Once again, Caleb thought he saw undulating tendrils stretching between Cuza and Sophia: the vampire's song made visible.

"You are not doing this to me again," she said slowly and deliberately as she struggled against the vampire's song. Caleb wondered if Cuza could see the wavering threads of magic curling away from Sophia until they melted into the mist.

With tremendous effort, she raised quavering arms, unclenched her fists, and jabbed her fingers toward the vampire. The air between them thickened as fog droplets coalesced into a twenty-foot-tall swirling cone that danced and spun as it closed on the surprised vampire. Sophia hadn't just summoned Wind; she'd created a tiny tornado out of thin air.

The cyclone hit Cuza, forcing him to stumble backward a few steps while it shredded his jacket and rearranged his slick black hair into a spiky mess. The vampire recovered enough to direct a lance of fire down at Sophia's bare feet, which also set the bottom of her bathrobe aflame.

Caleb ran to her and helped beat out the flames. Cuza, a triumphant look on this face, opened his mouth to speak, but frowned at the coughing, wheezing and spluttering noises coming from the motorcycle. Bela had wriggled from under the bike, dragged it upright, and was frantically working levers to coax the engine back to life.

Only a few seconds of distraction remained before Cuza lashed out again either at Bela or at Sophia. In that brief interval, there was no time for summoning spells. Caleb launched himself at the vampire. Cuza's arms shot out, reaching for Caleb's neck. Caleb tried to force the vampire to the ground; his momentum carried them both down, but Cuza twisted as he fell, landing on top of Caleb. The vampire's face, filled with cold hatred, loomed large in Caleb's fading vision as long, strong fingers dug into his neck, slowly crushing his windpipe. Caleb saw red, then black, while his ears sizzled.

"Your adventure in Romania failed," Cuza jeered at him. "Alexandru and his former wife are dead and gone: your doing."

"*You* killed Alexandru," Caleb rasped, each word requiring a prodigious effort.

"He deserved to die." Cuza laughed, but continued with what might almost have been tenderness, "Not Ana Maria. She was mine. She never loved you."

The iron grip on Caleb's neck eased slightly, not enough to free him from the terrible pressure, but enough for him to take in a breath. Then a second breath. On the third breath, he pushed his hands against Cuza's shoulders, planted one foot on the ground and levered his body over, so that he rolled on top of the surprised vampire with one knee pinned on his chest.

Caleb might have been a match for a vampire in hand-to-hand combat, except for the fiery pain in his ribs and the deep ache every time he breathed. In desperation, he thrust an arm out behind him, trying unsuccessfully to grab one of the wooden stakes in his back pocket. He needed all the help he could get in this fight.

With a tremendous shudder, Cuza thrust Caleb up and away, sending him tumbling over the pavement. On hands and knees, Caleb sucked in air, each lungful more painful than the last, and raised his head. Cuza stood four or five feet away, appearing uncharacteristically rumpled, the black suit flecked with dirt and shredded in places.

Caleb painfully pushed himself to his knees, wondering where he was going to find the strength to get to his feet. The vampire raised his arms slowly, enjoying Caleb's weakness and pain, and prepared to let loose another magical volley.

Two sounds exploded at the same time: a shriek from behind Caleb and the deafening growl of a motorcycle rushing toward him.

"No, you don't!" Sophia cried out and conjured a blast of wind that knocked Cuza flat on his back.

The German bike roared as Bela bore down on the prone vampire. Cuza tried to roll out of its path, but wasn't fast enough. The motorcycle ripped through one sleeve of the vampire's jacket and crushed his arm.

Caleb pulled himself to his feet, motioning weakly for Bela to come to a stop. Pain lanced through his chest and shoulder as he reached around to his back pocket. He wondered if he'd dislocated his shoulder, too. As his fingers closed around a wooden stake, the pain receded.

The vampire slowly stood. One of his arms hung limply at his side, the expensive fabric of his jacket was shredded, and his hand was a mangled mess. Caleb stumbled forward and locked eyes with Cuza.

"Get out of the way!" Bela yelled, gunning the engine. "I'll finish him off."

"Back off, junior," came a new voice from beyond the bright circle of light from the motorcycle's headlamp. Mickey ambled up to the bike, tapped on the handlebars, and then strode casually through the beam, dressed as usual in dark pants and a black leather jacket.

"You're late," Caleb panted between ragged breaths.

"Yeah, well, Her Ladyship had trouble deciding what to wear," Mickey said with a slight tilt of his head to one side, indicating a patch of darkness that resolved into Lady Agatha dressed in a long black trench coat and high, black leather boots.

Caleb couldn't stop the laughter from bursting through the tight wall of tension in his chest as he watched Lady Agatha stroll into the light, as if she were window shopping on Main Street. He hadn't been sure that she'd show up after he'd once again invaded her underground crypt to plead for her help. At least she hadn't armed Mickey with silver bullets and told him to shoot werewolves on sight.

Caleb's giddy laughter degenerated into a fit of coughing, while Cuza stared in disbelief as she ambled toward him.

"Yes, you are late," Cuza said, rearranging his face into a rough semblance of his usual haughtiness. "You see how these vicious dogs attack us."

Lady Agatha came to a halt an arm's length in front of Cuza. She looked over his disheveled hair, shredded jacket, and mutilated arm, shaking her head as if she were witnessing a crime against fashion. Mickey slipped behind Cuza, boxing him between them.

"Us?" She laughed, almost gaily, but there was steel underneath. "I am not being attacked, and I see no threat to myself. You, on the other hand, have made an extraordinary number of enemies."

"But these—these *wild animals*. They have killed one of our kind!" Cuza blustered, desperately trying to change the subject as he gestured with his good arm toward the headless body. "You are a fool if you think they can be trusted."

"Do not lecture me on whom to trust," Lady Agatha replied severely. "I told you that you were attracting too much attention, that your idiotic schemes would cause trouble. I told you once, twice, thrice."

"And I told you that you could go back to the shadows if you did not like my plans," Cuza shot back defensively.

Lady Agatha stared into Cuza's eyes for several long moments before nodding her head, perhaps with resignation or pity. Caleb wasn't sure how to interpret that gesture from one of the Undead. When she spoke, her voice held no trace of humanity.

"Because you come from a barbaric land, you do not understand that our kind must have rules, safeguards. In England, you would have been brought before the council for trial."

"Hah! I see no council here! You—" Cuza stopped abruptly when Mickey twisted his undamaged arm, pinning it behind his back.

"You should listen to her," Mickey cautioned, speaking into Cuza's ear. "Not that it's going to do any good."

"It is only I, dear Cuza," she said, stroking the vampire's cheek with her long, painted fingernails. "I shall be judge and jury."

For a few seconds no one spoke. Cricket song filled the void. Caleb had his eyes fixed on Cuza's rage-filled face, but he sensed movement as others joined him: Sophia on one side and Fintonclyde on the other. Around them, the mist had thinned to wispy shreds. Bela turned off the motorcycle's engine and headlamp, bringing back the deep shadows of the witching hour.

"Mircea!" Cuza called as he twisted, trying unsuccessfully to free himself from Mickey's grip. "Surely you won't betray me, after all I have done for you. You must stop her. You must stop this madness!"

Mickey barked out a laugh. "Thanks to you, I'm the last Arghezi on the planet. Yeah, I think you've done plenty for me already."

Lady Agatha took several steps back from Cuza, the heels of her boots tapping the pavement. She raised her arms to shoulder height, spreading them wide like an avenging angel, and intoned, *"Non unus ex nobis. Hoc est autem judicium: nunc et in aeternum. Quae in ignem mittitur. Fiat!"*

Caleb, who had studied Latin as a boy, couldn't get his addled brain to translate, but at his side Fintonclyde murmured softly, "You are not one of us. Now and for eternity. You are cast into the fire. So be it."

"Your words cannot harm me!" Cuza struggled more fiercely than before, but was unable to break free of Mickey's tight grip on his one good arm.

"Perhaps not. I am only judge and jury," Lady Agatha said, dropping her arms and turning toward Caleb. Perhaps her face now held pity, if that emotion could still haunt the Undead. "Mr. O'Connor?"

Caleb looked down at the forgotten wooden stake in his hand. Nodding grimly to Lady Agatha, he walked forward until he stood a foot from Cuza. Caleb raised an arm above his shoulder, the pain from his injuries and the weariness in his limbs forgotten.

"You will not—" Cuza began.

Caleb cut him off. "This is for Alexandru."

"For Alexandru," Mickey echoed. "And for Ana Maria, you bastard."

Caleb plunged the stake into the vampire's heart. Cuza's mouth opened in a silent "O" of surprise. Mickey released him, stepping away. Cuza clawed at the stake with his undamaged hand, long fingers curling around the protruding piece of wood. The vampire tugged at the stake with what must have been the last of his strength before slumping down into an inert heap at Caleb's feet.

Lady Agatha broke the silence: "St. Florian's Fire."

Caleb pivoted toward her, wondering how long he'd been staring down at the body of the vampire who'd destroyed people he'd loved and the castle that had been his home.

"That is the custom," Lady Agatha continued tersely. "I require your help to contain the fire. Arrange yourselves at cardinal points."

She swept her arm gracefully in an arc, pointing one long, spiky fingernail to four places in turn, each on the perimeter of circle with a diameter of about twenty feet. Cuza's body lay it its center.

"You'll have help," Sophia said quietly but firmly, moving to one of the spots Lady Agatha had indicated.

Caleb took his place, Sophia to his right, while Fintonclyde stood opposite him.

"Bela?" Caleb asked, gesturing at the remaining spot to his left. "You can do this. It'll be like a warding spell."

"Yeah, I'm good at those," the boy murmured, slightly shell-shocked. He flipped down the kickstand of the bike and limped heavily to the final place in the circle.

"Follow my lead," Caleb said as he concentrated on weaving a strong ward using the combined energy and power of all four of them. He wasn't sure what sort of magical fire the English vampire would conjure or if their shield would be sufficient to contain it.

Lady Agatha began to chant in Latin. Caleb couldn't make out the words as she paced outside their circle. Around the slumped body in the center, an unnatural, roiling pillar of fire bloomed. Transparent at first, the flame became opaque as it grew taller than the surrounding trees. Cuza vanished as the incandescent column flickered from red to yellow to white and threw off shimmering waves of heat, turbulent eddies that battered the magical shield.

Caleb struggled with the invisible lines of magic they'd woven together, knowing that if any one of them faltered, they all might be incinerated. He'd been too glib in telling Bela this would be a simple spell. *Would the boy be able to handle this?* His eyes flicked to his left, where Bela spread his shaking arms out wide. And Sophia who had been through so much… He glanced at her to his right. In the pulsating light of St. Florian's Fire, he saw her jaw clenched in concentration and her arms held rigidly at her sides.

In the space between Caleb and Sophia, a ghostly form wavered and then solidified. A tall boy with long dark hair in a ponytail, thumbs hooked in the pockets of his jeans, grinned at him, nodding his head toward the inferno. *I know you can do it.*

Lady Agatha pronounced the final words of the incantation. The shimmering, white-hot column of fire rushed up into the night sky like a rocket launched from Cape Canaveral. Caleb blinked at the sudden return of darkness, a brilliant after-image pulsing before his eyes.

The magical shield dissipated like autumn leaves carried away on the wind, leaving no sign of its presence except the exhausted faces and slumped shoulders of the four who'd fought to maintain the barrier. Sophia sunk to her knees, head in hands. Too exhausted and numb to go to her, though he knew he should, Caleb stared dully at the place where the fire had briefly burned like a tiny sun.

He'd expected to see a smoking crater or a pile of ash, but that patch of pavement at the center of the circle appeared no different than before, except that it was empty. He remembered saying goodbye to Ana Maria, giving her the eternal peace that she sought, and then consigning her body to the flames as she'd requested. He remembered breaking through the stony soil to lay Alexandru to rest in the tiny graveyard of Castle Arghezi. But for the vampire who had utterly corrupted Ana Maria and who had ended Alexandru's life, nothing tangible remained. Caleb didn't know what he'd expected at the defeat of the vampire Cuza, but not this feeling of emptiness.

Bela hobbled wearily toward him, shaking his head slowly from side to side. "Wow, that was…"

"I might have underestimated how hard that was going to be," Caleb said, throwing an arm around Bela's shoulders. "But you did it. Great job."

Around them, the crickets had fallen silent. A distant streetlight and a timid crescent moon provided scant illumination. Even in the dimness, Caleb could make out Bela's smile, hesitant at first, then blooming into a wide grin.

"Yeah, I—" Bela began, but stopped at the sound of approaching engines.

Headlights sliced the darkness: the single beams of two motorcycles and, a moment later, the twin beams of a pickup truck. All the Hellhounds had arrived.

The truck rolled to a stop about thirty feet from Caleb and Bela, its headlights pointed directly at them. The engine stopped and doors opened on either side of the truck. Caleb put up an arm to shade his eyes, squinting to make out the figures emerging onto pavement. Were there two or three?

The answer to Caleb's question came as a small figure pelted toward him, headlight beams flickering as the boy bobbed in and out of the light. Then something crashed into his legs, making him fight to stay upright. Looking down, he saw Rudy, arms wrapped tightly around him.

"See?" Bela said, shaking himself free from Caleb's arm. "I told you—I was going to tell you before that vampire got in the way—that Rudy's fine."

Caleb laid a hand on Rudy's head. The little boy stared up at him, anxiety written in the scrunched forehead and tight-lipped ghost of a smile.

"Hey," Caleb said softly, "it's going to be okay."

"You get the last of the vampires, mighty hunter?" Fang drawled out of the darkness.

The pack leader stayed out of the beam of the headlight as he approached, but Caleb recognized the swagger and the soft, Southern accent.

"We got the worst one, and your sons helped with a couple of the others," Caleb answered cautiously. After battling vampires, he doubted he'd have the reserves left to take on the Hellhounds, if they were going to fight him again over Rudy.

"Don't I get thanks for bringing your kid back?" Fang stepped closer and tousled Rudy's hair. "Turns out the kid don't like riding a bike."

"It was really scary riding with Bela," Rudy admitted sheepishly.

Fang shrugged. "He wouldn't make a good Hellhound, so..."

"I guess we'll keep him, then," Caleb said, smiling as Rudy squeezed him tighter.

"Well, I gotta go check out those vampires that my boys bagged," Fang said easily, as if he hadn't recently tried to kidnap the little boy clinging to Caleb. "And you tell that old man that he owes us for two more kills."

Fang turned and ambled toward Darius and Damien, who had parked their motorcycles near the truck. Caleb wasn't sure why Doña Flóres was yelling at them in Spanish: possibly for being too reckless or for not killing enough vampires. Bela did a fast hobble toward the Hellhounds, eager to check out the Undead trophies piled on the asphalt.

Caleb looked down at Rudy. "Come on, buddy. Let's see how Sophia's doing."

She sat on the pavement, head down and arms wrapped around her knees.

"Are you okay?" Rudy asked hesitantly.

Caleb held his breath, until she raised a tear-stained face to him with an expression of naked joy that almost stopped his heart.

"I'm fine," she sniffled, extending an arm to the little boy to draw him into a hug. "Just a little tired. You must be tired, too."

"No, I'm not!" Rudy answered defiantly, then yawned. "Well, maybe a little."

"We'll go home soon," she promised.

Caleb held out his hands to her and pulled her up. She stumbled to her feet, regained her balance, and threw her arms around him. He buried his face in her hair, breathing contentedly. After several long moments, he drew back slightly.

"What's wrong?" she asked. "I'm not still…"

He cupped his hands around her jaw. Her eyes were beautiful and clear with no remaining trace of the vampire's spell.

"You're fine, just fine."

"When we were in the circle," she whispered hesitantly, "you saw it, him, too?"

"Toby was here," Caleb said, briefly closing his eyes to savor the ghostly memory of his best friend. "I think he came to say goodbye to us."

Events began to blur for Caleb after that. The teenaged Hellhounds had brought back Vito's inert body with a tree branch jammed into its chest. There was an interesting story there, Caleb was sure, but the scrapes, bruises, and broken ribs that he'd been ignoring had caught up with him, and he was too tired to ask. Lady Agatha and Mickey had vanished into the waning night, while at some point, the agents had shown up. Through it all, Caleb didn't let go of Sophia's hand, and Rudy stuck close to both of them.

Fintonclyde reappeared, trailed by an uncharacteristically confused and uncertain Agent Hulstad.

"That was… unexpected, Mr. O'Connor. I don't know how to write my report or what to put in it." Hulstad squinted down at his little notebook. Bright light flashed as Agent Gallo paced around the dead vampires, taking pictures from all conceivable angles.

"Hmm. You've got a couple of inactivated BFIs," Caleb said, pointing to Cuza's former henchmen heaped together near the motorcycle gang. "After Gallo finishes taking pictures, we burn them. It seems straightforward to me."

"But where is Peter Brody?" the agent asked, perplexed. "And that fire, if it was a fire."

"Oh, you saw it?" Caleb said casually.

"We were observing from the perimeter." Hulstad cleared his throat. "And who was that woman?"

"Let's just say she had no love for Peter Brody and leave it at that." Caleb yawned. "Later you might get a better story out of me, but not now."

"You take Sophia and Rudy home," Fintonclyde said without any outward sign of the exhaustion that weighed on Caleb. "We will tidy things up here."

"Don't worry about Bela," Sophia said, noting Caleb's concerned glance toward the boy, who was talking excitedly with the motorcycle gang. "He's going to be partying with the Hellhounds till the sun comes up, but he'll be fine."

"At least until the police get here," Caleb said, worry creeping into his voice.

"I'm sure Agent Hulstad will sort it all out," she said with a tired laugh, squeezing his hand. "Let's go home."

Caleb gave in. Sophia always had good advice.

Chapter 28: The Wolf's Den

March 1993

ALEB HAD PAID THE taxi driver an exorbitant amount, plus a tip on top of that, to pick him up at the airport. He was on an expense account, after all. After collecting the receipt, he stood at the end of the driveway, readjusting his backpack.

The house on Roberts Avenue looked the same as the first time he'd seen it, when he'd been fifteen. Almost the same. Something was different. The siding was still painted salmon-pink with white shutters and white trim festooned with curly Victorian scrollwork at the roof line. Snowdrops and a few brave crocuses struggled amid islands of snow in the flower bed in front of the porch; the purple and yellow crocus were new since he'd left a week ago, but that wasn't what tickled his brain. Something else, then. Letting his gaze roam from the battered garage (he'd get around to painting it when the warm weather came) to the wide porch wrapped around the front of the house to the huge oak still bare of leaves towering overhead, he saw the new sign hanging above the porch railing. He'd known what she intended, had made suggestions about the colors and lettering. Seeing it now, freshly painted, he felt slightly uncomfortable.

WOLF'S DEN
BED & BREAKFAST

He'd objected to the name, but she had countered that he deserved some credit: she wouldn't be ready for the upcoming tourist season without his help painting, stripping floors, and tiling bathrooms, and without the money he'd loaned her when the plumbing renovations had blasted through her budget. *The name will stand out*, she'd said, noting that the other B&Bs in the neighborhood either went for floral names like Primrose Cottage or sea-themed names like Fisherman's Rest.

He was going to have to get used to the name, he thought as he trudged up the steps to the porch, especially if she'd already printed brochures. The front door was warded, as usual. The threat from rogue vampires had receded and the Hellhounds were back in their Florida stomping grounds, but Sophia insisted on keeping up the magical protections on the house.

"Sophia?" he called after suspending the ward, opening the front door and stepping into the hall. Both boys would be at school this morning. He wanted to give her warning about who had come into the house.

She appeared in the doorway at the end of the hall, a relieved smile spreading across her face. "Caleb, I didn't think you'd be back until after lunch."

He shrugged off his backpack, letting it and the duffle bag fall to the floor, and he walked into her embrace. For a few moments, he closed his eyes and said nothing, grateful to be out of the city where he'd spent most of the last week, and even more grateful to be inhaling the scent of her hair while running his hands down her back.

He wanted to do more than hug her, but she pulled away from him, saying, "Mickey's here for that thing we talked about. Remember?"

Over her shoulder, he saw the slim, dark-haired figure, leaning insouciantly against the doorframe.

"Hey, it's Secret Agent Caleb," Mickey said with a smirk.

Caleb scowled, reluctantly disentangling himself from Sophia. "I don't work for them, you know. I'm just a consultant."

Mickey chortled. "Consulting on how to take down immortals."

"That's not fair," he countered. "I give them training classes on how to recognize vampires and werewolves, but mostly I try to educate werewolves on how to avoid the Agency. You vampires are on your own."

Mickey laughed, about to say something more, but Sophia took Caleb's arm, pulling him gently toward the kitchen.

"Are you hungry? I can make you an early lunch or maybe just some tea," she said, blatantly trying to change the subject.

Entering the kitchen, Caleb spotted a plastic sheet spread across half the table, containing an array of unfamiliar tools surrounded by little plastic bottles, each with a different colored liquid inside, and, more ominously, a box of bright blue latex exam gloves.

"Tea, I guess," Caleb said, spinning around to face the door into the hall. "I'll just go get my bag and unpack…"

Sophia clucked at him. "Don't you want to just get it over with?"

Reluctantly, he turned to face her. "Well, uhm, I'll wait until after he's done yours. I'll go unpack now."

"Just finished up with the lady," Mickey replied smoothly. "Your turn next."

She crossed the kitchen, lifting her wavy brown hair above her shoulders with one hand. She turned her head so that he could see a fresh gauze pad taped across her neck.

"It wasn't so bad," she said, eyes sparkling with amusement.

"First, you gotta decide what you're gonna get. The lady here got a fleur-de-lis, two of 'em, of course," Mickey said.

At Caleb's puzzled look, Sophia explained, "Because of the French name."

"I always used to call him Frenchie. Drove him nuts," Mickey snickered. "Now for you, I was figuring a test tube or…yeah, how about a mouse?"

"A what?"

"Lady Agatha's idea," Mickey explained. "She figures that every immortal should have their own mark, something appropriate, you know."

"And how do your clientele—or should I call them blood tourists—like that?" Caleb asked, circling the table to give a wide berth to the ominous-looking tools.

"They love it. They pay money to get bitten by a real vampire, and then get a memento of the experience, which most of them don't remember anyway. And we'll know not to bite them again. Lady Agatha says we don't need to turn anyone else. Too much competition, you know?"

"I know we agreed on this scheme for other people, but no sane vampire is going to bite me again," Caleb objected, "so I don't see why I need to go through with this."

"What is your problem with getting a tattoo? You told the Agency that everyone who gets bitten by a vampire gets marked." Sophia set a mug of tea on the table, then glared at him with her hands on her hips.

"Tattoos probably won't survive the Night," Caleb said in a last-ditch avoidance maneuver. When Sophia and Mickey only stared at him uncomprehendingly, he explained, "The monthly transformation."

"Don't you remember all the tattoos the Hellhounds have?" she asked in a severe but mocking tone.

"Okay, fine. Fine." Caleb rolled his eyes at her, conceding defeat.

Mickey picked up a pad of paper and a pencil. "So, how about a little mousie, Chief? Seems fitting since the Doc bit you."

"No!" Caleb protested. "I don't want to be stuck with that on my neck. If you must, how about a book? Taking away her lab notebook was the beginning of the end, I suppose."

"Sure, Chief," Mickey said, seating himself at the table and starting to draw. "Shouldn't take long to get a design worked up."

"Great," Caleb said halfheartedly. "I'll just go unpack and maybe take a shower."

"Don't be too long," the vampire called, not looking up from his work. "I ain't got all day here."

Caleb stayed in the shower until his fingers turned prunish, aware that he was stalling. When he returned to the kitchen, Mickey scowled at him, while Sophia looked mildly amused.

"Sit," she ordered, picking up a chair and moving it around so that the back snugged up against the edge of the table. "If I had to do this, then so do you."

"Needles," Caleb mumbled. "I don't like needles."

She took his hand, pulling him toward the table, and then gently pushed him down into the chair. "Look at me, Caleb. You are one of the bravest people I know. After what you've been through, needles shouldn't scare you."

"Don't you have to be licensed to do this?" Caleb asked, turning his head to look at Mickey.

"Nah. The guy at Ink 'n Ice Cream over on Main Street showed me how. It's not too hard," Mickey said dismissively, coming around the table and thrusting a small square of paper in front of him. "How's this look, Chief?"

"That looks…" Caleb began, ready to reject it in order to stall for more time. Mickey had drawn an open book, about an inch wide, the pages crammed with tiny dots that looked like inscrutable writing in a foreign alphabet. "That looks a lot like her lab notebook."

"Of course, it does," the vampire said smugly. "I seen that thing dozens of times. Never saw the Doc without it."

"Oh, all right," Caleb said, giving in to the inevitable. "I guess that'll do."

Caleb heard the *thwack* of gloves being pulled on. Mickey returned to his side, hands covered in bright blue latex, and wiped his neck with a damp piece of gauze that smelled of disinfectant.

"Looks pretty smooth," Mickey said, running a gloved finger across a patch of Caleb's neck. "Of course, the puncture marks don't last forever, which is why you need the ink."

Mickey slapped something on his neck, then rubbed it with the wet gauze. Caleb winced, expecting to feel a prick.

"Relax, Chief. I'm just putting on the stencil. The real fun's coming in just a sec."

Sophia pulled a chair next to him and sat. Caleb heard metal objects clinking on the table behind him and then an ominous buzzing like a nightmare visit to the dentist.

"Speaking of Dr. Patel, you don't happen to know where she is, do you?" Caleb asked as the vampire approached him holding a thick black, buzzing cylinder that tapered down to a tiny point on one end.

"You're trying to distract me, Chief, when I got work to do," Mickey said with cheerful sadism.

"The Jax kicked her out, and the Agency hasn't been able to—" Caleb tensed, feeling a prick at his neck like a cat's claw that had been dipped in acid.

"Steady, there," Mickey murmured.

There wasn't just one cat scratching him, but more like a half dozen. Which was ridiculous, he thought, because the design was so small. How could you get so many cats attacking a square inch of skin?

"Tell me about your trip," Sophia said, attempting to distract him.

Caleb gritted his teeth, resigning himself to more punctures in his neck at the hands of a vampire. "There's a werewolf, maybe more than one, making trouble in Boston. I spent a day searching the city, but couldn't find any sign. I might have to go back down next full moon. Ow!"

"What else?" she asked.

"A couple in southern New Hampshire have a little girl who was bitten this summer. I haven't figured out the werewolf responsible yet. And I made contact with that pack in the Berkshires. Mostly good folks. They've adopted a few kids that they, uhm, converted."

"You worry about the children, don't you?" she asked softly.

"Raising a little werewolf isn't easy, even for werewolves," Caleb answered. "I've met so many cubs in the last few months, more than I thought I'd find."

"Hmm," she mused, "maybe you should start a summer camp for little werewolves."

Caleb blinked, afraid to nod his head, as the buzzing continued. The island was a good place for werewolves to run free on their Night, as he'd done growing up. And Fintonclyde had no plans for a camp next summer. In the last six months, he'd met plenty of exasperated parents trying to find ways to deal with their rambunctious werewolf children. Maybe he could give them a break for the summer, while helping the kids cope with the monthly change.

Caleb's mind had drifted away, and when he returned to the kitchen, the relentless buzzing had ceased. Mickey wiped a cloth over the stinging patch of skin on his neck.

"Are you done?" Caleb asked with hope in his voice.

"What? No, I just have to wipe away the…the…"

"B-word?" Sophia finished helpfully.

"Yeah, the blood," the vampire said sourly. "It's not easy for us when there's fresh you-know-what around. And, of course, werewolf you-know-what is kinda toxic."

"So, you're not done," Caleb said with disappointment and more than a little dread at another round of needles digging into his neck.

"Nah," Mickey said, starting the awful buzzing once again and bringing the tool close to his neck. "Got another thirty, thirty-five minutes to go, Chief."

"Sweet Selene," Caleb whispered.

Having vampires as allies might be worse than having vampires as enemies.

END

Cast of Characters

Werewolves

Caleb O'Connor: Down-easter, adopted by Clovis Fintonclyde at seven-years-old; lately returned to Maine after six years in Romania.

Bela Muscatura: Fourteen-year-old Romanian werewolf, adopted by Caleb.

Rudy Neustadt: Eight-year-old orphan from Bar Harbor, recently bitten by a werewolf.

Damien Fang: Leader of the Hellhounds, a motorcycle gang from Florida; usually goes by Fang.

Darius Fang and *Damien Fang, Jr.*: Fang's twin (but not identical) sixteen-year-old sons.

Doña Flóres Márquez: Cuban refugee and member of the Hellhounds.

Buck Holloway: Very large, very tattooed Hellhound with a bad temper.

Vampires

Cuza AKA *Peter Brody*: Romanian vampire who corrupted and invaded Castle Arghezi in the 1930s, then later tangled with Caleb in Romania.

Ana Maria Arghezi AKA *Lamia Borgheza*: Married to Alexandru Arghezi in Romania in the 1930s, then turned into a vampire by Cuza; later met Caleb in Romania, but died when Cuza attacked Castle Arghezi.

Mircea "Mickey" Arghezi: Came to Maine in the 1930s after being bitten in Romania by Ana Maria Arghezi; brother of the late Alexandru Arghezi; working for Lady Agatha.

Lady Agatha Pilkington: Came to Maine in 1919 from England, escaping the sinking Titanic; lived in Lilac House, a mansion by the sea, until it was attacked in 1942 by Clovis Fintonclyde, Alexandru Arghezi, and Antoine Daigle.

Guy de Mornay: One of Lady Agatha's devoted English gentlemen, also a Titanic survivor.

"Frenchie": Native of Maine, only recently Undead; working for Cuza.

Nina Patel, PhD: Scientist working on mouse genetics at the Jackson

Laboratory in Bar Harbor; recently turned into a vampire by Cuza.

Vito Mancuso and *Donnie Rizzo*: New York City vampires who came to Bar Harbor and now work for Cuza.

Humans

Alexandru Arghezi: Former MIT physics professor who grew up in Romania, but fled to the US when Cuza took over the family castle; mentor to Caleb in Romania; died when Cuza attacked Castle Arghezi.

Clovis Fintonclyde: Resides on Dragonshead Island off the Maine Coast near Bar Harbor where he tends a menagerie of fabulous and magical creatures; raised Caleb on the island after his parents couldn't care for him.

Sophia Daigle: Childhood friend of Caleb's; grew up in the tiny magical village of Tribulation, Maine, but now lives in Bar Harbor.

René Cousineau: Childhood friend of Caleb's; grew up in the tiny magical village of Tribulation, Maine; died attempting to break into a magically sealed old mansion, Lilac House.

Toby Byron: Childhood friend of Caleb's; died after attempting to break into a magically sealed old mansion, Lilac House.

Trudy Byron Matthews: Toby's mother, now married to Tom Matthews.

Tom Matthews: General contractor in Bar Harbor and regular at the Lobster Pot.

Dave Alroy: Unemployed sailmaker and regular at the Lobster Pot.

Hiram Hulstad: Senior Special Agent, Boston Field Office, in the Extraordinary Alien Registry (EAR), a black agency in the US Justice Department.

Dominic Gallo: Special Agent, Boston Field Office, in the Extraordinary Alien Registry (EAR), a black agency in the US Justice Department.

Acknowledgements

A work of fiction shouldn't be attempted without blind faith and very good friends. I confess to the former and gratefully acknowledge the latter, without whom you wouldn't have been able to read this tale. My editor Jay Nadeau knows and loves the characters, and doesn't hesitate to tell me when they are just not doing the right things. Her guidance has been key for the many years it took me to finish this book. Sarah McKelvey has been an exacting first reader. She read every chapter here (and many that never made it into the final version), and her advice on voice and characterization was always spot on. I am exceedingly grateful to Paul Eskridge, Catherine Keegan, Charles Nichols, and Alison Strack for tackling the full draft. They pointed out my mistakes and prodded me to go deeper, always deeper. Any remaining mistakes are entirely my own.

This is a work of fiction; thus, you should know that any resemblance to actual events or persons, living or dead, is entirely coincidental. The town of Bar Harbor, Maine and the Jackson Laboratory located there are real. However, for the purpose of the story, I have invented certain commercial establishments and residences in Bar Harbor and islands off the coast of Maine. As far as I know, there are no vampires currently working at the Jax.

About the Author

Connie Senior writes fiction because she can't help it. She wrote her first story, "The Haunted Space Station", in third grade. Since then, she accumulated various college degrees and worked as an environmental engineer and technical editor, but hasn't stopped spinning stories in her head: days spent on science, nights spent crafting tales of werewolves and vampires. She lives in Denver, Colorado, with her husband and a couple of elderly cats. *The Wolf's Den* is her second book, a sequel to *Only the Moon Howls*. Visit conniesenior.com for outtakes, extras, and new work or follow her on Twitter @WolfieTwin.